T0285515

WATCH
OVE
YOU

Watching Over You

a novel

Simon Delaney

RARE BIRD
LOS ANGELES, CALIF.

THIS IS A GENUINE RARE BIRD BOOK

Rare Bird Books
6044 North Figueroa Street
Los Angeles, California 90042
rarebirdbooks.com

FIRST NORTH AMERICAN HARDCOVER EDITION

For more information, address:
Rare Bird Books Subsidiary Rights Department
6044 North Figueroa Street
Los Angeles, California 90042

Set in Adobe Garamond
Printed in the United States

10 9 8 7 6 5 4 3 2 1

Library of Congress Cataloging-in-Publication Data available upon request

For Lisa, Cameron, Elliot, Isaac, and Lewis

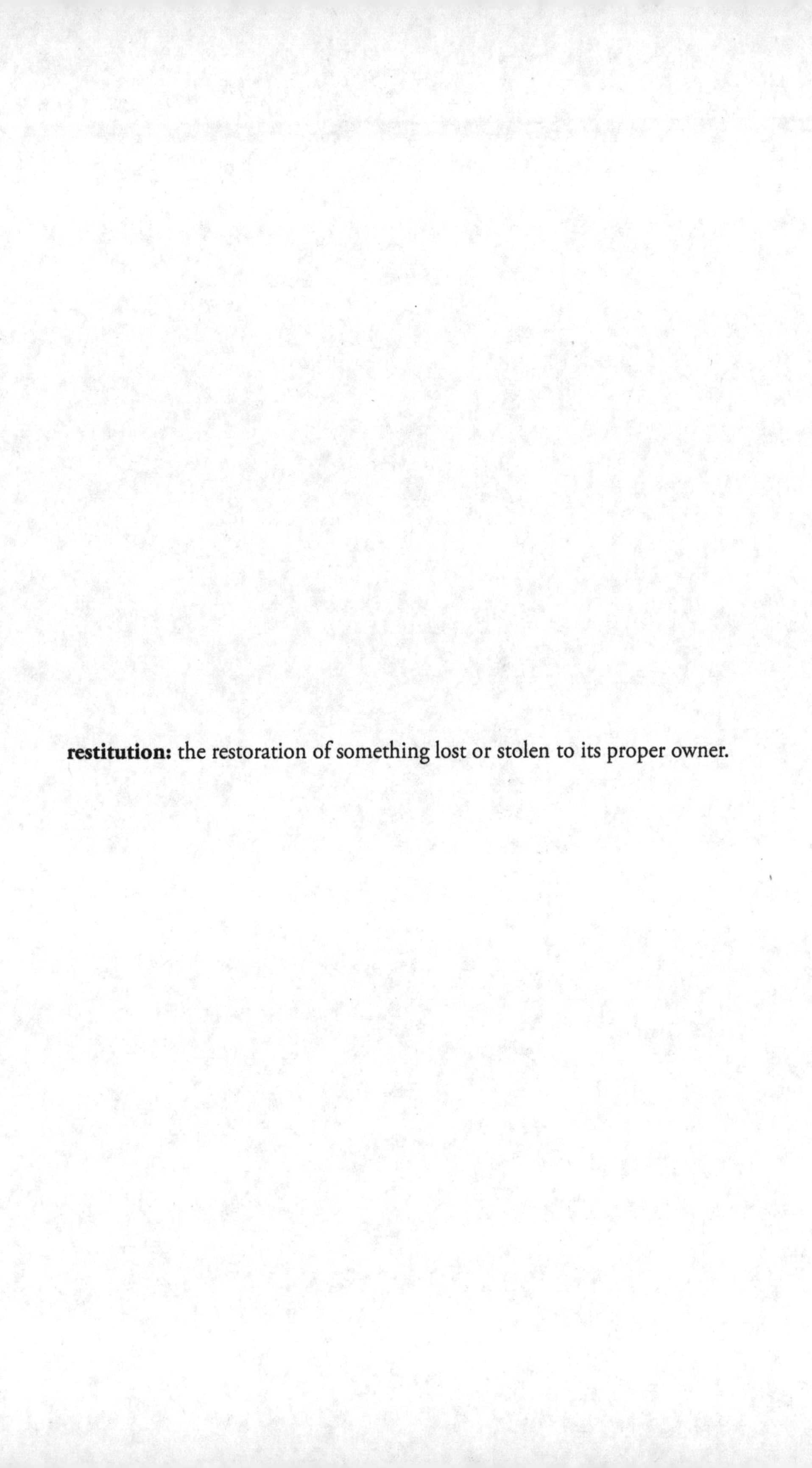

restitution: the restoration of something lost or stolen to its proper owner.

PROLOGUE

Paris, 1942

THE TWO GERMAN SOLDIERS dodged their way through the column of drab artillery vehicles that trundled along the Place de la Concorde. They did not slacken their pace as they climbed the short flight of steps at the Museum Jeu de Paume, a heavily fortified building on the banks of the Seine. The younger of the pair, but a military grade higher, Ronin Kohl had been close friends with his companion Karl Delitzsch long before they were paired together and put to work as part of a handpicked unit tasked with the removal of hundreds of precious works of art from locations that covered more than four countries. They had both been Hitler Youth, each had followed their father's footsteps into the party and, after meeting during basic training at the military academy in Dresden, had become inseparable as they progressed through officer training.

They saluted the sentry guarding the entrance and the double doors opened as if by their own volition. A passageway stretched before them, red-carpeted, flanked by two Roman statues and dimly lit by tall windows on either side. Beneath the gloomy ceiling of the room that had once been a tennis court for the seventeenth century nobility, lay rows and rows of gold-framed oil paintings, marble sculptures, and tapestries leaning against each other in the thick shadows. The place was deserted but the air itself seemed to vibrate with the dusky colors of the paintings. Ronin took quick steps and glanced behind at Karl whose spectacles glinted as his head swiveled left and right. His companion wore an expression of amazement, wonder, and pride.

Ronin could almost smell the power and opulence in the surroundings. It was a long way from the heavy fighting they'd both survived in Yugoslavia, Albania, and Greece. That guerrilla war still raged, and each had been lucky to come through it unscathed. And even luckier to have been reassigned to the newly formed Reichsleiter Rosenberg Institute for the Occupied Territories, or the ERR as it was more commonly known. Occupied Paris had its dangers, but it was like a holiday camp compared to what they'd been through in the last three years.

This morning their orders were to attend a briefing with their immediate superior, Bruno Lohse, who reported directly to Hermann Göring. Bruno Lohse was not a man to be trifled with. He was an art dealer but also a Nazi who had risen quickly through the party, and if he had a sense of humor, he kept it as well hidden as the treasures the Jewish population had squirrelled away. Today, Ronin and Kohl could hear almost every word he was shouting at the poor unfortunates currently in his office from outside in the corridor, despite the thick oak doors. He was in an even worse mood than normal. The Parisian Jews were not making it easy for him to do his job.

Lohse held daily gatherings with the heads of his various units of the ERR from 9:00 a.m. to 11:00 a.m., in the offices he'd sequestered in the Museum Jeu de Paume. Waiting in that corridor was akin to waiting to see your dentist, only minus the fun, and the anesthetic.

Finally, as the door to his office opened, a number of German officers funneled out, clearly having been taken down a peg or two.

"What's going on Walter?" Kohl said to one of the soldiers.

"He's not his usual self," answered Walter, looking a little shaken.

"Why?" asked Delitzsch. "Someone spill coffee on his latest Matisse?"

"Not quite," replied Walter. "He just heard his brother has been killed in action, right after being sprung in a raid in Antwerp."

"Shit," said Kohl, looking at his partner.

"Maybe not the best time to ask for a raise then?"

"Get the fuck in here you two!" Lohse screamed from inside the office.

"Probably not," said Delitzsch quietly.

Lohse was standing with his back to them, looking out the window at the river Seine below. The officers stood to attention at the desk, waiting for him to speak. He said nothing, and they stood there for what felt like an eternity.

"Sorry to hear about your brother," said Kohl, breaking the silence after several awkward minutes.

"Don't be," answered Lohse quietly, still facing away from the soldiers. "It was his own fault. He hadn't studied the reconnaissance properly, walked straight into a trap." Finally, he turned. "Sit," he barked. "I have a pressing mission for you and your unit."

"Our favorite type," answered Delitzsch.

Lohse opened a file, sifted through some documents, and handed them to the two officers.

"We've had intelligence directing us toward a potentially ripe section of Le Marais," he said. Le Marais was Paris's best-known Jewish neighborhood, a constant target for Lohse and his units since they'd arrived in Paris. "Within this specific area," he continued, laying out a street map of Paris on his desk and pointing to it with a well chewed pencil. "Our intelligence tells us that the lower section of Rue de Rosiers, between Rue Malher and Rue des Hospitalières St.-Gervais, was not sufficiently investigated. There are, according to our sources, *several* offices and homes that need to be revisited. Apparently, the Jews' methods of hidings their valuables have improved significantly since our original sweep, which means we need to take a deeper look into these properties."

"When you say *we*, you mean *us*?" said Kohl flippantly.

His partner threw him a look as if to say, "Are you fucking crazy?"

Lohse didn't acknowledge Kohl's question.

"There are two buildings in particular I want you focus on," Lohse said as he handed the soldiers a piece of paper with an address written on it. "Wait until nightfall," he added. "That area still has pockets of active Resistance units operating, if you encounter them, don't waste your time with arrests, just kill them." He paused and stared at them for a few seconds longer. "You have your orders. Now go."

Kohl and Delitzsch took the papers, stood, and saluted as Lohse lit a cigar and leaned back in his chair.

"Report back to me with a full inventory as soon as you have completed the order," he said as they turned to go. "Now I must telephone my mother and let her know there'll be one less at the dinner table this Christmas."

In normal times Rue de Rosiers, or "street of the rosebuds," was a bustling stretch of activity, home to a large majority of the Jewish community in Paris and had all the trappings of such a hub. The focal point for the local community was the synagogue at number twenty-five, a place that would be packed during services, which, as result, meant the nearby falafel shop was the perfect place to pick up the latest gossip, as well as freshly baked treats.

Another feature of this avenue was the large communal bathhouse Hammam Saint Paul. In normal times, this *schvitz* would be populated by the leaders of the various local community groups three times a week, where they held council meetings, with grievances being both aired and resolved. *These* were not normal times though. A once bustling thoroughfare was now an abandoned, bullet-ridden, and desolate street. Those business and places of public gathering were now empty, destroyed. The majority of the people who filled them were gone; many would never be seen again. Most were sent on trains to Poland and other areas around Europe where their unsolicited destiny awaited. Others fled, to all corners of the world, grabbing what they could, and leaving before the Nazi hit squads kicked their doors down.

Kohl Delitzsch, and the rest of their four-man unit, made up of Hans Müller and Artur Weber, two lower-ranked but first-rate soldiers, passed the now defunct metro station on Rue de Rosiers not long after sundown. The street was effectively deserted, save for a few manned German checkpoints dotted along the length of the avenue. When the unit reached the nearest checkpoint just outside the Saint-Paul Metro, they were quickly waved through. The German soldiers had been alerted to the unit's presence earlier that day, and *this* unit was afforded the same "access all areas" privileges that were normally reserved for members of the SS. Kohl and his men stopped momentarily to regroup by the entrance to the synagogue.

"Check the address again," Kohl said.

Müller pulled a piece of paper from his top pocket and read the details in a whisper, "Twenty-nine, thirty-three, and thirty-seven. All on the second floor of that block according to intelligence." He pointed down the street.

"Right," said Delitzsch. "Kohl and I will take the back stairs, you and Weber head up to the balcony and cover the front doors." He stared at Müller. "And not a fucking sound on approach, the Resistance still operates in this area."

The four-man squad headed down the avenue, splitting into two groups as they closed in on their target. Kohl started to climb the drainpipe to reach the second floor, Delitzsch kept watch.

"All clear," Kohl said as he reached the landing. Delitzsch headed up after him, and they surveyed the row of small windows facing them. "That one first," he said, pointing to the window farthest away from them.

They moved along the wall and got to the window, which was now just a broken frame, the glass having been blown out in an earlier raid. The two men entered the apartment through the broken window and were met in the hallway by Müller and Weber who had come in through the front door.

"Any problems?" asked Kohl as they started to make their way around the cramped two-bed apartment beginning their search.

"None," answered Weber. "There isn't so much as a mouse in these buildings."

"It's not mice I'm fucking worried about," replied Delitzsch as he pried open a door to a bedroom that had been blocked by rubble.

The apartment had already been destroyed, the infantry that had come before them had smashed their way through it, clearing out the families who were discovered hiding inside. Scattered across the space were the splintered remnants of tables and chairs, while once pristine but now torn curtains, framed the shattered windows. Delitzsch's feet crunched their way through the broken glass as he moved quickly from room to room.

"What are we supposed to be looking for in here? The place has been looted already, cleaned out, no?" asked Müller as he stood and looked at the debris.

"Fuck's sake, Müller," said Kohl as he pushed past him in the hallway. "Utilize that dormant organ under your helmet for once in your life. Just because someone *said* it's been done, doesn't always mean it *has*."

Müller had an expression on his face resembling a dog that had just been shown a card trick. Kohl exhaled and pointed to the ceiling in the hallway above Müller. Relatively unmarked from the previous raid, the ceiling was painted white, but Kohl had noticed something—a sixty-centimeter square of faintly cracked paint.

"I'll bet you two packs of cigarettes there's a makeshift loft up there," Kohl said as Delitzsch realized what his partner had spotted. He quickly went to find something to stand on.

Delitzsch and Weber dragged a tattered table into the hall from the living room. Kohl climbed onto the furniture and, using the butt of his rifle, started to tap away at the cracked paint. It wasn't long before not only the paint gave way, but the layers of plaster behind it too. Now covered in white dust, Kohl stood back slightly to reveal a square cut into the roof, with what looked like a hinge poking through the plaster at one end.

"See?" said Delitzsch, patting Müller on the shoulder. "That's why he's one of Göring's golden boys. This bloodhound could sniff out a gem blindfolded, underwater, from three kilometers away."

After some more thumping with his rifle, Kohl pushed on the now released square hatch, and it opened, flapping back, and revealing the entrance to a hidden loft space. As the crew entered the space one by one, they soon realized they had hit pay dirt. Using their army issue lighters, they found pieces of cloth, fashioned them into makeshift wicks, and then using some old wine bottles they'd found below in the apartment, they soon had the entire room bathed in soft light. They were surrounded by chests, crates, suitcases, and strongboxes, all left behind by the unfortunate tenants, presumably with the hope that they would one day get back home to retrieve them.

The four-man crew started to work their way through the hoard. They pulled all sorts from the room, from notebooks and diaries, toys, and oddities, to small pieces of jewelry and ceramics, as well as the odd small painting and sculpture.

"This'll get us a seat beside the Führer at the next convention," said Weber as they started to bundle everything into their backpacks.

"Only if any of this shit is worth anything," replied Delitzsch. "And you're hardly an expert on the subject," he added as he wrapped another bundle of items and packed them away. "You couldn't spell Botticelli, let alone recognize one."

The squad laughed, comfortable in each other's company, even in these most bizarre of circumstances.

As Weber and Delitzsch handed their overfilled backpacks down to Kohl, who had moved back down to the landing, Delitzsch spotted something in the corner of the attic. Another crate, tucked under a table, that they'd earlier missed. He pulled it out, opened it, and revealed some paintings, varying in size, six in total.

"Another one!" he shouted to the men as he pulled it toward the attic entrance. He lowered the box slowly down to Kohl.

"Right, let's wrap this up and fuck off," Delitzsch said.

They left through the front door of the apartment, their backpacks full, carrying two crates, one between two. Laden down, they were moving slowly when they reached the front of the building, emerging onto the first floor balcony that ran the length of the building. Kohl suddenly put his hand in the air, and snapped his fist closed, the sign to stop immediately. They stopped dead, and waited, watching their commander's hand closely. Kohl flashed two fingers, touched his ear, and pointed forward, meaning he'd heard something ahead of them. He signaled the men to back up. As the four men inched backward, he again closed his fist. They stopped. Kohl was now pointing behind them.

"What the fuck is going on?" whispered Weber.

"Shut the fuck up!" replied Kohl.

Just as he finished the sentence, a shot rang out, the bullet striking Weber in the center of his forehead, killing him instantly.

"MOVE!" shouted Delitzsch, and the three remaining men scrambled to take cover behind the low wall of the balcony.

A French Resistance sniper positioned on the roof opposite was now reloading and taking aim at the three remaining German soldiers. Kohl quickly looked around, assessing their options. The balcony had stairs at either end leading down to the street, and that looked like the only viable choice.

"On three, you and me head to that one," Kohl said to Müller. "You head to that end," he said to Delitzsch.

"Fucking Resistance," Delitzsch muttered as he prepared to bolt for the stairs.

Kohl held up his right hand, and counted down with his fingers: three, two, one, and then go. Kohl and Müller headed to the right end of the balcony, and Delitzsch to the left. As Kohl reached the stairs, four members of the French Resistance were charging up the steps, fully armed, guns trained on the Germans, while at the other end of the balcony a similar scenario was facing Delitzsch.

"Back!" Kohl shouted at Müller, who was now running back toward the middle of the balcony with Kohl behind him. The sniper took aim and hit the balcony with two quick shots. The three German soldiers, now surrounded, were running out of options. As they reached each other in the middle of the balcony, Kohl shouted to Delitzsch, "Jump!" and instinctively both he and Delitzsch make a hard turn and jumped over the balcony and down fifteen feet onto the street, leaving Müller and the two crates behind.

As they hit street level, shots rang out as Kohl looked back up to see Müller being gunned down by the approaching Resistance fighters. Delitzsch pushed his partner down the road, and they started to run, shots peppering the walls around them as they darted through the narrow laneways surrounding the nearby synagogue. Eventually, they reached a German checkpoint, and safety.

The Resistance didn't give chase. They knew they'd be outnumbered, and they'd had a good night, with two more Nazi occupier's dead. They recovered the two crates the Germans had abandoned on the balcony and quickly headed for their own sanctuary, the nearest safe house, less than a kilometer away, on Rue Pavée.

On the way, the Resistance group, originally made up of twelve men, split up to avoid capture, and by the time they reached the disused warehouse only four members of the squad remained, carrying the two crates. The upstairs office was a small dark room, filled with cigarette smoke, where the primary source of the smoke, their squad leader, Eric Purdue, was waiting.

"Well?" he said to the returning unit. "How did it go? Was the information good?"

"Spot on my friend," said Robert Morel, the most senior of the four Resistance members there.

They put the two crates in the center of the room and started opening the first of them, removing the selfsame items that Kohl, Delitzsch, and the now deceased Weber and Müller had pulled from the makeshift attic some forty minutes earlier. Purdue started to go through the contents of the second crate.

"Well well," he pronounced as he pulled six paintings from the crate one by one. "What have we here?"

They all looked at the bounty, which was now spread out across a large table. Six paintings, from six different artists, all with different subject matters, some portraits, some landscapes, but *all* beautiful.

"Which house were these taken from?" Eric asked his comrades.

"We followed the German squad and watched them leave number thirty-three," answered Robert.

"And who lived there?" Eric asked.

Robert checked through a copy of the most recent census, which the Resistance had secured through a friendly official in the local council offices now controlled by the Nazis.

"Rothstein," said Robert. "A Mr. and Mrs. Rothstein. One daughter, Edsel."

"Do we know what happened to them?" asked Eric. Robert checked through some other documents that were laid out on the table, lists collated by Resistance members with the help of the few remaining locals in the area, providing knowledge on the area and, more importantly, details about the fate of the residents who had lived there.

Robert looked up from the list. "The mother and father were marked for Belsen," he said.

"And the daughter?" asked Eric.

Robert again went back to the list. "Smuggled out with a group of teenagers and younger children, presumably to northern Europe," he replied. Eric stood holding the smallest of the paintings in his hands, gazing upon it adoringly.

"Well, the Rothstein's certainly have excellent taste," he said. "These paintings wouldn't look out of place in the Louvre. We'd best try and get word to little Miss Edsel Rothstein, and let her know that we have located her parents' possessions. I'm sure she'll be glad to know they're in safe hands now."

CHAPTER ONE

London, present day

THE DOOR OF THE coffee shop opened, and Michel headed onto Broadwick Street, coffee in one hand, phone in the other. He'd ignored the pastries menu on the wall behind the baristas. He didn't even want to think of eating this morning, couldn't rid his mind of the image that played over and over in his dreams of late, the image of him pulling the shutters down on his building for the final time. Sleep was such a luxury these days for Michel, let alone deep sleep that allowed him to dream. The past few weeks had pushed him closer to the edge, both mentally and physically, which meant that the for the last couple of nights, he'd passed out rather than drifting blissfully into a state of slumber. He walked briskly down the street, his head buried in his phone, checking emails. Turning right onto Poland Street, Michel picked up the pace. He'd just noticed the time on his phone and realized he was late. Left onto Noel Street, and then right onto Ramillies Street, Michel was now jogging. Already he was sweating; he could feel his shirt sticking to his back. Overhead, the sky grew dull, threatening a break in the unseasonably warm weather London had been enjoying.

"Please don't be there yet," he muttered to himself as he neared his destination. He passed the photographers gallery and swung right into Ramillies Place, where he came to a sharp stop.

"Fuck it," Michel said as he saw the van outside his building. The van's engine started, and it began to pull away. Michel ran and jumped out in front of the van with his arms out.

"Wait!" he shouted as the driver skidded to a halt.

"What the fuck are you doing, Michel?" shouted the driver as he got out of the van.

"Giorgio, so sorry I'm late, give me two minutes, I've got cash in the safe inside."

"I'm on a schedule, Michel, and I told you yesterday, no cash, no delivery. You said you'd be here at five thirty, yeah? You're not my only customer, you know?"

"I know, I know." Michel handed Giorgio his coffee to hold. "Give me two minutes."

Giorgio took the coffee and watched as Michel headed up the steps to the front door of his business, where he popped the key in and disappeared.

"*Stronzo*," said Giorgio to himself as he took a big gulp of Michel's coffee.

Rien Mais le Meilleur was an intimate forty-seat eatery tucked away on the ground floor at the end of Ramillies Place, and had been home, on and off, to Michel and his brother, Antoine, for most of their lives. Now a reimagining of the restaurant first opened by their parents in the late sixties, it had once been the toast of the London culinary scene. For almost thirty years it was one of *the* destination food spots in the capital, with people traveling from far and wide to eat some of the finest and most cutting-edge food available, all served in a convivial atmosphere. The dining room was beautifully appointed and under the guiding hands and watchful gaze of Jacques and Murielle de la Rue, Michel and Antoine's parents, Rien Mais le Meilleur flourished.

After their father died, and much to everyone's surprise and disappointment, the building was boarded up by their mother and the boys were dispatched to Paris to finish their studies—a move which the boys agreed to, motivated by despair at their mother's swift decision to abandon ship. The boys were to embark on their own paths, which both thrilled and terrified them.

They both put their heads down and succeeded, Michel as a concierge and maître d', and Antoine as a chef. Then finally, following a series of events that made them both rethink their lives, the brothers joined forces and returned to London, to reopen their parent's beloved restaurant. The brothers' reimagining of the business initially enjoyed a good run, especially in the early years, but the past eighteen months had been a downward spiral and now bankruptcy was staring them in the face. Their debts were out of control and Michel could now only buy supplies with cash. Almost all of their credit lines had been cut.

The downturn in business was one thing. Antoine's many passions in life—alcohol, women, and his love of gambling—were quite another. In contrast, Michel hadn't had a drink since he left Paris, and he had the same luck with women that Antoine had with the horses. The only bookmaker Michel was aware of was an old bookshop on Newburgh Street that specialized in first editions, one of Michel's lifelong passions. Antoine's habits were making an already bad situation perilously worse.

Scuttling through the dining room, Michel passed the cloakroom area, down the corridor past the kitchens, and through the door to the back office, *his* office. This small space was a postcard for mayhem, documents strewn all over the room, plates and glasses on the desk and the shelves, empty cigarette packets on the floor. He pulled a bunch of keys from his coat, found the smallest one on the key ring, and opened the top drawer of his desk. A yellow Post-it note was stuck to the front of a ledger. The list of numbers on the note were crossed out, except the one at the bottom—194239. He murmured the number repeatedly to himself as he headed to a picture on the back wall of the office. He took the picture down, revealing a wall safe. He started turning the wheel on the front of the safe, right, then left, until the lock clicked. He opened the safe door and pulled out a brown envelope, marked "RDF." He opened the envelope which contained a small bundle of cash and peeled off one hundred pounds, before locking the rest safely back up and running to the street.

"One minute and forty seconds," said Giorgio as he threw the now empty coffee cup at Michel's feet. "Not bad for a man your age."

"Here you go." Michel tried not to pant too heavily and therefore prove Giorgio right. "That'll cover us for tomorrow too, right?" He handed Giorgio the cash.

"Just about," Giorgio replied as he counted the money. "You know what my uncle always told me, Michel?" He pocketed the cash and began to lift two crates of fruit and vegetables out from the back of his van.

"No," replied Michel. "And I couldn't care less to be honest," he added under his breath.

"When a restauranteur starts paying you in cash for deliveries, it's only a matter of weeks before you'll be closing that account," said Giorgio as he left the crates at the top of the steps. "That's the fourth time in the past two weeks that you've paid me in cash." A smarmy smirk crept across his face. "You going to bother putting an order in for Wednesday?"

"We're not going anywhere, my friend," retorted Michel, with an even bigger smirk.

He stopped and called to Giorgio, who was just about settled back into his van. "And by the way, you might want to swing by the chemist on the way to your next delivery. That coffee you just drained was a hazelnut latte, and if your nut allergy is anything like your uncle's, you'll be shitting through the eye of a needle within the hour." Michel kicked the empty coffee cup back toward Giorgio's van. "*Buona giornata, amico mio*!" he shouted. He picked the two crates up, and headed through the front door of his restaurant, slamming it behind him.

Another day in paradise, he thought, as he headed for the kitchen.

CHAPTER TWO

THE RESTAURANT WAS A warren of a place, with a kitchen that once had the best equipment, the whitest tiles, and the shiniest chrome work surfaces in the entire West End. Now most of the equipment was held together with gaffer tape, the walls looked like they belonged in a pre-smoking ban pool hall, and the chrome surfaces resembled a DeLorean that had been driven off a cliff. This business was clearly on its last legs.

Michel stood and looked around. The kitchen was filthy, but the thought of heading back into his dimly lit office and trying to make headway on the company accounts, filled him with dread. With the kitchen staff not due in for another hour, he took his coat and jacket off, rolled up his sleeves, and got to work putting the newly delivered fruit and vegetables away in the kitchens fridges. He reached over to switch on an old radio that sat on a shelf above the sink. Antoine, being the older brother *and* the head chef, had control over *everything* within these kitchen walls, that was *his* domain after all, including, of course, the radio.

Antoine was so particular about what he was listening to while cooking that he'd pulled off the knob that was used to change the station, so your choice was limited to one. Antoine had the radio fixed to Classic FM, which, fortuitously, Michel loved, and so as "O mio babbino caro" from Puccini's *Gianni Schicchi* filled the air, he kicked into gear and set about cleaning the kitchen. Anything, he thought, was better than staring at a screen trying to balance VAT invoices.

Not long into his work, he heard a strange noise, an ugly, low, rumbling sound that stopped, and then started again seconds later. He switched off the radio and started to move through the kitchen. He nudged the large free-standing oven with his hip, the oven was now more than thirty years old and constantly breaking down, thinking that was the source, but no, the noise was still there. He walked slowly toward one of the two large walk-in fridges. The noise was getting louder. He picked up a carving knife and a rolling pin from the counter as he slowly approached the fridge door. Being a ground floor kitchen in Soho, one of the busiest parts of London, rats were familiar visitors to the fridges, so he was readying himself for anything as he got closer to the large door handle. Taking a deep breath, he opened it to find Antoine curled up in a crumpled three-piece pinstriped suit, asleep on the floor. Fortunately for Antoine, but not for the remaining stock on the shelves, his older brother had remembered to turn the power to the fridge off, before choosing it as his bed for the night.

"Why does he do this to me?" whispered Michel. He kicked Antoine in the legs. "Wakey, wakey!" he shouted. He ran to turn the fridge back on to save the last few trays of meats and cold produce.

Antoine stirred, opened one eye, rolled over, farted, and immediately fell back asleep. Michel took one of the trays of chicken livers, that were now perilously close to going off, and dropped them on Antoine's face.

"Get the fuck up!" he shouted as Antoine leapt to his feet wiping the reeking liver juice off his face.

"What the fuck!" Antoine bellowed.

"*You* can finish cleaning this kitchen up, then come to the office," Michel said as he left the kitchen. "We need to talk."

"Shit," said Antoine to himself. He'd planned to be up, showered, changed, and at his workstation *before* Michel arrived, but not for the first time, that plan went south, courtesy of a night filled with copious amounts of brandy and ginger ale.

"*Je suis vraiment désolé…*" whispered Antoine, now cleaned up and dressed in his chef whites, as he entered Michel's office carrying a tray, a peace offering of sorts: a pot of freshly brewed coffee, two china cups and saucers, and a small basket of croissants. He stopped and looked at his little brother, eyebrows raised as if to say, "Well?"

"Merci," said Michel quietly.

Antoine smiled and placed the tray on Michel's desk. He sat and started to pour the coffee.

"My famous lemon curd croissants, your favorite," he said as he placed one of the pastries on a napkin and offered it to his brother. Michel took it, helped himself to a huge bite, chewed, and smiled.

"How can a man so talented be such a fucking moron?"

"Practice," replied Antoine.

The brothers laughed. They sat in silence, drank their coffee, and ate their pastries. This was almost ritualistic, it was something they'd always done, something that started when they were kids, up in their bedroom above the restaurant. Every night toward the end of service, their mother would sneak a tray of pastries upstairs, then skip back down to the busy restaurant before their father noticed she *and* the pastries were gone. The boys had an old coffee percolator set up in the corner of their bedroom, a relic from the kitchens below, and they would brew a fresh pot, and enjoy their nightly treat together. It was a tradition they carried on right through their years studying and working in Paris, where they shared an apartment. It was a ritual they'd made sure to continue, to sit down at the end of the day, break bread, and go through the array of latest problems and obstacles, sorting out each other's personal lives, advising and counseling each other, and generally putting the world to rights. It was their *thing*. This morning felt different though. Something other than the sweet perfume of fresh pastries was in the air, and it needed to be addressed.

"This has got to change, Antoine," Michel said as he placed his empty cup back on the tray.

"I know, I know. Look, it was supposed to be a quiet night. I went to meet Davide in the Hibernian Club. He wanted to talk about a staff dinner he was planning to have here next week. Could've brought a lot of cash in."

"Could have?" Michel said. "So, I presume they're *not* going to be booking then."

"Well, not exactly," Antoine sheepishly explained. "We were about to agree a price, a group rate, when Davide offered to make it interesting, he'd pay double the price of the booking if I won, and I'd cover his tab here if *he* won."

"Won what?"

There was a long moment of silence, as Antoine paused before he delivered an answer he knew Michel didn't want to hear.

"The game of poker he wanted to play," said Antoine.

"Poker, seriously?" Michel shouted. "Here we are struggling for bookings, and you are handed an opportunity to get our restaurant fully booked with staff from one of the biggest financial houses in Canary Wharf, and you risk it on a fucking poker game? Why didn't you just take the booking and leave it at that?"

Silence.

"Because it *was* an opportunity, he was offering to pay an extra eighty quid per head if I won! That would have been an extra three grand on top of their tab, and they would have wiped our bar dry too!"

"But they're not fucking coming at *all* now are they!" roared Michel. "Jesus, Antoine, losing a six-grand tab, on a fucking poker game? That could've kept the doors of this place open for another couple of weeks!" Michel was disgusted with his brother, and not for the first time.

"No," said Antoine. "I didn't lose the poker game."

There was a further explanation coming. And it wasn't one Michel was expecting.

"I picked the wrong rooster," said Antoine.

"The wrong what?" said Michel, convinced he'd misheard his brother.

"The wrong rooster," answered Antoine.

Michel put his head in his hands.

"We left the club at two. I'd *won* the poker game," said Antoine, "but Davide wanted another drink, so we ended up at Mr. Dings."

"Jesus, not Dings?" said Michel, now knowing where this story was headed.

Mr. Dings was a notorious drinking den in Chinatown, offering late-night overpriced sushi and sake to those desperate enough to keep the party going. It was also home to one of the best attended illegal cock-fighting rings in the UK, something that Mr. Dings grandfather had started in the early thirties and had quickly become a Soho institution. Antoine went on to explain that Davide wanted another chance to win the bet, and so in a "double-or-nothing" move, with a tab of twelve grand riding on the outcome, it came down to one cock fight, and Antoine backed the wrong rooster. Davide won the bet, which meant his party of forty staff from the bank would be dining in the brothers' restaurant next week, free of charge.

"Right," said Michel calmly, after hearing all the evidence of the night before, "That's it."

"What's *it*?" said Antoine.

"I've spent the past eighteen months keeping this place going," said Michel, launching into a furious rant. "I've strung suppliers along with promises of payment, and I've even had to sell some of *my* own possessions to cover *your* gambling debts, pay the staff, and keep the roof over *our* heads, but no more, brother. No amount of lemon curd croissants can win me over this time. I'm done. *We're* done."

Michel sat at his desk, and spun the chair around, so he had his back to his brother. He was at the end of his tether. They were only a matter of weeks away from losing their business and their home. Antoine's behavior over the past couple of years had worn away at, and finally crushed, Michel.

"Brother," said Antoine. "Look, I'll clean up, I'll sober up, and I'll get us money. I don't know how or where, but I'll get it, pay you back, and get us back on our feet."

"No," said Michel. "You won't. You've made promise after promise before and never come through. So as usual, it's left up to me to sort this shit out, *your* shit, which through a DNA match means it's my shit too. This is different, Antoine, this isn't a small gambling debt, this is bigger than that, much bigger."

The brothers sat in silence. Each waiting for the other to talk. Antoine seemed to suddenly understand that this was serious. He was squirming in his seat, shifting from cheek to cheek, constantly on the move, fidgeting. There was a change in Michel's demeanor now, which gave Antoine a different feeling about this particular talking-to that was being dished out.

After what seemed an age, Michel fixed his glare on his brother and spoke. "There is one option left. But you're not going to like it."

CHAPTER THREE

Michel fidgeted as he stood and stared at his brother. Antoine, not moving a muscle, looked back at him, saying nothing, until it all got too much for his hungover head to deal with.

"Okay, brother, spit it out then," he said.

"Before I do," said Michel, "you need to be very clear in that pig-head of yours that what happens next is entirely because of you. We're here, in very deep shit, because of you. You have consistently ruined everything we set out to achieve and it cannot go on. Is that clear?"

"As my famous consommé. Now please, get on with it," Antoine replied rubbing his temples, his hangover now approaching warp-factor five.

"Well, as you know, for years we've turned down offer after offer from corporates, advertising, everyone—big offers, for you to put your name, and our Michelin star, behind a product or event?"

Michel knew that Antoine wouldn't like where this was going. Antoine had always hated the whole "celebrity chef" vibe, passionately putting down those peers of his who had cashed in and endorsed their own range of cooking utensils or released their own range of sauces or condiments. To Antoine, it was tantamount to sacrilege. It was selling out, and it wasn't why he'd become a chef. All those years training in the kitchens of Paris, the abuse, the blood, sweat and tears, the craft, the learning, the education, the skill of designing a dish, a menu, and having the public and the food critics love them. That was what life was all about for Antoine.

"No," said Antoine firmly as he got up and headed for the office door. Michel cut him off at the pass, and kicked the door shut.

"Sit down, shut up, and listen. Let me give you the facts of life, brother, as you clearly have no idea about them."

Michel had been shouting, spittle beginning to foam on his lips. He hadn't displayed so much ferocity since they were kids. He grabbed a box file from the drawers behind him and slammed it on the table in front of Antoine.

"According to this," Michel said, "we have enough money left to trade for approximately another ten days, and, after that, we're done, bankrupt." Antoine took the file and started thumbing through the contents, reams of "final demand" notices, letters from Inland Revenue, and lots of suppliers' invoices marked overdue.

"I had no idea, honestly," Antoine said. "I mean I knew it was bad, but not this bad."

"Well how could you know?" said Michel. "You've had your head buried in the sand for years. You haven't looked at these books in months, despite my protests, yet you've kept living and behaving like it was the week after we'd won our Michelin star, which was seven years ago! You've been celebrating that star ever since, and then when we lost it four years ago, that was *another* reason to drink. 'They're idiots, what the fuck do they know about food,' that's all you've spouted since, and I've had to listen to that shit for four years now, and honestly, I'm done with it."

Antoine felt like he was in the headmaster's office. He regularly had to take a verbal dressing down from Michel, but this was different. He could see his little brother was finally broken, spent.

The brothers had a bond stronger than most. They were more than best friends, they had always shared everything with each other, from toys to playground sweets, from birthday and Christmas presents to albums and even the odd girlfriend. They were tighter than most other siblings could ever hope to be. Because their parents were French, they also shared two languages, something that they would often use to their advantage in school when faced with a bully or an awkward teacher. They used French as if it was their secret language. They were connected in so many ways. As a result, they knew each other inside out—each other's moods, each other's likes and dislikes—and they were there for each other, always.

They were also connected by what happened when the boys were in their early teens. One afternoon Antoine returned home from school late, having played a football match, and stuck his head in the restaurant door, checking to see if Michel was around.

"He's been upstairs all day," said one of the waiters, when Antoine asked where his brother was. Michel had missed school that day, complaining of stomach pains that morning. Antoine ran upstairs to find Michel sprawled on the sitting room floor, where he'd passed out a few hours earlier. Antoine ran back down to the restaurant to alert his mother and father, who immediately rushed upstairs, and when they saw the state their son was in, called an ambulance.

Five months later, Antoine lay in a hospital bed beside his brother, both having been prepped for surgery, as Michel needed a kidney transplant. The brothers were a match, and naturally Antoine didn't hesitate in a bid to save his little brother's life. These brothers literally shared everything, even their kidneys. Michel had never forgotten what his brother had done for him, but recently he felt like he'd been forgiving Antoine for all the wrongs he'd done because of the sacrifice Antoine made for *him* when they were younger.

"All right," Antoine said. "What's this option? Let me hear it, but I'm telling you now, if you mention the words celebrity or *MasterChef,* I'll break your legs."

Michel flipped open his laptop, spun it around to face Antoine and said, "Read that."

Michel's email account was open on the screen, and Antoine ran his eyes rapidly over the section Michel had highlighted.

I hope you've given my offer some thought, Michel. It's a fantastic opportunity for you and Antoine to get away from it all, and it will give us, the TV public, a chance to see what makes the greatest French cooking dynasty since the Roux family tick. It'll be a fascinating watch. I look forward to hearing from you and your brother.

Best regards,

Alain Deschamps

Antoine finished reading and sat in silence for a moment. Michel was acutely conscious of the refrigerators humming in the kitchen below. Suddenly they sounded absurdly loud; their throbbing seemed to fill the building.

"Who the fuck is Alain Deschamps?" asked Antoine as he looked up from the screen.

Michel closed the laptop and moved around to the edge of the desk, close to Antoine.

"Alain Deschamps is a very, *very,* successful businessman based in Paris. He made his money as an art dealer, and now has a large stake in one of the biggest television channels in France, which, among other things, has a hugely popular food channel."

Antoine's face dropped.

"Before you say anything," Michel said, "let me give you some details. This isn't like any of the other Mickey Mouse shit we've turned down before."

"Go on," said Antoine.

"A four-part series, featuring you and me, six weeks filming around France, you cooking *your* dishes, us meeting the locals, me adding a little local history dotted in here and there, and us talking about our time training in France, *and* we end the series preparing a banquet in our old stomping ground, in Paris."

Antoine turned away from his brother. He spread his fingers against the edge of the table as though he were about to suddenly push it away. Michel watched as his brother closed his eyes and took a deep breath, appearing to try and swallow his distaste.

"We could do this in our sleep Antoine, *and* they've also offered to publish a cookbook based on the TV series, which would give you a chance to share your food with a wider audience, which means there could be bookings for tables here from all over Europe."

Antoine appeared to have stopped listening. The atmosphere in the room grew uncomfortable, but Michel kept going, laying out the blunt facts in a calm voice.

"Look, I know it's not your thing, but we've no options left, we've borrowed money from every shyster in London, we're on our last legs with suppliers, and we can't pay our staff to work past next Thursday."

Still, Antoine did not look at him. He stared at the opposite wall, his profile hard and stubborn. Michel thought he saw a belligerence take hold in his brother's mouth. Quickly, he continued.

"We could lock this place up for the six weeks, say we're refurbishing, and then when we get back, plough the money we'd get from the TV job into updating the kitchen and the dining room, and then relaunch, better than ever."

Antoine rubbed his forehead. The movement drew attention to his thick neck. Michel could see that he had put on weight in the past year, and that his face was flushed and bloated with exhaustion. He could see Antoine was taking it in. However, he knew what would get this over the line for him. He took a notepad, scribbled something on it and handed it to his brother.

With an effort Antoine peered at the note.

"Merde," he said.

"Exactly," replied Michel. "Who could say no to that money?"

Antoine's eyes widened. He folded his arms and stared at the table. Michel wasn't sure whether the gesture meant he disagreed with his brother or was considering the offer. The seconds ticked by. Finally, he looked up at Michel and grinned.

"Easiest two hundred grand we'll ever make, huh?" said Antoine.

"Exactly," said Michel, "and that's just our fee for the TV series. The production company will cover our flights, accommodation, expenses, and on top of that there's the book sales, *and* the inevitable bump in bookings the restaurant would get. Besides that, it'll do us both good to close this place up for six weeks, get some sun on our backs, cook and eat some great food, and meet some old friends. You could revamp the menu, get some inspiration, get your mojo back?" Michel could see that Antoine was warming to the idea, nonetheless Antoine seemed to be troubled by something else.

"But why us?" Antoine asked. "We've never done any of this TV stuff before?"

"That's exactly why," replied Michel. "It's *because* we've never done anything like this before. We've never put our heads above the parapet, the foodie audience doesn't know anything about us, about our dad, *his* success, and Christ knows, the people who watch these shows are screaming out for new faces. They want new blood on these channels, and who knows what opportunities it'll open up for the restaurant?"

Antoine pondered the offer that was in front of him and his brother. He let out a long sigh. "Dad would turn in his grave."

"Don't try and play that card, Antoine," Michel replied, clearly seeing the arrows coming. "You've managed to shit all over Dad's reputation in this town for the past few years. If he's going to move in that coffin, it'll be to track you down and give you a good kicking after what you've done to our family name."

"And there's no other option?"

"Nope," answered Michel.

"There's a sure thing running at Chepstow tomorrow in the three forty, I got a concrete tip from Larry the limp," said Antoine, in an attempt to lighten the mood, but Michel didn't laugh.

"Those days are over, Antoine," said Michel sternly. "This is our *last* chance."

Antoine nodded. He was in. He slowly cleared the table and left the office. Michel slumped back into his chair and put his head in his hands. He was relieved but exhausted, excited but terrified. He reached for his cigarettes on the desk and lit one. He opened his laptop, pulled up Alain Deschamps's email, and hit reply.

"I've spoken to Antoine, we're on board," he typed. "Get the contracts over as soon as possible, and we'll sign." He paused for a second, reread what he'd just typed, took a deep breath, and hit send.

No going back now.

CHAPTER FOUR

Paris, 1965

As a native of Paris, Jacques de la Rue was used to the hustle and bustle of this bohemian European capital. Having worked his way up from the lowly position of pot-washer to the exalted heights of head chef, he was more than comfortable in the heat of a demanding commercial kitchen. Paris and its food reputation were in full flight in the mid-sixties, exciting and revolutionary new dishes were setting as many global trends as the music and fashion of the day. While Yves Saint Lauren was paving the way with the revolutionary cocktail dress design, the Rolling Stones were heard loud and clear on every radio station from the Sorbonne to Marseille, lamenting their lack of satisfaction.

Jacques had put in a tough six months in his new job as head chef at a smart boutique hotel near the Place des Vosges. He had overseen all of the details, from the menu design to the table dressings in order to be ready for their opening night. A momentous and hugely successful summer was behind him. He had secured his place and reputation among the highest regarded new chefs on the Parisian food scene. These past months had also seen him fall in love.

With only one week to go in the crazily busy summer season, Jacques had already planned his post-summer holiday. He and his girlfriend, Murielle, whom he'd met five months ago when she was hired as a waitress at the new hotel, were heading south to Toulouse, to pick up a small barge, which would take them along the Canal du Midi toward Carcassonne, for a short but well-deserved break. Everything was planned as usual, with military precision, by Jacques. Jacques left nothing to chance; he didn't like surprises. He *was* planning a huge surprise for Murielle on the trip. He was going to propose, having fallen completely in love with this beautiful, smart woman.

She had an inkling; they had discussed the idea over several romantic walks through the park near the hotel where they worked, laughing and dreaming about their future together. One loose end was yet to be tied up though, and it was bugging Jacques. He had yet to ask Murielle's father for her hand, a tradition that stood firm even though this was the swinging sixties, and because Murielle's father was somewhat old fashioned. So, with a week to go before they were due to set off on their well-earned holiday, Jacques planned to leave work early one night, head over to the Sacré-Cœur area of Paris where Murielle's father worked and do the deed.

Jacques knew that Murielle's father would be in his office, as he was every night until eight, before heading back to Murielle's family home. Jacques would have to make good time to get across Paris tonight, as there was an international rugby match on at the Parc des Princes, so he knew traffic would be heavy. He went up to his room in the hotel and changed into his "good" suit, a linen suit that he'd picked up in a market some weeks ago, in preparation for tonight's meeting. Looking as formal as his limited wardrobe allowed him, he jumped in a cab and made his way through the busy evening Paris traffic.

While in the back of the taxi, Jacques checked his pocket, and breathed a sigh of relief when he saw that he'd remembered to bring the ring with him. The ring, which had been his mother's engagement ring, was to be the focal point of tonight's meeting with Ronin Kohl. Jacques planned that after delivering his now well-practiced speech, which he'd rehearsed in front of a full-length mirror in his room the night before, he would then show Mr. Kohl the ring, showing him that he meant business. Jacques clutched the ring box in his hand as the taxi neared the turn off on the Boulevard Barbès, drove down toward Rue Muller, and onward toward Kohl's office. Pulling up outside, Jacques leaned forward to pay the driver.

"Yes," said the driver as Jacques handed him the money.

"What?" replied Jacques.

"*I'd* say yes," said the driver, slightly blushing. "You've been rehearsing out loud all the way over here. I presume you're going to ask someone to marry you tonight?"

"I am," answered Jacques, embarrassed that he was so nervous he'd given a fully audible rendition of the speech and subsequent proposal to the driver. "Wish me luck," he said as he closed the door on the taxi.

"She'd be a fool to say no." The driver winked at Jacques and drove away.

CHAPTER FIVE

Present Day

JACQUES PRESSED THE BUZZER marked "Kohl and Associates" on the wall-mounted panel outside the building. The door buzzed, and in he went. He'd visited these offices months ago when Murielle brought him over to meet her father for the first time, and as Jacques climbed the stairs to Kohl's office on the third floor, he again ran through his prepared speech. By time he'd uttered the words, "And so I'm here to ask for your permission for your..." he'd reached the door of the office. He knocked and waited.

"It's open," said a voice from inside.

Jacques opened the door, closed it behind him, and turned to see Ronin Kohl, sitting at a large cumbersome looking draughtsman's desk, where he was busily putting the finishing touches to a drawing. Kohl was a stern looking man, spectacled, well-built, with tight cropped blond hair, and blue eyes. His face bore the marks of a man who had seen some troubling things in his time.

"To what do I owe the pleasure?" Kohl said, without raising his head from his work.

"Well," said Jacques. "Thank you for agreeing to see me, I know it was short notice, and I know that you are a very busy man."

"How's the cooking going?" Kohl cut across Jacques.

"The cooking?"

"The cooking. The café or whatever it is, how's business?" he said impatiently, not really caring what the answer was.

"You mean the award-winning *restaurant*, at the *hotel*, at which I'm *head chef*?" Jacques spoke with a little more edge than he'd planned.

Kohl clearly didn't rate Jacques, as a chef, as a businessman, and more importantly as potential husband material for his only daughter.

"It's going really well actually, we've had a busy summer, fully booked, and the restaurant is getting good reviews." Jacques sat on the sofa across the room from Ronin's desk.

"Good for you," said Kohl, with a beautifully measured patronizing tone, like he was congratulating a five-year-old on being able to spell the word "cat."

Kohl finished his work, flicked the lamp off above his desk and removed his glasses. He flipped his suit jacket on and sat beside Jacques on the sofa.

"Look, let's cut the soft shoe shuffle and get straight to the Charleston," he said "Why are you here?"

Jacques cleared his throat, but before he could speak Ronin jumped in again, "Let me guess, you need money?" Clearly impatient, Kohl reached for his wallet. He was not enjoying Jacques's company and wanted to wrap this impromptu meeting up as soon as he could.

"Why the hell would I need money?" said Jacques.

"Well, for one there's that suit. Looks like you've slept in it for a week. Then there's the cheap cologne, which I presume you bought at the same market as the suit, another bargain no doubt, and yet still not strong enough to mask the odour of the fish stew you've obviously been slaving over, and then there's the vain attempt to smarten yourself up, your hair looks like you've brushed it with a ladle. Do I need to continue?" Kohl spoke with such speed and dexterity as though *he'd* rehearsed it.

"No," said Jacques, calmly. "I don't need money, my restaurant is doing very well, I'm doing very well, thank you."

"So why the effort then." Kohl reached for the cigarette box on the table, took one, and offered the box to Jacques, which he took. Ronin took a long drag of his cigarette, sizing up his guest.

"It's about Murielle," Jacques said gently.

Kohl shifted uncomfortably in his seat and took another long drag of his cigarette.

"I know you're a man of convention, a man of tradition," Jacques said, checking every time he finished a sentence to see what reaction he was getting from his audience of one.

Nothing, not a flinch. Kohl sat and stared at the floor, occasionally looking at his watch. In what felt like an hour, just three minutes passed, with Jacques speaking about his love for Ronin's daughter, the times they'd shared together, his plans for their future, his plans for his business, and eventually his plans for a family.

Jacques was in full flow, nearing the crescendo of his speech, when Kohl abruptly cut in.

"Let me stop you there Jacques," he said as he stabbed out his cigarette, and stood face-to-face with Jacques. "If you're building up to ask me what I think you're building up to ask, the answer is no."

"But," said Jacques, trying to get ahead of what was coming.

"But nothing," said Kohl calmly. "There is no way that I will *ever* give my permission, let alone blessing, for my only daughter to marry you, a cook, a bottle washer, a glorified skivvy, and a Jew." Kohl landed on the last word like it was made of broken glass.

Jacques was stunned, not only by this man's words, but by everything this man stood for. Jacques family was Jewish and proud of it.

Kohl clearly had more to say, but his bigoted outburst had made Jacques's mind up. Jacques took one last drag of his cigarette, dropped it on the expensive Persian rug on the floor and stamped it out.

"No need to continue," he said. "You've answered any questions I might have asked of you, have a good night."

As the door closed, Kohl looked down at the small black smoldering mess on his rug and smirked to himself.

Outside, Jacques lit another cigarette, and started walking. As he approached the steps at the bottom of the famous Sacré-Cœur basilica, he spotted a familiar figure, sitting, waiting. It was Murielle. They'd arranged to meet not far from her father's office after Jacques's big meeting with him. She knew when Jacques asked her to meet her there earlier that day that he'd had something important to do, that he was going to her father's office to ask for her hand.

"Well?" Murielle said as Jacques sat beside her on the steps. "How did it go?"

Jacques took a minute as he lit her a cigarette and passed it to her.

"How do you think it went?" he said, with a smile on his face.

"Let me guess, it was a *nein*?"

They sat in silence as they considered the night's events, and its consequences.

"What now then?" she asked Jacques. He didn't answer. "Did you tell him about the baby?" Jacques shook his head.

"Funnily enough, the opportunity didn't present itself."

"So, what now?" Murielle said as she took Jacque's hand in hers.

"Time for plan B."

"There's a plan B?"

Jacques leaned down and kissed her softly, as if to say, "Don't worry, I've got this under control."

"We elope," he said.

"What, to Toulouse?"

"No, forget about Toulouse. London."

Jacques offered his hand to Murielle and lifted her off the steps and into his arms. He held her with an embrace that was intended to reassure Murielle that things were going to be okay.

They started to walk slowly, along Rue du Chevalier de la Barre, hand in hand, content. It was almost as if Jacques had planned this outcome all along, that this was the real surprise.

CHAPTER SIX

Paris, present day

LOCATED JUST BEHIND THE Hôtel d'Aubusson on Rue Dauphine in Paris' trendy left bank district, stood an impressive modern office block. Eight stories high, this glazier's heaven, with its polished steel, glass, and contemporary landscaping design, made this one of *the* most desirable office spaces in Paris. It was also one of the greenest buildings in Europe, complete with the latest in solar panel technology and state-of-the-art wind turbines, which meant that the building effectively powered itself. This impressive building was home to some of the top hedge funds in France, some of Europe's oldest and most respected law firms, and several Asian aircraft leasing houses. One of the most appealing things about this location for the companies based here was that the offices were discreet—numbers on doors, no company names, no pomp and ceremony, just numbers. Low visibility.

In the center of the spacious well-appointed lobby was a large security counter manned by three burly security guards, complete with war-zone type haircuts and matching earpieces. Two receptionists sat behind the counter, both of whom wouldn't have looked out of place on one of the famous catwalks during Paris fashion week.

Fabian Ritzier entered the building and approached the desk.

"How can I help you?" said one of the receptionists.

"Fabian Ritzier, from *Le Monde*, I have a ten thirty with Mr. Deschamps," replied Fabian.

"Perfect, one moment please." She tapped a number into her phone and waited. Then she spoke into her headset. "I have a Mr. Ritzier from *Le Monde* at the front desk? I'll let him know." She hung up. "Please take a seat, someone will be down for you shortly." She pointed Fabian toward the plush leather sofas in the lobby.

Fabian sat and opened his briefcase, checking he had everything he needed to carry out his impending task. Notepad, pencils, Dictaphone, and camera. He took a file from his bag and started to flick through it. He'd been sent by his editor to capture an exclusive and rare interview with Alain Deschamps, CEO of Deschamps International Holdings. It was to be a profile piece and was set to be published in an upcoming edition of his newspaper, *Le Monde*, one of the most respected daily publications in the world. Deschamps was one of those low profile, highly functioning one-percenters, beyond rich, self-made, and reclusive. This profile piece would finally put a face to the name. The French public and wider readers of the paper would finally get to see and know the local man who had risen phoenix-like from humble beginnings to become one of the richest men in France and one of the most influential people in his business. The art business.

Fabian read through his research notes, which contained rare photos of Deschamps in public, accompanied by the odd article about his sporadic and diverse moments of philanthropy, including his funding of several art colleges around France, Austria, and Germany, and his funding of a neonatal wing at the University Hospital of Bordeaux, the town of his birth.

Fabian's newspaper, along with every other major media outlet in the world, had chased Deschamps for an interview like this for years, with no results. Undeterred, Fabian happily took on this seemingly impossible assignment some time ago and set to it determined to get what numerous other journalists failed to, a sit down with this most elusive of power brokers. He sent numerous emails, requests, handwritten letters, and even attempted to doorstep Deschamps at a number of charity events but all efforts came to no avail.

Finally, he'd got his meeting. He'd wondered several times why he was suddenly granted this rare audience. The general consensus back in the *Le Monde* office was that Deschamps simply wanted to unveil another gift to the nation perhaps, or maybe he'd bought another racehorse from his friend Prince Khalid bin Abdullah of Saudi Arabia. Either way, Ritzier hadn't garnered the reputation as one of the finest journalists in the business because of his genteel manner. His interview style was tough, likened to a grilling in some circles. Regardless, this interview would hopefully give everyone a view of Deschamps that had never been seen before.

Fabian thumbed through a second file containing documents and files all marked "confidential," files from Interpol, the French finance ministry, MI5, and the FBI. Media outlets weren't the only people looking for a chat with Deschamps. This was the other side of Deschamps, one that had never been mined by any journalist. Deschamps clearly had encounters with the authorities in the past, most notably a high-profile, yet not widely covered, court case some years back from which he'd managed to walk free, scuttling out of the court, and into the back of an unmarked car, returning to anonymity with his criminal record remaining unblemished. It was never made public what Deschamps's full involvement in that case was, and how he'd managed to walk free. Fabian hoped today might give him the chance to find out.

The lift in the reception area chimed, and the doors opened. A slim, immaculately dressed young man approached the sofa.

"Mr. Ritzier?" said the young man.

"Yes," replied Fabian, standing and offering his hand.

"I'm Bruno Durand, Mr. Deschamps's PA, please follow me." He led Fabian back toward the lifts.

Bruno pressed number five on the panel, and up they went. There was no conversation, although Fabian noticed Bruno looking at him disapprovingly. Clearly, *he* didn't think this interview was a good idea. Either that or he was questioning Fabian's style choices—jeans, open shirt, and a sloppy corduroy jacket. Fabian couldn't care less either way. He'd received a similar withering look from a PA when he was being escorted into the Ecuadorian embassy in London to interview Julian Assange a few years ago, and that didn't stop or affect the interview, and more importantly for Fabian, it didn't affect the industry praise that he'd received for it. Another chime from the lift, and the doors opened onto the fifth floor.

They entered the reception area of Deschamps International Holdings and made their way down a long corridor. The floor to ceiling glazing gave Fabian a stunning view out toward Paris and the Seine, and as they wound their way around the corridor, he could hear music. "Tilted" by Christine and the Queens blared down the corridor. It was coming from Deschamps's office. They reached the office doors, where Bruno stopped and knocked.

The music stopped almost immediately, as they heard "Enter!" from inside the office.

It was the first time Fabian heard the imposing tones of Alain Deschamps, and now he was about to come face-to-face with him. Even though Fabian was a seasoned journalist, he felt the same twinge of adrenaline that he did the day he stood at the door of Julian Assange.

CHAPTER SEVEN

"Thank you, Bruno," said Deschamps as he brought Fabian into Alain's office. Alain then beckoned him to leave. Bruno paused at the door.

"You sure, Alain? I can sit in if you like?" he said.

"Fuck off, Bruno," said Alain firmly. "And get me and Mr. Ritzier some coffee and doughnuts from Henri's. I'm not serving this gentleman the vegan dishwater you normally conjure up."

"Certainly, Alain." Bruno sheepishly left the office, throwing Fabian a fierce look on the way out.

"I love Henri's doughnuts," said Alain. "Best patisserie this side of the Rhône." He approached Fabian, shook his hand firmly, and offered him a seat.

Some handshake, Fabian thought.

It was the first time Fabian got a good look at his interviewee. Deschamps cut an imposing figure of a man. Unshaven by design, he looked like he'd played a bit of rugby in his day. He was over six feet tall and cut an impressive figure in his three-piece, handmade, Dege & Skinner suit. Deschamps had two new suits shipped to him on the first Monday of every month from Dege & Skinner's studio in Saville Row, London, because, well, he could.

The two men settled around a large glass table in the center of Alain's office.

"Bruno likes to think he's my right-hand man," Alain said as he took out a silver cigarette case. "Truth is, he's as useful as a screen door on a submarine, but he's loyal." He lit a cigarette and offered one to Fabian.

"First thing I look for in a person, especially in business," he added.

"You can smoke in here?" asked Fabian.

"I pay fifteen thousand euro a week in rent for this office. I'll set fire to the carpets if I like."

Fair point, thought Fabian, as he smiled and took a cigarette. He was going to enjoy this encounter. Straight away Deschamps was showing no signs of being like the usual stiff, monotoned, buttoned-up CEO that he'd met numerous times over the years.

"So, I'm all yours," said Alain as he took off his suit jacket, put it on the back of his chair, and sat down. With his hand he lightly brushed his silver hair where it curled slightly at the edges. Fabian noted how dextrous and powerful his fingers looked.

"Great." Fabian took out his notepad and Dictaphone and placed them both in the center of the table.

"A Dictaphone?" said Alain. "Could you not use your phone to record this like every other self-respecting blogger in the twenty-first century?"

"I'm not a blogger, I'm a journalist."

"I beg your pardon, Mr. Bernstein."

"And," continued Fabian, "I'm old school." He took out his old Nokia 2210 and popped it on the middle of the table.

"Fuck me," said Alain, picking up the phone. "A prehistoric relic of the 1990s. I was a wizard at snake on these back in the day." He threw the phone back down on the table. "Anyway, where do you want to start?"

"Let's start with an easy one," answered Fabian as he clicked the record button on his Dictaphone. "Why have you recently bought a twenty-four percent share in TF1?"

"Wow. I thought you were going to start with where I went to school, what I did for kicks in my teenage years, etc.?"

Fabian didn't reply, his original question stood.

TF1 was the biggest and most respected TV network in France, a huge media organization, with a variety of programming spread over a number of channels, as well as rolling news and sports. Not, you would think, the natural habitat for a reclusive art dealer.

"We'll get to the family stuff later," said Fabian. "This is one of the many things about you that intrigues me, the diversity of your business interests. Why does an art dealer want to get involved with a media group. Is it just another investment opportunity, or is there more to it?"

"In fairness, it's a good question, I just thought you'd want to buy me dinner first, rather than jumping straight into the heavy petting," Alain replied. He seemed surprised yet impressed by Fabian's line of questioning. "The truth is, yes, it's an investment, and I hope it's a sound one, but the real reason is I want another platform to expand my brand through." Alain lit another cigarette.

"Your brand?"

"Yes," replied Alain. "I want to bring my brand, my art to the masses, and what better way than by getting in on a board level with a national network, through which I can make programming suggestions."

"Suggestions? More like demands surely?"

No response. Alain paused to draw on his cigarette. A wreath of smoke hung over his head. He stared at the journalist for a while.

"So, you want to make television shows," Fabian asked in a less aggressive tone of voice.

Deschamps nodded.

"About art?" asked Fabian.

"Not just art," replied Alain. "All branches of the arts, theater, music, food, culture, wine, opera, etc. All those things that when stitched together make up the fabric of a nation's identity."

Very poetic, Fabian thought. But something about Alain's tone didn't sit right with Fabian. Why would a billionaire suddenly have an interest in making TV shows? He was not talking about investing in shows, he was talking about making them. Fabian decided to park this line of questioning for the moment and try a different tack.

"Okay, let's go back to the beginning then," he said, in attempt to make sure his interviewee didn't pull the plug before he got to the good stuff. "Born in Bordeaux, moved to Paris at the age of three, is that right?"

"Correct," replied Alain. "My family moved to Paris from Bordeaux because of my father's work. He was also an art dealer, so no surprise that I followed him into the business. I was after all surrounded by art for as long as I can remember. My father had a small workshop in the garden of our house in Bordeaux. I still remember he and some friends packing everything up so carefully the day we relocated to Paris." He drew on his cigarette and stared at the smoke. His eyes watered slightly.

"He and his friends took such care and pride as they set everything up again in our *new* home in Paris, a small building that also served as an office and a gallery," he added.

Fabian took notes, even though his Dictaphone was capturing every word.

"Tell me about your father, did he instil a particular work ethic in you?" he asked.

"Well," replied Alain. "Like every father of that generation, he was strict, *some* would say more than others, and as it goes, I got the odd beating like most nine-year-olds who did or said things they shouldn't have, but I always just stood there and took it, mainly because most of the time I deserved it. To be fair to my father, though, he instilled more than just a work ethic in me, he taught me about respect, about business, and more specifically how to get a deal done."

Alain's stream of consciousness was interrupted by a knock on the door.

"Enter," said Alain.

Bruno appeared with a tray, containing two takeaway coffees and a box of doughnuts, six in total, all different flavours, just the way Alain liked it.

"Anything else I can do?" asked Bruno politely.

"Yes, fuck off again," answered Alain and stubbed out his cigarette.

Bruno straightened up, fixed his suit jacket like he'd just been denied entry into an exclusive nightclub, and left.

Alain took one of the coffees and began to tuck into the doughnuts. He seemed almost child-like in his pleasure at eating. After a pause, he offered his guest one.

"Not for me thanks," said Fabian.

There was a side to Deschamps that Fabian wanted to dig into further. And he knew that when he got to it, Deschamps might clam up or, even worse, call a halt to the interview. Before Fabian had a chance to get the next question out, however, Alain interrupted.

"Let's take a walk," he grunted as he rose from his seat, brushed the powdered sugar off his shirt. "I want to show you some something."

Fabian nodded and got up and followed Alain. They were now standing at the back wall of the office behind Deschamps's large, uncluttered desk. Alain put his left hand up to a panel on the wall, which scanned his fingerprints, and a door in the wall slid open. *Right*, thought Fabian, *either he thinks he's James Bond or he's just another billionaire showing off his gadgets*. Either way, whatever Fabian was going to see on the other side of this door had been seen by very few and was clearly off-limits to the public.

Fabian's interest in this man was peaking even higher than before.

CHAPTER EIGHT

THEY ENTERED THROUGH THE door, which slid closed behind them.

"What I'm going to show you," said Alain as they made their way down the corridor. "Is the reason I do what I do, the reason I've gotten up at four a.m. every morning and worked harder than anyone else. This is my *private* collection, something that I've spent most of my adult life putting together, something that means more than just art to me." They wandered down the plush dimly lit corridor and finally entered a small square room.

Mounted on a wall facing the two men, were six custom built glass boxes, each individually lit, each containing a painting. One box, at the end of the row, was empty. Fabian scanned the paintings as they approached them, from left to right, recognizing some of the artists, but not all. Gustav Klimt, Van Huysum, and Memling were among the artists on view. Two comfortable armchairs were positioned in the center of the room, facing the wall of paintings. Alain sat in one and offered the other to Fabian.

"This is how these are meant to be enjoyed," he said as he settled into the armchair, and gazed at his collection, looking on them lovingly, with a proud yet contained smile on his face.

They both sat in silence and took in the wonder of what was in front of them. After several minutes of viewing, Fabian decided now was the moment to broach the topic he'd wanted to ever since he first took on the task of bagging the interview with Deschamps.

"Tell me about the Delitzsch family," he asked.

A long silence. Alain's profile looked brutish against the magnificent paintings, like a rugby player who had been in too many scrums, his facial scars more suited to a man who was paid to protect the paintings as opposed to a man rich enough to own such delicate pieces of art.

The art dealer slowly turned his chair around to face Fabian. To the journalist's surprise, he was smiling. But the gaze he fixed on Fabian was fanatical in its intensity.

"Bravo," he said. "You've clearly done a deep dive. I was wondering how long it would take you to get *there*."

"Honestly, it's the main reason I'm here," Fabian replied. "To get to the real you. I'm not interested in your philanthropy, your charity work, or even your business conquests. My editor is, but I want to know why and how you are what you are, and why you have always denied your past."

The faint smile dissipated from Alain's face. He stood up and walked toward the paintings, observing them closely. He moved slowly down along the collection as he spoke.

"Denied, is a strong word, Mr. Ritzier. *Safeguarded*, I would have said."

Alain took a long pause.

"To save you the embarrassment of scratching around for your next question, let me fill in some of the blanks in your research. You're right, I am indeed from the Delitzsch family. My father changed his surname in the mid-fifties, just after we'd moved to Paris. He didn't think a German surname with such *connotations* would help him greatly in trying to set up and run an art dealership in the same city that was pillaged of some of its finest pieces by assorted members of the *organization* he'd been associated with, falsely, might I add, some fifteen years earlier."

The reason the name Delitzsch would strike such a discord with the Parisian public was simple. Alain's father was a ranking member of the Nazi party who served their leader diligently as an army officer during the Second World War, and was part of those first battalions to enter the French capital. This was the period that Alain's father, and a small group of fellow officers, made their mark.

Much has been written about the looting of some of the world's greatest treasures by the Nazis during World War Two, which was led primarily by Hermann Göring, a prominent admirer and thief of art. Delitzsch and his cohorts played a significant part in this legacy of ritualistic and organized crime.

After Delitzsch had arrived back in Paris in the 1950s, having survived the war and fled to Bordeaux in the process, he'd changed the family name in an attempt to blend into the local population and business community in the area known as Les Bain. He and his co-conspirators moved what remaining treasures they had, from Germany, through France, into Bordeaux, and finally into the little workshop at the bottom of the Delitzsch garden. Those paintings that Alain watched his father and his friends move carefully into a truck in preparation for their family's move to Paris could have had amongst them some the greatest works of art known to man. Paintings that had been missing since the early 1940s. Those paintings arrived in his father's new studio in Paris but were never put on public display. They were sold to eager underground buyers across the world, and crucially they established Delitzsch as a major player in the art world, more specifically, the art *underworld*. Most of the major art robberies, forgeries, and illicit movements of stolen works that occurred in Europe after the war, all had a link to the Delitzsch studio/gallery in Paris. But none were ever proven.

One of the many skills that Delitzsch picked up as a high-ranking officer in the German army were the dark arts of avoidance, espionage, forgery, and bribery. Delitzsch learned the most powerful of all: having enough money to pay people in high places to remain on his payroll, in his pocket, and therefore be willing to look the other way.

To the outside world the Delitzsch Gallery was a simple, understated boutique studio, which serviced a small book of clients, where bog standard landscapes and portraits sold for no more than a couple of hundred euros at a time, therefore keeping the business under the radar of the authorities. Nothing could have been further from the truth about this small, atypical, nondescript gallery.

"I know all about the rumors that circulated about my father's gallery," said Deschamps as he made his way down the line of paintings. "And I gather from your line of questioning, so do you. But let me assure you, Mr. Ritzier, my father's way of doing business died along with him twenty years ago. I'm a different proposition, I like conducting *my* business ventures with different methods, all perfectly legal and above board." Alain stopped and faced Fabian.

Fabian didn't believe that parable for a second. Deschamps's business methods may seem legit in the eyes of some, but to the French government and the European authorities, like watching a graceful swan treading water, only *part* of the business was visible to the naked eye. The frantically paddling feet of the swan's underbelly was what interested Fabian and the authorities. That was where the dirt was. That was where the gold was, literally.

"Are these paintings what I think they are?" asked Fabian, staring at the five framed works of art in front of him.

"What you think they are?" answered Deschamps. "I'm guessing from your expression that you think these are lost treasures from World War Two, maybe belonging to a certain infamous collection?"

Fabian nodded in agreement. Alain smiled and continued his lecture.

"These are indeed priceless treasures, ones that I have managed to locate, recover, and ones that shortly will be handed back to the world," he added.

"How so?"

"In three months' time, an exhibition will take place here in Paris, at the Hôtel Drouot, where on display as part of this exclusive auction, will be a number of recovered lost treasures from World War Two," said Alain. "But these, these paintings are yet to be unveiled. To this very day this collection is still believed to be missing, some even question the collection's very existence. So just before the auction, I will alert the authorities, and then offer them to the state, accompanied by all of the original paperwork, expert authentication, in other words with full provenance, thanks to the years of work and research carried out by my team and I. They will then go on display for all the world to see, and go on to be sold, and for my troubles I will ask for only two things: one, to remain anonymous, and two, receive a *small* commission on the sales, a finder's fee so to speak." He sat back in his armchair.

"I have, after all, done their work for them. Interpol and the likes have been looking for these masterpieces for seventy years and have come up empty-handed as usual," he added.

"Let me guess, these paintings may have at one time passed through your father's workshop in Bordeaux or his gallery in Paris?" asked Fabian.

"Let's just say that there may possibly be a connection between these paintings and my family," replied Alain. "Only me, my mother and father, and those friends who helped him on that day saw *those* paintings leave our house in Bordeaux. Maybe these are those very paintings, maybe not, maybe they are part of a completely different, yet much *prized* collection. Who knows? But one thing is for sure, all will be revealed at that auction, that I can guarantee you."

"So, what are you waiting for? Why wait for another three months to declare them, and why do it anonymously?"

Alain smiled at Fabian.

"Anonymity from the public I definitely want, they don't need to know that I've donated these. However, I'll insist that the authorities inform those in the art world of exactly who found and donated them. That will go some distance to clearing my family's original name, and put paid to the cross I've had to bear for forty years, my father's legacy, and as to why wait? Well as you can see one box is empty, one artist, one painting from this particular collection remains adrift." He stood up suddenly from his chair.

"And which painting is that?" asked Fabian.

"A Pierre Bontemps piece. The title of which doesn't concern you for the moment."

Alain was referring to the grandson of the renowned French Renaissance sculptor, who produced a number of stunning paintings throughout his career.

"A beautiful painting," Alain continued "Which has proved to be the most difficult to track down, but, after a lot of investigation and research, I've finally located it, and it won't be long before it's here, where it belongs, and then, and *only* then, will I present these treasures, this particular collection, as one to the authorities."

Fabian stood and moved toward the paintings.

"I get the feeling *I'm* going to have something to do with this grand reveal, this master plan of yours?"

"Very astute of you. You are here to document the journey, to give this story credence, and you will be here to see the last painting arrive, which if my plans conclude as hoped, should be in around eight weeks' time, right here in Paris, and you and your newspaper will be getting the world exclusive."

"Okay, I'll bite," said Fabian. "What happens next?"

"Get your camera out and photograph these gems, with me standing next to them of course."

Fabian reached for the camera in his bag, took it out, and asked Alain to stand in line with the paintings. In a way, he felt oddly detached from what was happening in this secret room of priceless artworks, as if he had strayed into a dream. Alain positioned himself in front of the only empty case and posed pointing toward the other five. Click, click, click. Photographs done. *This is going to knock their socks off back at the office*, Fabian thought, as he packed his camera back into his bag, and headed to the door, with Alain leading the way. As they reached the office, Alain stopped and turned to face Fabian with a mechanical smile.

"Just to make myself clear, Mr. Ritzier," he said as he moved a little closer to Fabian. "Your confidentiality in all of this is crucial, if any part of this plan gets revealed now or at any point before the auction, the last painting won't make it here, and if it doesn't, I'll burn the others. They either *all* go to that auction, or none will, and that all depends on you." He took another step closer to Fabian.

"You are not the only one taking photos in here," Alain said in a flat tone as he pointed to a discreetly placed security camera above the paintings, a camera that was now pointing straight at Fabian.

Silence. The air in the room seemed to change as Fabian stared back at the art dealer's furtive expression. Alain had his eyes fixed on Fabian, not a muscle in face twitched.

"You can trust me," Fabian said, momentarily paralyzed by the intensity of his interviewee's gaze.

"I know I can," said Deschamps as an almost smug smile broke across his face. "That's why I asked for you specifically, I mean, you don't think I didn't do my homework on you, do you? I spoke to Assange, amongst others, and you're here," said Alain.

Fabian smiled with relief and thought he may just have met his match here. "Well one final question before I leave," he said as he gathered his things before heading to the office door. "Why call me in now, I mean I've been chasing this interview for two years?"

Alain looked out of the window and down to the banks of the Seine. He wore a look of intense patience.

"One of the greatest abilities to master in business, indeed in life, is timing," he said. "You were no use to me, until now. Also, one year ago, to this day to be precise, my mother passed away."

"Sorry to hear that," offered Fabian.

"I shared her last few hours, at her bedside in the hospice," said Alain. "Her last words to me were, 'Make it right, Alain, make it right.' And that's precisely what I intend to do."

Fabian looked at Alain. Fabian's expression said "I understand," but inside, he thought, *Bullshit.*

"Thank you for your time," Fabian said. Before leaving, he held out his hand and Alain shook it. There was something dismissive about the art dealer's gesture, as though he wanted the journalist to be gone as soon as possible. As the door closed, Fabian had a final glimpse of Alain, seated at his expansive desk, as still as a statue.

Fabian stood at the lift and noticed Bruno, hovering nearby.

"Get what you came for?" Bruno asked in a perfectly pitched snotty tone.

"More than I could have imagined," replied Fabian as the lift door opened.

Back in his office, Alain sat at his desk and clicked on the mouse in front of his desktop. The huge screens lit up in front of him. He logged in to his email, and dozens of new messages flooded in. He quickly scanned through them and spotted the message he'd been waiting for. It was an email from Michel de la Rue. He read Michel's reply.

"Perfect," Alain whispered, and leaned back into his chair.

His plan was right on track.

CHAPTER NINE

Paris, 1942

When the small band of Resistance members uncovered the six paintings in their safehouse in Paris, they were determined to protect them from the surrounding Nazi forces, and others.

There was a huge appetite for these pieces among the art world, collectors knew that these would be prized even more when the war was over, and so, exhibitions were held in France, during the Nazi occupation, all with the blessing of the French government. Collectors from all over Europe would gather and secure ownership of these once hidden gems, now readily available works of art, at hugely discounted prices, with *most* of the money going back to the French government, and subsequently (and supposedly) redirected to fund their war effort. This was frowned upon, not just by the majority of the art world, but by the general public. In fact, it was universally shouted down, but of course, that didn't mean these fire sales were not going to continue happening.

The Resistance were determined not to let this happen to any treasures that they got their hands on, so in order to protect the pieces, they would often split them up and disperse them to various safe houses dotted across the other allied countries, with the intention of having them returned after the war and eventually reunited with their original owners. This, unfortunately, didn't happen on the scale that they'd hoped, but some made it back, much to the delight of those families.

The night that this small band of French freedom fighters liberated these paintings from the Germans, they took their newly found six works of art from the crate and discussed the bounty that lay in front of them. Having grabbed the stash from the hands Karl Delitzsch and his Nazi ERR unit and made their way through and around the numerous perilous checkpoints on the way to their hideout, each of the members of this unit were now personally invested in the fate of their bounty. The sense of excitement in the room was matched by a greater amount of tension, as a number of the men stood guard at the door and windows overlooking the streets below. These paintings were far from safe.

"What's the plan for these?" asked Robert as he placed them all on the floor in front of his squad leader, Eric Purdue.

"Strange," said Eric Purdue as he looked at the paintings. "These all came from the same apartment, right?"

Robert nodded.

"But they have nothing in common," Eric said as he walked up and down surveying the art, stopping to take a closer look at each one. "They are all by different artists, different styles, some are portraits, some landscapes, they're even different sizes. This is an incredible collection. Whoever put these together knew what they liked."

"Rothstein," said Robert, referring back to the list of names of the previous tenants who occupied the address that the paintings had been lifted from.

"Yes, Rothstein," replied Eric as he pondered the paintings. "They knew what they liked, but these are such strange bedfellows, such obscure friends, don't you think?"

The men suddenly stopped talking as they heard voices coming from the street outside. Eric looked at the man standing guard at the window. He had his finger placed over his lips. Down below he could see a German patrol unit of four men making their way down the alley. Robert pointed at the paintings and gestured to Eric to pack them up. Eric shook his head sharply, telling his men not to move a muscle. All eyes were on the guard at the window. He held his hand in the air for what seemed like an age. Eventually the patrol below passed the building and carried on down the alley away from the Resistance hideout. He nodded at Robert. All clear. Eric breathed a sigh of relief and wiped sweat off his forehead with the sleeve of his coat.

"*Obscurum amicis*," said Robert in a low voice, pointing at the paintings. Silence. Eric hadn't a clue what that meant, he'd been a carpenter before the war broke out. Robert, on the other hand, had been a history teacher.

"It's Latin," Robert said. "Means 'obscure friends.'"

"I like that," replied Eric, giving his friend a thumbs up. He headed to the table to pick up a small box of wood turning tools.

Sitting on the floor, Eric took the first painting, the smallest, and flipped it over, and began to carve the letters O and A into the back of the frame. As he did, Robert sat at the table and catalogued the paintings from one to six, listing the artist, the subject matter, and the original owner's name. After an hour or so, having completed the job of marking each painting, Eric stood and started to move the paintings around the room.

"The best way to keep these paintings together," he said as he addressed the onlooking squad, "is to separate them." Robert looks at him quizzically.

"That doesn't make any sense," he said to his superior officer.

"Listen to me," replied Eric. "These vultures, the Nazis, and those cutthroat art dealers are all on the lookout for pieces of art like these, so it is our *duty* to make their task more difficult, *impossible* in fact."

Robert stared blankly at him.

"Why make their job easy by putting all six of these together?" Eric continued. "If these get discovered together, the owners will have lost all six, all at the one time. *But* if we separate them, and they happen to fall into the wrong hands, it will mean a loss of one only piece to the owners, therefore giving them a chance of salvaging something from their original collection, when this war is over, no?"

"So, where do we send these then?" Robert said, agreeing with his boss.

Eric consulted a file of notes on his desk.

Eric handed Robert the file, which was a list of addresses. "These are safe houses across Europe, friendlies, that will receive and store goods from us, no questions asked, and hold them until further instructions."

"Madrid, Antwerp, Lisbon," Robert read aloud from the piece of paper.

They started picking up the paintings one by one and allocating them to a certain crate, each labeled for delivery to one of the addresses on the list. They took great care to wrap every piece and placed them in the crates alongside other works of art, ceramics, and jewelry that the Resistance had managed to salvage. After almost an hour the paintings were all packed away, except one.

"Right, last, but by no means least, this little gem," said Eric as he picked up the remaining painting and headed to the only remaining crate that had available space. Robert added notes to the list as Eric spoke.

"Portrait, consisting of a woman and two children, to my untrained eye it looks like a mother and two sons," said Eric.

"Artist?" asked Robert.

"Bontemps." Eric read the label on the back of the canvass. "Entitled, *Veiller Sur Toi*," he said as he placed it carefully into the crate. He slowly placed a lid on the top of the crate, and gently tapped the nails into place, securing the contents.

"Destination?" asked Robert as he prepared to enter the final piece of information onto the list. Eric read the label on the lid of the crate aloud.

"Brooks Coffee Importers Co., Ramillies Place, Soho, London," he said.

This collection of paintings, which had previously hung on an apartment wall in Paris, were now being split up among six different crates and were about to embark on six separate journeys across the continent.

The Obscurum Amicis Collection

River Landscape *by Salomon van Ruysdael,* Two Riders on the Beach *by Max Liebermann,* The Convalesced Woman *by Ferdinand Georg Waldmüller,* Portrait of Carl Sternhiem *by Ernst Ludwig Kirchner,* Landschaft bei Paris *by Albert Gleizes, and* Veiller Sur Toi *by Pierre Bontemps. The six paintings that made up the collection known as the* Obscurum Amicis.

Originally owned by Laurence and Rebecca Rothstein, these six works of art had graced the walls of their apartment in Paris for years. Some of the paintings having been inherited, and had traveled with the Rothstein's from Poland as the couple hastily relocated ahead of the German invasion in 1914. The remainder of the collection was made up of pieces that had been bought in and around Paris over the next forty years. Each painting had caught the eye of the couple for different reasons. Some were bought as investments, some because of their subject matter, some quite simply because they struck a chord with either Laurence or Rebecca. It was a collection that had been lovingly put together, and brutally torn apart. Removed from the walls of their Paris home by a Nazi ERR squad, they then fell into the hands of a French Resistance squad, who in an effort to preserve them, split them up.

What had become of these paintings since they disappeared into the Paris night back in 1942? Details of the journeys and destinations of the paintings were rumored over the years, but never confirmed. Their whereabouts had never been established.

Alain Deschamps was now so convinced that he knew more about this collection than any other person, he considered himself the world's authority on the subject of the Obscurum Amicis. *Over the past twenty years, he had dedicated his life to tracking this collection down, utilizing his wide network of underworld contacts. And he'd had more success than all of the aforementioned police agencies put together. Alain was well aware that money could buy you anything, and the most important commodity to gather when pursuing a mission like this, was information, and Alain had the ear of some of the most influential and persuasive criminal organizations in the world. After almost two decades, his self-set task was almost complete.*

He hadn't just located the six paintings, he'd already taken possession of five of them. A huge amount of research, money, and time had been invested by Alain and his team, which was headed up by his long-time consigliere, Mr. Hassan, who personally clocked thousands of air miles and spent fortunes of Alain's money greasing the palms of those people and organizations who could provide them with the right piece of information that could lead Alain and him toward finding any of his target paintings. Locating these lost works of art was a painstaking process, but Alain was determined to reunite this collection. As it turned out, locating them proved to be the easier part of this mission. Stealing them, proved to be the tricky part.

Cue Mr. Hassan, who once again would have to delve into his rich armory of unscrupulous skills that Alain had so often called upon.

The six crates that the paintings were shipped in in 1942 were all marked with an address, each one destined for a recognized safe house within one of the many Allied countries around Europe and the world. All six crates made it to their separately allocated destinations. The French Resistance had done their job; they had relocated the paintings, far away from the treacherous theater of war where they'd been stolen from. But the Resistance not only sent the paintings, they also sent orders.

Those orders instructed that the cargo to be stored safely until the war was over, at which point the paintings temporary caretakers would be contacted and arrangements would be made to get the six paintings back to Paris and returned to their rightful owners. But arrangements were never made, word never came, and the paintings simply sat where they'd been dispatched to, far away from Paris.

CHAPTER TEN

London, 1965

THE FIRST COUPLE OF years after Jacques and Murielle arrived in London were difficult. Having effectively left their worlds behind them in Paris, cutting all ties with family and friends, they were starting from scratch. Before leaving Paris, Jacques had looked into the possibility of eloping to London. He had a hunch Murielle's father would react the way he did to his marriage proposal, so he had to have some plans in place. Jacques had contacted an old friend he'd worked alongside in the market in Paris years ago, Tomas Bechet, who was now in London, working as a sous chef in a hotel near Paddington Station.

"There's always space for another talented chef!" he told Jacques when he rang him a week before leaving for London.

Perfect, thought Jacques.

When they arrived in London, Jacques and Murielle set up home in a studio apartment just off Edgeware Road, a ten-minute walk from the bustling Paddington area. Murielle was almost five months pregnant when they arrived, so Jacques made sure she was comfortable, as he headed out to work fourteen-hour shifts at the hotel alongside Tomas. Both Jacques and Murielle knew basic English; Murielle had studied it in school, and Jacques had been taught by his grandfather, who insisted he learned basic phrases as a child. They had money coming in and a roof over their heads. But they'd soon need a bigger roof and more money.

On the fifth of February 1966, their first-born, Antoine, came into the world. A healthy bouncing baby boy gave Jacques even more focus and made him more determined than ever to make a success of it in London. Antoine's arrival was tinged with sadness, as the couple weren't surrounded by the usual comforting blanket of family, friends, and in-laws, those people who not only share in your newfound joy but offer support as you try and keep working to provide for your new family. Regardless, they made it work.

One person who was there for them, to not only share their workload, but to bask in the joy that a newborn brings to a house, was their downstairs neighbor,

Mrs. Rothstein. Only a month after Antoine was born, Murielle declared herself happy and healthy enough to find a job and with Mrs. Rothstein happy to babysit, she quickly found a job at a small flower shop beside the tube station at Lancaster Gate. Mrs. Rothstein was not only the perfect neighbor, she became a close friend, never complaining about the odd late arrival of Murielle when collecting Antoine after she'd finished work. She never hesitated to help when she knew Jacques and Murielle were swamped with work.

Truth be told, the couple were great for her too, her kindness and favors were reciprocated. Jacques helped out with any tasks she needed done in and around her small apartment. Murielle always picked up anything Mrs Rothstein needed at the shops, and they were there if she fell ill and needed company on her frequent trips to the doctor or physio at the local hospital. Mrs. Rothstein had no family and could only walk with the aid of two walking sticks, and appreciated the help they offered her. Her only company was her beloved cat, and because Jacques and Murielle were in London having cut all ties to *their* families, it was almost as if the couple and their vulnerable neighbor were meant to cross paths, meant to find each other.

The simple fact that Murielle felt comfortable enough to leave her baby with Mrs. Rothstein while she went to work, spoke volumes. And Murielle needed to go to work. Although Jacques was working long hours, the pay wasn't great, so two pay packets were needed, especially as they were planning to move out of their studio into a two-bedroom house. That ambition was a pipe dream, but a dream nonetheless.

Antoine was eighteen months old when the couple turned the key on 17a Marshall Street, a two-bed apartment above an auctioneer's office in the heart of Soho. The new move also coincided with a change of job for Jacques. He was installed as head chef at a new funky French bistro on Argyll Street, close to their new address. This meant a bump in salary for Jacques, which in turn meant that Murielle could now stay at home, and concentrate on raising their first born, and focus on *her* new bump, their second child, who wouldn't be long in arriving.

Murielle's days were filled with young Antoine, taking him for regular walks in the nearby St. Anne's Churchyard, a favorite destination for her and Antoine. Murielle made sure that every day, she took the time to check in on Mrs. Rothstein, their previous neighbor and dear friend, who had done so much for the couple. Mrs. Rothstein's physical condition had deteriorated, and she was now pretty much housebound, which meant that the visits from Murielle and Antoine were welcomed even more than before.

Murielle had a real connection with Mrs. Rothstein. She admired her, having faced such physical difficulties in her life from an early age, which clearly didn't stop her from getting on with life. Murielle admired her determination, her spirit, and she in turn admired Murielle. Mrs. Rothstein knew it wasn't easy for Murielle coming to a new city, pregnant, without a full grasp on the native language, while setting up a new life for her and her family. Mrs. Rothstein faced the same challenges when she herself arrived in London back in 1942, albeit under very different circumstances.

Every other evening, on his way home from work, Jacques would swing by Mrs. Rothstein's house, fill her fridge with leftovers from the restaurant, change the litter in the cat's tray, and sit and chat. Mrs. Rothstein cherished the company more than the food. Even though the food was beautiful, she loved listening to Jacques talk about his dreams for his family. Jacques talked at length about his ultimate dream, to one day open his own restaurant. Mrs. Rothstein would reciprocate, telling Jacques about her early days in Paris, the disease that left her looking and feeling older than she actually was, and about her forced move to London, but she mainly spoke about her brief marriage to Thomas, her beau. Her face would light up when she spoke about him.

Jacques's thoughts of opening his own place were fanciful, nigh on impossible really, given the property prices in London, let alone the start-up costs, etc., but both he and Mrs. Rothstein loved to talk about it so much that between the two of them they had the menus written and the décor chosen.

Early September saw the arrival of baby number two, another boy, Michel. Antoine was thrilled that he now had a little brother, a playmate, someone he could share his adventures with. And that, they did. All in all, normality had set in; Jacques worked long hours, the boys and Murielle were happy spending time in each other's company, Antoine had started school, money was coming in, and their fridge was full.

This was all unsettled by a phone call Murielle received one Thursday morning. She had just dropped Antoine at school, and she and Michel were getting ready to head out to the playground.

"Hello?" Murielle said answering the phone, while zipping Michel's coat up. "What?" she said as she stood up. "Oh my god, when? No, thank you for letting me know, I'll come over as soon as I can."

She hung up, and immediately picked the phone back up and started to make a call.

"Chez Dorian, good morning, how can I help you?" said the voice at the end of the phone.

"Phillipe, it's Murielle, can I speak to Jacques?"

"Of course," he said. "One moment please."

She waited, her hands now trembling.

"Murielle?" Jacques said into the phone. "Are the boys okay?" She *never* rang him at work.

"The boys are fine, it's Mrs. Rothstein."

"Ah, she wanted me to look at her boiler, tell her I'll get around to her later this afternoon when things settle down here."

"No, Jacques, a sergeant from Charing Cross Police Station just phoned, she was killed this morning."

Silence.

CHAPTER ELEVEN

The mood in the restaurant kitchen had suddenly turned somber.

"Christ, what happened?" asked Jacques.

"She was out walking, going to the pharmacy to collect her prescription, and she slipped on the path, fell straight onto the road, and was hit by a car," Murielle answered.

"Jesus. Where have they got her?"

"She's in the hospital. They want you to go over and identify her."

"I'll go straight away."

The next couple of weeks were hard for Murielle and Jacques. They'd suddenly lost a dear friend, the woman who'd practically taken them in when they arrived from Paris, had become a confidant of both, had taken care of their children, and given them so much more than company. Consequently, they'd cared so much for her over the years, she had been the obvious choice and hugely flattered when she was asked to be godmother to both Antoine and Michel.

Mrs. Rothstein had no family, so Jacques and Murielle immediately took on the responsibility of arranging her funeral. When the time came only they and their two small boys, and the priest stood at the graveside. Jacques read an excerpt from "Stop All the Clocks" by W. H. Auden, one of Mrs. Rothstein's favorite poets, as Murielle laid a beautiful wreath packed with her favorite flowers, lilies, near her headstone. As the couple stood with their boys watching Mrs. Rothstein being laid to rest, it was obvious that both of them were thinking of their own families, and their lives back in Paris, which at times like this, they dearly missed.

The funeral also made them grateful of what they had. Over the following months, life went back to normal, Jacques frantically pushing new dishes out on his ever-expanding menu. Murielle was busy with the boys, Antoine was thriving in school, so she was able to pick up some part-time work in a local dentist's office as a receptionist, leaving baby Michel with a friend she'd met at the local church group. All was back on track, but again, as life has a habit of doing, things changed with the arrival of a letter early one morning. Murielle placed it on Jacques's plate just before serving breakfast. "Schuster, Hempenstall & Dawlish" was the sender's name printed on the back of the envelope.

"What's this now?" Jacques asked as he pushed the letter aside and replaced it with a freshly boiled egg.

A boiled egg, toast, cut into soldiers, and tea, Jacques's breakfast of choice since he was a small boy, and Murielle had kept this tradition going for him, mainly because that was as far as her culinary skills went. He took his knife, which was covered in butter and used it to tear open the letter. He started to read.

"Very curious," he said as he put the letter down and rose from the table.

"What is, the egg?" asked Murielle wondering if she'd screwed up the simple breakfast again.

"It's from Mrs. Rothstein's solicitors," said Jacques, in a puzzled tone.

"Mrs. Rothstein had a solicitor?"

"Seems like she had, and they've called you and I to the reading of her will, next Tuesday morning at ten."

The offices of Schuster, Hempenstall & Dawlish were located at sixteen Woodseer Street, near the famous Brick Lane Markets, in London's East End.

Murielle and Jacques sat waiting in the reception area, both curious as to what they were about to hear.

"If she's left me her cat, I won't be responsible for my actions," he said.

"Mr. and Mrs. de la Rue? Mr. Schuster will see you now," said the receptionist as she showed them toward an office door.

"Good morning," said Mr. Schuster as he greeted the couple from behind his desk. "Let's get this going, shall we? I have a court appearance at eleven, and I can't be late for Judge Morrison."

Schuster continued, thumbing through the paperwork on his desk.

"Mrs. Edsel Rothstein, last will and testament." He read through the first lines of the document, scanning the contents as he worked through it. "Ah, here we are, yes, a letter that Mrs. Rothstein wished to be read aloud before disclosing the contents of her will." He opened a small envelope and began to read aloud from the note.

"'*Having arrived in London at such a young age, with no family, no English, in fact nothing more than the clothes on my back, I am more aware than most that help, though often needed, is seldom offered, but when it is, it is greatly appreciated. So many people during my early years in England offered me kindness in the form of accommodation, work, a meal, or a simple conversation. My beloved Thomas and his family were a godsend, and my heart has never recovered from them being taken away from me so cruelly. I had thought I could never see or feel anything worse than the loss of contact with my parents in Paris, only to be riddled with grief again just as I had regained myself and found my new life in London. For me, finding the love and kindness that only a family can bring, for a third time in my life was truly a blessing. And that is who I want to now help, provide for, and hope that they will then pass the gift of family onto their own.'"*

Murielle wiped a tear from here eye, as she could hear the words in Mrs. Rothstein's voice. Jacques gently took his wife's hand in his as Schuster finished reading. He folded the letter and put it back in its envelope.

"On to the main event then," Schuster said, with all the emotion of man who'd just read the first two pages of the telephone directory. He clumsily opened a large legal document. "Here we are," he said, clearly in a hurry. "So, I, Edsel Rothstein, etc., bequeath the following to J and M de la Rue of 17a Marshall Street, London."

He looked up, as if he was seeking confirmation that those were the people sitting in front of him. Jacques got the hint and slipped his driver's license onto the table in front of the onlooking solicitor. Mr. Schuster looked this over and seemed happy that he'd got his man, *and* woman.

"Quite the windfall, isn't it?" Schuster said. "She had no blood relatives left in this world, obviously, we checked to make sure the will wouldn't be contested, and it seems you two are all she had."

The couple looked at each other.

"Quite the windfall?" said Murielle, looking for a little more detail. "What exactly does that entail?"

Mr. Shuster scanned through the document and stopped.

"Well, from what I can see here, she's left you seventy pounds from her post office savings, a cat called Milky, and a building on Ramillies place."

The couple were stunned into silence.

"Sorry, did you just say a *building*?" asked Jacques.

"A building, yes, and a cat," replied Mr. Shuster.

"Mrs. Rothstein was a woman of means," he continued, noticing the couples puzzled looks from across his desk. "She says here that you were tenants in a building of hers on Edgeware Road?"

"Tenants?" answered Murielle. "No, we were neighbors, we presumed she was just another tenant."

"No, she was the *landlord*," replied Mr. Shuster. "And according to this, she left *that* property to the cats and dogs' home in Battersea. The other building was going the same way, but according to my records she made an adjustment to her will some two years ago, to make provisions for her godsons? It seems she took her responsibilities of godmother very seriously."

The couple looked at each other in total bewilderment.

"And that other building," asked Jacques. "What and where is it that exactly?"

"Let me see," said Shuster as he flicked through the scattered papers. "A two-story, three-bedroom house, including a retail space on the ground floor and a cellar, on Ramillies Place, Soho."

The couple sat open mouthed scarcely able to fathom what had just happened.

"Jesus," said Jacques in a soft voice. "She must have really liked my potatoes dauphinoise."

"She clearly liked it," Murielle said with tears in her eyes, "but she *loved* Antoine and Michel."

Jacques and Murielle stood outside the building on Ramillies Place later that day, accompanied by their two boys, and Milky the cat, whom they'd collected on the way, from Mrs. Rothstein's neighbor.

The building was boarded up, it hadn't been lived in for years, and required a lot of major work to turn it back into the place it once was. The couple stood hand in hand, with Michel in Jacques arms and Antoine standing holding on to his mothers' overcoat.

"I can't believe this," said Murielle. "What the hell are we going to do with all of this space?"

"Create something incredible," replied Jacques as he squeezed his wife's hand a little tighter. "That's what she'd want us to do."

"With seventy pounds?" Murielle said. Jacques laughed.

"I sat for hours, days on end, chatting with Mrs. Rothstein, talking about my dream, my dream for *our* family, for a family business," he said as he moved toward the steps in front of the house. "To be honest, I didn't think she was listening to me half the time. But obviously she was."

Jacques picked Milky up and sat on the cold wet steps. He took a cigarette from his pocket, and lit it, looking back at his family.

"This?" he said, pointing up toward the first two floors. "Is going to be the home of our dreams, and this..." He pointed to the ground floor part of the building. "Is going to be our restaurant, *our* future."

Murielle looked at the building, taking it all in.

"Don't forget the cellar," she asked jokingly.

Jacques stood and took his wife's hands in his and flicked his cigarette across the street.

"Yes, the cellar, well that my darling, is where we'll store all our treasures."

River Landscape *by Salomon van Ruysdael*

...made its way to the small border town of Oberpallen, a well-established smuggling stronghold used by the Resistance during the war, thanks to its location on the Belgium/Luxembourg border. The painting found shelter in the basement of the Saints-Pierre-et-Paul Church, which had been the focal point of the Resistance activities in the area. It remained in the basement, untouched and safe, until 1975, when the newly ordained parish priest of the church discovered it and, taking a liking to it, decided that it should be shared with the local church attendees. The priest took the painting from the crate and placed it on the wall of the lobby of the church, alongside posters advertising local events.

Not the safest of places to put a painting worth almost three hundred thousand euro, but of course no one was aware of its value, let alone its significance. It hung on the wall of the church lobby gathering dust for almost twenty-one years, until the development of a new shopping village nearby meant that the church was to be leveled then relocated, rebuilt on a new site in Bricowelt less than a kilometer away from where it had originally stood. When the new church opened a year later, everything from the original building was put back in its place within the new building, except for the dust covered painting that once hung in the old church's lobby.

The parish priest that had placed it there over twenty years earlier, had since passed away, and as a result the paintings absence from the new place of worship didn't raise a single eyebrow from the now aging congregation.

CHAPTER TWELVE

London, present day

MICHEL PACED UP AND down outside the restaurant. His suitcases were on the bottom step, all neatly arranged in a pile, *a la* Felix Unger, along with his laptop bag.

He looked at his watch for the third time in the last five minutes. Michel needed a piss badly, but he'd already locked the building up, and couldn't be bothered going through the routine of unlocking doors and resetting alarms. It was 8:37 a.m., and he'd told Antoine to be up and ready and at the front door at 8:30. Not having heard a stir from Antoine's room earlier on, he went in to check, and to wake him, but he wasn't there.

Fuck it, he thought, *he's changed his mind about the trip, and skipped town*. Michel was in a rage. But he was still determined to go ahead with the trip. *One de la Rue would be better than none*, he thought, as he worked through a range of excuses for turning up to film a cookery show minus his brother, the chef.

Although nowadays mornings weren't Antoine's strong suit, they *used* to be back in the days when he was in full flight in the restaurant kitchen, when he had a goal, a purpose, a drive. With all of those gone, mainly because of his own actions, he was now as reliable as a modern-day exit poll. Michel and Antoine still lived above the restaurant, which some might say would have made it easier to be on time for a meeting on the steps of his own home and workplace, but those people had clearly never met Michel and Antoine. Michel was down at those very steps at 8:00 a.m., a full thirty minutes early, a Michel de la Rue trademark. Antoine was nowhere to be seen, which was one of *his* trademarks.

Finally, at 8:50, Michel heard the recognizable sound of Antoine approaching. This usually involved a lot of swearing, coughing, and the odd burst of flatulence.

"Morning, little brother," said Antoine as he arrived, throwing his duffel bag on top of Michel's cases knocking them over. He then stepped over them, sat on the curb at the edge of the road, and started to roll a cigarette.

"Where were you, I checked your room earlier and thought you'd gone on the lam!"

"Please, the only lamb I'm concerned with is the one we'll cook on a beach in the north of France in a couple of weeks," Antoine said. "I couldn't sleep last night after what you'd said to me, and so I got up early, packed, and fancied taking in some air, that's all."

Michel shook his head, his brother never failed to surprise him.

"And I wanted to see Larry the limp, told him to put my last forty quid on that nag running this afternoon at Chepstow," he said.

Michel looked at him as if to say, "You didn't, did you?"

Antoine looked backed and laughed.

"Fuck's sake, I'm only kidding!" This made Michel smile and then laugh.

Antoine hugged his brother. He was in, for the trip, and for turning things around. Michel hugged his brother, relived that he wasn't facing this filming adventure on his own. And maybe, just maybe, he had his brother back.

"What the fuck have you got so many bags for?" Antoine asked. "Looks like you've packed to emigrate, complete with the fixtures and fittings."

"Not quite."

"Right, let's get this show on the road!" Antoine stood and stretched his body.

"Thing is, the taxi I booked for eight thirty has now buggered off, so we have to wait for another one," said Michel, his frustrations brewing. "I swear, if we miss this train, I'll make you walk to Dover."

The boys were due to catch the 9:40 train from St. Pancras International, which would take them to the car ferry at Dover. There, they were due to meet, for the first time, the film crew who were going to accompany them on their gastronomic adventure through France. The trip, much to Michel's delight, had been planned down to the last detail—trains, boats, hotels, etc.—and those timetables must be adhered to or the trip would quickly descend into chaos. Michel, a huge Michael Palin fan, was treating this like he was Phileas Fogg, heading off on his personal eighty-day grand tour.

Antoine, on the other hand, was along for the ride. He hoped he had to do as little as possible. He had visions of dining in some of the finest restaurants France had to offer, sampling lots of the best wines in the world, all the while being chauffer driven from location to location and staying in the best hotels in the country. All without putting his hand in his own pocket. Nothing, however, could be further from reality.

The taxi pulled up, and the boys loaded their bags in. Before they knew it, they were at St. Pancras Station, and headed for platform seven, where the Dover train was ready to depart. The boys settled into their seats on the train, in economy class, ahead of the ninety-minute sojourn through London and down to the Southeast coast of England. Michel had his usual array of books on the journey, including *Hemmingway's Chair*, his favorite Palin novel that he planned to reread. Antoine, as unprepared as ever, had brought nothing to occupy himself except his thoughts, which he now decided would be a good time to share with Michel.

"Tell me more about this Deschamps character," Antoine asked. "How do you know him? How did he approach you about all of this?"

"You know," said Michel as he put his book down and turned his attention to his brother. "If you'd paid attention to me last week when I explained all of this, you wouldn't have to ask me that."

"I understand that, brother. But as you've come to realize, if the conversation doesn't include key words such as 'dead cert,' or 'yes, she *is* single,' just go ahead and presume I'm not listening."

"I'm still looking into him." Michel took a notebook from his laptop bag. "But there's a lot more to him than meets the eye," he said to himself as started flicking through his notes.

Michel wasn't quite ready to share what he'd found out about Alain Deschamps with his brother, not yet.

Two Riders on a Beach *by Max Liebermann*

...traveled for almost ten months, having a few short stops along the way, as it made its long journey north from Paris to the small fishing port of Bodo in the northwest of Norway. The location of the port, and its proximity to the Sjunkhatten National Park, made this a smugglers paradise during the war. The vast National Park, which boasted hundreds of acres of trees and natural wildlife, was the perfect place to conceal the numerous caches of weapons that came in through the nearby port en route to the Resistance fighters on the war front. These weapons and other pieces of smuggled merchandise ended up spread amongst a number of small wooden cabins that were dotted along the lakeside of the huge inland Heggmovstnet Bay that sat to the west of the national park. Having arrived at the lake via Bodo, the painting was stored away safely in a cabin owned by a local politician, awaiting collection. As the war came to an end, none of the pieces of art had been called for, collected, or moved on, and so they sat, untouched, almost ignored.

After the war, this bay area in Norway became a tourist hotspot, with the well-heeled visiting in their numbers to partake in the various levels of water sports and fishing that were on offer. It was a particularly popular spot for visitors from Asia. In 1998, the newly renovated cabins, or exclusive holiday homes as they were now advertised, where the painting was hanging, were rented by a Japanese businessman and his son visiting Scandinavia as part of a round-the-world trip. The son, who was studying graphic design back at university in Sendai, Japan, threw his eye on the painting. His father made an offer to the owner of the cabin that they were staying in and, not even being aware there was a painting on the wall of the cabin, the owner agreed to the offer of forty euro. The painting swapped hands and began winging its way to Japan. It hung on the wall of the son's university dormitory until 1999, when during a New Year's Eve party, it disappeared. His father had paid the equivalent of a decent bottle of sake for it, so the son didn't even bring it up the next time he saw his father.

The painting was actually worth just under €1.2 million. If the son had known that, maybe he'd have locked the door to his dorm room.

CHAPTER THIRTEEN

Paris, present day

Six months before Michel received the offer from Alain Deschamps to film a TV series, he met the man himself for the first time, over a plate of stale canopies.

Michel was attending a lunch for *Variety*, the children's charity, which had its roots firmly in the entertainment industry. Known as the showbiz charity, its events were often high-profile ones, aiming to raise huge amounts of money for the beneficiaries of their work. Michel's attendance at this event was driven by one main objective: this would be good for the restaurant, he thought, and would keep at least the public perception up that his and Antoine's business was alive and well.

The event was being held at The Dorchester, one of London's most exclusive hotels and was due to be attended by the great and good of the London food scene. Having scraped together the money to buy a ticket, and having borrowed a tuxedo from a colleague, Michel rocked up early as usual.

Walking through the lobby of the hotel, he was greeted by a large doorman standing guard at the door to the ballroom where the event was taking place.

"Ticket?" said the bouncer with all the charm of a border crossing guard in war-torn Syria.

Michel produced his ticket. Having checked but probably not read it, the bouncer opened the door for him and in he went.

He took his seat at his allocated table way back from the stage. Michel hadn't contributed nearly enough to the charity to get a seat closer to the stage, where he would have had the chance to rub shoulders with the likes of several aging soap stars, two ex-England footballers, and a now long-forgotten runner-up of *Dancing with the Stars*.

Almost an hour passed, and Michel was now mingling, doing his best to keep up appearances, telling people "Yes, Antoine is great, doing his best cooking in years, yes give us a ring whenever, you know, we should be able to fit you in, things have never been better," etc., etc. All lies, of course, except the one about being able to fit people in, that he *could* do, in their droves. He was scrambling around the room, bouncing from one monotonous encounter to the next, when something he saw suddenly stopped him in his tracks.

There, sitting at the bar, deep in conversation, was a former colleague from Paris, Lucy, whom he hadn't seen in what felt like a lifetime. He hadn't seen her since the night she stormed out of his apartment after another blazing row, bringing their long relationship to an end. It had been coming, in fairness. They'd met while they were both working as concierges on the front desk at the exclusive Mandarin Oriental, a beautiful large hotel located just minutes from the Louvre. They fell in love almost immediately, and enjoyed an idyllic romance, culminating in them moving in together. There was even talk of an engagement at one point, but it never came to pass. She was then, and was maybe still, the love of his life.

Michel couldn't believe it; he'd heard rumors that she'd left the hotel business some time ago, and he wondered why she was here at an event populated by people from the hospitality industry. Regardless, there she was, and she hadn't changed at all, in fact she looked better, more relaxed, happier even.

The last year they'd spent together in Paris they were both surrounded by stress brought on by their work situations. At that point they were working at different hotels, and they seemed to be constantly arguing. It all bubbled up like a well shaken, primed, table-ready bottle of Veuve Clicquot and popped on that fateful night years ago back in Paris. Their relationship was as dead as the cheap Liebfraumilch on offer at the lunchtime event they were now both attending. When they split up, it wasn't the most acrimonious of breakups. They were still in the same trade, but were working in different countries, so the opportunity to meet and possibly resolve their differences, or have "the talk" never arose. Maybe this was the time to address that. In fairness a lot of Evian had gone under the bridge since then.

Taking a deep breath, Michel straightened his velvet bowtie and headed toward Lucy. She seemed deep in conversation with a man she was talking to at the bar. Michel butted in.

"Excuse me, Lucy?" Michel said as he reached the pair.

"Not now, mate, we've plenty of wine," said the man, waving Michel away, clearly mistaking him for a member of the hotel staff.

"He's not a waiter, Andrew," Lucy said as she looked, stunned, at Michel.

"Oh, sorry, mate," said Andrew as he offered his hand to Michel by way of an apology. "Andrew Cairns, regional director Cairns Meats."

"Nice to meet you, Andrew," Michel replied. "I'm a big fan of your Cumberland sausage."

A beat.

"We don't do a Cumberland sausage?" said Andrew, clearly confused by Michel's attempt at humor.

Lucy laughed quietly; she got it. "Andrew, can we pick this up later?" she said dismissing Andrew, and offering Michel the now vacant seat at the bar.

Andrew left, looking back at Michel with a puzzled expression.

"Well, well," Lucy said. "Of all the charity events in the world, you had to walk into mine."

Casablanca was the first movie they'd been to see together, on their third date. Michel immediately got the reference and played along.

"What about us?" Michel said.

"We'll always have Paris," Lucy replied.

Michel felt relieved that they had slipped so easily back into their almost nerd like fascination with that movie gem.

"How long has it been?" she asked.

"Three years, two months," replied Michel. "I think, I mean I don't know exactly, can't be exact, you know, exactly." He tried to play it cool but came off sounding like Dustin Hoffman's Raymond Babbitt.

Lucy called the barman down to her.

"Two cosmopolitans, please," she said.

"Eh, just one, and a virgin bloody Mary for me please," said Michel cutting in.

"Long night?" Lucy asked.

"Long three years," he answered. "So, sticking with the clichés, what brings you here?"

"Work," she replied as their drinks arrived.

"Cheers," Michel said as they clinked glasses. "So, you're back in the hospitality game then. Which hotel chain are you currently shackled to?"

"Not quite, I did rejoin the hospitality flock, but not for long. I left the hotel business for good about eighteen months ago. Got fed up with the long hours and the shitty pay." Michel smiled at the on-point description of his line of work.

"You still putting out fires for your big brother?" Lucy asked.

"I am, but these days I need a bigger hose."

They sat without talking for a couple of minutes. There was an awkward vibe—these unplanned reunions were seldom enjoyable, let alone comfortable.

"Lucy," said Michel as he leaned in to tackle the elephant in the room. "Do you think we should have stuck at it, you know, made it work?"

Lucy moved to answer when they were interrupted by a loud announcement from the MC on stage in the ballroom.

"Ladies and gentlemen, please welcome one of our guest speakers, and main sponsors of today's event, Mr. Alain Deschamps!"

A round of applause rippled across the room, as the speaker took to center stage.

"Excuse me," said Lucy. "My boss is up, I better pretend to pay attention." She left Michel and moved toward the side stage area.

Michel sat at the bar nursing his drink, and watched Lucy's boss regale the crowd with stories, one-liners, and amusing anecdotes. When he'd finished his speech, Alain left the stage, and headed straight to talk to Lucy who was waiting side stage. As Michel watched them chat, they started to walk toward him at the bar.

"Michel, I'd like you to meet Alain Deschamps, CEO of Deschamps International Holdings, and my boss, so be polite," she said. The men greeted each other as Lucy stepped away.

"I'll check and see if the room is ready," she said to Alain as she left them.

Michel watched Lucy as Alain slapped him on the back and sat beside him at the bar.

"Monsieur, a large Courvoisier for me, and whatever Mr. de la Rue is having," he barked.

Michel was shaken by Alain's over-familiarity. Immediately, he was on his guard.

"Are you in the business?" Michel asked.

"Entertainment? I'm new to it," Alain answered. "I've just entered the murky waters of broadcasting, in France, and am looking for new opportunities. What has you here? You're clearly not in the fashion business." He pointed to Michel's tux.

"No, the catwalk spat me out like a fur ball a long time ago," Michel answered. "I'm a restaurant owner."

Alain burst into laughter.

"I know who you are Michel, and I know what you do."

Michel was taken aback. He hadn't a clue what was happening, and yet Alain seemed fully aware of Michel and what his business was.

The room filled with the sound of an eight-piece big band, launching into "Ain't That a Kick in the Head" and people started to make their way to the dance floor. The party it seemed, had just kicked up a gear, either that or the Liebfraumilch had taken effect.

"Can we go somewhere a little more private and talk?" Alain asked. He stood up from his chair at the bar. "We can bring our drinks with us."

Michel stood, and saw Lucy just ahead of them, holding a door open for both him and Alain. The two men headed over and entered into a small room, a private suite, and sat at a table that had three place settings, complete with wine glasses and a carafe of water, as if this meeting had been preordained. Lucy joined the two men at the table.

"I've got a business proposal for you." Alain said.

"A business proposal, you could just phone the restaurant and make a booking like everyone else?" Michel replied.

Alain nodded his head. "That's not what I meant."

"What is it you mean?"

Alain pointed to Lucy.

Lucy looked at Michel, gave him a reassuring smile, and pulled her chair closer to the table.

"I've been working for Alain for the past eighteen months, as his 'special projects director,'" she said. "I travel the world on his behalf, seeking out new markets, new opportunities for his corporation."

"Bit different to giving Chinese tourists directions to the *Mona Lisa*," Michel said.

"After you and I..." Lucy said, pausing to change tack. "After we went our separate ways, I eventually changed direction, moving into marketing, and then into public relations. Alain plucked me from my position with one of the oil families in the Middle East, with whom he has a working relationship."

"She's a very impressive woman," said Alain chipping in. "Listen, Michel, as I said back at the bar, I've recently invested in a television channel, and Lucy here has been charged with overseeing that investment, specifically to provide me with potential content ideas, and she has." He paused. "You," he said.

"Sorry, me?" replied Michel, looking a little confused.

Alain wore a serious expression, but a smile still twitched on his lips. He appeared to be amused by Michel's response.

"I've invested heavily in a network television channel in France, and one of the things I want to do as part of my entry package is relaunch their existing food channel."

"Right, and again, what has this to do with me?" replied Michel.

"A friend of mine recently dined at your restaurant and told me repeatedly that he hadn't had French food as good as that, outside *Paris*, since as far back as he could remember. Lucy heard him mention this at a meeting some months later, and when she asked him the name of the restaurant, her eyes lit up."

Michel looked at Lucy, and she gave him a nod in return, signifying that this was all true.

"Lucy mentioned that she knew the restaurant he'd dined at, your restaurant, and she filled me in on you and your brother, you know, your story."

"Did she?" Michel asked.

"Don't worry, I didn't tell him everything," Lucy said. "Just the story about how your parents had opened it back in the day, and how you boys had taken it over, all general stuff, no personal details were shared, I can assure you."

Michel believed her.

"Go on," Michel said to Alain.

"So, I got to thinking, you and your brother, who is by all accounts an amazing chef, coupled with your parent's backstory, and your front-of-house skills, not to mention your encyclopedic knowledge of Paris and France, all add up."

"To what?" asked Michel.

"To a great television series."

Michel took a long moment and poured himself a large glass of water from the carafe at the table. He sat back and smiled.

"Do you know how many offers we've turned down over the years? Huge offers from retailers, for endorsements, from various UK production companies for television opportunities, and we've always turned them down."

"He does know about those," answered Lucy. "He's knows about all the offers, but you didn't need to accept them back then, now you do."

That stung. Lucy was always one for getting straight to the point, straight to the heart of the matter; it was one of the many things Michel loved about her, no bullshit. Michel couldn't hide the fact that he and Antoine did indeed need a huge cash injection now more than ever, but he decided to try and play his cards close to his chest.

"Lucy has the details of what I'm proposing," Alain said. "It's a great offer, one that would be good for all of us; you'll get a more than decent payday, and my first commission for my new channel will be a hit, everyone's a winner." Alain got up from the table, knocked back the remainder of his drink, shook Michel's hand firmly, and walked away.

"See you in the car, Lucy!" he shouted as the door closed behind him. Michel detected a hint of triumph in the way he left the room.

He looked at Lucy for a long moment.

"What the hell was that all about?" he asked. "I mean it's a lot to take in, Lucy, for starters who is this guy?"

"He's a very rich, very influential person," replied Lucy. "And as he said, he's constantly looking out for opportunities; he's a philanthropist, an investor in businesses, in people, people like you and Antoine."

More silence as Michel sat and pondered. He had a peculiar sense of inevitability, that he was destined to be dragged into Alain's gravitational pull no matter how much he resisted.

"Alain is making you and Antoine an offer for a TV series, where you and your brother travel through France, cooking Antoine's dishes, and visiting some regional food festivals, etc. And he wants to pay you both handsomely." Lucy offered after a moment.

Michel looked at her.

"Look what I didn't tell Alain when he asked about your business, is what I found out when I dug into your financials," she said. "He isn't aware of any of that; if he was, the offer would be minuscule, believe me. I know you're in the shit Michel, deep in the shit; you're what, probably a year or two away from closing?" She leaned forward and patted his arm as if to comfort him.

Michel's expression darkened.

"I also know what that restaurant, what that building means to you and Antoine, especially you, and that you'd do anything to keep it open. Well, here's your chance."

Michel looked at her; she knew him so well. He couldn't hide anything from her, never could. Lucy spoke softly, reassuringly.

"I wouldn't do something like this if I didn't care about you, Michel. You and me were great together, *and* a disaster together." They both smiled.

"That's why we split up, nothing more nothing less, but that doesn't mean that I can't still look out for you, the way you did for me back in Paris; if it wasn't for you and the help and advice you gave me when I started my training at the hotel with you, I would never have received that job offer in Dubai. Look, here's the offer." She handed him a piece of paper. "Alain said he'll be in touch with you when he gets back to Paris, to find out whether you're interested or not. Either way, Michel, take a couple of days and just think about it."

Lucy rose from the table, hugged Michel, and left. She stopped at the door and turned back to look at Michel.

"And, hey, you and Alain? Could be the start of a beautiful friendship."

She winked at Michel, like Bogey winking at Bergman, and left. Not for the first time, she had taken Michel's breath away. After she'd gone, Michel sat for a while, staring at the door, his jaw clenched as if he were biting down on something painful.

The Convalesced Woman *by Ferdinand Georg Waldmüller*

...was another piece of the Obscurum Amicis collection that was destined for holier climbs. The crate that housed the painting almost didn't survive its journey, as the fishing trawler it ended up on was all but destroyed by huge waves, caught in a storm just as it came to dock in the old harbor town of Corfu, Greece. Fortunately, a large group of fishermen who were taking shelter in the nearby sheds on the harbor pier, were able to pull all the crew and the floating debris from the wreck ashore. The crate, which was addressed to the Palace of St. Michael and St. George less than a kilometer and a half from the harbor, finally completed its journey, hauled into the church by three burly locals. The awaiting clergymen, which included one ex-pat French Resistance fighter, took the cargo and placed it in the huge safe at the nearby Casa Parlante Museum, as the church he served in had no such facility.

The priests made the right decision, as the painting remained safe, in the safe, right up until the summer of 1998, when during a well-planned robbery, the safe was blown loose from its footing in the basement and removed completely. However, all of its contents were emptied and left behind, scattered around the floor of the basement, all bar one item, a solitary painting. It was as if someone came looking for that piece specifically.

CHAPTER FOURTEEN

Dover, present day

"NEXT STOP DOVER PRIORY," said the announcer. Antoine nudged Michel, who had been asleep for the final thirty minutes of the train journey.

"Come on, brother," said Antoine. "Time to go and meet our film crew, let's just hope there's a few decent lookers in the bunch."

He passed Michel his bags and they moved down to the train doors. The train slowly pulled in and stopped, the doors opened, and the boys disembarked.

"How do we know who we're looking for?" asked Antoine as they made their way down the platform.

"The producer said they'd have a sign."

They made their way off the platform and into the large concourse in the station, where the brothers looked around in search of their TV crew.

"Heads up," said Antoine as he nudged Michel again. He'd spotted something or, rather, someone.

The boys headed toward a young man who was holding a sign marked *The Deli Rew brothers.*

"Spelling isn't this guy's specialty," Antoine said as they approached the man.

"Best behavior, Antoine, first impressions and all that," replied Michel. "Hi, Michel and Antoine de la Rue," Michel said as they got to their man.

Silence.

"Eh, Michel and Antoine de la Rue," repeated Michel pointing at the sign the man was holding.

The young man put his finger in the air to shush Michel, and then frantically whispered into his phone. The brothers looked at each other puzzled by his behavior.

"Good afternoon, please follow me this direction, I have interesting cars awaiting and many people for you to liaise with upon them," the phone blurted out.

Antoine looked at Michel.

"Google Translate," said Michel.

"Wow, this is going to be a long six weeks," Antoine said as he threw his arm around his brother and they followed the young man out of the train station toward the car park.

CHAPTER FIFTEEN

London, 1968

DUST. DUST EVERYWHERE. SCAFFOLDING hugged the front of the building on Ramillies Place, as the building site buzzed with various tradesmen swarming in, out, and around it like worker bees servicing their queen.

There was a constant hum of noise, as carpenters, plumbers, and electricians banged, hammered, and smashed their way through walls, floors, and doors. Murielle and Jacques now ploughed all of their time into turning this forgotten building into a warm secure home for their family. No small feat, given on top of that task they were attempting to create a shiny, new, modern, contemporary restaurant on the ground floor, which would be Jacques's new kingdom.

The private area of the house, where the family would be living, was to be Murielle's kingdom, and with her passion and skill for interior design, she'd charged herself with overseeing all of the plans. She had an amazing eye for detail, having studied design in Paris. She also had a keen love of fashion and style and had already begun picking up pieces around the flea markets of London, which she stored for further use as the house edged toward completion.

Jacques had left his previous job pretty much as soon as they'd been informed of their windfall courtesy of Mrs. Rothstein. He was now fully focused on making this new project work, making his dream come true, and in honoring Mrs. Rothstein's memory, returning this building to what it once was.

What it was back in the day, was a bustling business, a coffee importers, originally opened in 1902, and run by a family who lived above their booming business, much like Jacques and Murielle were planning to do. The private quarters above the business had once been a beautiful, immaculately appointed home. Jacques and Murielle wanted to replicate that. Remnants of both the business and the family who were there before them were evident all over the now derelict site. From small residues of the original wallpaper still clinging to some of the corners of the walls in the living areas, to the remains of an oak counter in the old shop area of the building on the ground floor, to signs of fire damage in the cellar. Fragments of the previous tenants' lives and business peeped out from behind the dirt everywhere the new owners looked. One part of the building was a veritable Aladdin's cave for foibles and oddities.

This room was where Murielle spent most of her afternoons. While the construction work was happening above her, she happily spent hours sifting through and sorting decades of cellar rubbish, trying to find the odd pearl that she could rescue, restore, and then reinstate around the house above. Like Jacques, she was also was acutely aware of honoring the memory of their late friend Mrs. Rothstein.

Jacques entered the cellar down a makeshift ladder, with a flask of tea and two plastic cups in his hand. The cellar was dark and damp, lit by a temporary single swinging lightbulb, and it still had the lingering smell of roasting coffee beans from years ago.

"Union break," he said as he approached his wife, turned over a broken wooden box, and put the cups down on it. He pulled another two larger wooden boxes toward him and offered his wife a seat.

"What a place," he said as he looked around the room and started to pour the coffee.

"It's amazing," Murielle answered. "I keep finding things that are mind blowing, and when you look at them, touch them, it's like transporting yourself back thirty years or more." She handed him an old newspaper. "Look."

"*The Evening Standard*," said Jacques as he blew the dust off the old newspaper and noted the date, September first, 1939. He began reading aloud, "'Germany invades and bombs Poland, Britain mobilizes.'"

"Incredible, isn't it?" said Murielle. "The more I learn about the history in this city, in this building, this room, it's astonishing."

"In fairness darling, most of the stuff you've found down here has more of chance of ending up in the dump rather than on display at the Victoria and Albert Museum."

"I know that," replied Murielle. "I just find it all so fascinating. It's the thought of what else could be down here that keeps me coming back down. I mean look at this." She got up and pulled a heavy wooden crate across the floor from the far side of the room.

"What's that?" asked Jacques. "Another box of ancient rubbish?"

"No, it's a wooden crate. I was waiting for a strong man to come down here and help me open it." She fluttered her eyelids at her husband.

"Well, I could ask Angelo to come down and help you if you like?" replied Jacques, referring to the overweight builder with serious halitosis and bad teeth.

"No, he's knee-deep in pipework in the kitchen, best place for him." She moved slowly toward Jacques. He raised his eyebrows as he watched her. They were now face-to-face. Jacques leaned in to kiss his wife but Murielle placed her finger on his lips. She took a step back, picked up a crowbar and placed it in his hands.

"After you open the box," she said in a tone that usually resulted in her getting what she wanted. Jacques took a deep breath, finished his coffee with a single gulp, grabbed the crowbar and stood over the crate.

"If I open this and it's another box of prehistoric coffee beans, I'll make you drink it." He struggled to break through the lid.

"I look forward to it," said Murielle, fully expecting it to be exactly that, as she'd already opened four such crates over the past two weeks.

Jacques finally popped open the wooden lid, to reveal the contents.

"Right," he said, looking blankly into the box.

"Well? Liberica or Excelsa?" She was referring to two of the many types of coffee beans they'd discovered in the cellar previously.

"Well, it ain't beans, that's for sure." He brought the crate over to the makeshift table.

"What the hell?" Murielle said as Jacques pulled out a framed painting from the crate.

"And it's not alone." Jacques pulled three small pieces of ceramics from the crate. Murielle stood scratching her head.

"This building baffles me," she said as Jacques started to head back to the makeshift ladder leading out of the cellar.

"Well this is a mystery you'll have to solve on your own, darling, I've two toilets to plumb and an oven to install." He disappeared back up the ladder.

Murielle stared at the painting and the small ceramic pieces, and then looked around the room, it was in a truly sorry state. Jacques was right, time was of the essence, but she couldn't take her eyes off the contents of the newly opened crate in front of her.

True to his word, two weeks later, their new restaurant, Rien Mais le Meilleur, was ready for its first night of trading.

A pristine blue and white striped awning hung over the cellar entrance, with the name of the restaurant embroidered proudly across the center. Subtle lighting along the handrails either side of the steps, led to a double door. Inside, the dining room was stunning, with leather banquette seating running along both walls, small square tables with seating for four at each, were perfectly positioned in the center of the space. The old oak counter they'd found when they first got into the building, was now restored, and was pride of place near the door, reimagined as a waiter's station. The tables were covered with immaculately pressed white tablecloths, and each table was adorned with an array of sparkling cutlery, a table lamp, and small square crystal cut ashtrays. In the corner of the room, sat a baby grand piano, the couple's biggest investment, given the location of the restaurant in the heart of London's West End, Jacques was clearly aiming to attract the surrounding theater crowd.

The walls were a smoky tanned leather color and dotted along them were various pieces of art. Situated closest to the kitchen, was the best table in the house, the chef's table, that prized location for any guest, where their evening's dining would be elevated as each course was served to them by the head chef himself, at a premium price of course. On the wall behind these prized seats, lit beautifully, hung a painting. It was the painting Jacques pulled from that dusty crate down in the cellar some weeks earlier.

Murielle took it upon herself to restore the frame as best she could, and she did, lovingly. Now it had pride of place in their newest creation, the home and restaurant of their dreams.

She, and the painting, it seemed, had found their rightful place.

Portrait of Carl Sternhiem *by Ernst Ludwig Kirchner*

...made its journey from Paris across the English Channel, headed north, then west into the countryside of Wales. Arriving in Abergavenny, a sparsely populated, rural farming area, the painting had followed a well-worn path for art lovers in the UK. The huge private house called Llanvihangel Court was at an earlier period in its history owned by the fourth Earl of Worcester, Edward Somerset. It was always a house that accommodated a much-admired art collection, and the estate's owner at the time of delivery, a Mr. Bennett, was more than happy to house it, in this sprawling grade one listed building. It sat near the top of one of two grand staircases, which led to the private rooms of the Bennett family. Mr. Bennett was a keen supporter of the war effort. His two eldest sons had both taken the King's shilling in the Great War, so he thought nothing of often sending funds to London, as a gesture of support of his friend Mr. Winston Churchill, who had spent some time in the house in Wales, before he became Prime Minister. Another way that the Bennett family helped was by taking in works of art that they knew belonged to dislocated families across France, and pledged to hold them, making sure that they played their part in the restitution of such pieces when the war was over.

The painting hung on the wall of this magnificent sandstone building for over five decades. Some years later the nephew of the latest owner, a Mr. Lamington, attended an "invite only" game of Texas Hold'em poker at the house. It was part of a private hire, which saw a group of wealthy Middle-Eastern businessmen take over the building for the weekend. During the final hand of the two-day tournament, Mr. Lamington having lost everything he had come to the evening with, was talked into staking a painting of his choice in a last-ditch attempt to save face, and his ever-decreasing bank balance. He lost the hand, and chose a painting to be handed over. The businessman, a burly Middle-Eastern man, who won the painting in that final hand of poker made his way into the Welsh night leaving all of his other winnings in his room. The painting, which he now clung to, was what he had come for.

CHAPTER SIXTEEN

London, 1965

THE FIRST FEW YEARS of the business were a whirlwind. Great word of mouth, and more importantly for Jacques, a shining review in *The Times*, meant they were practically booked out at least five nights a week. Jacques was flat out in the kitchen. Staffing was a constant problem, finding good chefs and waiters became an enormous headache, which meant he was at his workstation, known in the trade as *the pass*, every night. "The pass" is the area of the kitchen where the head chef stood and examined each plate before it went out into the dining room to the waiting guests. If the dish wasn't as Jacques planned and designed it when it got to the pass, it didn't go out, simple as that. In the beginning Jacques was a little forgiving of his new chefs, his *brigade*.

"We are all learning together, eh?" Jacques would say as he'd help the chef correct their mistake on the plate, but as time went on, and the pressure mounted to maintain the high standards he himself had set, his patience drifted away like a paper boat leaving a small child's hand as they pushed it across a lake. Lately, if the dish wasn't up to scratch, the chef responsible would often find themselves scraping it off the nearest wall where Jacques had flung it in disgust, or they might find themselves locked in the walk-in fridge for ten minutes.

Having got through those early chaotic years of the business, and with the restaurant now flourishing, and routines in place, the de la Rue family found their rhythm. Jacques worked long hours downstairs, while Murielle was now part of the buzzing local social scene, spending some of her days attending lunches and other gatherings with similar powerful other-halves, while the boys were coming to the end of their schooling and counting the days. At the age of sixteen, Antoine and Michel were both put to work in the restaurant, and with Antoine showing a flair for the kitchen, he instantly became his father's protégé, while Michel, who had a talent for eating but not cooking the food, was dispatched to the dining room and started as a waiter under the tutelage of Mr. Florien, the restaurant's highly regarded maître d'. The daily hustle and bustle of the restaurant meant that there was rarely a private moment to be had by anyone in the family. The kitchen was in full flow from six a.m., with chefs baking breads, taking deliveries in, and starting the *mise en place* for lunch, which was the most important part of any chef's job, the preparation of the food and ingredients ahead of that evenings service.

"If the *mise en place* is not done correctly, service will quickly turn to shit!" This was another mantra that Jacques would bellow out if his brigade hadn't got their prep completed to his high standards. Meanwhile the front of house staff would be busy cleaning down from the previous day's service, in preparation for another fresh onslaught of patrons.

More often than not, Jacques wouldn't surface in the morning until after ten, having enjoyed the latter part of the previous evening with the guests at the chefs table. Murielle would be up early every morning, making sure the boys got out to school on time, after which she would slip out to meet a friend, or take in some much needed retail therapy. The couple hardly spent a moment alone together, but dreams were hard work, and if you wanted to make them a reality, this level of disruption was what the couple were committed to, all to make *their* restaurant the place-to-be in London's hottest food destination.

Landschaft bei Paris *by Albert Gleizes*

...was the painting that traveled the farthest from Paris. The crate that it was housed in took to land, sea, air, train, bus, and horse and cart, before reaching its final destination. By the time it was delivered to the Mohun Bagan Athletic Club in Kolkata, India, the crate had almost disintegrated. It had taken thirteen months to complete its journey, and the crate looked like it was about to turn to dust and collapse. A Mr. Blanc collected the crate and brought it across the bustling city, passing by the world-famous Eden Gardens, home to the India national cricket team, and into his office at the old Calcutta Town Hall. Mr. Blanc, another ex-pat French Resistance member, now worked as a senior clerk in the town hall and had agreed to take this delivery into safekeeping. However, when he opened the crate, he was expecting ceramics or perhaps jewelry, certainly not a painting. Mr. Blanc, not being blessed with the honest traits of his fellow Resistance members, and now being so far away from war, was more interested in moving on whatever items he was sent, in order to pay for his increasing opium habit. He didn't believe in restitution. He believed in feathering his own nest, and so quickly began looking out for a buyer for the painting. His efforts weren't exactly exhaustive; he passed it off to a small-time opium dealer based in the south of the city, near St. Paul's Cathedral, in an effort to repay a debt he owed to that same dealer. Mr. Blanc received the required forgiveness from his debt after he'd handed over the painting, both vendor and buyer being totally oblivious to the paintings real value.

The painting spent a decade or more in India, eventually being used as a part payment in a long-drawn-out feud that the small-time opium dealer had got involved in. After changing hands several times amongst the lower end of India's underworld, it ended up hanging on the wall of a larger opium exporter, a man of real means, who was based in Chakraberia, west of Kolkata. The painting remained with him until the early 2000s, when he, his family, and his opium enterprise were brought to their knees by members of the notorious D-Company, who were, and still are, one of the biggest crime syndicates in India. Shortly after D-Company acquired the painting, they entered a business partnership with a Paris-based logistics wizard, and when a member of the Paris corporation paid them a site visit not long after, he spotted the painting, and subsequently it was traded as part of the sign-up terms with him and his organization. They were to hand over the painting, as a sign of their commitment to this new enterprise. In return, their opium and other illegal cargo would secure safe access to major shipping routes all across Asia, Europe, and South America.

The deal was signed, and the painting was handed over to the representative of the Paris-based corporation, a Mr. Hassan.

CHAPTER SEVENTEEN

London, 1986

THURSDAY AT THE RESTAURANT was an important day. For Jacques, Thursday meant only one thing. Fresh fish. He would leave the restaurant each Thursday morning, normally at the crack of dawn, and head with his sous-chef to Billingsgate, the biggest fish market in the UK. There, he and his right-hand man would sift through what was on offer, make their selections, and order enough stock to carry them through the next seven days. Only the *best* produce would make it into Jacques's kitchen.

The market opened at 4:00 a.m., and Jacques would always be there at four on the dot to get the best position to talk to the fishermen and be in prime place when the auctions started. For years, Jacques had yearned to go on a fishing trip with one of his suppliers, Greg Balding. He was one of Jacques trusted suppliers and managed a small fleet of trawlers that were based and fished from a bustling harbor town on the coast of Cornwall.

Greg, a former skipper, who only occasionally went out on one of his boats now, was always waxing lyrical about being on the open sea, trawling for prawns.

"There's nothing like it," he'd repeatedly say to Jacques, offering him a spot on one of his trawlers. "You have to experience it, Jacques, whenever you like, mate, you name the day." Eventually, Jacques named a day.

He traveled down to the busy fishing village of Padstow on a Wednesday night after his restaurant had closed and enjoyed a lively late night in one of the local hostelries with Greg and his boat crew. The next morning at the crack of dawn they ventured out to spend the day fishing on the choppy English Channel.

The next morning, the restaurant was busy as usual with preparations for the day ahead going on at a pace. Antoine was manning the kitchen. His dad was due back before dinner service, and he wanted to make sure that he and the team were ready when he got back.

"You know my old man," Antoine said to the rest of the chefs in the kitchen as they worked through their *mise en place*. "There's probably been a hip flask or two drained during the fishing trip, so let's have everything shipshape before the big man gets back to the pass, yes?"

"Oui, chef!" answered the brigade in typical military fashion.

Michel was helping Mr. Florien get the dining room ready for service. He hoovered, while other waiters polished cutlery and dressed tables. Murielle was on Bond Street, collecting Michel's birthday present, a pair of gold cufflinks, engraved with his initials.

Back at the restaurant, they were now well into lunch service, with almost a full house, the dining room buzzing with the sounds of happy diners enjoying their food. In the kitchen, Antoine was getting the groundwork done for that evening's dinner service. The radio that sat on one of the shelves in the kitchen blared out "The Power of Love" by Jennifer Rush. She was accompanied, out of tune, but loudly, by most of the kitchen staff, who resembled a tone-deaf version of an overgrown Vienna boys' choir. In the midst of the organized mayhem, the phone on the back wall of the kitchen rang.

"Kitchen, Elliot speaking," said Elliot Toner, one of the sous-chefs. "Sure, one minute." He left the phone down on the counter. "Chef, phone!" he shouted across the kitchen.

Antoine danced his way over to the phone, pausing to dip one of the chefs across him, in a smooth dance floor pick up move he'd perfected in the nightclubs of Soho.

"Hello?" he roared down the phone. "Hi, Greg, you boys stop for pie and mash on the way back up here?" He fiddled with the long flex on the phone. "What?" He paused, his face dropping suddenly. "Turn it off, Elliot," he shouted pointing at the radio.

No response.

"Elliot, turn the fucking radio off!" he roared.

Elliot jumped to attention and ran to switch the radio off. Antoine hung up the phone and stood at the counter, frozen to the spot.

"What's up?" Elliot asked.

Antoine stood motionless. His eyebrows were raised slightly, the closest he came to expressing a strong emotion. The rest of his features were blank.

The kitchen brigade had now stopped working and all eyes were fixed on Antoine.

"Chef, what's wrong?" Elliot said.

Antoine seemed to deflate in front of their eyes, he reached out to grab the counter that he was leaning against as he crumpled slowly and sunk onto the floor. The crew looked at each other as Antoine attempted to speak.

"My father's dead," replied Antoine, barely able to get the words out of his mouth. He cleared his throat and tried again. "My father's dead," he repeated in a whisper.

Hours later, the family gathered around the chef's table in the restaurant. Lots of empty glasses and wine bottles crowded the table. Murielle, Michel, Antoine, and Mr. Florien had now been joined by Greg, Jacques's friend who'd been on the fishing trip with him.

"It all happened so quickly," said Greg, who had driven to London from Cornwall in the early of hours of the morning and was now reliving the events of the fishing trip.

"We'd been out for two hours, all was well, and then a squall of a storm hit the boat out of nowhere. I was standing beside Jacques, and I got called to go to the front of the boat to release a jammed chain. As I got to the front of the boat we were hit by a huge wave, we all clung on, and when it passed, I ran to the back of the boat, and when I got there…" he said, stopping to take a drink. "He was gone, just swept away, he was there one minute, and gone the next."

The coastguard was alerted, and the search went on for three hours, but Jacques body wasn't recovered, and the search was called off due to the bad weather.

Michel comforted Mr. Florien, who was in tears. Antoine sat and stared into space.

"He was so young," he said, in a mumble to himself.

Murielle was numb; she was barely in the room. The man she had loved more than anything in the world, given her life to, given two sons to, was gone. She just sat there and smoked, her eyes filled with tears, nodding her head every so often.

The silence in the room was deafening, people moved around the space slowly, refilling their glasses, lighting cigarettes, and grazing on their food meant for those customers who had booked for that evening's now canceled service. All the while, Murielle sat, motionless. Antoine moved beside her and toped her glass up. He put his arm around her, she felt stiff, taught with anxiety. He squeezed her shoulder reassuringly. She looked at her eldest boy, and took his hand in hers.

"What am I supposed to do now? I can't run all of this on my own, he did everything, I can't do it, I just can't," she mumbled.

"Mum, don't think about that now, that's not important, we're here, we'll do whatever you need. Whatever you want to do, me and Michel are right behind you."

Murielle stood and emptied her glass, and left to go upstairs.

Antoine looked at his little brother, who was watching Murielle leave the room. They caught each other's eyes.

"Is she okay?" Michel asked.

"I've no idea, brother, I've no idea."

CHAPTER EIGHTEEN

Dover, present day

MICHEL AND ANTOINE WERE a little stiff and groggy from the train journey but were soon on their toes as they headed to meet their film crew. A light rain started to fall as the brothers were led toward them by their linguistically challenged new friend. They exchanged looks.

"*These* are the people we're spending the next six weeks with?" asked Antoine. He appeared to have already not just sized them up but made up his mind he didn't like any of them.

"Be polite," said Michel as they reached the group.

"Bonjour mes amis," Michel said, in an attempt to break the ice and show that he and his brother were comfortable to converse in his mother tongue.

"Excuse me?" said the first man whose hand Michel shook.

"Oh sorry, I presumed you were French," Michel said, realizing that the looks he got when he'd fired his opening salvo weren't because his fly was open.

"We're all English," offered one of the crew.

"How to make friends and influence people," said Antoine, stepping in to dispel his brother's growing embarrassment. "A book that Michel has never read, unfortunately," he continued. "I am Antoine de la Rue, and this is my little brother, Michel."

One of the group offered his hand.

"I'm Donald Foulkes, your producer and director," he continued. "And this is our crew, firstly our cameraman, Phil Best."

Phil shook the brothers' hands. Michel noticed Phil had what can only be described as the most pronounced gunner-eye he'd ever encountered. Antoine went to make a comment.

"Don't," said Michel as he looked at Phil, who was now looking back at both of them, at the same time.

"Next, our sound guru, Stephen Duxbury. Stephen, say hello!" said Donald. Stephen had headphones on and was chewing gum. Donald kicked Stephen in the shins to get his attention.

"The fuck what was that for?" shouted Stephen.

"Say hello to the *talent*," Donald said, referring to Antoine and Michel.

"Hello, talent!" Stephen shouted, not even removing the earphones for the introduction. "Either of you allergic to gaffer tape? I'll be using a lot of gaffer tape on you, for your mics."

The brothers both shook their heads.

"Great," said Stephen. "See you on the dance floor." He and Phil the cameraman headed off to load the last of their gear into the crew van.

"Last, and by very means least, this is our fixer and guide, Olly Bailey," Donald said as he introduced the boys to the man who greeted them back at the train.

"He's our fixer?" asked Antoine. "This poor sod can't even speak English!"

"Yes, he can," answered Olly, in a broad Yorkshire accent, much to the brother's surprise. "I can actually speak four languages, although my Russian isn't exactly where I'd like it to be, but I get by," he said, with a strong hint of fuck you.

"Then what was all that about with the whole Google Translate floorshow back at the train station?" asked Michel.

"I was just testing the Wi-Fi in the train station," answered Olly. "Turns out it's pretty good in there." Olly headed off to join Phil and Stephen over in the crew van.

"Right, let's saddle up," said Donald. "We're on a tight schedule, don't want to miss the ferry."

Antoine and Michel started to head toward the crew van.

"No, hang on," Donald said. "That's the *crew's* transport, *this* is what you guys will be traveling in for the trip; we've already rigged it with lipstick camera's, GoPro's, microphones, and the like." Donald pointed to another van beside the crew vehicle.

"You're kidding me?" said Antoine as he looked over at the van. "We'd be lucky to make it to the ferry, let alone all the way to Paris in that rust bucket!"

The lads stood looking at a 1985 Volkswagen T25 Camper Van, blue in color, with a white roof, that doubled as a sleeping area, topped off with a white trim, white bumpers, and a white radiator grill.

"Jesus," said Michel as they approached the campervan and started inspecting it closer.

"It even has a pull-out awning!" said Donald.

"Well at least we won't get soaked while we sit by the roadside waiting for the AA," said Michel.

"Come on, it's in great nick!" said Donald offering encouragement. "This would outdrive our van, *any* day." Antoine looked over at the crew van, a 2019 Toyota Land Cruiser, top spec, shining like a new brass button on a recently dry-cleaned blazer.

"Well, why we don't take *yours* then, and put your theory to the test?"

"Funny, very funny," replied Donald. "Look, this is a warts-and-all documentary, and filming starts now, and ends when you finish service at the banquet in Paris in six weeks. Now put on your big boy pants and let's get on with it, we've a boat to catch." He jumped into the crew van.

"Well," Michel said. "This is going be a laugh-a-minute." They threw their cases into the campervan. "You have any idea how to change a tire, just in case?"

"I reckon it'd be handier to know how to rebuild an engine, given the noise this thing is making," Antoine replied as they set off, following behind the crew van.

Phil was hanging out of the back of the crew vehicle, filming the boys, and the cameras in the brothers' van whirred into life. Donald gave the boys a thumbs up from the back seat of his vehicle. Antoine flipped him the bird in response.

"Right chaps," Donald said over the radio as Antoine picked up the walkie-talkie in their van. "We're rolling!"

The brothers were silent as they drove along. They didn't say a word. They were not sure what to say, in fact they were not sure what to do at all; this was completely alien to them.

"Chaps?" said Donald over the walkie-talkie. "This isn't a silent movie, you know?"

Antoine pushed the button on the walkie-talkie.

"Well, what the fuck do you want us to talk about?" he asked, a genuine question, as he and his brother had never done this before.

"Talk about where you are, what's around you, what you're about to do, you know, keep the viewer informed!" Donald said enthusiastically over the radio. "Start with the itinerary, it's in the glove box, read that out loud, and see where that takes the conversation."

"That's a good idea in fairness; it'd be good to know what the fuck he's planned for us," Antoine said.

"I read the itinerary two months ago, when it was emailed to us both," replied Michel.

"Right," said Antoine. "My email mustn't be working properly."

"Bullshit," said Michel. "You just didn't bother your arse reading it, well now's your chance, go on, give us your best Anthony Bourdain." He handed Antoine the itinerary from the glovebox.

"Right, watch and learn, little brother." Antoine started to read the itinerary aloud, putting on a voice like he was announcing the Oscar nominations: "'This six-week culinary adventure will take the de la Rue brothers, that's us, from Calais to Paris, they'll check in at some of the more *interesting* food festivals that France has to offer, and they will share their knowledge of the produce and famous recipes of the area, as well as a little local history. The trip will culminate in the brothers preparing a six-course tasting menu for an invited audience at the residence of the British ambassador in Paris.'"

"Beautifully done!" screamed Donald from the walkie-talkie.

"You see?" said Antoine. "I'm a natural."

Michel raised his eyes to heaven, and smiled as yet again his brother managed to nail it, first take, much like everything else he'd put his hand to in life.

Fifteen minutes and one pit stop later, to fix a camera that had slipped off its mounting on the windscreen inside the brothers' van, they arrived at the car ferry and boarded the ship. They had a two-hour crossing ahead of them, and then their first staged filming segment was scheduled. The crew were to film the brothers attending a food festival in Oye-Plage, a small town near Calais, where they'd meet locals, taste food, and cook a dish themselves, on the beach. Sounded straightforward enough, but of course, it wasn't.

Oye-Plage played host every year to one of Europe's biggest *naked* food festivals, which took place on the nearby beach, and it was not the food that was naked, no, it was the guests, the chefs, and all attendees.

Donald, being the over-concerned producer that he was, had decided *not* to fill the brothers in on this particular detail until they neared the location; he certainly wasn't going to tell them during the channel crossing. He didn't fancy swimming back to Dover with a sound boom-pole protruding from him.

CHAPTER NINETEEN

As the brothers and their crew dawdled along on the car ferry, 310 kilometers away, in an apartment on the second floor of 28 Rue Gabriel-Laumain, Fabian sat in his apartment at his desk scribbling in a large notebook. He'd lived in this apartment for ten years, having moved to Paris after graduating from college in Lens. He'd made the place his own, with souvenirs from his travels worldwide dotted around the rooms.

He was getting a start on the Alain Deschamps profile piece, but he was finding it difficult as to what angle to take. He knew that his editor and the wider readership expected a standard piece, that customary, predicted copy, that featured in magazines abandoned on the tables of every doctors waiting room in the world, that standard two-page spread featuring the CEO of a faceless corporation that most readers hadn't heard of, accompanied by the typical bland set of photos. Dull. Predictable. Two things that Fabian's articles could never be accused of being were dull and predictable.

Fabian's articles were in-depth and showed the reader a side of the interviewee that they hadn't seen before, that they hadn't expected. This piece felt different though; he knew what his editors and readers wanted, but *he* wanted to write about the dark side of Deschamps. Fabian had done an even deeper dive into Alain's past than he'd let on at their meeting. But he was missing one thing. Proof. Fabian, like most respected journalists, craved proof, and so did his editors. *Maybe more coffee would help*, he thought. He left his desk and headed to his kitchen, lighting the smallest gas ring on his cooker and heating a pot that sat above it. As he took a cup from the kitchen counter, the buzzer on his front door rang.

He wasn't expecting anyone. The buzzer went again, clearly the visitor lacked patience. He left the now bubbling pot and headed to his front door. When he opened it, a familiar face greeted him.

Lorenzo Pieters was a regular visitor to Fabian's place of work, *Le Monde*. Fabian had seen him there, meeting with Fabian's editor. He'd been introduced to him once when Lorenzo turned up to pay his respects to a senior staffer at their retirement party in the paper's offices. Pieters was a serious man with a serious job. He cut a small figure in the doorway of Fabian's apartment, his slight physical stature in no way matched his dogged and at times fiery personality. Fabian knew of this man's power and connections throughout the larger European community of lawmakers.

Lorenzo was head of Interpol's Stolen Works of Art Unit. Based in Lyon, at Interpol's headquarters, Lorenzo and his handpicked team, spent their days monitoring the biggest movers of stolen art works in the world. He and his team had an outstanding strike rate. Over the past three years, since he'd taken the helm, Pieters and his unit had recovered works of art valued well into the billions, from sculptures to Fabergé eggs, to rare ancient jewelry. They had reunited people, families, governments, and countries with treasures that they had all considered lost and long gone. His latest project, and specific target, involved paintings, specifically a certain collection of paintings.

"Lorenzo," said Fabian. "To what do I owe the pleasure of a home visit?"

"This isn't a social visit, Fabian," said Lorenzo. "Is that fresh coffee I smell brewing?" He sniffed and entered the room.

"No, it's a new coffee flavoured infuser I'm trying out. Good, isn't it?"

Lorenzo didn't laugh. Fabian didn't expect him to.

"Would you like a cup?" asked Fabian, already knowing what his visitor's answer would be.

"That would be great, may I sit?"

"Make yourself at home," answered Fabian as he headed back to the kitchen to get his guest a cup.

"Nice apartment." Lorenzo sat on the sofa. He popped a briefcase onto the small coffee table in front of him and opened it. Straight down to business.

"Yes, it's not huge, but it's perfect for me." Fabian returned to the living room with the coffees. "So, what's this about?" he asked, taking a seat at his desk, and closing his laptop as he did.

"I'm going to get straight to it and spare you the usual bullshit small talk." Lorenzo took a large file from his briefcase. "You've been spending a little time with an old friend of ours recently, I see." He took some photos from a file and handed them to Fabian.

Fabian took a look through the four photos he'd been handed, which were long lens shots of Fabian entering an office complex on Rue Dauphine.

"Right," said Fabian. "What do you think I was doing in there, and why would that pique *your* interest?"

"Not *what*, Fabian, *whom*," answered Lorenzo. "As I said, Fabian, let's avoid small talk, shall we?" Lorenzo watched Fabian sift through the photos.

"Of course," agreed Fabian.

"Alain Deschamps," said Lorenzo. "We know you've met him, spent time with him, and I'd like to know what you and he discussed?"

"Well, as I'm sure you've already gathered from your friend, my editor, the interview will be published in less the ten days, I can arrange a copy to be sent to you, or maybe you have an online subscription?"

Another failed attempt at lightening the mood. Lorenzo smiled and looked around the room. His eyes seemed to be scanning the room, like a hawk searching out its prey, which made Fabian nervous.

"You know, I could just take this from here, take it back to the station, and get the answers I need," said Lorenzo, referring to Fabian's Dictaphone on the coffee table in front of him.

Rookie error from Fabian.

"You could," said Fabian. "Or, as you said, I could just tell you, therefore cutting through the small talk."

Pieters shifted in his chair and looked at his watch. He was getting restless. He hadn't the time to waste on coffee and pleasantries with a journalist, but as always, Pieters was doing what he needed to do. One of his greatest skills was reading a situation, acting on it accordingly, and getting the desired result. Today wasn't going to be any different.

"Can I ask you a question first?" said Fabian.

"Please do," replied Lorenzo. "Good coffee by the way."

"Deschamps. I presume he's been on your radar for some time?"

"For many years," replied Lorenzo, putting his coffee cup back on the table. "He became my reason for getting up in the morning quite some time ago."

"Well, as you know, I was sent in to do a profile piece on him, an exclusive." Fabian lit a cigarette. "But I got more than I bargained for. He's a layered character, wouldn't you agree?"

"That's one way of putting it," answered Lorenzo. "If by layered, you mean a man who presents one face, one image, while hiding several others, then yes, he's as layered as the piles of lacquer applied onto a fake Da Vinci."

Lorenzo took a cigarette from the box on the table and lit it. He paused before his next question.

"Did he tell you about the upcoming exhibition in Paris, at the auction house?" he asked.

Fabian nodded.

"Then you know what he's planning to do, or at least what he *says* he planning to do."

"He *outlined* a plan."

"Oh I'm sure he did," replied Lorenzo. There was a moment's silence. Lorenzo slowly took another sip of his coffee, never taking his eyes off Fabian. He was beginning to form an opinion of the man.

Lorenzo got up and walked around the room. He stopped in front of the framed piece of movie memorabilia on the wall that dominated the living space.

"Tony Stark," he said. "Now there's a man whose set of skills I could do with in my unit. But I have to make do with the tools that I've been given."

"Seems to me the team you have are performing well," said Fabian, commenting on the impressive record Pieters' squad had.

"They are, but we don't get the results we do just through our own work. We rely on a network of information gatherers, friendlies all over the world who help us with our lines of inquiry."

"And I'm guessing that I'm about to be asked to join that exclusive club, am I right?"

Lorenzo smiled, nearly laughed.

"Tell me, did Deschamps give you the grand tour while you were there?"

"I saw the inside of his office, if that's what you mean?"

"So, he didn't take you down his tunnel of light, to show you his hoard then?"

Clearly Lorenzo knew more than Fabian thought he did about his recent meeting with Alain. Fabian considered this for a moment and decided to go with full honesty and be up-front with Lorenzo.

"He did."

"So, you had a private audience with the *Obscurum Amicis*." Fabian stared blankly at Lorenzo.

"It's been years since I studied Latin in school," Fabian said. "You'll have to help me out here."

"The *Obscurum Amicis* or 'Obscure Friends' are a collection of six paintings, known to have been stolen during a single raid by a Nazi ERR squad in Paris, June of 1940," Lorenzo explained as he paced the room. "This collection of paintings got their name not because the subjects of those paintings were similar or by the same artist, but because these six paintings were bundled together in that raid, therefore becoming odd bedfellows, or, obscure friends. Those paintings have traveled the world; we know they were split up at some point and dispersed to various private collectors, but they have never seen the light of day, either in a gallery, a museum, or on a private collector's wall. They've remained unseen by the public, and the authorities for that matter."

Fabian's mind was racing.

"So, you're telling me that I had a private viewing of these rare 'Obscure Friends,' in an office, about sixteen kilometers away from where we're sitting?"

"No," replied Lorenzo. "You had an audience with fakes, forgeries, replicas of the *Obscurum Amicis*. But we happen to now have the information that Deschamps, or Delitzsch Jr. as we like to call him, has the *real* paintings, locked away in an unknown location, and is preparing to complete his collection, by adding the sixth and final member of that exclusive group to his hoard. At which point he'll offload them to a single buyer and *not* hand them over to the authorities, as I'm sure he told you he was going to do."

Fabian nodded in agreement.

"Well, this is where you come in, my friend," Lorenzo said. Fabian lit another cigarette and stood.

"I'd better get some fresh coffee on," he said as he headed back toward the kitchen.

"Good idea. But before you do, did you happen to bump into this person while you were in his office?"

Lorenzo joined him in the kitchen and handed him another photo. Fabian studied it carefully. It was another long lens shot; this time it was one of Alain Deschamps having lunch at a street side café, accompanied by a woman.

"No," answered Fabian. "Who is she?"

"Lucy Carter."

"And where does she fit in to all of this?"

"Well, let's just say that she's become a person of interest," replied Lorenzo. "For both of us."

Veiller Sur Toi *by Pierre Bontemps*

...had a practically sedate journey to its location in comparison to its companions. It headed to London, to Soho, to Ramillies Place, to the Brooks Coffee Importers Co. It was received and placed in the cellar of the building, by a Mr. Harry Martin, a long-time warehouse employee of the Brooks family. There it sat, safe and undisturbed, until 1968, when during the removal of the old foundations of the building during renovations, it was discovered and opened by Murielle and Jacques de la Rue. Murielle instantly felt connected to the painting, loved it, and hung it on the wall of their newly opened restaurant.

Unbeknown to both, it seemed Murielle and her father Ronin Kohl had a similar taste in art.

CHAPTER TWENTY

Northern France, present day

On their second full day of filming, Antoine and Michel stood on a pier, naked as the day they came into the world, save for the aprons provided by their producer. Michel couldn't have felt more uncomfortable if he tried, he cringed at the idea when Donald finally mentioned it as they approached the first filming assignment and had a knot in his stomach all day. The brothers stood there and looked at the crowds in front of them, who were also naked, not that that comforted Michel, who was clinging on to his apron strings for dear life. The only people who weren't bereft of clothes were the film crew. This was the first of the many planned staged setups for the documentary series, and things couldn't have started in a more bizarre fashion.

They had arrived in Oye-Plage and were joined by almost two hundred festivalgoers, who were all here to celebrate the sardine, the small oily fish that originated in Sardinia but that now fed and economically sustained a large part of this region of France.

The brothers were positioned on one of the small jetties protruding out into the sea. A trestle table was set up in front of them, laid out with ingredients and cooking utensils. Donald and the crew stood opposite the brothers, behind the camera, two cameras in fact, one stationary on a tripod filming a wide shot, manned by Donald, and another in the arms of Phil, the main cameraman, which enabled him to move in between the two brothers, and then onto the food. The crew were poised and ready to capture what Donald hoped would be the first in a series of gastronomic masterclasses.

Donald had high hopes for the brothers now, particularly of Michel, after the team had spent the earlier part of the day filming out and about in the nearby town center, as the brothers moved in and out of the markets, and perused through what was on offer. This part of France, like so many others, was heavily reliant on its food tourism trade. Small towns were proud of their food markets, each and every day these places would come alive as locals and tourists buzzed their way through the various stalls, gorging on the finest ingredients and dishes that that region was most proud of. Antoine was in heaven, stopping at each stall, touching and smelling the endless array of meats, fish, and vegetables that were on offer. His mind was in overdrive, as he spoke about creating a different dish each time he picked up a new ingredient. He regaled the crew about the food and drink that this specific part of France was famous for. It had Flemish influences, he told them, and he couldn't wait to cook a regional speciality, beef braised in Flemish beer, and had the crew salivating as he described *ficille Picardie*, a ham and mushroom crêpe baked in a rich cream sauce, and featuring the finest cheese in the region, *Mariolles*. Alongside Antoine's culinary ramblings, Michel easily slipped into even more detail about the local area, its people, its ingredients, and its food traditions. They were both in their element, and the camera captured it all. *So, a successful start, and maybe, just maybe, these boys had TV presenter potential*, Donald thought.

Donald quickly landed on a particular shooting style for this project, realizing that if he and the crew stayed out of the way, the brothers forgot about the cameras, and their inhibitions left them, and they just started being themselves: two brothers talking food and history.

"Right," said Donald. "Michel, we'll start with Michel filling us in about where we are, and then we'll pull back to reveal you both, and the stunning location, and then Antoine we'll get straight into the cooking. Sound like a plan, chaps?"

"Great, wonderful," replied Antoine with a level of lethargy that suggested he'd rather be anywhere else in the world than standing here, with his bare hairy arse on display to the gathering crowd behind him.

"Let's just get this done, shall we?" said Michel to Donald, wishing to speed things up, so they could get back to the campervan and get dressed.

"Roll it up!" said Donald, and the crew did just that, sound and cameras rolled, they were now recording. "In your own time, Michel."

Silence. Nothing from either Michel or Antoine.

They seemed to be distracted by something happening on the beach behind the film crew. Considering that there was a huge crowd of naked people surrounding them, it would be easy to get distracted, but the boys weren't looking at the overweight naked revelers playing netball on the beach. They were transfixed by a tall middle-aged man with a long beard, who was strolling along the beach, taking his pig for a walk. A pig. On a lead.

"Action!" shouted Donald at the brothers.

The brothers didn't flinch, glued to this anomaly on the strand.

"Action!" Donald shouted, trying to snap the lads out of their trance.

"Is that Roussel?" said Michel to Antoine. Antoine squinted his eyes to see.

"I think you're right," answered Antoine as he stepped forward to take a closer look.

They recognized the pig-walker as a man that the brothers knew well, having shared a kitchen with Antoine back in the day in Paris.

"Hang on, Donald," said Michel as he moved toward the beach. "Françoise! Françoise Roussel!"

The man with pig stopped, looked around, and saw two naked chefs waving frantically at him from the pier.

"Mes amis!" he shouted back and started to head in their direction.

"Fellas, what the hell is going on?" Donald shouted.

"An old friend, haven't seen him in years, give us a minute here," Antoine answered as they moved down the steps on the pier and onto the beach to greet their old pal. Antoine and Michel greeted their old pal with aplomb. An awkward silence followed as Antoine and Michel remembered they were both naked.

"I don't believe it," said Antoine, breaking the moment. "How long has it been?"

"Too long my friend, too long," Françoise replied.

"What are you doing here?" Michel asked as he took a pack of cigarettes out of his apron and lit one.

"I live here, man, I'm a local!" Françoise replied. "Been here for almost eight years now. Last time I saw you naked, Antoine, it was the night we graduated from catering college."

"True," replied Antoine. "And if memory serves me right there was a pig or two there that night as well!"

"Speak for yourself," replied Françoise. "How's London, you still cooking up a storm over there?"

"There's a storm alright," answered Michel as he looked at Antoine. "But not much cooking."

"But we have a plan, we'll be back on top before you know it, right brother?" Antoine said.

"Right," said Michel, with not much conviction.

"What about you, you still throwing pans around the kitchen?" asked Antoine.

"No, god no," replied Françoise. "Packed that in years ago. Moved down here, bought a small farm, spend my days surrounded by nature, farming and hunting. Beats the shit out of being stuck in a hot kitchen for twelve hours a day."

"Man, you've got it licked," said Antoine, pining for a similar solitary self-sufficient existence.

"Is this part of your daily routine then?" Michel asked. "Walking your pig on a nudist beach?"

"Wait, this is a *nudist* beach?" Françoise replied. The three men laughed again, delighted to be back in each other's company.

"This is Aggie," said Françoise, referring to the pig at the end of the lead. "My most valuable employee." The brothers looked at each other quizzically.

"Employee?" asked Antoine.

"Before you ask," replied Françoise, cutting in before the brothers thought he had completely fallen off the deep end. "Truffle farming. That's my business, and this seventeen-stone bag of bacon fat is that best truffle hunter in this part of the country."

Makes sense, Michel thought, impressed with Françoise's entrepreneurial spirit.

"So, what's with the camera crew?" he asked the brothers.

"It's a documentary for a new food channel here in France," Antoine replied. "*His* big idea," he added as he pointed to his little brother. Michel clicked his fingers; he had an idea.

"Donald!" he shouted back toward the crew. "Get over here!" Donald moved to join the three men on the beach,

"You ready to get back to it?" he asked.

"This man," said Michel. "And more importantly this *pig*, should be on our show, best truffle hunter in the business, the pig, not him," he added, pointing to Françoise. "Could be a great piece of, what did you call it back on the ferry, 'color' for the show?" Donald looked at the pig and then at Françoise.

"Not a bad shout, Michel," he answered. He turned to Françoise." How far away is your farm?"

"About eight kilometers," replied Françoise.

"Okay, right, we have time," said Donald looking at his watch. "We could swing by your place tonight after we finish filming here, and maybe get some filming done with you and Aggie in the morning, and be back on track by tomorrow afternoon?"

"Fantastic," declared Michel. "So we'll see you tonight, Françoise?"

"Perfect," Françoise replied. "I'll stick something on the spit-roast." Hastily, he covered Aggie's ears.

"Right, shall we get back to it boys? The sardines, remember?" Donald said to the brothers as he shook Françoise's hand and headed back toward the film crew.

"Appreciate that, Michel," said Françoise. "It'd be great to get some publicity for my farm."

"Anything for an old friend," replied Michel. Truth be known Michel fancied sleeping in a warm bed in Françoise's farmhouse tonight, as opposed to watching his brother snore less than four feet away from him in their battered campervan.

Having repositioned themselves back at the cookery set-up, Antoine dazzled the small crowd around him, and the crew, as he whipped together an amazing dish, one from his large repertoire, a Mediterranean sardine pasta dish, with lemon, capers, and chili. During the cooking demonstration Michel ably assisted his brother with the cooking, while regaling the crowd and therefore, the TV viewers, with a little local history from the area, finishing the segment by teasing the viewer with the promise of the brothers visit to a nearby truffle farm later in that episode.

It was great television, as the brother's breezed their way through the ten-minute segment without skipping a beat. As the crew all tucked into the dish after the filming was completed, they made various noises of pleasure, and gave Antoine several thumbs-up signs as they devoured the dish he'd cooked. Donald stood back and surveyed the scene. His talent laughing, his crew full of joy *and* sardines, and naked revelers partying away in the background. *Maybe this would work out after all*, he thought.

Dressed and back on road, the brothers and the crew drove toward Françoise's farm. In the crew van Phil was at the wheel, while Olly and Stephen caught up on some sleep in the middle seat. In the back seat, Donald was watching the footage from the beach shoot, having just uploaded it to his laptop. As he watched the footage, he couldn't help but be impressed with the brothers.

They had an obvious natural rapport, which shone through the screen, Antoine's culinary skills were plain to see, and a joy to watch, and Michel's knowledge of French food and French history was as educational as it was entertaining. The de la Rue brothers were a great combination, at least they appeared to be to Donald.

Up ahead, in the campervan, Antoine was on driving duty, while Michel sat in the back on the small pull-out sofa, tucking into the remainder of the dish that Antoine had served up for the locals earlier on. Michel savored each bite of the dish.

"You know what, Antoine," he said as he wiped his mouth with a napkin. "You really are an incredible chef."

"Merci," replied Antoine as he looked at his brother in the rearview mirror. "You always did like that dish. Remember the first time I cooked it for you?"

"How could I forget," replied Michel. "The smell of sardines lingered for about a week."

"We almost get booted out of the apartment for that!" Antoine laughed at the recollection.

"Well, that, and the constant late-night parties, and the fact that we didn't make the rent every second month," he added.

"Happier times, brother, happier times," said Michel as he put the empty bowl down on the table. He lay back on the small sofa and closed his eyes. As the campervan trundled along, Michel quickly drifted off to sleep, and began to recall those earlier happier times with a smile on his face.

CHAPTER TWENTY-ONE

London, 1987

After the jolt of Jacques death, life changed very quickly for the de la Rue family. Murielle spent the first few months after his death pining for the man she was devoted to. After some time she decided, not flippantly, but with a great deal of thought, to close up the restaurant. Without Jacques it had lost all meaning to her, this business and home that she had once helped build with her own hands, was now unimportant, and she wanted to wash her hands of it, for now, and start a new journey. The truth was the restaurant was more Jacques's dream than hers. Without him, her connection to the business was gone. She was a shell of the woman she once was. Her strength, her passion for life had waned. She wanted away from this building. She announced her plans for the closure of the business at a staff meeting some months after Jacques had been buried. The anxious staff gathered and sat around the restaurant. Murielle took center stage to deliver the news.

"So, this is what is happening," she started. "For reasons I don't need to explain to you, I'm closing the business, *and* the house, for the foreseeable future at least, and making a fresh start away from here."

Antoine and Michel stood at the back wall of the dining room. Their mother had already informed them of her plans earlier that morning.

"Today will be our last day of trading, until I decide what I'm doing with the place long-term. Tonight, I will lock the door on the restaurant, and in two days I will lock the door on the house." Her voice croaked a little as the severity of her decision seemed all the more real, now she was saying it out loud.

"Where are you going to go?" asked one of the waitresses innocently.

Murielle smiled gently at the girl.

"Scotland," Murielle answered.

"So, what becomes of all of *us*, to *this* place?" Mr. Florien asked. "Just because *you're* throwing your life down the toilet doesn't mean this place, *and us*, should follow you down the plughole." Mutterings of approval and a smattering of applause from the other staff gathered in the room.

"Mr. Florien," said Murielle quietly as she approached him.

The maître d' shifted uncomfortably in his seat. He and Murielle had never been particularly close, he was hired by Jacques, and spent more time making passes at her and the guests then attending to the normal business of the day. She put up with him because Jacques adored him, protected him. But now he didn't have Jacques to fight his corner, and Murielle could let her true feelings for Mr. Florien be known.

"I couldn't care *less* what you think of *me*, or what I'm planning to do, but if you *want* to continue your protest, feel free. But *always* remember, I need to make only *one* phone call to *your* wife, and you'll have to worry about more than just looking for a job, because I'm pretty sure after I tell her what I know, about what, and *who* you did, in this very room, your wife might try her hand at rearranging your testicles." Her voice turned cold. Mr. Florien fell silent, firmly put in his place.

"Jesus," whispered Michel to Antoine. "I'm seeing a side of our mother I didn't know existed."

"Now, if there's no further questions, get yourselves back to work, we've one more service to do." The staff scuttled away to resume their duties. Murielle walked toward her sons and beckoned to them.

"Follow me," she said, heading toward the back office.

"Are you two going to be okay?" she asked. She sat behind the desk and busied herself moving files and papers around, not looking up at her sons. There was an air of determination about her.

"Of course we will, I mean, nothing *we* say is going to change your mind, so we'll just have to get on with it," said Antoine patting his brother on the back. "Anyway, it'll be an adventure if nothing else."

"I wouldn't call catering college an adventure," said Michel. "We're hardly heading off to trek across the Himalayas." Michel wasn't a fan of change, he liked routine, so he was far from enamoured by the idea of leaving the sanctity and security of his home *and* friends.

"One step at a time, brother," said Antoine. "Come on, Paris, you and me, in our own apartment, we'll make new friends, and you never know, you might even find a girl stupid enough to date you over there?"

"Fuck you!" replied Michel as he punched his brother in the arm.

"Boys, please," said Murielle as she stood and took the painting down from in front of the wall safe. "It's all been arranged, you'll be met from the train, brought to your new digs, for which I've paid the rent for the first three months, after that it's up to you, you'll both have plenty to do with college, improving your French, but you'll need to find work, to pay your bills." She took an envelope from the safe. The envelope was marked "RDF."

"RDF?" asked Michel.

"Rainy day fund," replied Murielle. "Your fathers' idea, money to be used only in an emergency, on a rainy day as such, and god knows it's chucking it down out there at the moment." She handed the boys a bundle of cash each.

"This will help you get set up properly," she said. "And look, I'll come over and visit after I get settled, and of course I'll let you know what I plan to do with this place in the long term, when I have time to sit down and figure this all out, but for now it's time for you two to stand on your own two feet." There was a genuine smile in her tone.

She was going to miss her boys, of course she would, but she needed to push them, so that they could learn to be men, and find themselves, now that their hero and role model was gone. The boys got up to leave. Michel stopped at door of the office.

"Mum, do you *hate* this place now?" he asked.

Murielle stopped what she was doing and stared at her two sons. She took a sharp intake of breath as her eyes filled a little. She moved slowly toward Michel and put her hand under his chin.

"No, darling," she replied. "I don't hate this place. I just can't face it without your father, which is why I want you two to get away from here, from all of *this*, and start again, become the men your father was. I'm not ready to run this place, maybe you two will be after your studies, we'll have to wait and see." She kissed Michel lightly on the cheek and moved back to finish clearing the mess on the desk.

Michel stood and looked at his mother. *She* was his real hero, he'd never told her that, but she knew; she could see it in his expression, in his eyes, in the way he looked at her. They smiled at each other as Michel turned and gestured to Antoine that it was time to leave. The boys slowly moved down the corridor, stopping to look back at their mother, as she continued to tidy their father's desk. Little did they know, that would be the last time they would see her.

CHAPTER TWENTY-TWO

Paris, 1987

THE BROTHERS QUICKLY SETTLED into life in Paris, finishing their college courses, perfecting their French, all while taking on part-time work. They did all this, not through a desire to follow their mother's wishes, but to help them forget. They were both deeply affected by their father's passing; they were in their own ways exceptionally close to him. And they were hurting. But they found comfort and solace in each other's company and through the distractions that college and work offered.

They shared a small apartment on Rue de Beauce, from where they buried themselves in their studies, and eventually in their work. Michel, having specialized in front of house during his time at catering college, had now been placed at a nearby hotel, the Hôtel du Vieux, located not far from their apartment, on Rue de Bretagne. He loved his work; he was a people person and thrived when dealing with the general public, which given his allocated position front and center at the concierge desk, gave him ample opportunity to mix with the onslaught of visitors from all corners of the world.

On his days off, Michel would spend time in the Historical Library of the City of Paris, on Rue Pavée, a short ten-minute walk from their apartment. This was where he nurtured his love of reading, in particular first editions. Here he would sit for hours, surrounded by glorious silence, and here he grew his love and appreciation of the great romantic writers, Byron, Margaret Mitchell, and Jude Deveraux. Michel was, at heart, like his mother, a romantic.

Antoine, on the other hand, lived for the hustle and bustle of Paris. He was intoxicated by the energy of the professional kitchen, and he was intoxicated by the fairer sex. He had finished top of his class, head and shoulders above any of the other new chef talent that was emerging from the school. Having cooked alongside his father in London since an early age, he'd had a head start on most of his classmates but didn't take that early learning lightly; he put his head down in college and worked hard. Emerging from college, he became sought after. After bouncing between several restaurants, he chose a job that saw him become part of an energetic brigade of chefs, including his best friend at college, Françoise Roussel, at the popular L'Art Brut Bistrot, located on the busy Rue Rambuteau. Antoine, Françoise, and his fellow chefs would often finish work at 1:00 a.m., and then head to various watering holes around Paris; they had their favorites. They had many in fact, and they had the two main things they needed to enjoy them: money in their pockets and youth.

Having fallen into somewhat of a routine, the brothers' lives in Paris were hectic, but organized. Michel made sure of that. Every second Sunday, as they both enjoyed a rare but regular day off, he made sure they'd spend it together, reading the Sunday papers, taking a stroll through the nearby Jardin Anne Frank, taking the time to talk, to recount the previous few week's events, and occasionally the subject of their parents would come up. They would both share memories of them as a happy couple and take the opportunity to laugh and cry, together.

They also used this time together to keep each other informed on their mother's latest movements. Murielle would call the apartment once a week and update the boys about her new life in Scotland. The brothers would take turns answering the call, but over time, the calls became less frequent.

Michel was at his desk in work one afternoon, dealing with an irate American couple who were complaining about the amount of time they'd had to queue to see the *Mona Lisa* at the Louvre.

"I mean it was ridiculous," said the wife, loudly. "We must have stood there for fifty minutes." Her voice became more irritated with every sentence. "And we hadn't eaten since we'd had breakfast here."

"Which by the way, was miniscule," added her husband from behind her, where he'd spent most of his life.

As Michel was preparing to launch into a well-practiced apologetic verse from his training handbook, which would culminate in the offering of a twenty-five-pound voucher to spend at the nearby shopping arcade, a young woman approached the desk, and was seemingly in a hurry.

"Excuse me," she said, trying to get Michel's attention.

"One moment, Madame," Michel answered without looking up.

"We were here first, lady," said the American tourist, with the amount of care and consideration normally afforded to a child who'd just broken your car window with their football.

"Here you go," said Michel as he handed the voucher to the disgruntled guest. "Enjoy with our compliments and apologies once again," he said as they walked away.

"Wonder if they'll accept this in McDonald's?" the husband said as they waddled across the lobby.

"How can I help you?" Michel said as he looked up at the young lady. He was now seeing her for the first time. He couldn't speak. She was stunningly beautiful and had a smile that could melt a heart at ninety-one meters, a smile she was now unleashing at Michel.

"Well, I'm hoping *I* can help *you*," she said, pointing to a badge on her lapel. Michel looked at the badge, which read "trainee" under her name, "Lucy."

"Ah, wait, you're the new assistant concierge?" he asked, not believing his luck.

"Well done," Lucy replied as she moved in behind the desk, beside Michel. Michel's day, and his life in Paris, was about to get a little more colorful.

Over the next few months, Lucy and Michel's work friendship developed into a romantic relationship, one that would see them spend every waking hour with each other, both at work, and at home, with Lucy eventually moving out of her studio apartment, and into the brothers' altogether larger two-bed apartment. It was palatial compared to her dingy studio abode. Antoine was now rarely at home, spending most nights at Françoise's place or at the apartment of the latest notch on his headboard, so Lucy being in the brothers' apartment wasn't an inconvenience. In fact Antoine loved it.

"See?" he said one night to Michel over dinner. "Didn't I tell you you'd fall in love in Paris?

Michel smiled back at Antoine, "That you did, brother, that you did."

A year had passed in Paris, when one evening in the brother's apartment, the phone rang. It was, Michel presumed, their mother's now bimonthly phone call, not having heard from her in nearly five weeks.

"Hello?" said Lucy into the phone. Michel came from the bedroom having just showered and looked over at Lucy. "He is, who can I say is calling?" she said in her best concierge tone.

Michel smiled as he looked at her. He dried his hair with a towel and sat on the couch beside the phone.

"I'll pass you onto him," Lucy said as she handed him the phone and sat beside him on the sofa.

"Who is it?" he mouthed to Lucy before speaking into the phone.

"A Mr. Lewis Ralph?" she whispered back to him, taking the towel off his head and throwing it onto the floor.

"Who the hell is Mr. Lewis Ralph?" he whispered back as she started to kiss him.

"Ask him yourself," she said, clearly wanting to continue what they'd started in the bedroom. Michel stood up from the couch and took the phone with him.

"Stop!" he said to her in a playful manner as he turned his attention to the phone. "Michel de la Rue, can I help you?" He imitated Lucy's tone attempting to show her who was the best concierge in the apartment.

Lucy didn't take her eyes off Michel, who suddenly seemed to crumple in front of her eyes. In the space of two minutes she watched him morph from playful to pitiful, as he collapsed in a heap onto the floor of the apartment, the phone still in his hand. Mr. Lewis Ralph was calling from the British embassy in Paris. He had received a call two hours earlier from the police in the UK, from Scotland, to be precise. Mr. Ralph was calling to let Michel know that his mother had been among four people killed the previous night in a road traffic accident on the outskirts of Aberdeen.

Among the dead was one Nigel Dinsdale, a man who had befriended Murielle and become her confidante. It was a name the brothers hadn't heard before. According to the police Nigel was at the wheel and was heavily intoxicated at the time. Those next few hours, days, and weeks were an utter blur for the brothers. They hastily returned to the UK, where they visited the crash site in Aberdeen, laying flowers at the exact spot of the fatal accident, and then proceeded to bury their beloved mother in London. They grieved with friends, and eventually visited the now boarded up building that was previously their home. In the space of a year the house had been boarded up by the council in London, as it had run into such disrepair; and squatters had taken occupancy. Murielle simply locked the door and left, leaving the place unoccupied and vulnerable.

Garnering what small details they could from people in Aberdeen who'd known their mother *and* Nigel Dinsdale, the two had spent more and more time together, and that time was by all accounts, spent in a haze of alcohol. Nigel, a failed actor from London, had bumped into Murielle in Scotland, which was now his home. They had first met at an opening night in the West End where he'd be appearing in the ensemble of *Jesus Christ Superstar*. They quickly became friends in Scotland, and proceeded to embark on benders that would make the days of Caligula look like a Noel Coward garden farce. Michel and Antoine blamed Nigel for everything, not only for the car crash, but for turning their mother into something she wasn't, for making her forget about everything she'd once cared for in her life: her business, her home, her husband, and most importantly of all, her boys. Michel and Antoine felt that Nigel's influence had effectively destroyed their mother's life.

The brothers soon discovered that when Jacques died, he had no will in place, and so the business and family home, instead of automatically going to Murielle, had to go into probate, and Murielle had to prove her right to it—not a difficult process being his wife and next of kin, but a lengthy and costly process. So, instead of Murielle inheriting everything immediately, she would have to wait, and she eventually got nothing. She tried to get a resolve on the probate process by engaging a lawyer in London that Nigel had recommended. The large legal fees quickly ate through the little money she had, but incompetence on the lawyer's part meant that the case didn't get resolved in the courts before she died, which meant that the house was still in probate, and *should* now pass down to her sons. The brothers were blissfully unaware of this at the time of their father's death, imagining their mother had received the proceeds from the will, including the house, and was spending her days living off the inheritance, which was mainly made up of their property in Soho, and a small life insurance policy on their father. They presumed she spent her days enjoying her life. They'd heard nothing from their mother to suggest anything different. They simply heard nothing from their mother.

The fact that the brothers' had lost touch with their mother was never discussed between them. Ignorance they thought incorrectly, was bliss, but it turned out to be misery. Now, because Murielle had no will, the probate on the property in Soho continued. Red tape had meant that the house and business, which now should have been passed down to Antoine and Michel immediately, was still lingering in probate purgatory. *Not for much longer*, thought Michel, as he took on the task of getting back what was rightfully his and Antoine's.

Michel retained the services of an inexperienced, cost-effective, but eager and efficient law firm in Paris, having quickly dismissed the one his mother had previously been using in London. Lewis Ralph from the British embassy offered his services to advise Michel on what the brothers next steps were, and Michel and Antoine were grateful for his help and advice. Having secured new lawyers, this meant the probate case moved up a gear, in fact it moved through several gears. The strain that their mother's passing and the continuing legal battle over their rightful inheritance put on Michel's and Antoine's lives almost broke them, but it didn't. It did the opposite. It seemed to galvanize the brothers, made them stronger, closer. One relationship however, was a casualty.

Lucy came from work one evening to the boys' apartment, bristling with excitement. She had news, great news, she thought, news that would potentially put a smile back on Michel's face, a smile that had practically disappeared after that fateful phone call with Mr. Ralph some time ago. Antoine was asleep on the couch. Lucy tiptoed past by him and headed to the kitchen.

"Michel?" she said in a forced whisper as she made her way through the apartment, "You home?"

"He's in his room," said Antoine, with one eye open, and now reminded that he had a hangover.

Lucy entered the bedroom to find Michel sitting on the edge of the bed, with what looked like a letter in his hand.

"You are not going to believe what I've just received," she said excitedly as she started to change out of her uniform. "Do you remember that Saudi entourage that stayed in the hotel for three weeks last month?" Michel didn't answer.

"I mean how could you *not*?" she continued, now sitting on the end of the bed. "They had us running around like headless chickens, fetch this, fetch that, tickets for this, reservations for that, room service, hookers, car service." Still no reply from Michel. The letter in his hand was shaking, as were his hands, his eyes were fixed on the piece of paper.

"Well, it's seems our endeavors on their behalf, have paid off, for once," she said. "Because I've had a call from the head of HR at the Conrad Hotel Group in Dubai!" Michel hadn't budged. "Are you listening to a word I'm saying?" she said raising her voice at Michel.

"What? What are you saying?" he replied. "So, you had a call from a HR department, big deal, it's probably an offer of a cheap holiday."

"For *your* information, they've offered us a job, *both* of us, in their new hotel in Dubai, top package, accommodation included, with bonuses to follow."

"Lucy," said Michel softly as he stood up from the bed and handed her the letter.

"What's this?" She began to read the letter. "It's from your solicitor, what's it about?" She looked up at Michel, her face now racked with confusion and concern.

"It's the probate, it's come through, the house in London is ours, mine and Antoine's," he replied as he sat back down on the bed. "We've finally got back what was rightfully ours. Finally, after years in the courts, it's ours."

"Christ, have you told Antoine?"

"He's asleep, I'll tell him when he wakes up."

"So, what does this mean?" she asked.

"It means we can go home, and I dunno, fix up the house, reopen the business, *our* business, the restaurant, my *father's* restaurant, bring it back to life."

"And when you say *we*, do you mean me and you, or you and Antoine?" she asked with a little edge. Michel looked at her quizzically.

"Well, all three of us," he answered. Lucy smiled and walked toward Michel. She handed him the letter back.

"As usual," she said. "You've made the decision for me. I'm expected to just give everything up here that I've worked so hard for, and in the process turn down the opportunity of a lifetime to work for one of the richest families in Saudi Arabia, and head back to London, which I couldn't wait to get the fuck away from, and start again? Not a fucking hope." Michel stood there stunned as Lucy threw the letter back at Michel and left the bedroom.

Antoine was now sitting up on the couch, with a glass of water in one hand and two headache tablets in the other. Lucy burst past Antoine, grabbed her coat and headed for the front door. Michel came tearing out of the bedroom.

"Lucy, will you wait, please!" he shouted. "Wait a minute!"

Lucy stopped at the door.

"Where are you going?" asked Antoine.

"Dubai," said Lucy as she slammed the apartment door behind her.

Antoine passed the water and the headache tablets to Michel.

"I think you might need these more than me," he said.

CHAPTER TWENTY-THREE

Paris, present day

One week after Fabian had a visit from Lorenzo Pieters, he again found himself at the offices of Deschamps International Holdings. He and Lorenzo sat in an unmarked car outside on the street, ninety-one meters from the front of the offices. Both men sat silently and smoked as they watched people come and go from the building.

"You having second thoughts?" asked Lorenzo.

"Not at all," replied Fabian. "Just going through this whole thing in my head."

"Don't overthink things," said Lorenzo. "You are simply going in for a follow-up meeting, nothing out of the ordinary about that."

"Easy for you to say, you aren't the one going face-to-face with Deschamps under false pretences," Fabian said as he put out his cigarette. Lorenzo laughed quietly.

"All goes well, I'll soon have plenty of face time with Deschamps." said Lorenzo.

Fabian checked his laptop bag, fidgeting around to find some chewing gum.

"When this is all over, think of the story you'll have written," Lorenzo offered as Fabian clipped his bag shut. "Just go and do your job, simple as that, we'll take care of everything else."

Fabian took a deep breath, opened the car door, and stepped out on the street. Lorenzo started the engine and rolled down the passenger window.

"As soon as you have an idea of where this Lucy Carter fits into all of this, the quicker we can move on," he said as he sped away, leaving Fabian standing alone.

He looked up at the impressive office structure and made his way toward the entrance.

Under the instruction and guidance of Lorenzo, Fabian had requested a follow-up to the original interview he'd had with Alain a couple of weeks earlier. His request had been granted, and he was told to report to the office, where he would once again be face-to-face with the reclusive entrepreneur. This time, the meeting was under a wholly different guise, at least from Fabian's point of view. Fabian's editor had been briefed by Interpol about their journalist's new task, and of course he and the paper gave Fabian's new assignment their blessing. Pieters met with Fabian several times over the past week in the Interpol offices, and had brought him up to speed on where he and his team were at in terms of the Deschamps investigation. Pieters explained that Deschamps and his movements had been on Interpol's radar for more than five years.

In 2015, Pieters and his team had been alerted after a painting had surfaced in eastern Europe, a painting that had been on a priority list that sat on Pieters' computer. The list consisted of known Jewish owned pieces of art that had been looted by the Nazis during World War Two. This painting in particular sparked an investigation which turned into a personal quest for Pieters, one that continued to this day. Pieters immediately flew into Budapest and made his way east to Debrecen, Hungary's second largest city, where the painting was waiting for him in the Hajdu-Bihar County Police Headquarters. When he arrived to view it, local officers informed him that it had been discovered hidden amongst a large shipment of drugs that had been intercepted at Hegyeshalom, the old border station between Hungary and Austria. The drugs and the shipment were destined for Paris. Pieters was told that the drugs were seized as part of an investigation into a large drug ring based in Málaga, Spain, that moved narcotics across most of mainland Europe and into the UK. Pieters recognized the small mark on the bottom right-hand corner of the back of the painting. This mark told him *this* was one of a collection of six paintings, known as the *Obscurum Amicis* set, which up until that very moment Pieters had believed to be a myth, an old soldiers' tale from the Second World War, but here was the proof that the myth was in fact a reality.

This painting hadn't been seen in over seventy years. The small mark, made up of two letters, O and A, had been carefully engraved into the right-hand corner on the back of the frame, and that was all that Pieters needed to see. This was huge for him and for his team because he knew that with this painting secured and identified, it confirmed that the list on his computer was genuine, and not a myth, that this collection of paintings *actually* existed, was out there somewhere, and now could be recovered. This painting, however, didn't remain in Pieters' hands for long. A raid on that Hungarian border post three nights later, saw it once again disappear into the night. After they had let the painting slip through their fingers, Pieters instructed his team to focus solely on the recovery of the entire collection. As a result he and his team embarked on a journey that would take them across Europe.

As he sat in his office back in Paris, Pieters pondered the notion that if he managed to recover all *six* paintings, he could potentially be installed as the new head of Interpol. Promotion and *notoriety* beckoned.

CHAPTER TWENTY-FOUR

Paris, present day

FABIAN SAT IN THE lobby of the office building, thumbing through notes given to him by Pieters. Among the notes were photocopies of the two lists that French Resistance squads had taken time and care to write in 1942. These pieces of paper, which had come into Interpol's possession via a veteran of the French Resistance, were the basis of Pieters whole operation over the past five years. Pieters himself had tracked down the surviving members of those Resistance squads to garner information about Nazi looting during World War Two.

These lists, containing the most valuable of information, were given to Pieters by Robert Morel, whom he'd tracked down and visited, spending time with him in a nursing home in Rennes, where Robert was originally from and would later be laid to rest. Robert had kept these lists for years, as a memento, one of his many souvenirs from his time in service for the Resistance during the war. He also hoped that one day the information provided on them could be of help to those Jewish families now looking to be reunited with their forefathers' treasures. For sixty years no-one came looking for the information. But finally, Robert's hopes were realized, the day Lorenzo Pieters came to visit his nursing home.

As well as having to find out more about Lucy, Fabian was also tasked with once again gaining entry to the private collection housed in Alain's office, in an attempt to confirm if the five paintings housed on the wall had any connection to the *Obscurum Amicis* collection. Fabian had familiarized himself sufficiently with the information provided to him by Interpol on the collection; details of the artists and their subject matters. Fabian was confident that a brief visit to the small room where Deschamps's paintings were hanging would be enough for him to confirm Pieter's and Interpol's suspicions. Pieters had his reasons to think that the versions Deschamps had in his private office were fakes, and that the *real* versions were safely stored away in one of Alain's many secure holding areas he had dotted across the European continent. Pieters was also convinced that Deschamps was involved in more than stolen art.

That was part of the third and final strand to Fabian's visit. He was to try and garner more information about Deschamps and his business. "Information is power," Pieters had told him as he left Fabian's apartment a week ago. The lift chimed in the reception area, and Fabian braced himself for another icy greeting from Bruno, Alain's diligent assistant. But instead of the slim sartorially dressed man emerging from the lift, Fabian got quite the shock.

A radiant blonde woman, again, immaculately dressed—it must have been a requisite when you worked for Alain—briskly walked toward him. It took him a moment to recognize her. She was the woman in the photo Pieters had shown him. It was Lucy Carter.

"Lucy Carter, head of Special Projects," she said as she shook Fabian's hand firmly. "Apologies, I'm afraid Alain can't make today's meeting, he was called away to Geneva on urgent business."

Fabian face couldn't mask his disappointment. He thought that he'd lost his chance to get access to Alain's private viewing room. He was also thinking that Alain might be suspicious. Fabian had ignored two phone calls from Alain in that past week, before he'd requested the follow up meeting, and was now regretting not answering.

"I'm afraid you'll have to make do with me," Lucy said as she pointed toward the lifts.

"Oh, right," replied Fabian as he started to follow her.

"I'm sure I can provide whatever information and color you might need to complete your piece for your paper," Lucy said as they stepped into the lift. "Alain filled me in on how far you'd got to in the last meeting."

Fabian had done some other specific research over the past week, which centered around the person he was now standing next to in that lift, Lucy Carter. Pieters had asked him to look into her and her background, beyond what Interpol had already garnered, and find out more about what she did within Deschamps International Holdings. Her title of "head of special projects" was a little vague for Pieter's taste; he wanted details. Fabian started his research how most people do these days, online.

Starting with LinkedIn, he'd found Lucy's profile, and was able to view Lucy's career path, right from when she graduated from university in York, to moving to Paris and starting a career in hospitality, spanning several different hotel groups and ending up in Dubai, where she'd spent the longest period of her career, up to joining Deschamps International Holdings back in 2018. This gave Fabian the professional picture of Lucy, but he needed to see the other side, the private side, because that was where he was more likely to paint a picture of the woman herself. Scouring through the dozens of Lucy Carters on Facebook, he eventually found Lucy's profile, Lucy had used the same LinkedIn profile picture on both social media sites. Fabian was able to read about her music interests, which said a lot about her, Fabian thought, as he read through them: George Michael, Garth Brooks, Elbow, Supertramp, and, most bizarrely of all he thought, Barry Manilow. She had an eclectic taste in music, and, it seemed, in men. She was listed as single on Facebook. How could a woman this successful and beautiful be single, he thought, but it also didn't surprise him, she was after all a corporate machine, dedicating the majority of her time and efforts to her career.

From the public posts on her page, that drive and ambition was evident. A scattering of photos with her parents and siblings, a couple of skiing holidays in St. Moritz, and a handful of photos of her socialising with various friends. One photo in particular caught Fabian's eye.

It was a picture of her with two men, sitting on a sofa in what looked like a standard Parisian apartment, the trio all smiles, huddled together. The two men in the photo didn't interest him, but what was on wall behind the trio in the photo did. As Fabian pushed in on the photograph on his screen, he could now make out a large, framed photograph on the wall of the apartment behind them. *That* photograph was in black and white, and featured another grouping of what looked like three friends, sitting around a table in a restaurant. It looked like it had been taken in the sixties given the way the people in the photograph were dressed. What had caught Fabian's eye, though, was the painting that hung on the wall behind the people in the photo, and as he pushed farther in, the painting revealed itself. It looked very much like the Bontemps painting *Veillier Sur Toi* from the Obscure Friends list. The more Fabian looked at it, the more he was convinced it was.

The people in the black and white photo were Murielle and Jacques de la Rue and Mr. Florien, and it was taken on the opening night of Rien Mais le Meilleur, in London, in 1968. The people on the sofa in front of this photo were Antoine and Michel de la Rue and Lucy, and this photo was taken back in the day in Paris, in the brother's apartment.

Lucy was now firmly in Fabian's sights, and with her boss not on-site, he had the chance to dig deeper into Ms. Carter, and potentially get closer to a piece of the *Obscurum Amicis*. This was exactly what Lorenzo Pieters had instructed him to do.

CHAPTER TWENTY-FIVE

MICHEL WOKE IN A warm comfortable bed. He hadn't had such a good night's sleep since he and Antoine crammed themselves into the dingy campervan back in Dover. Their old friend Françoise Roussel's centuries old farmhouse provided the perfect place for slumber. It was located in the middle of the countryside, surrounded by nothing but silence.

Michel left the small bedroom and made his way down to the large communal farmhouse kitchen, where he was due to meet the crew and his brother, to prep and talk through the day's filming schedule that lay ahead of them. When he got to the kitchen there was no one there. He did, however, hear voices out in the yard. Michel poured himself a coffee and, still in his pyjamas, headed toward the door leading out into the yard. When he cracked open the door and entered the large farmyard area, he was greeted by a scene reminiscent of a daytime parochial television crime drama.

There were two police cars, an animal wrangler, a group of young men, all screams and hand gestures, an old man laughing and frantically waving a walking stick, and two pigs trying as best as they could to breed, amid all the commotion. Donald sat quietly on an upturned wheelbarrow amidst the chaos, with his heads in his hands. Michel spotted the rest of the film crew all lined up along with Antoine, handcuffed, and being giving a dressing down by a member of the local French police. Françoise appeared to have passed out and was tied to the roof of his Citroën C4.

"What the fuck is going on here?" asked Michel as he walked over to Donald.

"Your brother." he replied. "*That's* what's going on!"

Michel threw a look over at Antoine, who caught his brother's eye. "Sorry," mouthed Antoine at Michel.

"Have you *any* idea of the amount of shit that he's landed me in?" asked Donald as he stood up and moved toward Michel. "I've got to sort this mess out, as well as try to keep the film crew and you two on the road!"

"Hang on a second, why are shouting at me? I've been asleep in my room!" Michel roared.

"Sorry, Michel," replied Donald. "It's been a bloody nightmare these last few hours. I was asleep too, until I got a call from the police at three a.m."

"What happened?"

"Ask him."

Antoine walked slowly toward Donald and Michel.

"Let me explain," he said as he reached the now fuming pair. "But first, coffee." He pointed toward the farmhouse.

Antoine dawdled toward the kitchen, followed by Stephen, while Olly and Phil untied Françoise from the roof of his car, and having taken him down off the roof, they then followed the rest of the group back into the farmhouse. Françoise's feet dragged along the ground like he'd just been tranquillised by a hunter.

"This should be good," said Donald as he and Michel wandered inside.

Antoine poured coffee for the gathered ensemble and moved around the table dispensing French toast and paracetamol to each of the suffering men. There were various moans and groans emanating from Françoise, who was slowly starting to come to, as he lay on a pull-out bed in the corner of the kitchen.

"So," said Antoine. He sat himself down in a large armchair in the corner of the kitchen. "You know last night when we all came back from the pub, and I asked Françoise if he fancied a nightcap?"

"Yes," replied Michel. "At which point Françoise said there was nothing to drink in the house, and so we all went to bed?"

"Well," said Antoine. "*You* two went to bed, but the rest of us were convinced that there must be something else to drink in here; I mean what self-respecting French farmer doesn't have his own version of home brew, huh?"

"Christ," replied Michel.

"Indeed. So, we went looking out into the barns, I mean he *had* to have a still somewhere, right lads?"

"I said I didn't want anything else to drink," offered Phil as he swallowed the tablets laid out on the kitchen table. "But willpower isn't my strong point."

"Neither is observation clearly," said Olly, pointing to the fact that Phil had just swallowed two of Françoise's vitamin tablets. Phil immediately spat them across the room like they were cyanide.

"So, what happened?" yelled Michel as he handed Phil two headache tablets.

Antoine settled at the table and began to explain.

Over the next thirty minutes Antoine laid out in detail the events of the previous night. Earlier on in the pub, Françoise had told the group about a recent set-to he'd had with a neighbor, a *rival* so to speak. Every spring, in the picture-perfect town of Sarlat in the southwest of France, there was a festival held, La Fête de la Truffe, or "the festival of the truffle." The main focus of the festival was the crowning of *le roi des chasseurs de truffes*, or "The king of the truffle hunters," a title that Françoise and his nemesis neighbor Emile yearned for. Antoine, egged on by the film crew, came up with a plan to make sure Françoise, and his swine, would take home the crown. Françoise also said that his neighbor had a stash of an illicit home brew that they could lay their hands on after they'd taken care of his neighbor's prize-winning pig. Antoine devised a plan, but of course that plan, like most plans Antoine had, went south. Ineptitude, coupled with devouring the neighbor's home brew stash, several falls through barn doors, all alerted the neighbor Emile and his five hulk-like sons. Soon the merry band of makeshift plotters were caught, and dragged back to Françoise's farm.

When the police arrived at the farm, they surveyed the scene, and handed out a ticket to Françoise for breaking the peace, but worse for Françoise, they banned him and Aggie for life from entering the upcoming competition.

"Just another average Friday night then?" said Michel as Antoine finished his retelling of the previous night's events. Françoise stirred from his slumber.

"When are you guys leaving?" he asked.

"As soon as fucking possible," replied Donald as he rounded up the crew and got them to clear up and start moving out of the farmhouse. "I didn't think babysitting was going to be part of my brief."

"Welcome to my world," Michel answered as he watched Antoine throw up into a nearby hedge. Antoine looked up at Michel and gave him a thumbs-up sign, and then vomited again. *Same old story*, thought Michel.

CHAPTER TWENTY-SIX

Lucy escorted Fabian to her office on the second floor of the complex that housed Deschamps International Holdings' head office. The floor housed Deschamps's most prized employees, and the trappings of holding such a position in his organization were clear—an open plan area filled with the latest in barista style coffee machines, bean bags, and huddle areas that wouldn't look out of place in Google HQ. Fabian was hoping this time with Lucy would give him a chance to determine two things, just how much was Lucy aware of Alain's business dealings with some of Europe's most notorious crime families, and, was *she* involved at any level. Lucy offered Fabian a seat on one of the sofas in her spacious corner office. Fabian sat and again got out his journalistic paraphernalia in order to document the meeting.

"Alain brought me up to speed with what you two had covered in the last meeting," Lucy said as she sat behind her desk. "I can't imagine you need much more detail, but I'm happy to help."

"I just need to fill in a few blanks, and I'll have everything I need to finish the article," replied Fabian.

"Can I get you a coffee?" Lucy asked as she pressed a button on the phone on her desk. Fabian wasn't thirsty *but* to get the chance to see Bruno get the hump as he was asked to fetch coffee for him again, was too good an opportunity to turn down.

"That would be lovely, thanks."

She picked up the phone and addressed Bruno on the other end.

"Two coffees, please, as quick as you can."

Fabian could almost hear Bruno huff and puff from down the corridor.

"How long have you been working here?" he asked. Lucy looked at him with a confused frown on her face.

He already knew the answer from his research, but he wanted to test the water and see how talkative Lucy would be. She took a moment and gave Fabian an unyielding look.

"We're not here to talk about me, are we?" she said. Her answer, and the tone that it was delivered in, gave Fabian an indication that this wasn't going to be a walk in the park.

"Not at all, just making conversation," replied Fabian, in a genial manner. The awkward moment was thankfully broken by a knock on the door of the office, and Bruno entered, carrying a tray with two coffees on it.

"No Henri's pastries today?" asked Fabian.

"Not today, no," answered Bruno. "They are just for special occasions." He left the office, slamming the door on his way out.

"Charming," Lucy said. "He doesn't like me."

"I don't think he likes anybody, except maybe his mother, and possibly Lady Gaga," Fabian said, raising a laugh from Lucy.

"I've been here for nearly two years," Lucy said, she now seemed comfortable enough to answer a general conversation opener like the one Fabian asked her.

"You like it here?" he asked.

"Sure," she replied. "Staff are friendly, with the exception of Bruno, facilities are top class, so I suppose there are worse places than Paris to be working in, it's an incredible city."

"Isn't it just? It's been my home for a long time." Fabian kept it light and conversational. Lucy got up from her desk and took her coffee to the nearby window, where she peered down to the bustling leafy streets below her.

"I can see why so many people want to make this place their home, I don't think I'd want to leave if I'd ever put down roots here," she said. Fabian stood and joined her at the window, looking out across at the Paris skyline.

"Then why did you up sticks and move to Dubai three years ago?" he asked.

Lucy put her coffee cup down on the windowsill, turned and shot a look at Fabian.

"I'm sorry?" she said, confused by the reason for his question. Fabian returned to the sofa and took out his laptop. He started tapping on the keyboard, and as he did, he beckoned to Lucy to come and join him. She didn't move.

"Can you tell me what the hell is going on here? How do you know I've lived in Paris before, and how do you know that I went to Dubai?" The tone in her voice had risen.

"Well, anybody can find out that information," replied Fabian. "They just need a bit of common sense, an inquisitive nature, and decent Wi-Fi." He again gestured to come and sit on the sofa beside him. "Let me show you."

Lucy reluctantly sat beside him. Fabian opened the Facebook app on his laptop.

"Watch," he said as he typed. He entered Lucy's name in the search bar. Within seconds her profile popped up and Fabian quickly took her on a virtual tour of her life, stopping first on a photo of her and her family back in England, just after they'd arrived from the US where Lucy was born. Photos of her and her father, who was in the military, then some of her backpacking around Asia, then more images of her enjoying university life in York, and then photos of her in Paris. He then moved onto a photo of her at work in the hotel in Paris, which had been taken by a colleague, then onto some photos she'd taken of the departure gates at Charles de Gaulle Airport en route to Dubai. In less than two minutes, he'd given her an edited version of the past fifteen years of her life.

"Do I need to call security?" She reached for the phone on her desk. Fabian quickly jumped up and stood opposite her.

"No," he said. "Nothing like that. I'm not here for *you,* this is about *Alain.*"

"You're here for Alain, what does that even mean?"

Fabian took a look back through the glass doors that led into Lucy's office; he wanted to make sure his favorite coffee server wasn't lingering around, taking everything in.

"Look," said Fabian. "There's more to your boss, and his business activities than meets the eye." Lucy took a moment and then laughed gently.

"Mr. Ritzier, I'm not sure who you think you're dealing with here, but I didn't come down with the last shower. Do you not think I did *my* research into Alain and this company before I took the position? I know he's had run-ins with revenue, and customs, but all of that is being dealt with in the courts, by people who are far more qualified than you and I."

She left her desk and headed to the door of her office. She stood holding it open for Fabian; she now wanted him to leave. He didn't move.

"Look, Mr. Ritzier," she said. "I'm not sure what your motives are here, I know you're a respected journalist, but this kind of ambulance chasing is laughable, just leave, finish your profile piece with the information you've already been given, and if any of it is libellous, we'll see you in court."

Fabian stood and looked at her. His next move, his next sentence, had to land with Lucy, had to grab her attention, because if he left on this note, he might not get back in here, into the belly of the beast.

"You're clearly an intelligent woman," he said. "And not easily taken for a fool."

Lucy raised her eyes, far from enamoured by the attempt at flattery. But her heart was pounding in her chest. She collected herself, clenching the fingers on her right hand, a technique she'd used on many occasions working in hospitality dealing with irate guests. This was different though; this was a different level of stress.

"As you said, you did your research into Alain, into this corporation, and yet you didn't see any red flags? Nothing that might have made you stop and think about leaving a perfectly good job and career in Dubai, to jump ship and join this company?" he said.

Lucy's demeanour started to change slightly. She didn't like her career choices being questioned.

"His connections with crime families around Europe, his connections with dirty oil money in the Middle East, his connection with the Nazis through his late father, none of that made you think, no, I won't take the huge salary increase, I'll stay where I am?" Fabian continued.

Lucy closed the door slowly and started to walk toward Fabian. As she stood in front of him, she folded her arms, and fixed him with a determined glare. She cleared her throat. Just before she was about to speak Fabian cut her off.

"Did you ever ask yourself, why did he headhunt *me* for this position?" he said. "He could have picked any number of PR gurus for this job, but he picked you, a former concierge, *why*? Did you honestly think a man *that* busy would take the time to nurture a practical PR virgin into someone who could head up a new division for him?"

Lucy took a step back and sat on the edge of her desk. He was landing punches, he was making her think. She now looked like she had more questions than answers. Fabian moved back to the table, picked up his laptop, and put it in on Lucy's desk. He reopened her Facebook profile.

"*This* is why he wanted you here, *this*, and no other reason," he said, pulling up the photo of her Michel and Antoine on the sofa in the brother's apartment in Paris. "He wanted you here, so he could get to *this*." He zoomed in on the photo, to reveal the photo behind them, the photo of the brother's parents sitting with Mr. Florien. Lucy stared into the screen, her eyes widening as she became more and more baffled by what she was seeing and hearing.

"What the hell would Alain want with Michel's parents?" she asked.

"It's not *them* that he's interested in, it's *this*." He zoomed in closer on the photo to reveal the painting displayed behind Jacques and Murielle.

"A painting?"

"Yes, a painting, and he hired you to help him get access to it."

Lucy looked at Fabian. He nodded his head and raised his eyebrows. Lucy was frozen.

He closed the laptop sharply, grabbed her coat from the back of her chair and handed it to her.

"Let's go somewhere a little more private," he said as he opened the office door. "These walls have ears, and eyes." He pointed to the security camera above her. Fabian quickly gathered his things as Lucy moved slowly toward the door. As they walked down the corridor toward the lift, he took his phone from his pocket, and typed a text message: "We're on the move. Meet you at Boulevard de la Bastille in thirty mins."

Over in his office, Lorenzo Pieters phone beeped. He read the text, clicked his fingers at the three colleagues who were sitting near him and said, "Let's go, he's bringing her in." Minutes later Pieter's and his Interpol colleagues were in their car speeding across Paris.

CHAPTER TWENTY-SEVEN

London, 1942

EDSEL ROTHSTEIN WAS SIXTEEN years old when she was removed from Paris in 1942. Her childhood had been shattered three years earlier with the outbreak of World War Two. Being the only child of Laurence and Rebecca, she'd enjoyed her parents' full attention, and because her parents were people of means, her father was a doctor and her mother a teacher at a private school in Paris, she was treated to regular trips to the opera, museums, art galleries. Her mother rarely left her side, from the moment she was born to the night they were separated in 1942.

When Edsel was born, she was quickly diagnosed with polio, and as a result spent the first eleven months of her life in hospital. After several operations and months of treatments, she came through the illness and was discharged to go home, she had made such an effect on the nurses and staff of the hospital since her birth, that they lined the corridor as her mother proudly carried her in her arms toward the front doors of the hospital, and into the waiting embrace of her father. Edsel was a special little girl, she was fighter, full of determination, a trait she inherited from her parents. But her battle with polio was far from over, and the physical scars of the disease were there for all to see. She had developed acute flaccid paralysis, which meant that she couldn't walk on her own without the aid of a walking frame.

Over the next couple of years, her parents worked hard at helping her improve her physical condition with the help of the best physical therapist's money could secure. By the time she was of the age to attend senior school, she could now move around with just two walking sticks to help her. She was schooled at an exclusive Jewish school not far from her home, her mother and father making sure that she was given every opportunity in life despite her physical difficulties. But the world changed in 1939, and because her parents were educated and wealthy, and lived in an affluent part of the main Jewish quarter in the French capital, it was only a matter of time before the Nazis singled them out for special treatment.

Her parents had been removed from their beds by the Nazis during a nighttime raid on their apartment block on Rue de Rosiers. In the melee of the raid, Edsel was smuggled out by a neighbor, hidden, and eventually smuggled onto a truck, where she and a dozen other Jewish children were driven off into the night away from the Paris theater of war. Her parents were destined for an entirely different fate in Belsen. Edsel would never see them again.

Edsel and other occupants of the truck ended up in a village called Walton-on-the-Naze, near the seaside town of Dovercourt, on the southwest coast of England. Dovercourt had burst into a hive of activity in 1939, as the movement of Jewish refugee children from all over Europe resulted in their port being used as a landing point, where the children arriving from Poland, Czechoslovakia, and Austria were met by would-be foster families, rehoused, and kept safe until the war was over. This mass movement of Jewish refugee children, known as the *Kindertransport,* eventually relocated over ten thousand children over a nine-month period.

Edsel and her group were transported through France and the Netherlands, ending up at the port of Ijmuiden, in the north of Holland. They were then boarded onto a passenger-freighter, and taken over to the UK, to Doverport, to safety. There, they were met by British families, who had first heard of this scheme back in November 1938, when on the BBC Home Service, Viscount Samuel put out a public appeal looking for families to help these dislocated children. Hundreds of families answered the call. Edsel was greeted off the boat by Mrs. Lisa Martin, a mother of six, who had previously taken some of the *Kindertransport* into her home.

Mrs. Martin lived in Walton-on-the-Naze, but Edsel wasn't going to be living there. Edsel was taken by train into Liverpool Street Station in the heart of London, and then on to Mrs. Martins' brother's home, on Shoreditch High Street. Mrs. Martin knew that Edsel would have a better chance of getting work in central London, even with her physical impediment. Having no English, Edsel struggled to settle in, but over the following months she was accepted as one of the Martin family, and with their help and support, she soon became capable of conversing in their native tongue. Because she was sixteen, she was quickly sent to look for work, and being a bright, polite, smart girl, she found a job in no time, a job that she would become eternally grateful for, as it not only provided her with an income over the next few years, but this job was to be the place where she would meet her future husband.

Thomas Brooks and his family had run the Brooks Coffee Importers Company since the turn of the century. Thomas was the youngest of the three Brooks children and the only boy, so he was earmarked as the future head of the company, and at a young age was installed as a clerk, worked his way up, and eventually became manager of the offices and shop on Ramillies Place. Edsel had been recommended to the Brooks business by Mrs. Martins brother Harry, who worked there, and who knew that they were looking for more employees. Edsel was employed upstairs, working in the Brooks' private house, above the business, as a junior chambermaid. This was physically challenging work, particularly for Edsel, but she set about it like everything she faced in life, with determination and grit. These qualities made those around her admire her even more, and she quickly became a favorite of both the staff and the family who employed her, they took her under their wing, and helped her develop her English, and her work ethic. Soon Edsel and Thomas fell in love.

She stayed in service with the Brooks family until 1949, and after a long relationship with Thomas, they married toward the end of that year, and were planning a family and a long and happy life together. These plans turned to ash however, when tragedy struck the Brooks family. While Thomas and Edsel were away enjoying their four-day honeymoon in Jersey, a fire started in the cellar of the warehouse, quickly tearing through the entire building. Two generations of the Brooks family were lost, Thomas' parents, his siblings as well as several warehouse and kitchen staff, including Edsel's adopted Uncle Harry Martin. Nine people lost their lives on that fateful day. Thomas never recovered from the mental scarring brought on by the tragedy, grieved deeply for the loss of his family, and slowly became a shell of the man Edsel had married. He eventually was taken into psychiatric care, where, under little or no supervision, he took his own life, less than two years after marrying his bride Edsel.

At such a young age Edsel was again left with nothing. Her new family, like her family back in Paris, had been taken away from her. She'd lost everything *except* the building in Soho. She was the only surviving member of the Brooks family, so the business and building came directly to her through Mr. Brooks Sr.'s will.

She had little interest in it, however, the building was so damaged in the fire that she moved into a small flat nearby, rarely visiting the building over the subsequent years, as it was too painful for her. She had no idea what to do with the place and turned down many offers for the damaged building, and never sold it. When asked once by an over-eager estate agent what her reluctance to sell was, she mentioned something about finding "the right people," as she put it, to move it on to. She went on to lead a solitary, reclusive life, merely existing in her small flat, where she filled her days tending to her cat, rarely venturing out. It was only when she had a knock on the door from her newest neighbors Murielle and Jacques de la Rue years later, that she began to come out of her shell again, finding friendship and solace in them and their young family.

Thomas Brooks' father had been more than happy to offer Edsel a job in his house when she first arrived in Ramillies Place. Both he and his wife had tried to do their bit for the cause during the First and Second World Wars, contributing money and support to the allied war effort during both campaigns. His help extended beyond that, as he was also a fervent supporter of the French Resistance. His father had served in France during World War One, and so an affinity to the country and the people of France was deep rooted, and when Edsel Rothstein turned up on his doorstep in 1942 seeking work, he felt an instant connection to her, to her homeland. Having a French father himself, he felt by hiring her, and nurturing her, he was giving something back to the country of his father's birth. He and Edsel would often converse in French while she carried out her duties around his house, and when his son professed his love for her some years later, Mr. Brooks Sr. instantly blessed their union, and was overjoyed that his family once again would have French blood in its line.

Mr. Brooks Sr.'s efforts to support the cause extended beyond cash donations, he offered his warehouse and his shipping connections to the Resistance, regularly sending and receiving shipments of arms to and from Paris. He also provided space in his warehouse to hold "goods" that the Resistance would send for safekeeping. On a cold morning in the late spring of 1943, Mr. Brooks warehouse staff received under the cover of night, another shipment from Paris, which they quickly stored away in the cellar of the business in Ramillies Place.

The shipment consisted of two crates made up of various personal belongings from families who had been moved on by the Nazis. These crates were buried, stored deep in the cellar, safe from harm, ready to be moved upon further instruction on a moment's notice. Those two crates were never collected, they sat in the cellar, gathering dust. During the fire that consumed the building some years later, they were far from safe, and only one crate survived the inferno. One crate was discovered after new foundations were being dug during renovations and dragged across the floor of the cellar by Murielle de la Rue, and opened by her husband Jacques, which contained the remnants of one of Edsel Rothstein's parents most prized possessions.

Edsel was blissfully unaware that lying among the pieces in that crate, in the cellar of the very building she'd been sent to in 1942, the building that she'd walked away from in 1949, was one of her father and mother's most cherished items, a painting that hung on the wall of Edsel's childhood home in Paris.

As Murielle pulled that painting from the crate that day, little did *she* know the journey it had taken to get there, and the significance and connection it had to the woman who passed that building down to her family. Murielle instantly fell in love with the picture, the subject matter struck a chord with her. A simple portrait piece, featuring a woman and two small boys, just like her and her two small sons. The way the woman in the painting looked at the boys rang true with Murielle, nurturing, protective, and loving, the very same way she looked at her boys.

Murielle made sure that after she'd restored the piece, it would take pride of place on the wall of her young family's new restaurant, and it did. But Murielle, much like Mrs. Rothstein, also had no idea of *her* own connection to the painting. After all, it had been stolen by Murielle's father, Ronin Kohl and his ERR squad, from Mrs. Rothstein's parent's apartment, some thirty years earlier. It was Ronin Kohl's refusal to grant permission for Murielle and Jacques to marry, that had driven the couple to London, and eventually to this building in Ramillies Place. Once again, a member of the Kohl family had their hands on this painting.

After the fire that swept through the lives of the Brooks family, the building lay dormant for years, until Edsel Brooks, neé Rothstein, passed it on to Jacques and Murielle. They were in her mind, "The right people to take it on and love it," Mrs. Rothstein said in her will, adding, "I only hope they get to enjoy it with their new family for longer than I did with mine." Murielle and Jacques quickly and lovingly brought the building back to life, just as Mrs. Rothstein had hoped, but soon *their* troubles landed upon them.

CHAPTER TWENTY-EIGHT

Dubai

ALAIN DESCHAMPS WAS A regular visitor to the Middle East, making trips to this part of the world since the mid-1990s. He would make at least three trips a year, each for two weeks at a time, to Saudi Arabia's capital city, Riyadh. For a well-heeled international entrepreneur, to arrive at the King Khaled Airport was luxury personified. The first time Alain landed in this desert jewel, he felt at home. Greeted at the Royal Pavilion, the uber-VIP area, Alain was whisked through this beacon to Islamic architectural design and into the central meeting area, where he was met by Ahmed Hassan, his trusted advisor, right-hand man, and problem solver. Alain first noticed the heat. It was a dry heat, not like the skin pinching heat of a Paris summer, this was different, it made him feel like he was in an Indiana Jones movie. His mouth was dry, and his eyes felt dust filled. Temperatures consistently hovered around forty degrees. Alain, coolly dressed in a linen suit, fedora, and Steve McQueen Persol 714 sunglasses, could only imagine how hot the worshippers queuing to attend services at the on-site mosque were. Since that first trip, he routine remained the same; he made sure that he always stayed at the same hotel and the same room, suite 701, at the Ritz-Carlton Hotel. The hotel was a favorite of his for several reasons.

Firstly, it was only a forty-minute drive from the King Khaled Airport, which meant he could be off the plane and in the sauna in his spacious hotel lodgings within the hour. Alain was a germaphobe and cherished the act of cleansing himself completely, particularly after a long flight. He didn't suffer the perils of long-haul flights that any other of the regular travellers. Alain would arrive fresh and well rested, having been wined and dined during the flight in first class, or on a number of occasions, by private jet, arranged for him by his man on the ground in Riyadh, Mr. Hassan. Another reason why he loved the location of the hotel was that it was situated opposite the diplomatic area of the city, which is where, through Hassan, he had an office and was therefore surrounded by the people who held the strings to, and could connect him with, the real powerbrokers in this influential part of the world.

His daily routine on these trips ran like clockwork. Breakfast in his suite, then chauffeur driven to his office where he would spend the bulk of the morning taking meetings, then lunch at the nearby Kingdom Center, before returning to his office until late afternoon and finally back to the hotel for dinner, with whomever had taken his fancy that day, or whomever needed a little five-star persuasion to get a certain deal done. His long patronage at the hotel was rewarded with several perks, his own butler, a personal chef, and twenty-four-hour access to the concierge, who would satisfy his every whim, day or night. Alain knew the general manager and key staff by name, and every member of staff knew who he was.

On a trip to Riyadh a couple of years back, Alain's routine took its normal form. Meetings, followed by dining, followed by more meetings, all the while being catered for and pandered to, by the regular staff of the hotel. On returning to the hotel one evening after a particularly busy day, Alain got to the concierge desk, and expected to see his old friend Mr. Abdullah, the concierge who'd looked after him for years. Alain checked his watch impatiently as he stood at the unattended desk. It was after six and he had dinner booked in the hotel restaurant at seven, but wanted time to get himself ready, which typically involved an in-room massage.

"Can I help you, sir?" said a voice from behind him. Alain turned to see a beautiful young woman, resplendent in the hotel's uniform, beaming at him. She walked behind the concierge desk and smiled at Alain.

"Sorry," Alain replied. "I'm waiting for Mr. Abdullah."

"Ah," replied the lady. "I'm afraid Mr. Abdullah has left the hotel."

"Shit, will he be back later?" Alain asked.

"Sorry, no, he's left the hotel group, he's been transferred to our sister hotel in Doha."

"Right, I didn't know anything about that." said Alain, thrown by the new information. "And you are?"

"Lucy Carter, the new head concierge," she replied with a broad, warm smile. Alain smiled back at her.

"Pleased to meet you Ms. Carter, I'm Alain Deschamps."

"Yes, I'm aware of you, Mr. Deschamps," Lucy replied. "I've been fully briefed on all of our most important clients, and you were one of the first that I was made cognizant of."

Alain was impressed by the way Lucy operated, a friendly face and manner, professional, and easy on the eyes, exactly what he was looking for. For the past few months, he had been struggling to fill a new position at his organization back in Paris, he was diversifying, moving into new strands of business, and was on the lookout for key staff that could help him with this transition, and he always looked for these particular personnel without the aid of a recruitment agency. If someone was going to fill a key position that would involve working closely alongside Alain, he wanted to hand pick the candidates. Having sat in front of and interviewed several candidates, none of which he connected with, he had a thought. Maybe this lady would be open to a new opportunity, even though she had clearly just started one. Regardless, and as always when it came to matters like these, he'd need to do his homework on her first, and that would involve Mr. Hassan.

Alain had dedicated most of his adult life to finishing the work his father had started. He earned his fortune a long time ago, building on what funds his father had left him after he'd passed away. His father, Karl Delitzsch, had played a huge part in his life, not only building a successful business to the point where he could leave his only child a small fortune after he died, but by teaching him the basic lessons in life as a parent, such as how to behave in and around others. He taught him about the values that *he'd* adhered to as a child, mainly to develop an undying respect for his seniors, in life and in business. Unfortunately for Karl, his respect for those seniors he'd served blindly, was misplaced. Like so many others that joined the ranks of the Nazi army, they were ordered to do and say things, to carry out orders, without question or reason. And Karl did.

Karl carried out atrocities against the Jewish people and nation, with regular and unnerving ease. His orders and work during the war became his son Alain's obsession *after* the war. Karl and his ERR comrade Ronin Kohl, set up and successfully ran a criminal organization based in Paris, which specialized in the movement of stolen works of art. Alain Deschamps, or *Delitzsch Jr.* as he was now referred to by Interpol, was carrying on his father's work, and had taken it to the next level, into the twenty-first century. Not that his father ever recognized that fact. He would constantly remind Alain and those around him who would listen that he'd given Alain a sufficient nest egg to build his business, that Alain couldn't have done it on his own, that he always needed his guiding hand. Alain resented this, and it stuck like a thorn in his side to this day.

Alain's company, Deschamps International Holdings, was now a major player across the world of organized crime. If something needed moving, something that would traditionally alert the authorities if sent through the normal logistical routes, then Alain's company could get the job done, for a large commission. With a client list that stretched across the globe, from Japan to India, working on behalf of clients such as the Yamaguchi-Gumi in Japan, the Arellano Felix Organization in Mexico, and in India alongside the notorious D-Company, Deschamps was shipping and smuggling narcotics, people, works of art, and weapons, on a large scale. It was a multibillion-euro business.

Alain's father hadn't seen this growth, this giant of an empire that his son had built, nevertheless Alain swore as he sat at his father's death bed, that he'd make right one of his father's biggest regrets, *Derjenige, der entkommen ist* or "The one that got away." His father was referring to a shipment that he and his crew had let slip in 1942, one of the few that got away from him and his relentlessly proficient unit. A collection of six paintings that Alain later learned was part of a collection known as the *Obscurum Amicis.*

Alain was driven to get these paintings back, whatever it took or cost. His first port of call was Ronin Kohl, but Kohl had suffered in later life, the traumas of war finally catching up with him, tormented with depression and what is now diagnosed as post-traumatic stress disorder. He was little use to Alain in terms of getting information from. Kohl died not long after Alain's father passed, alone, in a small apartment in Berlin, where he'd retired shortly after his and Delitzsch's partnership had been dissolved. Alain didn't let that stop him, there were other contacts he could tap into and other ways of finding out about the legend of these paintings. He'd already located and recovered five, and only had one to go.

Alain wanted to give the impression that he was atoning for the sins of his father, by finding and returning the collection to their rightful owners. In reality he had no such plan. He was going to reunite this collection and sell them to the highest bidder on the black market. As part of this new public perception of his business, and because he was branching out into the legitimate commercial world, Alain needed to refresh his roster of employees. He wanted new faces, ones that wouldn't trigger any alarm bells in *any* jurisdiction, people with clean records, good attitudes, and ones that with the right training, could become huge assets for his business going forward.

Lucy Carter might well fit into that bracket, Alain thought, as he sat at his laptop and began to carry out some preliminary research into her.

Later that year, Alain was back in Saudi Arabia. The doorbell rang in Alain's hotel suite. He left the bathroom where he had been shaving and went to answer. He was in his bath robe, partially covered in shaving cream, hair just washed, but not dried. He looked a state, but headed straight to open the door, without checking his appearance in the nearby full-length mirror. This was because he knew who was at the door, and this person had seen him in far worse states than the one he was currently in. Mr. Hassan stood in the doorway, immaculately dressed as always, ready to serve his lord and master.

"You're late," said Alain as he opened the door to his long-time obedient collaborator. Hassan looked at his watch.

"I'm three minutes late, Alain," replied Mr. Hassan as he entered the bedroom and headed straight for the living quarters. "Hardly a federal crime."

"Three minutes, three hours, it's still late, right?" said Alain, with a little grin brewing on his face.

"Right, I'm late, but I'm here now," answered Mr. Hassan as he opened his briefcase and started pulling out some documents readied for Alain's signature, and a very special bottle of cognac.

"Ah!" replied Alain. "You never fail me, my old friend." He whipped the bottle off Mr. Hassan, fetched two glasses, and proceeded to crack the seal on the bottle. Alain poured, and the two men clinked their glasses.

"Right, to business," Alain says, aware that he had a dinner date in forty minutes, and still hadn't had his manicure.

"Must be serious," said Hassan. "You normally don't crack open a bottle like this unless there is something wrong."

"Nothing is *wrong*," replied Alain. "I'm just going to ask you to do something I've never asked of you before, that's all."

Hassan sat up straight in his chair and put his drink down on the table. Given the array of barbaric contracts that his employer had tasked him with over the years, whatever Alain's latest request was going to be, it required his full attention.

"I have two meetings set for tomorrow," said Alain as he refilled both of their glasses. "Both meetings are crucial to the outcome of the many years of my work, *our* work, and need to be handled correctly, which means I don't want you in the room." Hassan shifted in his seat. That wasn't what he'd expected to hear.

"Have I suddenly become incapable of behaving correctly at these meetings?" replied Hassan, a little put-out. "I've sat in meetings with you and some of the most dangerous people in the world, with heads-of-state, with military generals, what makes you think I'll be any different with whomever it is your meeting tomorrow?"

"Don't take that tone, Ahmed," replied Alain. "You know that you are the only person I genuinely trust, you've proved that to me over the years, but tomorrow is different. I'm keeping you away from these meetings in an attempt to protect you, provide you with some distance."

Hassan didn't react. He sat looking stoically at his boss. Alain drained his glass and stood from the table. He moved to the balcony in his suite and beckoned to Hassan to follow him. The two men stood on the balcony looking out at the Riyadh skyline.

"We aren't far away from completing this," Alain said. "I know you've been beside me all the way, but I need to ask you this one thing, I want space tomorrow, let me conduct these meetings on my own, believe me, it'll be worth it in the end."

Hassan took this in, and straightened himself, like any good soldier.

"Of course," he replied. "Whatever you need." The men shook hands, and Alain showed his consigliere out of the room.

The following morning Alain set off into the heart of Riyadh, accompanied only by his driver, a local chauffeur whom Hassan had vetted. His first meeting took place in a high-rise office, in one of the many sprouting skyscrapers in the shiny new financial district. The meeting lasted less than thirty minutes, and as Alain climbed back into the car, he smiled to himself. If and when he finally secured the collection, he had now completed the sale of the *Obscurum Amicis* to a faceless pension fund run by two of the largest crime syndicates in eastern Europe. Meeting one had been a success. Onto the next, and more important meeting.

As the driver sped away from Riyadh and out into the surrounding desert, Alain's phone beeped. A text message appeared on his screen. He read the text to himself, "Hope the meetings are going to plan, H." He smiled to himself and popped the phone back into his jacket pocket. Ninety minutes later, the car swung into the compound of the impressive King Abdul Aziz Al-Kharj Castle, in the center of Al-Kharj. Alain's door was opened, and he was greeted on the steps to the building by two heavily armed men, who led him down a long corridor, resplendent with the finest marble floors. They stopped outside two large doors. One of the men frisked Alain, and then stood eye to eye with him.

"The ambassador is a busy man, you have fifteen minutes."

"Start the clock," replied Alain as the door opened, and he entered the palatial room.

"Ambassador Kaie," Alain said, offering his hand. "It's been a while."

"Good to see you again, Alain," Kaie replied. "Let's make this quick, shall we? I'm on flight to South America in ninety minutes."

"Absolutely," replied Alain. "I trust you got the details of the property?"

"I did, all is in order, some small details to sort out, but the path is clear."

"Perfect," replied Alain as he opened his briefcase.

Later that night as Alain lay on the sun lounger on his balcony, his phone beeped. It was Hassan, again. "Apologies for questioning you yesterday, won't happen again, hope today went well, H."

Alain typed and sent a reply. "My day went as I'd hoped, and yes you're right; it won't happen again."

CHAPTER TWENTY-NINE

France, present day

After the incident filled night at the truffle farm, Michel could sense that their producer was determined to get this band of merry, yet *hungover* men, back on track as quickly as he could. The next stop on their food tour was the town of Goyencourt, and this would mark the halfway point on the journey to Paris. It would be a two-day jaunt from Françoise's truffle farm to Goyencourt, so the team had plenty of time to recover and prepare for their next big filming sequence, at *La Fête de la Fraise*, "the festival of the strawberry." Donald had earmarked a number of beauty spots along the route, where the crew would stop and film the brothers out and about, taking in the local amenities, mixing with the natives, and sampling the best local produce on offer in this scenic part of France.

The first of these diversions involved one such local food producer, Gerard du Pont, who owned and ran a family farm that produced some of the most sought after goat cheese in the country. The farmhouse was a beautiful, picturesque home where outside Gerard and his family appeared to greet the film crew. The crew were invited to enjoy an incredible breakfast spread, with all of the dishes featuring the famous *Chabichou du Poitu,* the goat cheese that Gerard and his family had been producing for almost forty years. Antoine gorged his way down the table, as the smells of caramelized leeks and melted goat cheese caused various sounds of exaltation to emanate from him. The brothers spent the day helping Gerard feed the goats, and watching the rest of his family work, as they demonstrated the entire process of taking the goats' milk and turning it into their award-winning cheese. As always on these types of food shows, the sequence involving the presenters milking the animal provided much hilarity, and after what had happened back at the truffle farm, the entire crew needed a morale boost, and true to form Olly the fixer ended up with a black eye after he got a kick from a less than impressed goat that he was attempting to coax into position.

The day's filming continued with something none of the crew ever thought they would witness, a session of goat yoga, during which the brothers were positioned on mats, in the middle of the biggest barn on the farm, surrounded by Gerard and his family, meditating and performing yoga, with two goats in the center of a circle. The crew could barely contain their laughter as they watched Michel and Antoine squirm around, decked out in suitably garish workout attire, which had been bought earlier by Donald in a flea market in the village near the farm.

The visit to the farm culminated in Antoine cooking lunch for the family, and, he wowed the hungry crowd with a dish using Gerard's home-produced goat cheese. Michel watched on proudly as Antoine served up another crowd-pleaser from his repertoire, goat cheese pasta salad with toasted almonds. Michel had opted to sit this sequence out and let his brother have the limelight. As the sun began to set, Michel watched his brother, a true artist, as he threw the almonds in the pan, flicking the pan theatrically over the open flames, rolling and cutting fresh pasta, creating clouds of flour dust around him, and delicately handling the prized goat cheese. It was like watching Buddy Rich, the continuous movement, the control, the power, the deftness of touch, culminating in a masterpiece being created. Michel watched Antoine's face as he asked Gerard and his family to taste the dish, and, like watching a father seeing his child score a goal, as Gerard gave Antoine a thumbs-up, Antoine's face was filled with pride and humility. Michel longed for more of these moments with his brother, watching him at his peacock best, like the old days.

As the crew started packing up the vans for the next leg of the journey, Donald sat on the opened tailgate of the crew van, with his laptop in front of him, watching the daily footage, or "rushes." He watched with a huge smile on his face, enjoying the banter between the brothers and Gerard, as well as the stunning French countryside, even the yoga sequence looked great.

One thing that Donald noticed in the footage was a change in Michel's demeanor. He'd seemed a little distracted over the past few days. Maybe he was still cringing from the thoughts of what had happened back on Françoise's farm, but they'd all seemed to shake that off. This was different. He was spending a lot of time in the back of the campervan, alone, taking phone calls, always away from nearby listening ears, not joining the crew for their various lunch and dinner breaks. Donald thought he'd broach the subject on the drive to their next destination.

The Old Mill of Vernon was where they were headed. It was a sixteenth century mill, that had been destroyed and rebuilt no fewer than three times, first during the Franco-Prussian war of 1870, again in 1940 during World War Two, and one final time in 1944. The mill was stunning, perched over the water's edge. It looked like something from a Shakespearean sonnet—chocolate box beautiful—and Donald thought this would make a perfect background as once again Antoine served up another winning dish, this time featuring flour that this mill would have produced back in the day.

The crew drove along the carriageway toward Giverny, where the mill was located. The normal seating arrangements had been changed, with Donald swapping with Antoine, saying that he'd wanted to run through the upcoming schedule with Michel, but really, he just wanted to check in with him. Antoine was riding in the crew van, and less than thirty minutes into the drive, he and the three-man film crew had already re-enacted the infamous van scene from *Dumb & Dumber*, and were now working their way through the equally well-known car scene from *Wayne's World*, complete with Queen soundtrack and requisite head-banging.

Ahead in the campervan Donald was driving, Michel sat in the back, busily tapping away on his laptop. There wasn't much in the way of conversation, none in fact. The radio in the campervan was stuck on a regional French channel, which meant the music on offer wasn't helping much either. Donald turned the radio off.

"Not a Sasha Distel fan?" he asked Michel. Michel stared at his laptop screen, which had his full attention. He didn't hear Donald, or Sasha for that matter.

"Is there something I should be aware of?" Donald tried again, this time a little louder.

"Quite a lot," replied Michel to himself, and then he said to Donald. "Nothing that you can help me with, thanks."

Donald looked in the rearview mirror and saw that Michel now scribbling into a notebook.

"You know," Donald said. "Part of my brief as the show's producer means that I'm obliged to wear several hats during the filming process, babysitter, director, driver, editor, timekeeper, *and* therapist. Michel looked at Donald's face in the mirror, his wide eyes and open expression were the face of a man who loved to help, even if those needing the help didn't want it. Donald continued on.

"If there's something that you *think* I could help with, try me, I'm here to support my cast and crew." Donald's genuine offer of an ear to bend surprised Michel, he'd presumed most people in showbusiness were self-absorbed, but not Donald it seemed.

Michel closed the notebook, put away his laptop, and joined Donald in the front of the campervan.

"Sorry," said Michel. "Just trying to sort out some of the shit we left behind in London." He wearily rubbed his eyes and let out a sigh. He nodded his head and looked out the window for a long moment before he turned back to look at Donald.

"I understand," said Donald, realizing that that was the extent of the information Michel was going to offer, but glad nonetheless that conversation had returned to the van. "We all have stuff we can't shake, no matter where in the world we run to."

"Ain't that the truth," replied Michel. Donald lit a cigarette and offered one to Michel.

"You know, Michel," said Donald. "You and your brother are doing a great job on the show so far, you've a real flair for this presenting thing."

Michel shrugged his shoulders. "Appreciate that," he said. "To be honest I thought we'd both stink the place out."

"Really?" said Donald. "Well, if it makes you feel any better so did me and the crew, but you've produced the goods on camera, and that's all that matters. Seems like the crew have taken to Antoine." He pointed to the crew van behind them. Michel took a peek back at the crew van and saw three bare bums mooning the other poor unsuspecting motorists on the carriageway.

"Indeed," said Michel. "Antoine has had his arse out for most of this trip." Both Donald and Michel laughed, glad that the mood in the van was now filled with levity and not with an awkward silence. Michel's phone rang, he took it from his jacket pocket, and looked at the number on display.

"Sorry," he said as he started to move to the back of the campervan. "I need to take this."

"Fire away." said Donald.

"Well?" said Michel into the phone, trying to keep his voice down. "Did you get any further?" Donald watched the exchange via the rearview mirror.

"Really? That's fantastic," said Michel. "Em, let me find out, hang on a minute. Donald, what's the name of the next town we're stopping in?"

"Nearest town to the mill is Bois-Jérôme-Saint-Ouen."

"Did you hear that? Can you send it to the post office in that town, and I'll pick it up there? Perfect." He hung up from the call and climbed back into the front seat beside Donald.

"Everything okay?" asked Donald, slightly concerned by the conversation he'd just heard.

"Spot on," replied Michel. A slight smile broke on his face, like a weight had just been lifted from his shoulders.

CHAPTER THIRTY

Paris, present day

Fabian and Lucy made their way across the tree-lined street outside her office and jumped into a taxi and headed toward central Paris. The heavy rain lashed against the body of the cab causing the windows to fog up. Lucy used her sleeve to clean the window to give her a better view of which direction the car was heading.

"Where are we going?" asked Lucy, now very aware that she was in a car with a man she'd just met, heading god knows where. Fabian read a text on his phone and leaned forward to give the driver the address.

"Hôtel Marceau Bastille," he said, and sat back in the seat. "We're going to meet a friend of mine. He can bring you up to speed on your boss."

Lucy clenched her cigarette lighter in her hand.

"Is Alain in danger? Has he done something wrong?"

Fabian pulled his laptop from his bag and dropped it on Lucy's lap.

"Here," he said, lifting the screen up. "We've about fifteen minutes before we get to the hotel, have a look through that, it might answer some of your questions."

Fabian clicked on a file on his desktop marked "AD" and Lucy started to read. The first thing Lucy saw was a document from Interpol. Alongside a picture of Alain was a list of what looked like phone numbers. She read down the list and spotted her number, several times, all marked with an asterisk. As she flicked through the documents, she saw photos of Alain, some on his own, others with various colleagues, some of whom she recognized, all company people from within his organization. Her eyes stopped when she got to a photo of her and Alain, the one that Lorenzo had shown Fabian back in his apartment weeks ago.

"What the fuck?" she said under her breath, closing the laptop. "Have you been following me?"

"Not me," Fabian answered. "Interpol."

Lucy could feel her blood run cold, what the hell was she in the middle of?

"You seen enough?" asked Fabian. He took the laptop back from her and put it back in his bag.

"I'm not sure *what* I've seen," she replied.

"Relax, you're not the focus of attention here," Fabian said.

Lucy took a pack of cigarettes from her bag and went to light one.

"Sorry, Madam," said the driver. "Not in here."

Lucy put the cigarettes back in her bag and took out a vape. She held it up to the driver as if to ask, is this one okay? The driver nodded, and she took a large drag of the electronic cigarette, blowing a plume of mango flavoured smoke out of the open window.

"Who is this friend of yours were heading to meet?" she said to Fabian.

"Someone who can answer all of your questions. And no doubt they'll have a few questions for you." That didn't help Lucy's anxieties.

The taxi headed down the Boulevard de la Bastille, swung right into Rue Jules César and came to a stop outside the hotel. Fabian paid the driver, and as he and Lucy headed up the steps to the hotel entrance, Lucy stopped.

As he moved back down the steps to her, she took out her phone and quickly snapped a photo of the departing taxi, then swung the phone around to capture a shot of Fabian, and finally she took one of the large hotel signs above the entrance door.

"What are you doing?" asked Fabian.

"Just making it easier for the police, you know, when they try to piece together my final movements," Lucy answered, popping the phone back in her bag.

"We are *meeting* the police," said Fabian as he held the door to the lobby open for her. His answer didn't make her feel any better. He led Lucy through the lobby and into the lifts. They got out on the third floor and headed for suite 306 on the top floor. Fabian knocked on the door, and when it opened, Lucy's anxiety levels peaked.

They were led into the living area of the suite by a heavily suited and booted Interpol operative. The suite was bustling with people sitting at desks, feverishly tapping away on laptops. At the heart of the room was a wall of screens, all showing various angles on buildings. All very high-tech and eerily quiet as the Interpol operatives went about their business. The screens also displayed what looked like flight tracking, lines and dots beeped as they moved across the monitors.

The suite had been sequestered by Interpol as Pieters' investigation into Deschamps stepped up a gear. Having presented enough evidence to his seniors, Pieters had been given the go-ahead to move to the next step of his investigation, ST3, or surveillance Tier 3, which as a result meant that Pieters had been given more money, equipment, and manpower, some of whom were now stationed in this discreet hotel suite, away from the Interpol offices, and were now focused on Deschamps. Pieters stood with his back to Lucy and Fabian, surveying the information on the screens.

"Agent Pieters?" said the couple's burly escort. Pieters turned to the couple and offered his hand to Lucy.

"Ms. Carter, pleasure to meet you, Lorenzo Pieters, head of Interpol's Stolen Works of Art Unit," he said. Lucy shook his hand and looked around the room again.

"Nice to meet you, why am I here, am I under arrest for something?" she asked, cutting straight to the point.

"Please, have a seat," replied Pieters. The three sat around a large table in the center of the room, facing the wall of screens. "No, you're not under arrest," said Lorenzo. "How much has Mr. Ritzier filled you in?"

"I've shown her one of the files you'd sent me," replied Fabian.

"Let me walk you through this, Ms. Carter," Lorenzo said as he clicked his fingers at a nearby operative sat in front of the bank of screens. The operative tapped quickly on his keyboard, and the screens in front of Lucy changed. They all now showed Alain at different times in different locations.

"As I'm sure you've now worked out, we've had your boss, Mr. Deschamps, and several of his key employees under surveillance for some time," he began as Lucy and Fabian watched the screens closely. Lucy again pulled the cigarette lighter from her pocket and began to fidget with it. She looked around the room at the many operatives, screens, badges, and guns. She could feel her temples throb, she wanted to be anywhere but here. Lorenzo tapped loudly on the desk.

"Ms. Carter," he said like a schoolteacher. "What you may not be aware of is exactly what *kind* of work your employer is actually involved in. And more to the point, some of the people that he's involved with." Lucy sat up straight as she saw an image of herself on the screen alongside Alain and another employee. She took a sharp intake of breath. Lorenzo stood and circled the table.

"Lots of interesting characters on show here, Ms. Carter. I'm sure you'll agree," Pieters said. "Although I'm beginning to doubt you even know who some of these people are?" He wrapped his knuckles on the desk again and pointed to the screen. Lucy looked up to see a photo of Alain and a heavyset unshaven man, sitting outside a restaurant opposite another man, who looked like he was taking notes. "I presume you know who the man on the right is?" asked Lorenzo.

"I do, that's Ahmed Hassan, Mr. Deschamps's global head of security."

"Head of security," he said with a smile on his face. "Not the job title I would give him, but you're *technically* correct. And the man to the left of Alain?"

"No idea," she replied.

"That is Kabir Batra, one of the most senior men from an organization based in India, called D-Company. This man and his organization are believed to have been behind the terrorist attacks in Mumbai in 1993, as well as other atrocities. All of their endeavors are funded through their opium syndicates in Asia. This photograph was taken some years ago in Kolkata, not long before a certain piece of art was stolen as part of a hate campaign Mr. Batra had launched against another dealer, all under the instruction and supervision of Mr. Deschamps. And in return Deschamps would guarantee secure shipping routes for D-Company and their opium throughout Europe."

Lucy shook her head in disbelief.

"So, what you're telling me is that Alain is an opium dealer?" she asked Lorenzo.

"No, he's much more than *just* an opium dealer." He clicked his fingers and drew her attention to the screen.

The image on the screen changed, and Lucy and Fabian were now looking at another photo, in which Alain was standing in a train compartment, again accompanied by Mr. Hassan, but this time he and his head of security were pictured with two women.

"These two well-dressed ladies," said Lorenzo. "Are Himara Sato and Yui Tanaka, senior officials at the admissions office at the Sendai University in Japan."

Lucy watched as the photographs changed, and she saw the women being handed a briefcase in exchange for an envelope.

"Let me guess, more opium?" she asked.

"No, a key," replied Lorenzo. "To a dormitory at the university's student accommodations, where two days later, on New Year's Eve, *another* painting was stolen." Lucy turned to Fabian.

"So, your adding art thief to opium dealer?" she said. Fabian looked back at Lucy and nodded. "But he's an art *dealer*. And a very successful one at that. Why would he need to *steal* paintings, when he runs one the most successful galleries in Europe, a business he's run for years, *legitimately*, I might add."

Lorenzo got up from the table and went to the coffee machine that sat on a counter near the window in the room.

"Coffee?" he asked Fabian and Lucy. They both nodded yes. Lorenzo took three cups and started pouring the drinks.

"Ms. Carter," he said as he finished pouring the coffee. "I'm surprised at your line of questioning." He spoke with a serious tone. "This man is a committed career criminal, second generation in fact. He runs one of the biggest and most connected criminal organizations in Europe. And *you're* the head of his "Special Projects team," and yet you can't understand why you're here?"

"If you think I've done something wrong, then why am I not in a police station, surrounded by our company's lawyers?" She stood her ground and maintained her innocence.

"Because we *know* you haven't done anything wrong, save for a few parking tickets, but nothing that would warrant you being taken to a police station. As far as I can make out, your only serious crime was your choice of employer, and I can't charge you with that, can I?" Pieters replied.

He handed out the coffees, and then dropped a large file on the table in front of Lucy, marked "L Carter." She opened it to reveal several long lens shots of her coming in and out of her apartment, in and out of Deschamps's office block, socialising with friends, along with transcripts of phone calls she'd made to friends, colleagues, and family members. A lot of detail.

"Look," he said, sitting down at the table. "We know you're clean; we know that you have no connection to the underside of what your company is involved in, which is the reason you're sitting here with me and not in a holding cell. You could be of great *help* to us, to our investigation."

Lucy allowed herself to relax slightly, safe in the knowledge that she *hadn't* done anything wrong. She took a sip of coffee, her mouth was bone dry. Pieters watched Lucy closely, trying to gauge if she was taking this in or not.

"Deschamps," he said, "has been systematically stealing certain works of art over the past fifteen years." He flipped his way through the rest of his presentation on the screen. "From the UK, to Greece, to Luxembourg, he's orchestrated one the longest and biggest art heists in recent years, which he now hopes to complete with the theft of one more painting, this one." He nodded to the nearby operative, who punched up the photo of Lucy, Michel, and Antoine, sitting on the sofa in the brother's apartment. The operative zoomed in on the photo, where they could now see a framed photo on the wall behind Lucy and the brothers. The image came to rest and she could now see the Pierre Bontemps painting *Veiller Sur Toi.*

Lucy stared at the screen, her mouth slightly open. She was immediately transported back to that apartment. She could remember the day that photograph was taken. It was just after she'd moved in with the brothers, and they'd celebrated with an amazing dinner that Antoine had prepared in the apartment, followed by a couple of bottles of wine. Michel had wanted to show off his latest toy, a camera which you could set a timer on and take a shot of yourself, an early *selfie*, so to speak. The resulting photograph was now displayed in front of her, on the one-and-a-half-meter square screen in this temporary Interpol office. She couldn't speak. So Pieters did.

"First question," Lorenzo asked. "The two people on the sofa with you, their names?"

Lucy thought for a moment before answering. She still wasn't sure what she'd gotten herself into here and was concerned she might be getting her once boyfriend and his brother in trouble. But as far as she was aware, *they* hadn't done anything wrong either, at least not wrong enough to have Interpol chasing them. She looked at Fabian.

"The best option is always the truth," Fabian said. "It's the easiest thing to remember."

Lucy took another mouthful of her coffee before settling herself.

"Michel and Antoine de la Rue."

Lorenzo nodded to another operative, who typed the names into his laptop.

"How do you know them?"

"Michel and I worked together for a while, in a hotel, here in Paris."

"You *worked* together?" Lorenzo watched Lucy as she nodded back to him. "And where was the photo taken, your apartment?"

She looked at Fabian again.

"No," answered Lucy. "Their apartment, on Rue de Beauce, but they haven't lived there for years, they moved back to London, as far as I know."

Pieters nodded again to the operative, who took note of this new information.

"And the people in the framed photo, sitting in front of the painting?" asked Lorenzo.

"Murielle and Jacques, their parents."

Fabian reached over to refill Lucy's cup.

"They both passed away, years ago," Lucy added.

"Do you know anything about that painting in the photo?" Fabian asked.

"Not much, I think it hung on the wall of their restaurant in London, the one the boys have been running since their parents both passed away."

"Have you been to the restaurant?" Lorenzo asked.

"Sorry," Lucy said as she stood from the table. "Is there a bathroom I could use?"

"Of course, second door on the left," replied Lorenzo, pointing down the corridor.

"Excuse me," Lucy said as she headed out of the room.

Lucy entered the bathroom, locked the door behind her, and sat on the edge of the bath. She took her phone out of her purse and typed a text. "Need to talk, ASAP." She sat and waited for a reply.

CHAPTER THIRTY-ONE

As the film crew finished their lunch, Donald's phone beeped.

"Right, chaps," he said. "Just got a text from the owner of the mill; he'll meet us down there in thirty minutes."

"Ah come on, Donnie," said Stephen. "This is the first nice place we've eaten lunch in on the whole trip."

"I've just ordered a crème brulé," added Phil.

"Alright, keep what's left of your hair on, you can have another five minutes," said Donald, happy enough himself to sit for another short while. The crew were sitting in the grounds of the Fondation Monet, Giverny, the home and gardens of Claude Monet. It was a blissful location, and Donald was happy to sit for another few minutes and take it in, while Phil wolfed down his dessert.

"Can we make a quick pit stop on the way over there?" Michel asked Donald as they started to head for the vans.

"Sure," replied Donald as he stood to pay the bill. "But make sure it's quick, we've only got three hours access to the mill."

A short ten-minute drive from Monet's house was the village of Bois-Jérôme-Saint-Ouen, a quiet, ornate village, which sported a small grocery shop, a post office, and a bakery. The two vans pulled up outside the post office. Michel started to get out of the campervan.

"Make it quick," said Donald as he watched Michel jump out of the campervan.

Inside the post office, Michel found himself standing alone in the small shop, he knocked gently on the counter which ran the width of the room.

"Salut?" he said hopefully. No answer. "Anyone home?" This time a little louder.

An elderly gentleman appeared through a door behind the counter, looking a little worse for wear, having just woken up from his daily afternoon nap.

"Can I help you?" said the man as he rubbed his eyes and crumbs from his beard. "If you're looking for directions to Monet's house, you've passed it on the road in, about six kilometers back that way." He seemed fed up with giving those directions.

"No, no thanks," answered Michel. "We've just been there; no, I'm picking up a letter that was sent here for me, registered post, from Paris?"

The man scratched his head and looked at Michel like he'd just asked him to explain the three secrets of Fátima. He didn't move.

"A letter, sent by registered post?" Michel said. "From the British embassy?"

"Ah, the letter!" the man replied as the sound of the penny dropping could be heard as far away as Monet's house. "Of course, monsieur, one moment please, your name?"

"De la Rue," replied Michel. The shopkeeper produced a letter from under the counter.

"Can I see some identification please?"

Michel took his driving license out and slid it onto the counter.

"Bien sur," he replied, and handed the letter over to Michel. "Must be very important, delivered here by motorcycle, arrived early this morning." Michel shifted from foot to foot, peppering to get his hands on the envelope. "Do you work for the embassy?"

"Something like that," replied Michel as he popped the letter in his pocket and bade farewell to the dozy attendant, who was already halfway back to his makeshift cot at the back of the post office.

"All sorted?" asked Donald as Michel jumped back into the campervan.

"I think so," replied Michel as the vans pulled out.

As the convoy trundled their way through the village, Michel looked back at the van that Antoine was traveling in and gave him a thumbs up. Antoine reciprocated.

The crew were spellbound as they drove through the narrow streets of the medieval village, which was decked out in all its festival splendor. Each house along the route was framed with colorful flower displays and bunting, this was their chance to bang the drum for the strawberry, the celebrated fruit that brought thousands of people into the village and surrounding areas on the same weekend for the past thirty tears. Noise from the hungry crowd was matched by that of the local jazz ensemble, who blasted out the joyous "When the Saints Go Marching In" from the nearby stage. As the crew passed the town square close to road that led to the mill, their vans stopped in traffic as the crowds thronged around them, all heading to see the star attraction, the one hundred and twenty-eight stone strawberry tart, that was being assembled by a feverish troupe of pâtissiers.

The crew set up the camera and sound equipment for filming on the banks of the lake surrounding the mill, while Antoine and Donald were busy setting up the cooking station where Antoine would serve up one of his most loved deserts from his restaurant menu in London, strawberry and mint mille-feuille with honey ice cream, which of course featured the highly regarded local fruit. Yet again Antoine held his audience spellbound as he started with a platter of ingredients, and created another mouthwatering dish, paying homage to the locals cherished star, the strawberry.

"You noticed anything strange about Michel lately?" Donald asked Antoine as they started to clean down Antoine's table.

"I've been noticing strange things about him since he was in short trousers," Antoine replied with a smile. "Why?"

"Nothing," replied Donald. "Just doesn't seem to be himself these past few days."

Antoine stopped what he was doing and looked over at his brother who was standing looking out over the water. Michel was motionless. He spotted Antoine and Donald looking over at him. He gave them a placid wave.

"Let me have a word," he said to Donald. As Antoine got closer to Michel, he noticed his brother was reading a letter. Michel looked up and seeing his brother approach, quickly put the letter back in the envelope and in his pocket.

"Penny for your thoughts?" said Antoine.

"Oh, you don't want to know." Michel moved toward the edge of the riverbank and sat down.

"You know, you were always a fucking terrible liar. That's what makes you such a bad poker player." Antoine took a pack of cigarettes out and offered his brother one.

"True," Michel replied. "You and Dad were the professionals at that, poker *and* lying."

Antoine chuckled quietly to himself.

"You got your lying skills from Mum, she was a terrible liar as well, awful at hiding bad news too, which made you both terrible card players."

Michel smiled at the memory of them sitting as a family around the little kitchen table back in their bedroom in London, playing cards into the small hours of the morning, just him, his brother, and his mother and father. God he missed those days so badly.

"We won our fair share of games," Michel said.

"That's because Dad and I took pity on you and Mum. You ever hear of anyone winning a hand of Texas Hold'em with a pair of sixes?" The brothers laughed and sat together taking in the countryside around them. The soundtrack consisted of birdsong as the sun flickered across the still water. On the far side of the lake, framed by centuries old willow trees, sat at small abandoned lodge with a little pier, the perfect spot for some fishing.

"So," said Antoine after a few minutes of peace and tranquillity, and smoking. "What's in the letter?"

Michel sat for a moment. He could feel the letter burning in his pocket. He was angry with himself that his brother had noticed it. His eyes flickered as he weighed up the potential scenarios involving him disclosing the contents to Antoine.

"Antoine we've only a week or so before we get to Paris and finish the trip and the shoot, and then we can get paid, and get back to London."

"Thanks for the breaking news, but that's not what I asked you."

Michel looked at his brother.

"Antoine, there's *another* reason I wanted us to come on this trip. I mean originally, I wanted us to come for the very reasons I explained to you back in London, to make enough money to relaunch our restaurant, but something else came up, before we left, that changed things."

"Is this a fucking riddle?" asked Antoine, losing patience with his brother.

"It's not a riddle," said Michel. "Just give me another day or two and I'll be able to explain everything to you."

"Jesus, it's always like a game of Cluedo with you, just tell me who the fucking letter was from?" Antoine towered over his brother.

"Alright!" replied Michel. He stood and took the letter out of his pocket and handed it to Antoine. Antoine opened the envelope, took the letter out, and began to read.

The letter was from the British embassy in Paris, and it looked like a photocopy of some sort of room itinerary. It was a photocopy of a page from the embassy's house diary, listing upcoming events at the embassy in the various rooms that were on site, and available to hire by those wealthy or influential enough to hire them. Rooms were also available to film crews, that could also hire them out as a filming location. Under the date of Friday, fifteenth of July, an entry read, "TF1, private hire of orangeries and kitchens, for the purpose of filming."

"That's us and the crew isn't it?" asked Antoine.

"Yes, it is. That's the day we are due to film there, to cook lunch for the British ambassador. It's also got the guest list on there, look." He pointed to the reverse of the page. Antoine turned the page over and read aloud.

"Ambassador Dunscombe, the Minister for French tourism Mrs. Henry, Head of content at TF1, Mr. Bellion.

"A guest list, and there's a dozen or so names on this list, what am I supposed to be seeing here?" Antoine asked.

"It's not whose name *is* there; it's whose name *isn't*."

Antoine looked blankly at his brother.

"Oh, for fuck's sake," said Michel. "Who approached us about this job, who booked us, who's paying us a small fortune to be here?"

"Deschamps."

"Correct, Deschamps." said Michel. "Deschamps told us that he would be front and center at the lunch on the final day of filming."

"So his name isn't on the list, so what, he obviously can't make it, so fucking what? It's one less cover for me to cook."

"Antoine, unlike you, I thought it was a little strange that the person who's put this whole thing together, and explicitly told me he'd be at the final banquet, is not on the final guest list."

Antoine shrugged his shoulders. Michel was losing his patience with his brother.

"You've been reading too many conspiracy theory articles, my brother," said Antoine, dismissing Michel and walking away.

"Wait!" said Michel as he grabbed his brother by the arm. "Look at this." Michel pulled his notebook from his jacket pocket, opened it and handed it to Antoine.

"I did a little digging into our new employer Mr. Deschamps. And I found out a lot of things, a *lot* of things, that if we'd known before we signed the contract would have made us run in the opposite direction, but we were too far down the line to back out of the deal."

Antoine started to read as Michel moved in closer to him.

"I wanted to find out where Mr. Deschamps will be while we're dishing your French onion soup out to the great and good of Paris on July fifteenth," he said. Antoine read Michel's notes aloud.

"Dorchester Hotel London, booking confirmed, two nights, two double rooms, from the thirteenth to the fifteenth of July," Antoine paused. "What is this?"

"I phoned around some hotel contacts back home, keep reading," Michel answered. "I asked them to find any rooms booked under the names Delitzsch or Kohl."

"Hang on, Kohl?"

"Aha," said Michel.

"Mother's maiden name," Antoine said. Michel nodded, hoping that Antoine was now seeing the light, or at least a glimmer of light.

"What the fuck is going on?" asked Antoine, now totally perplexed. Just as Michel moved to answer him, his phone beeped. Michel took his phone from his jacket pocket and read the text message. His eyes widened as he read it. Michel dialed Lucy's number straight away, and it rang, and rang, and rang.

Back in the hotel room in Paris, Lucy could feel her phone vibrating on the table beside her. Lorenzo was in the center of the room, eyeing up the various monitors on the wall. Fabian noticed Lucy slide the phone out of her purse. She clumsily knocked the phone against her coffee cup. She winced.

Lorenzo turned sharply and looked at Lucy. "Who is it?" he asked her as she looked at the phone.

"Michel," replied Lucy hesitantly as Pieters approached her.

"Interesting," Lorenzo said. "Answer it, And then pass the phone to me. It's about time I introduced myself to him and filled him and his brother in on what part they can play in all of this."

CHAPTER THIRTY-TWO

Geneva, present day

Alain sat on the terrace of his room at Le Richemond, a boutique hotel nestled in the governmental hub of Geneva, the Swiss capital. He was enjoying the silence of the early morning, the sunshine, and the continental breakfast, one of the many things that the hotel was famed for. His almost meditative state was broken by a loud knock on the main door to his suite. Alain folded his newspaper, left the terrace, and opened the door to find Mr. Hassan standing in the hallway.

"You want some breakfast?" Alain said as he made his way back out onto the terrace.

"No," replied Hassan. "I grabbed something earlier on my way to see Jean-Pierre at the trade department." Hassan was currently negotiating a rezoning development contract for Alain in Switzerland, which would see Deschamps's company increase their Swiss property portfolio substantially.

"Any problems with the planning procedures?"

"Nothing a large envelope can't sort out," replied Hassan.

Alain smiled at just how easily these middle management civil servants could be bought off.

"Have you spoken to our friend in London?"

"Earlier this week," replied Hassan.

"Good, and how is Mr. Knowles?" asked Alain. "I presume everything is in place?"

"You know Frank. Not a lot going on behind the eyes, but he's always proven to be the right man for the job. He's getting his crew together as we speak." Mr. Hassan opened his briefcase and took out his laptop. He sat beside Alain on the terrace and positioned it so they could both see the screen.

"So," said Hassan. "Frank is all set, his team will carry out surveillance immediately, and as per your instructions, he and the team can be in position within six hours, after we give them the go-ahead. These guys don't need much advance notice. His crew have been given the plans and schematics for the building; they are familiarizing themselves with those as we speak. And of course, I'll be joining them the night before the capture, to make sure all is going to plan."

"Good," replied Alain. "And the route to Paris and beyond with the payload?"

"I've spoken to our friendlies at the port. We have the usual payoffs to make there, and at the channel tunnel, but we've made provisions for that. The cargo will be picked up and taken straight to our holding area in Paris, at which point I'll personally escort it out to its final destination."

Alain stood and sipped his latte surveying the park the across from the hotel, which given the time of year, was looking its best. Pink blossom trees gleamed against the manicured lawns, which were surrounded by miniature water features. Tourists and locals shuffled through the park sipping takeaway coffees from one of the many little food trucks located amongst the gardens.

"Hard to believe we're so close to completing a life's work my friend," he said to Hassan. "Completing something my father started over sixty years ago," he added.

"He would be very proud of you." Hassan replied.

"I suppose he would," replied Alain. "I'm not doing this to serve a maniacal leader like he did, I'm doing it to for my own reasons, my own endgame."

Hassan looked at Alain admiringly.

"I look forward to hearing about it," said Hassan, knowing fully well that there were always some details of Alain's plans that were held back, even from him. The two men looked out at the Geneva skyline, a view filled with shining office blocks housing some of the biggest corporations in the world.

Alain felt at one with his plan. A plan that was meticulously conceived and was slowly being executed. He was beginning to feel excited about what lay ahead for him.

"When was the last time you checked in with Karsten?" asked Alain.

"Earlier this week," replied Hassan. "He sent me the live link so you can check in on the assets." He took a USB key from his pocket, slid it into the port on his computer, then tapped on the keyboard, opening a secure email server. He then opened an email from Karsten and clicked on the link within. Alain watched the screen as the live stream loaded, and he could now see the assets, *his* assets. Five paintings from the *Obscurum Amicis* collection. There they were, all hanging safely on the wall of the bunker where Alain had stored them ever since he stole the first of the five years earlier.

Berchtesgaden, an atypical German town in the Bavarian Alps on the Austrian border, was the birthplace of Karl Delitzsch, Alain's father. Alain's family had held sway in the town for decades, with a series of Alain's relations holding the position of mayor of the town. To this day, a Delitzsch still held a seat on the local council, meaning that Alain could continuously access his extended family, and more importantly access their powerful influence amongst the locals. This part of Germany was steeped in history—Nazi history. To the south of the town, lay Hitler's eagle's nest retreat, the Kehlsteinhaus, which today is a restaurant that boasts stunning Alpine views. The nearby Obersalzberg Museum chronicles the dark history of the surrounding area.

Among these regular tourist destinations, was the decommissioned Berchtesgaden Salt Mines, once a flourishing national industry that had operated since the twelfth century. It now sat empty, with sparse pockets of tourists occasionally taking tours of the previously bustling industrial site. The site was a network of corridors, rail tracks, tunnels, and rooms, sprawled across four kilometers, all at an average depth of over one hundred meters. Most of the mine was inaccessible and unsafe, with only a small portion deemed safe enough for visitors. Alain's father had often spoken about this place to him, regaling him with stories of him and his brothers as young children being fascinated by the place. It became an adventure playground for them, as well as a future place of employment for them and most of the men in the surrounding area, before they were called to serve their country in the First and Second World Wars.

Alain's family, and in particular his uncle Karsten, an ex-miner himself, still lived in the town, and this uncle held a seat on the local council. He had secured, on his nephew's behalf, access to a small portion of the mine. Many palms had been greased along the way; it had cost Alain a lot of money, but fortunately for him, his uncle had inherited the familiar family traits of dishonesty and bribery and a desire to make easy money through illegal channels. So, when Karsten's nephew came to visit him some years earlier, and put the following proposal in front of him—to take a small space within the mine and house certain "personal effects," at a nominal annual fee—his uncle arranged its sanction. He gave Alain the certified ownership papers, the access, *and* the security to protect it, as Karsten also served as a volunteer member of the local police force. From early in his career as a master thief, Alain would regularly send the efforts of his crimes which included jewelry, ceramics, foreign exchange, paintings, documents accompanied *every* time by Mr. Hassan. They were transported and deposited in the four-meter by four-meter room, hidden far below the surface, deep in the network of corridors in the mine.

Mr. Hassan had made many trips to the town over the years. He invested in some property there, on Alain's suggestion, and eventually made it his home, which meant that no alarms were raised by his constant movements to and from the town. He was now after all, a German citizen, making border crossings a mere formality. Karsten had made sure the room deep in the mine was secured beyond the levels of any of the other rooms in the complex. It was situated at the end of a twenty-one-meter tunnel, far from the tourist route at the southwest end of the sprawling site. Karsten had personally overseen the room fit out, which included a far-more-than-necessary strong door, high-tech alarms, and security cameras discreetly fitted both outside and inside the room, all at a huge cost, all paid for by Alain.

"So, everything is set," Alain said as his colleague closed the link on the laptop and finished his coffee. "And the whereabouts of our duo?"

"Everything is going according to plan, the duo and their film crew are currently..." He paused and opened the GPS tracking system on his screen, and then zoomed in on a small blue flashing dot, over a map of France. The signal from the dot was being beamed via the GPS device fitted to the underside of the crew van, which Donald was currently driving.

"On the move from Giverny, heading southeast toward Paris." Mr. Hassan answered. "Barring any diversions, they should get to Paris within the next thirty-six hours."

"Perfect," replied Alain. "Give the instruction to Frank and the crew to assemble in London, and proceed as planned with stage one."

"Will do." Hassan picked his phone up to call Frank.

"You'd better get yourself to the airport," said Alain. "I want you over there to supervise the extraction. We're too close now to fuck it all up now in the final furlong." His voice had a deadly serious tone.

"Understood." Hassan gathered his things together and left the room.

"Nearly there," Alain said to himself as he sat back down on his terrace to finish his newspaper and his breakfast. The plan had, as Mr. Hassan said, gone according to schedule thus far. This complex strategy, this journey to his endgame, had been finalized in Alain's mind not long after he'd hired Lucy Carter.

While the de la Rue brothers were due to be away from Soho filming, this would give Alain and his team plenty of time to study their building and its surroundings, and plenty of time to break in and search the premises for Deschamps's holy grail, the Pierre Bontemps painting. It would also give them ample time to clean and cover their tracks and get the newly acquired piece away from London and over to Berchtesgaden, and into the mine, where it would be reunited with its five original companions.

The final part of Alain's grand plan, his escape, his endgame, had yet to be revealed to anyone, but in his own mind, it was fully mapped out, and the very thought of his own final destination brought a smile to his face.

CHAPTER THIRTY-THREE

When Frank Knowles got the call from Mr. Hassan, he quickly sprang into action. A former member of the armed forces, he was perfectly suited to this type of operation, having first come to the attention of Mr. Hassan back in India, while working as a mercenary helping secure small holdings along the India-Pakistan border in the ongoing opium war in the region. He had retired early from the army, and like a few others in his ranks, he decided it was time to leave and join the private sector. He was now a gun for hire, a mercenary, who fought not for a cause, but for the highest bidder, and Alain Deschamps was generous with his compensation.

Hassan recruited him into Deschamps's private security detail, whom he had now loyally served, exclusively, for ten years. Knowles was part of a tight crew of four men, all ex-servicemen, all recruited by Hassan. Over those years they had carried out various missions on Hassan's orders. This efficient crew were unwaveringly loyal to Hassan and Deschamps. They jumped into action as soon as one of the aforementioned called.

"Yes?" replied Knowles into the phone as he and his fellow crew members sat in a van on Ramillies Place, watching their target building.

"As soon as stage one is complete, move to stage two as planned," said Hassan down the phone.

"Copy that," replied Knowles. "We'll meet you at the prearranged location at 1600 hours on Tuesday."

"Good." Hassan hung up the phone.

"Right, boys," said Knowles to the lads in the van. "Time to take a closer look." He jumped out of the van and headed toward the building. Working quickly and efficiently, the four men, dressed in Thames Water crew uniforms, set up a temporary roadblock around a manhole cover outside the address in Ramillies Place. They erected a sixty-centimeter square screen, complete with Thames Water branding, around the manhole, and traffic cones on either side of it, with two of the men remaining above ground to divert traffic and any nosy locals. Knowles and Andy Griffiths, his lieutenant, opened the manhole cover and entered the sewer. The two men switched on the lights on their military issue headlamps and made their way down the wet rusty staircase. When they reached the bottom, Knowles pulled a small map out of his side pocket.

"Right," he said, shining his light on the map. "According to this, we're looking at nine meters north, then east for two meters, that should put us under the cellar."

"Copy that," replied Griffiths as he headed down the long tunnel. They moved north, and then swung right, headed in an easterly direction, stopping under where Knowles had calculated the cellar of the building should be. Above their heads was a small sewer grate, well out of reach of the two men.

"Get the camera out," said Knowles. Griffiths dropped his backpack onto the floor and took out a small pinhole camera, no bigger than a marble, which was attached to a long extendable rod. After a few clicks to straighten the rod, with the camera attached to the end, Griffiths hoisted it up toward the grate. Knowles crouched down looking at a monitor Griffiths had handed him, showing him what the camera could see above him.

"On you go," Knowles said as Griffiths moved the camera up through one of the narrow gaps in the grate. On the screen, Knowles watched the dark cellar appear. Griffiths moved the camera left and right, inspecting all of the walls in the cellar.

"Nothing," said Knowles. "We need to check the ground floor." He gave Griffiths the signal to wrap up and move on. As the two resurfaced to the street level through, the men guarding the area pointed to the vacant building nearest the restaurant. Knowles nodded, and all four headed to alley that ran between the restaurant building and its closest neighbor. Halfway down the alley, Knowles, checking his schematic map, spotted a wall mounted vent, leading into the ground floor of the building. He stopped and pointed upward, showing his partner the vent. Griffiths joined Knowles as the other two men took a position at either end of the short alley, again on lookout duty. As Griffiths got the camera back out, and up into the vent, Knowles watched the screen.

"Move into the room," he told Griffiths as he guided the camera in past a gap in one of the wall mounted banquette seats. "Rotate."

Griffiths slowly made the camera turn slowly 360 degrees, giving Knowles a fuller view of the room. "Stop," he said. "Back two clicks."

Griffiths moved the camera back.

"There," Knowles said as the screen in front of him showed what they'd come to find. The camera, pointing toward the chefs table in the dining room of the restaurant, revealed a painting on the wall. "Snap it," said Knowles as Griffiths clicked on his handheld device, queuing the camera to capture the image.

"Got it," said Griffiths.

"Wrap it up," said Knowles as he started to pack away the screen into his backpack. The four men quickly disbanded the temporary stand around the manhole outside and made their way back into their van and away from Ramillies Place.

"So why can't we just get in, get it, and that's the job done," Griffiths said.

"That's why you never made officer grade." Knowles scolded his partner. "Don't ask stupid fucking questions, just follow the orders given, there are reasons why we can't go in and get the target now, reasons that neither you nor I need to be aware of, our mission for today was to confirm the location of the piece, which we've just done. We move in to remove it only when Hassan instructs us to, no sooner."

As the van sped through Soho and out onto Tottenham Court Road, Knowles sent a photo of the painting to his boss. Mr. Hassan was sitting at gate 107 at the airport in Geneva, patiently attempting to complete his latest sudoku puzzle. His phone beeped in his suit pocket. He swiped the screen on his phone, opened the new email, and saw the captured picture sent by his collaborator in London. He typed in a reply, reading, "Good. Move on to next phase, I'll be in touch as soon as I land," and hit send. His flight to London had just been called for boarding.

CHAPTER THIRTY-FOUR

Paris, late 1980s

As well as inheriting a love of literature from his mother, Michel had always had an interest in art. During his college years in Paris, Michel didn't take the well-worn path of most students, that of late nights parties and skipping lectures. Michel never missed a class, handed every assignment up on time, and consequently sailed through every exam. His spare time was spent immersing himself in Paris and all it had to offer, culture-wise. The library was his go-to place, his happy place. It was there that he'd met Myles O'Sullivan, the Irish-born architect that would go on to become a dear friend, and future designer of their rebooted restaurant in London.

Michel's idea of a late night was being allowed to stay in the library with Myles way past closing time, which he was allowed to do because the chief librarian, a sweet elderly spinster by the name of Ms. Morin, had taken a shine to him over the years, to the point where she'd given Michel a key, so he could come and go as he pleased. Just as long as he locked up and left some pastries on her desk for her when she clocked in for work the following morning. Ms. Morin introduced Michel to some of the giants of the literary world and was happy to share her love of the arts, which opened a whole new world to Michel. Michel was that type of man, if he committed to something, albeit a hobby, an interest, he went all the way with it.

His happiest times were spent in "research mode" as Antoine called it. Antoine could always tell when Michel was knee-deep in a new subject, a new obsession, as he'd mope around the apartment zombie-like, having burned the midnight oil in the library and then been up with the lark so he wouldn't miss his first college class. Ms. Morin would tell him a little about a particular artist, and Michel would jump in, reading up on the artist's career, their works, their successes and failures. After completing a certain body of research, he would then sit in the library and share this newfound knowledge with Ms. Morin and Myles, and anyone else who cared to listen. Antoine happened to land in one of these sessions in the library one night. He'd dropped in to borrow some money from Michel on his way to a night out, but quickly left cash in hand, bored to tears.

Above all else, Michel committed most of his time in the library to reading about the generation before him. Having lost both of his parents at a young age, their early lives fascinated him. He hadn't been given much information from his parents while they were alive, and as a result he knew little about *their* parents, his *grandparents*. So he took it upon himself to find out more, using the scraps of information that he'd gleaned over the years as a starting point.

He knew that his mother was German, and that his father was French, and he knew that they'd met in Paris in the 1960s, but that was it. His parents spoke very little about how and where they'd met, and why they'd ended up in London. Murielle never spoke of her parents. She had told her two sons that they'd both been killed in the war in Berlin during the early days of the campaign in 1939. A lie, but Michel and Antoine weren't to know that. Jacques on the other hand, provided a little more information about *his* parents, talking fondly about *his* father.

"The best gift my father gave me, was his work ethic, nothing better than an honest day's work, remember that boys," he said to Michel and Antoine many times during their childhood years. Both brothers had taken that advice on board. They worked hard in school and college, and were determined to succeed in life, another trait they inherited from their father, determination.

The amount of information Michel had on his mother's side of the family was tantamount to nil. He knew his mother was an only child, same as his father, and he knew her maiden name, Kohl, but that was it. One night in their apartment, he brought the topic up with Antoine over dinner.

"You ever wonder think about our grandparents?" he asked Antoine as they sat at the kitchen table, surrounded by empty plates, and two half empty wine glasses.

"Course I have. I wish Dad was still alive so we could ask him more. Grandad sounded like a real character."

"Really? What did he tell you about him?"

"He would talk about him while we were prepping for service," Antoine said, remembering back to his early chef days working alongside his father in London. "He always smiled when he spoke about his dad, he was his hero." Antoine topped up their glasses. "He worked as a bookbinder, I think, somewhere here in Paris. He was great with his hands according to Dad. Suppose that's where he and I got our knife skills from!"

"I never knew that," said Michel, realizing that he'd missed out on moments like that with his father because he was stationed out in the front of house.

"According to Dad, not only did he *bind* the books, apparently, he was something of a bookworm. He'd often bring machine rejected samples home to read, which I guess is where *you* got your appetite for the written word."

"I guess so," replied Michel. Maybe he *had* got his love of books from his grandfather, but while he was in Paris, he was determined to find out more about both sets of grandparents. Of course, the best place to start any research project was in the library.

Over the years Michel and Antoine spent training and working in Paris, Michel would occasionally dig up another nugget of information about their family history, and he would often sit waiting up for Antoine to come in from work to share the latest discovery with him. He'd been able to locate the bookbinders where his grandfather *and* father had both worked, Wildenstein's, having checked through numerous census records and maps in the library archive. The brothers made the short trip, a sort of pilgrimage, to the address where the factory had stood, but alas, it was long gone, having been redeveloped for a social housing project in the late 1970s. The boys stood at the site and pictured what the place must have looked like back in the day, and pictured both their father and grandfather entering and leaving the building.

"Thank you, Michel, what an incredible way to spend a morning," Antoine said as he put his arm around Michel's shoulder, proud at his brother's detective work.

An altogether more poignant moment came sometime later when Michel discovered where his father's parents were buried. Antoine and Michel arrived early one morning at the Montparnasse Cemetery, in the south of Paris, and having spoken to a clerk in the office at the entrance to the graveyard, they located and paid their respects at their grandparents' burial place. The brothers sat on a bench beside the modest grave for nearly two hours. They laid flowers, they prayed, and they talked about their family. The dates on the headstone showed that their grandparents had passed away long before either of the boys were born.

"What do you think they would say to us if they were here now?" Michel asked his older brother.

"I think they'd be proud, Michel," Antoine answered. "From what Dad told me, they'd had a hard life, mustn't have been easy living here during the war."

"Can you imagine it?" Michel asked.

"No, not worth thinking about."

"True, but we can't forget, let alone ignore what happened here. I mean it's not that long ago that this city was on fire, this country was torn apart."

"I know, I know." Antoine stopped to take that thought in. "Is it any wonder why mother never spoke about *her* father and mother?"

"What do you mean?" Michel was well aware that his maternal grandparents were German but had no idea of their involvement in the war, if any.

"I don't know," replied Antoine. "I've always wondered about why she never mentioned them, never spoke about where they were or what they did during the war. Did that never jar with you?"

"No, never gave it much thought," he replied. He was lying, as it totally consumed him. Michel watched Antoine stand and ready himself to leave.

"Well," Antoine said. "Maybe *they* should be your next research project." He smiled at his brother. "Just what did dear old grandad Kohl *do* during the war? There's your next task." He laughed and started to walk down the avenue away from the grave.

"Maybe," said Michel to himself. He stood and ran to catch up with his brother.

There was no doubt, this *was* going to be Michel's next research mission.

As their time in college in Paris came to an end, and the boys both entered the workforce, Michel had to spend less and less time at the library. He was now fully focused on his career, as was Antoine, both putting in serious hours, leaving little free time to indulge their interests, Michel's being reading, and Antoine's being partying.

But Michel's itch to research for new information on his family never faltered.

CHAPTER THIRTY-FIVE

London, some months before the film shoot.

When the boys moved back to London after finally settling the probate case surrounding the house and restaurant, Michel would occasionally spend time in the nearby London Library on St. James's Square. He tried to recreate those moments of serenity through learning that he'd had so many of in Paris, sitting alone reading, researching a newfound artist or completing another branch on his family tree. As time went on, and the restaurant became less and less busy, Michel found that he needed this place of solace more than ever. He'd been frantic in the restaurant for the past two years, trying to keep the place open, dealing with his brothers mounting problems, as well as fending off suppliers and other creditors who were now literally banging down his door on a daily basis.

In the library, he would lose himself in the world of Francisco Goya, Samuel Morse, or Johannes Vermeer, or through accessing German census records in search of his maternal grandparents. He craved this time away from the restaurant, which had now become an albatross around his neck.

After meeting with Alain Deschamps at the charity lunch in The Dorchester hotel, Michel was at a low point. That meeting with Deschamps was bizarre, made even more so by the fact that he'd bumped into Lucy, the one person in the world whom he'd truly loved, and lost. He had always blamed himself for their breakup, and rightly so, he'd been selfish, too caught up in his own problems to notice that the most significant relationship of his life was dissipating in front of his own eyes. But of course he'd never told Lucy any of that; he never had the opportunity to do so, and as Lucy said those words on the night they broke up, "He'd made her mind up for her," he'd realized what he'd lost. Her.

This was all running through Michel's head in the days and weeks after that charity lunch.

Some months later as he sat in his usual spot in the London Library, stared at his notebook, pencil in hand, but he had nothing to write. His thoughts were scattered. He stared at the blank page. He needed a new point of focus, a new person, place, or thing to research, to distance himself from his those thoughts. Clarity. That's what he was seeking. Sticking out of the corner of his notebook, he noticed the edge of a business card. He pulled the card out and looked at the name on it. "Alain Deschamps, CEO, Deschamps International Holdings." He stood and took his notebook to one of the vacant counters in the library which had a desktop computer on it. He opened the internet browser on the screen. He typed the words "Alain Deschamps" into the search engine. Michel's eyes widened as he started to look down through the pages and pages of results that came up.

Well now, he thought. *Looks like I'm not the only person interested in you, Alain.* He grabbed his pencil and started scribbling.

It didn't take Michel long to realize that he wasn't dealing with your standard run-of-the-mill CEO here. In the past when Michel was fielding offers for him and his brother's services, commercial opportunities at the height of their success, those offers came through PR agencies. The first difference that he noticed was that *this* offer from Deschamps came straight from the horse's mouth, albeit with a helpful nudge in the right direction from Michel's ex-girlfriend. When Michel started to dig into Deschamps's company, and his past, he soon started to question his own level of eagerness to take Alain's money and sign up for the filming assignment. He pulled together as much information as he could from the various searches into Alain Deschamps. That night after the dinner service, in the privacy of his bedroom he could reread and study what he had uncovered.

When Michel got back up to the house that evening, Antoine was upstairs in their own kitchen, putting together a little light supper. The restaurant below had been locked up for the night; they'd only had four customers in that evening, so Antoine made the call to send the skeleton staff home earlier than usual. Michel knew supper was almost ready, as the sounds of Wynton Marsalis emanated from the kitchen, Marsalis was one of Antoine's favorite artists; this was his *cooking* music, music he created to, and if the radio was on, and this was playing, it normally meant a beautiful home-cooked meal wasn't far away. As Michel approached the kitchen, he put the folder with all of his research in it on the small table in the hall. He didn't want Antoine poking his nose in and discovering what he'd been working on that day at the library. Antoine had taken some persuading in order to get him to agree to do the documentary for Alain, and Michel wasn't about to hand him the evidence that could potentially spark him into changing his mind at the last minute. This TV job was, Michel thought at the time of accepting it, the only realistic way that the brothers could secure the short-term future of their restaurant, *and* their home. He knew Antoine well enough to know that if he smelled a rat, he would pull the entire venture. They'd very quickly be back to square one, staring bankruptcy in the face.

What Michel had found out about Deschamps wasn't damming enough to share with Antoine yet, and certainly wasn't enough to harbor the thought of pulling out of the deal, but it *was* enough for him to think he needed to do some more digging. There were a lot of questions about Alain Deschamps that Michel needed to find answers to before he reached the point of telling Antoine.

"How was your day?" Michel asked as he entered the kitchen and sat at the table.

"Same as usual," replied Antoine. "Started with an almighty hangover, and went downhill from there." The brothers tucked into the food Antoine had prepared.

"How many covers tonight?" Michel asked, in an attempt to keep the conversation light over dinner.

"Two tables of two," Antoine replied. "I let the kitchen lads go early and did the service myself. Was back up here at nine thirty." The brothers sat and ate, comfortable in each other's silence as always, the radio in the background providing the only sound.

"You know this offer couldn't have come at a better time, Michel," said Antoine, pouring each a glass of wine. "I've been thinking about what we could do with the money, revamp the kitchen maybe, give the dining room a new lease of life, what do you think? In fact, I started jotting down a few ideas while I was down there tonight." He handed Michel a sheet that he'd sketched some new dishes on.

It was the first time in years that Michel had heard Antoine talk about the future, about moving forward, about the restaurant, about something other than his latest list of personal problems.

"They look amazing," replied Michel with a broad smile on his face, delighted to see this version of his brother, and best friend, in front of him again. He certainly wasn't going to bring up his reservations about Alain now. The two sat for a couple of hours, enjoying the food, the music, and each other's company, forgetting about all of their recent and current troubles, talking about ideas for the revamp, the new menu, and their upcoming filming in France. It was just like the old days.

The next morning, Sunday, meant the restaurant was closed, Michel took full advantage of the day being his and left the house in Soho and headed to another favorite haunt of his, a small bookshop on Newburgh Street. As well as having an incredible selection of reading materials, the bookshop had a small reading section upstairs, complete with an expresso machine and only two tables. It was never crowded, which meant he could while away most of the day, practically undisturbed. Today, however, he'd arranged to meet someone in the bookshop, with a view to widening his delve into Alain Deschamps. Michel and his brother were due to head off on their TV adventure soon, time was of the essence.

One of the things Michel insisted on when he signed himself and Antoine up for the TV job was they were to be paid thirty percent of their fee up front. Michel stood firm on this during the contact negotiations for two reasons. One it would show that Deschamps was serious about his commitment to the brothers, and two, he could then use some of that money to pay off those suppliers and other creditors that were high on his list. Then they could keep trading, with a somewhat lighter slate of creditors. Alain agreed, and the money was wired to their business account the following week. This meant the trip to France was *actually* going ahead. He didn't tell Antoine about getting some of the fee up front, he was afraid that Antoine would take his portion and piss it against a wall. He was prepared to let Antoine splurge some of the fee, but only when they got back from filming, with the job complete, and even then, he'd make sure that Antoine didn't get his hands on the bulk of the money. He wanted to ensure they'd have enough to pay their remaining creditors off and get started on the full relaunch of their restaurant.

Third Story Books on Newburgh Street in Soho was where Michel had arranged the meeting. Being a Sunday, Soho was as quiet as it could be. As Michel climbed the old wooden stairs to the third floor, he could already smell the freshly brewed coffee. He loved coming to this place, as it was slightly off the beaten path, and never busy. Owned by a middle-aged man, the eccentric and utterly fascinating Cameron Stapleton, this old school coffee shop-come-reading hangout, hadn't changed much over the years. It was cramped, the books were disorganized, spread across rows of shelves and tables, and Michel loved every inch of the place. It was also one of the best places to find first editions, Cameron being very well connected in the literary world. His father was an accomplished writer and had spent time and partied with the likes of Hemmingway and Noël Coward.

Michel took up his usual spot, the table near the window which sported a huge picture of Oscar Wilde on the wall above it. He ordered an espresso from Cameron, who was very excited to show Michel his latest acquisition, a first edition of Charles Dickens' *David Copperfield*, which he'd managed to track down and buy from a retired American soap actor. Michel for once, wasn't that interested in Cameron's story. He was preoccupied with the meeting he was due to have. Normally, he and Cameron would sit chatting, Michel listening attentively as Cameron regaled him with the story of landing his latest rare book. Not today though, and Cameron sensed this, giving up on the conversation and leaving Michel alone at the table. Michel heard footsteps coming up the stairs and looked to see who they belonged to. As the footsteps reached the top of the stairs, the man looked around and spotted Michel.

"There you are," he said, walking over to join Michel at his table.

"Good to see you again," Michel said as he rose to greet his old friend with a warm hug. "Coffee?" Michel offered his guest a seat and a drink.

"Please," the friend replied. "An Americano."

Michel called over to Cameron who joined the two men at the table. "Another espresso for me, and an Americano, please."

"Aren't you going to introduce me?" Cameron asked. It was beyond unusual that Michel had company.

"Sorry, of course, this is Lewis Ralph," he said as Cameron shook Mr. Ralph's hand.

"A new face, lovely to meet you," Cameron said, and scurried off to make the coffees.

Lewis Ralph had worked at the British embassy in Paris for almost twenty-five years, before retiring and returning home to England. He'd worked under eight different ambassadors in his time, serving them all diligently. The bulk of his duties involved looking after the welfare and needs of British citizens that both resided and were holidaying in the French capital, passport problems, customs issues, and the like. One day many years ago, he had to track down and contact the relatives of an English woman who had been killed in a car crash in Scotland whose sons lived in Paris. Lewis Ralph called on the brothers' apartment that evening, and spoke to Michel to inform him and his brother of their mother's death. He and Michel had stayed in touch after the phone call. He was always there for the brothers and helped Michel with travel arrangements to and from London for the funeral and provided crucial help in recommending a lawyer when it came to sorting out their mother's probate case. Mr. Ralph would check in on the brothers occasionally, and Michel would often use Mr. Ralph and his contacts to help him sort problems for various guests at the hotels where Michel worked.

When Mr. Ralph retired and returned home to England, Michel invited him to dinner at the restaurant, and he became a regular, with him and his wife spending many a happy evening there in Michel and Antoine's company. Michel and Mr. Ralph also shared some common interests, art and literature.

"So why are we meeting here?" asked Mr. Ralph. "Something wrong back at the restaurant?"

"No, not at all, well nothing other than the usual mayhem, I just wanted to run something by you, out of earshot of Antoine." Michel took a folder from his laptop bag. "I wanted to pick your brains about something, *someone*, in fact, whose business is based in Paris. I thought you might be able to shed some light on him for me."

"Oh really?" Mr Ralph took his coat off, and put it on the back of his chair, clearly settling in at the thought of being handed a shiny new project. He didn't like to sit still and, being retired, he craved being given a task, a point of focus, something other than tending to his extensive miniature Japanese garden at home.

"What do you know about this man?" Michel said as he handed Mr. Ralph his folder. Mr. Ralph opened the folder and saw a picture of Alain Deschamps, along with various newspaper articles Michel had printed out. He looked up at Michel.

"Right. Interesting topic. What exactly have you got to do with Alain Deschamps?"

"We've just signed up to do a television series for him."

"A television series? But this man is an art dealer, at least that's what it says on his tax returns, what has he got to do with television?"

"He's just got into the business, bought a sizeable share of TF1," replied Michel. "And we are his first TV project, his first venture into TV production. Me and Antoine."

"Not the finest company you could have chosen to keep. This man has quite the reputation. I've had many dealings with this Deschamps over the years."

"I thought you might, that's why I wanted to talk to you." Cameron dropped two coffees off at their table as Michel and Mr. Ralph settled into a deep conversation, one that was to enlighten Michel as to whom he and his brother had just committed to work for.

It was very useful to have a contact in the British embassy, and Mr. Ralph was the first name that came to mind when Michel started digging into Alain Deschamps.

By the time they were finished talking, the small bookshop was closing. Michel and Mr. Ralph had not only moved close to working out *why* Alain had chosen Michel and Antoine for this project, but what his real motive was. More importantly they started to formulate a strategy, a course of action, and a plan, that they hoped would put paid to Alain's intentions.

CHAPTER THIRTY-SIX

Paris, present day

LORENZO TOOK THE PHONE from Lucy and held his finger up, as if to tell Fabian and Lucy to be quiet. *He* was going to do the talking.

"Mr. de la Rue," he said into the phone. "Good afternoon, my name is Lorenzo Pieters, and I'm here with your friend Lucy."

Michel didn't answer straight away.

"Michel, can you hear me?" Pieters asked, getting impatient.

"What's going on, is Lucy okay? Who are you?"

"Lorenzo Pieters, from Interpol. And Lucy is perfectly fine, she is here assisting us with some inquiries."

"Let me speak to her, now," Michel said, his heart beating in his chest.

"By all means." Lorenzo handed the phone back to Lucy.

"Michel?" Lucy said. "I'm fine, and he's right, I'm helping Mr. Pieters with some information about a friend of ours."

"Deschamps?"

"Yes, why, did you hear something? Has Alain been in touch with you?" Lorenzo took the phone back from her.

"Michel, I'm putting you on speaker phone, if that's okay?" Pieters said as he pressed a button on Lucy's phone. "We need to *share* information at this point, Michel, all of us."

"Fine," replied Michel. "So how do I know you are who you say you are?"

"At this stage, Mr. de la Rue, you'll have to take my word for it. Until we meet face-to-face at which point, I'll happily furnish you with my credentials," he added sarcastically.

"Michel," said Lucy. "I'm sitting in a hotel suite surrounded by Interpol operatives, believe me, I've seen his credentials, he is who he says he is."

"Right," replied Michel, after a long pause. "So, what's going on, why are you calling me?"

"Well, if you could answer Lucy's previous question," said Lorenzo. "That would be a great start. Has Deschamps been in touch with you recently?"

"I haven't seen him in the flesh since I met him for the first time some months ago in London, with Lucy," answered Michel. "Ever since, we've only been in contact through email; we're not due to meet him again until we arrive in Paris in a couple of weeks."

Pieters looked over at one of the operatives sitting at a computer screen. The operative looked back at him and nodded, all clear. Having now got hold of Michel's phone number, the Interpol agent had quickly run a scan of his previous phone calls, both made and received, and none of Alain's phone numbers appeared. Michel was telling the truth, so far, at least about not talking to Alain recently. Pieters paused and thought about his next question.

"We have reason to believe that you are connected to something that Deschamps wants to get his hands on, something that is part of a bigger plan that he and his team have been working on for quite some time," replied Lorenzo. Silence.

Without knowing it, Pieters had just given Michel confirmation of everything that he and Lewis Ralph had suspected.

CHAPTER THIRTY-SEVEN

During Michel and Lewis Ralph's initial meeting and subsequent research into Deschamps, they had burrowed through dozens of documents from Michel's early investigations. After that meeting Mr. Ralph took their inquiries to the next stage, and called in favors from other ex-embassy staff, former members of the French police force, and one or two contacts that he'd made in Interpol over the years. Another reason why Michel had called in Mr. Ralph was the fact that he was somewhat of an expert on the subject of World War Two, having studied history at Cambridge University, going on to do his thesis entitled "Restitution—Post WWII."

Lewis Ralph was well aware of Alain Deschamps. During his time working at the embassy in Paris he had heard all sorts of rumors about his operation and had even taken the time to visit Deschamps's modest gallery in Paris, where he was far from impressed with the mediocre collections on show. He always wondered why Deschamps was held in such high regard in the art world, when all he seemed to have on the walls of his gallery were middle-of-the-road, bog-standard portraits and landscape. Occasionally though, there would be one stand-out piece, the work of a master, which would draw the crowds into the gallery and bring affirmation to Deschamps's reputation as a serious art dealer. Digging into the background of the Deschamps Gallery, Lewis discovered stories of shipments arriving under the cover of darkness and various private viewings being arranged for clients who, like the shipments, were never seen in broad daylight.

Through his studies in college Mr. Ralph was also very aware and passionate about the amount of art and artefacts that were stolen from the Jewish population during World War Two. While working at the British embassy he had spent time with family members of those who were originally part of the Jewish community that had been so violently displaced. It was then that he began to hear various stories and legends about stashes of art which had somehow been smuggled out of the city by the French Resistance. One such stash, stuck in his mind more than others.

On an official visit to a nursing home in Paris, he and the sitting British ambassador were meeting with several war veterans, mainly from the allied side, who had served their country and were now convalescing. It was the fiftieth anniversary of the end of the Second World War, and the Ambassador was keen to thank those soldiers who had given everything to attain peace across Europe. While talking to one particular French soldier, Mr. Ralph was distracted by another man sitting near a large bay window, who was waving at him. The man, in his late eighties, was clearly keen to get Mr. Ralph's attention. Lewis approached the man and asked him if he was okay.

"Most well," said the man, gesturing for Lewis to sit beside him, which he did. He sat and spoke to that war veteran for over an hour. Lewis was engrossed. As it turned out, he was not a soldier, in the formal sense. He wasn't in receipt of a government pension, for he was in fact a former member of the French Resistance. During that hour he regaled Lewis with many stories of daring-do. Lewis was enthralled.

One story the man relayed to him stuck with Lewis, the story of the *Obscurum Amicis*, a legend of World War Two, which Lewis had vaguely heard of before. This man claimed he and his squad of Resistance members had lifted the collection directly from a Nazi ERR squad.

Over the preceding years, Lewis dipped in and out of research on the topic of these paintings, reading whatever he could get his hands on. His research eventually led him to Alain Deschamps and his Paris gallery. Lewis had heard rumors that Deschamps and, in particular, his father Karl Delitzsch, had some part to play in the legend. Never did Lewis think that the conversation with an ex-Resistance soldier would amount to anything significant, but when he sat in that coffee shop in London talking to Michel many years later, it did. This former soldier was the same man that provided Lorenzo Pieters, some years later, with copies of the lists of paintings he and his brigade had handled. Paintings that Pieters and Interpol were now trying to secure.

Lewis Ralph did eventually come face-to-face with Deschamps during his time in Paris, in a courtroom setting. When Lewis and Michel compared notes, research documents, and the files they had both put together over the week after they'd met for coffee, they concluded that Deschamps wanted something that belonged to Michel and Antoine, that had belonged to their parents, that had originally belonged to the previous owner of the building, Mrs. Edsel Rothstein.

Being a regular at Michel's restaurant, Lewis was aware of the painting that hung on the wall in their dining room above the chef's table. Before Michel and Antoine left to begin their filming commitments in France, Mr. Ralph, with Michel's permission, had *Veiller Sur Toi* authenticated and valued, by a London based art dealer Lewis brought to the restaurant one evening. He wanted to verify it was genuine, and then attempt to trace its provenance.

Michel had his own reasons to have it authenticated, which he was now explaining while on the phone to Lorenzo Pieters. Michel agreed that they shared the same end goal—to take Deschamps down—and agreed to work with Lorenzo to reach that goal.

Back in the hotel room, as Fabian, Lucy, Pieters, and all of the operatives listened to Michel offer this information, the mood changed. After Michel had stopped speaking, Lorenzo looked around the table.

"Michel, you have been more than helpful, and I'm beginning to understand why Deschamps is so interested in you and your brother. We need to meet, soon. I'll text you an address shortly," he said to Michel.

"Fine," Michel replied. He hung up the phone.

"Very interesting," said Pieters. He put his phone in his pocket and looked at Fabian and Lucy. "I'm looking forward to meeting Michel, sounds like he has more to say about your boss, Lucy. So, we need to pool our information and resources and confirm a final plan for Deschamps." He stood up from the table and signaled to two of the other operatives in the room. The two men started packing up their laptops and other documents around them.

"Fabian, you're going to document everything as we move on. I'm sure your editor wouldn't say no to the world exclusive detailing the demise of Alain Deschamps?"

"I can smell the Pulitzer from here," Fabian replied.

CHAPTER THIRTY-EIGHT

"WHAT ABOUT ME?" ASKED Lucy, wondering if her presence was still needed.

"I need you to come with us when we meet Michel," replied Lorenzo. "He needs to be reassured that we're all on the same side here, in the meantime, go back to work, business as usual."

"You want me to go back to work, look Alain in the eye, and pretend like nothing is going on. That's what you're asking me to do?" Lucy was flipping her cigarette lighter over and over in her hand.

Lorenzo pulled his chair closer to the table.

"I'm not asking you, I'm telling you, and if our operation goes to plan this will all be over in a matter of days."

Lucy slammed the lighter on the table.

"And what if it doesn't go to plan!" she shouted, standing from her seat. Lorenzo and Fabian were taken aback by this sudden outburst. Lorenzo stood and picked up the lighter. He approached Lucy.

"Lucy," he said in a reassuring tone. "We have everything in place to make this operation a success, and Michel can help us get this over the line, that's why I *need* you to do this, you have to trust me." He placed the lighter back into Lucy's hand. She looked to Fabian. His stern expression didn't help.

Lucy was trembling. There was so much going on inside her head. The thoughts of going back to that office and meeting Alain was making her stomach churn. Her toe tapped on the floor as her mind raced. All she could think about was Michel. She lit a cigarette and took a long drag.

"Okay," she eventually replied. "Whatever I can do to help Michel, and you."

Lorenzo smiled, and shook Lucy's hand. Fabian and Lucy started to make their exit from the hotel room.

"I can drop you close to your office," Fabian offered.

"Not too close," Lucy replied as she stopped at the hotel room door, and looked back to Pieters.

"Where and when are we meeting Michel?" she asked.

"When? Friday. Where? Maybe you could suggest somewhere that he'd feel comfortable, somewhere informal, quiet, and away from prying eyes?"

Lucy buttoned her coat as she thought about a possible venue. After a moment she answered Pieters.

"I know just the place."

CHAPTER THIRTY-NINE

Michel stood on the bank of the small bay, which lapped up against the old flour mill. The silence was broken when his phone beeped. Michel read the text. "24 Rue Pavée, 11am Friday, See you there, Lucy." Michel knew that address by heart; it was the address of the library that he'd spent so much time in in his early years in Paris.

There were a couple of days filming with his brother and the crew to get through before that Friday. He figured all he had to do was try and keep things as "normal" as possible try not to spook Donald or Antoine, then get to the meeting at the library, at which point everything would be explained to both.

The brothers had one more festival to attend before they arrived in Paris and the culmination of their filming trip—the banquet at the residence of the British ambassador. Antoine had thoroughly enjoyed the time in France, he was loving the freedom the trip gave him, not just freedom from the drudgery of the professional kitchen, but the freedom of being able to design, cook, and to present new dishes to the crew and to the public. He loved company, and despite his early concerns about the crew, they'd really hit it off.

The two vans pulled away from the site of the Old Mill of Vernon and drove through the outskirts of the Giverny region, heading toward Paris. All was calm amongst the small film unit. This pleased no one more than Donald, who, much like Antoine when they all first met, hadn't high hopes for the series. But, after a number of weeks, and with almost thirty-eight hours of television filmed and uploaded, he was confident that he was about to deliver an accomplished and polished series. He had been in weekly contact with the commissioning editor at TF1, a Mr. Tallon, sending him clips of the rushes to view. Mr. Tallon seemed pleased with what he saw. Just one more food festival to film at, and then the crowning glory of the series, a high-class banquet serving Michelin star food to a grateful and enthusiastic audience.

The penultimate filming sequence was at the town of Rosny-sous-Bois, less than thirty kilometers east of Paris. This festival, La Fête de la Gastronomie, centered around a huge open space in the nearby Parc Jean Decesari.

Even though the atmosphere among the crew was jovial, Michel was far from relaxed as they approached their destination.

He was anxious, hoping that all of what he and Lewis Ralph had planned would go off without a hitch, and that was *before* Interpol came on his radar. He was trying to work out whether it was a good thing or not that the authorities were now on board, and whether or not it would wreck what he and Lewis had planned. Michel couldn't help but drift into a somewhat happier frame of mind as they neared Paris. He started to see landmarks that he recognized, transporting him back to his college days. He loved this city; it killed him that he and his brother had to leave it some years ago, but circumstances demanded they return to London.

"You okay, brother?" Antoine asked as he looked over at Michel in the passenger seat of their campervan. Michel didn't answer; he was miles away, in another world. "Michel? You okay?" This time Antoine slapped his brother on the arm. Michel jolted to attention.

"Yes, sorry," he replied. "Sorry I was a million miles away."

Michel smiled nervously to himself as he gently rested his head against the window. He was exhausted.

"Might try and catch a little sleep," he said in an attempt to stop Antoine asking any more questions.

He'd been distracted for most of the van journey, but now the reality of what was about to go down over the next few days, both in Paris and in London, was starting to sink in.

CHAPTER FORTY

Mr. Hassan was no stranger to London, having traveled there since the mid-1990s as part of his brief as Alain Deschamps's consiglieri. Deschamps International Holdings had an office in London, which was nothing more than a front, another off-the-shelf company that Alain had acquired, with the sole purpose of putting another layer of red tape between him and the authorities. He bought their premises in Canary Wharf, one of London's central business districts on the Isle of Dogs, for several reasons. As an investment, of course, property was hardly a risk these days but primarily it provided his accountants with another layer of filters. In total there were thirty-four subsidiaries of Deschamps International Holdings, dotted across seven different countries, each providing another level of filtering when it came to passing dirty money in at the bottom, only for it to reappear, squeaky clean at the top, the top being Alain's corporate headquarters in Paris.

The office in London was empty of staff and consisted of nothing more than a nameplate on a wall. It was a big open-plan site, taking up one complete floor, and had very little infrastructure, apart from one corner office, Mr. Hassan's. This office was where Hassan would take delivery of any sensitive items, and also where they had a secure IP address, which meant the movement of monies was easily done, with no one looking over his shoulder, virtually and in reality.

Mr. Hassan called Frank Knowles and his lieutenant Andy Griffiths to a meeting there, to go through final plans for their current London mission. Knowles and Griffiths had previously confirmed the location of the painting within the building on Ramillies place. They'd pinpointed various security systems, namely shutters on the front of the building, a basic alarm, as well as a number of security cameras both inside and outside the property, none of which appeared to be functional. Hassan briefly greeted them and they sat in his corner office.

"Friday is still a go," Hassan said as he handed both men a photograph of the painting. "As previously discussed, this is the only item we are removing from the site. We want to cover our tracks and leave the site for the police to assume that this was a run of the mill robbery. Take the usual steps in this regard."

"Copy that," replied Knowles. Hassan leant in close to Knowles' face.

"Let me make myself perfectly clear, this isn't a standard operation, this requires absolute precision, and what I don't need is you and your team taking your foot off the pedal, no mistakes, no fuck-ups." He stuck his finger into Knowles' chest, and held his gaze for several moments. "Clear?"

"Crystal."

Griffiths sat up in his chair. Hassan was not a man to be flippant around, either in what you said, or with your body language.

"We know we have the place to ourselves, there's no one else on-site, so we can take our time, acquire the piece, and leave. Understood?" said Hassan, loosening his tone a little.

"Yes, sir," both men replied.

"Fine. I'll meet you on site at 1930 hours."

Knowles and Griffiths headed sharply back to the lifts, leaving Hassan alone in the office.

CHAPTER FORTY-ONE

IN THE COMFORT OF his Paris office, Alain sat facing the large iMac screen on his desk, ready to watch a live feed of what was due to happen that night in London, via a bodycam that Mr. Hassan would be wearing over his uniform. He was also able to communicate directly with Hassan through a small earpiece he was wearing. Alain had cleared his diary of meetings that afternoon. He wanted no disruptions, no distractions.

"All set?" Alain asked. He could see the restaurant in London in all its glory in front of him on the screen.

"Standing by," answered Hassan as he signaled to the other men to cross the street.

The five men moved toward the side of the building on Ramillies Place to a laneway, and slowly moved down in single file. At the end of the laneway Knowles and his team erected a temporary screen around a manhole as on their previous visit. Hassan lifted the manhole cover off and set it to one side.

"You two with me," he said to Knowles and Griffiths. "You two keep us posted on any movement," he said to the other two men. Again as their previous visit, Knowles knew there was another manhole cover less than fifteen feet away from where they were, situated in the back yard of the restaurant building. Scaling down through the sewer, Hassan stopped and waited for Knowles and Griffiths, and when they arrived down, Knowles took the point position. Without speaking, he signaled forward, and the men moved slowly, together, until Knowles lifted his hand to stop.

He pointed above his head. Looking up Hassan could see another manhole cover. Knowles climbed up the ladder, pushed the manhole cover out of his way, and jumped out of the sewer, pulling both Hassan and Griffiths up after him. The three men now stood in the yard at the back of the building, looking at two doors in front of them, both were reinforced fire doors, and to the far right, was a small staircase leading down to the cellar entrance. Knowles pointed to those stairs and the three men headed down to the cellar door. The two men on watch outside in the laneway, packed up the temporary screen, and made their way back onto Ramillies Place. They put the gear into the back of their marked Thames Water Services van and sat waiting for further instructions from the men inside the building. Knowles lifted his backpack off and took out a variety of cutting tools and started work on the lock of the cellar door. The old door didn't offer up much resistance. Less than a minute later the men were ready to enter the cellar.

Hassan gave Griffiths the go ahead. Moments later the three men were standing inside the cellar, having closed the door behind them.

"Knowles, take the top floor," he said. "Griffiths, stay here in the cellar and do what you need to do. I'll head to the ground floor and secure the package." Both Griffiths and Knowles got to work.

Hassan followed Knowles up the cellar stairs to a door, which led them into the service kitchen of the restaurant on the ground floor of the building. Knowles continued out through the kitchen and up the stairs to the private residence. Hassan left the kitchen and entered the dining room. He headed straight toward the chef's table where the target, the painting, was located. Hassan was carrying a portfolio case, which he laid on the chefs table and zipped open. He then turned his attention to the painting. Six hundred kilometers away, Alain was watched Hassan's every movement on his screen.

"There she is," Alain whispered. "Take her down, gently, let me see the back," Alain said to Hassan, who slowly started to move in toward the painting. The painting wasn't large; it only measured sixty centimeters by forty-five centimeters, and wasn't heavy, most of the weight was in the frame. Hassan laid the painting face down onto the open portfolio case. Alain looked at the back of the frame as Hassan's view slowly revealed the telltale letters O and A on the bottom right-hand corner.

"Beautiful, now pack it away," said Alain.

Hassan flipped the painting over, placed it snugly into the portfolio case, and zipped it up.

"Let me know when you're both finished," Hassan said in his headset to Griffiths and Knowles.

Up on the first floor, Knowles was going from room to room, making a mess, turning over the odd small piece of furniture, tearing curtains and flipping mattresses. Down in the cellar, Griffiths was making an equal mess. Minutes later Hassan joined Griffiths in the cellar, quickly followed by Knowles.

"Do it," said Hassan to Knowles, who again went for his backpack. He opened a pouch containing used syringes and dotted them across the cellar floor, leaving a sufficient trail of random jumbled DNA to send the Metropolitan Police on a wild-goose chase. Griffiths had taken possession of the syringe's a few days earlier, having paid a crowd of junkies with some cocaine in exchange for some of their dirty needles.

"Move out," said Hassan, and the three all headed out of the cellar door. Within minutes they were back in their van.

"Continue with the exit plan as agreed," said Alain.

"Copy that," replied Knowles, and the van moved away down Ramillies place.

Alain closed his laptop and sat back in his large office chair. His heart was beating fast, and a smile broke across his face. All he had to do now was wait until the package made it securely from London to Paris, then after setting eyes on it himself, he would send it on its way to Berchtesgaden, where after many years, the painting would be reunited with its original companions. Alain could be forgiven for thinking that his work was almost complete. He had left no stone unturned in the recovery of these artworks, made sure that all bases were covered, that nothing could or would lead the authorities to his doorstep.

Up to now, everything had gone smoothly. There was of course the odd speed bump, but nothing that couldn't be ironed out by Mr. Hassan and a large brown envelope, a bank transfer, or, if needed, a visit from Knowles and his squad.

CHAPTER FORTY-TWO

London

Almost a month earlier, Michel and Antoine had been busy packing up the house and locking down the restaurant in London ahead of their filming trip to France. After a long day of cleaning the kitchen down Antoine had crawled up the stairs to his bed, not having done that amount of physical work for a long time. Michel had made sure Antoine was asleep before he made his way out the front door of the house and sat on the bottom step of their stoop. He looked at his watch. Right on cue a familiar car swung onto Ramillies place stopping outside the restaurant. The window rolled down revealing Mr. Lewis Ralph.

"Did you get it?" asked Michel.

"It's in the boot," Lewis replied. Michel seemed mightily relieved.

"Great, swing round to the back, and we'll get it inside while Antoine is asleep."

"Did the payment go through?" Lewis asked.

"Did it this morning," Michel answered as he stood heading back into the house. "And thank you," he added. "You know, not just for the money, but for all the help, everything."

"I just hope you know what you're doing."

Michel paused for a moment.

"You and me both," he said as he closed the front door and made his way down and out to the back of the restaurant.

Michel opened the door into the backyard and watched as Lewis pulled his car in.

Lewis opened the boot. He pulled out a flat object, that had been covered with a blanket, and handed it to Michel. The two men went into the cellar and closed the door behind them. Michel placed the object on a table in the center of the room and slowly pulled the blanket away.

"Jesus," he said as he saw what had been covered up. "It's perfect," he added.

"I should hope so," said Lewis, looking at the object. "Or you've just blown three thousand pounds of my pension," he added.

As Michel pulled the remaining corner of the blanket away from the object, he revealed it in all its glory. An exact replica of the painting that sat fifteen feet above their heads on the wall behind the chef's table in the restaurant's dining room.

"It's incredible," Michel said as he took the painting in. "I mean, who could tell the difference?"

"Well not you or me," replied Lewis. "But then again, we're not the ones you're trying to fool, right?" Lewis shook Michel's hand and headed back to his car and pulled away into the crisp London night.

Michel moved quickly back into the restaurant with the replica painting. He stopped at the door and listened. He heard the familiar sound of Antoine snoring. Perfect, he thought, he could now take his time with the next delicate part of his plan. Michel put the blanket wrapped painting on the chef's table, and moved to the wall. He slowly took the painting down and placed it on the table next to its doppelgänger. He stood and looked at the two paintings side by side.

Like a mirror image, he thought to himself.

He sat at the table and started to remove the original painting from its frame, taking his time, making sure not to damage either the painting or the frame. After almost an hour, he had replaced it with the replica. He returned the replica to the wall behind the chef's table. He slowly rolled the original painting up and put it in a cardboard tube he'd brought up from the cellar. As he got to the door of the dining room and went to turn out the lights, he looked back at the replica now sitting on the wall, where the original had hung. This was a gamble, a huge one, and it was being made by the only de la Rue man who'd never placed a bet in his life. Michel turned the lights off and headed up to his bedroom. He took the cardboard tube containing the rolled up original and placed it carefully into his suitcase. As he lay in bed, too tired to sleep, his phone beeped. A text message lit up on the screen.

"Hope you're happy with the result," Michel read. "BT."

"*I* am, but it's not me who needs to be convinced," he typed. A moment later his phone beeped again.

"I've managed to fool the world once before remember?" the message read.

"It's not the world I'm worried about, it's Alain Deschamps," Michel mumbled to himself as he lay back and closed his eyes.

CHAPTER FORTY-THREE

Paris, early 1980s

Bobby Thewlis was a master of his craft. At the peak of his powers he was regarded a world authority in his field. What began as a hobby, soon became his job, and quickly turned into his passion and an obsession. Thewlis had spent the majority of his career in the classroom, working as an art teacher in a variety of secondary schools across the south of England. Born in Norwich, he moved to London to study art at the University of the Arts in High Holborn. Thewlis, like most artists, dreamed of having his work talked about, amongst those in the much revered art circles, to have his work held in high esteem. Thewlis, unlike most artists he studied with, achieved this, although not in the usual manner or form.

Having spent several years teaching, unhappily, he quit his job, packed a bag, and headed to Paris, to develop his skills, to follow what he believed to be his true path in life. What little money he had saved meant his early days in Paris were spent taking both language and art classes, and sitting on the banks of the Seine painting.

He made small money taking menial jobs, which afforded him time to spend doing what he loved more than anything, painting, honing his craft. He spent his weekends amongst fellow artists at Place du Tertre in Montmartre, where tourists and locals could swarm around the main square, watching artists create, ponder, and discuss their latest works. Another reason Thewlis and his fellow artists made the weekly pilgrimage to this venue was that it gave them the chance to potentially sell their works, funding their artistic endeavors, and negating the need for them to hold down regular, menial jobs. The weekend vigil to Montmartre was what Thewlis looked forward to most. There he could simply paint, improve his work, and develop his own style.

One spring Sunday morning, Thewlis had taken up his regular pitch on the main square, close to the Chez Eugène restaurant. Even though he was deep in concentration working on his latest piece, Bobby noticed that a man was watching him closely. The man left the square for a while and returned, standing behind Bobby just over his shoulder and watching him paint. Bobby was well used to this, most of the tourists would hover around the artists, never intending to buy a painting, treating the square like an open-air gallery. That was fair enough; they didn't *have* to buy a piece, but everyone knew that this was how these artists survived. Bobby didn't really mind these people. He wasn't like most of the other artists, who all looked like they were suffering while painting. Bobby enjoyed the process and was happy to take and answer questions from whichever direction they came. As Thewlis was nearing the end of his day's painting, he noticed the same man reappear again. The man had now found a chair and was sitting close, watching intensely as Bobby painted.. Most of the artists had left for the day; there was a chill in the air and only the hardcore artists were left now. As Bobby finished up, he started to clear his things, a slow ritual that included washing his brushes, cleaning down his pallet, and gently wrapping his canvas. The man spoke as Bobby tinkered with his equipment.

"Chagall, Dubuffet?" the man said.

"Pardon?"

"Your influences?" said the man. "I can see flashes of Chagall in there."

He pulled his chair beside Bobby, but didn't take his eyes off the painting. Bobby looked at the painting intensely.

"I *like* Chagall," said Bobby. "But then again, who doesn't?"

"Indeed," replied the man. "Shame most people don't have the resources to own one."

"Most of the tourists here today look like they couldn't even afford a piece by me, let alone Chagall," said Bobby.

"Well the day isn't over yet," the man said as he took his wallet out of his pocket. "How much?" He pointed to Bobby's painting.

Bobby was taken aback.

"Make me an offer," replied Bobby. The man sat back in his chair and studied the painting one more time.

"Twenty."

"Thirty," replied Bobby.

The man took another long look at the painting, and extended his hand out.

"Twenty-five, and we have a deal," he said. Bobby quickly shook the man's hand, glad to have made the sale, his first in three weeks.

"Got myself a bargain I reckon," the man said.

"Well, I don't know about that, but I appreciate the business," replied Bobby. He removed the painting from his easel, and began to wrap it for its new owner.

"Do you do commissions?" the man asked.

"Not to date, no, but I wouldn't say no to the work. What have you got in mind?"

"I've always fancied having my own Chagall."

"But you can't afford it, right?"

"Something like that," replied the man. "Thing is, I know a lot of people who can't, seems a shame to deprive them."

"I'm not with you," said Bobby as he zipped up his coat and put his scarf around his neck.

"Why don't we grab a bite, and I can explain," said the man, pointing toward the nearby café. "I believe this place is famous for its croque monsieur?"

"Best in the city by all accounts." They moved off toward the café. "I'm Bobby Thewlis by the way," he said to the man.

"Alain Deschamps," he replied as he pushed open the door to the café.

CHAPTER FORTY-FOUR

London, present day

After meeting years ago in Paris, Alain and Bobby became well acquainted. Bobby earned a substantial living, having been convinced by his new patron that by producing a line of high-end forgeries, Alain could move them on for a large profit through his Paris based studio/gallery.

Bobby's works, which had been painstakingly put together in a small studio room where Bobby lived in the east of Paris, eventually found their way onto the walls of Alain's gallery, at which point Alain would close the sale with the unsuspecting clients, having provided full provenance and certification from various art experts. Those experts were on Deschamps's payroll and would happily certify anything, for the right price. Bobby's reproductions of some of the most famous paintings in the world ended up on the walls of private collectors from Asia to North America, some fetching upward of half a million pounds, for which Bobby received a two percent commission. Never more.

Bobby was very aware of his junior position within Alain's operation, and over the years it started to get under his skin. Not being compensated sufficiently ate away at him, resulting in a growing level of mistrust for his only patron. Bobby felt he and his work were hugely undervalued. His partner took all of the plaudits and most of the money as a result of Bobby's toil, and over time Bobby's protests became more and more vocal. Alain wearied listening to Bobby's complaints. Having grown his operation over the years, Alain no longer relied on *just* Bobby to produce the forgeries. Over time he'd recruited several artists and forgers, but the quality of Bobby's work was head and shoulders above the other artists. However, as a result of Bobby's now constant bickering, Alain began to cut the amount of commissions Bobby was receiving.

Bobby, now a daily source of complaint, would constantly call and even doorstep Alain at his gallery, threatening at one point to reveal to a potential customer that he was the real artist of the piece they were about to purchase. It almost came to the point where Alain would have to call in the services of

Mr. Hassan, but thankfully for Bobby, it never came to that. The fate Alain bestowed on Bobby was worse than a bullet in the head from Hassan.

When Alain Deschamps decided he was done with you, you didn't get a farewell party and severance payment. Alain wanted to put Bobby out of business, *his* business. Not only would Bobby no longer be working for Alain, Alain made sure he'd never work for anyone. Alain commissioned Bobby to do a painting by the renowned artist Jean-Baptiste-Camille Corot, a notoriously difficult painter to forge. Many artists had tried but failed to reproduce the levels of skill and lightness of touch on display in Corot's work. Bobby loved a challenge, and Alain knew this. He knew that this commission alone would keep Bobby busy, and quiet, for months. Bobby thought this commission would be his crowning glory, the one that would put him on the global map as a forger of note, one that would have his forger peers talk about him in glowing terms. Alain's plan was that the replica was to be placed into auction in the Hôtel Drouot auction house, having been authenticated by one of the many experts on Deschamps's payroll. Bobby got to work, and after seven months when it was finished, he delivered it as normal to Alain's gallery. Alain thanked him profusely and said of the painting that it was Bobby's finest work to date. The date of the auction was set for three weeks later, and Bobby took up a position at the back of the room as the piece sat on an easel beside the auctioneer. It was the main attraction at that day's sales event. It was valued at almost two million pounds, and if it sold at the asking price, this would net Thewlis around forty thousand pounds, his biggest commission payment to date. Enough he thought to finally get him out from under the shadow of Deschamps. Bobby wanted to do this final piece, leave Paris, retire back to the UK, and live off his ill-gotten gains in blissful obscurity.

The painting sold that day for just over 2.5 million pounds, and over the next few months, Bobby sat and waited for his windfall to arrive from Alain. Normally his commission would arrive no later than one week after a confirmed sale, but it never came. What did come was a knock on his door a matter of weeks later. When he answered it, he was greeted by a couple of plain clothes detectives, accompanied by uniformed officers.

They were there to arrest Bobby, who had been identified as the master forger behind the painting that had been sold in Paris a few months earlier. The person who had bought that piece, had had their own independent expert look into the painting shortly after the sale, and having found some small discrepancies, he alerted the auction house, and the authorities. The police didn't take long to track down the gallery who donated the painting, the Alain Deschamps Gallery. Alain, having planned this all along, quickly gave Bobby up, as part of a plea bargain which saw their investigations go no further into the Deschamps Gallery.

Bobby was represented by a court-appointed solicitor. He was sentenced to six years in prison, served two, and was released back into society, eventually returning back to London. Bobby wanted to retire back home in a blaze of glory, but instead he returned under a cloud of darkness, his reputation in tatters. His career, if you could call it that, was over.

He took a small flat in London's East End, settled into a life of anonymity, but carried on painting. Over the following years he had approaches from journalists offering him money to tell his story. All were turned down. He would also be visited from time to time by the British flying squad, eager to see if another forgery they'd uncovered was made by his hand. He cooperated with them as best he could, but never gave up any of his former colleagues.

He was harboring a grudge toward Deschamps, for good reason, and that grudge would fester. Bobby just wanted to paint for his own reasons, and to be left alone. The grudge turned into hatred, and disgust, at himself mainly, that he'd let himself be sold down the river as easily as he was. A life of solitude and desolation lay ahead of him. But when he had a knock on the door one morning a number of years later, the light was soon to return to his day.

CHAPTER FORTY-FIVE

London

Lewis Ralph and Michel stood in the rain at Bobby's door waiting for an answer. Lewis knew Bobby from old, having been part of the legal team in the British consulate in Paris that helped convict Bobby. Lewis hated the fact that Deschamps had walked away a free man from the charges that saw Bobby Thewlis imprisoned. He'd always felt like the authorities missed a beat, having passed up the chance to dig further into the Deschamps Gallery. Lewis had met Bobby on several occasions while he was in custody in Paris and had always found him to be amicable, polite, soft-spoken, and cooperative. When Bobby eventually answered the door, he instantly recognized Mr. Lewis Ralph.

"Oh dear, what have I done now, Lewis?" he asked.

"Nothing, Bobby, we just want to have a chat, that's all."

"We?" said Bobby referring to Michel.

"Michel de la Rue," Michel said, offering his hand. Bobby shook it unenthusiastically.

"Have we met?" Bobby asked.

"No," replied Michel. "But we have someone in common. Alain Deschamps."

Bobby's face changed, like a cold breeze had swept across it.

"Can we come in?" asked Mr. Ralph. Bobby hesitated for a moment, and then swung the front door open and walked away down the hallway. Lewis and Michel followed Bobby into the house, and sat and talked with him for almost two hours in his dingy sitting room. At the beginning of the conversation, Bobby's answers were staccato. He still didn't trust Mr. Ralph, even though he'd been the fairest of the prosecution team that eventually helped convict him. But as the meeting went on, as Michel and Lewis laid out their proposal, he soon became deadly interested in what they had to say.

Bobby had turned down many propositions over the years, but when this one was laid out in front of him, he signed up immediately, not for the money, but for the chance to finally get one over on the man who had ruined his life, his career. After the three men had finished talking, Bobby led his two visitors down the hall toward the front door. All three shook hands, and said their goodbyes.

"So," said Mr. Ralph. "You're happy enough you can get it done in that timeframe?"

"Normally, not a chance," Bobby replied. "But because of who this is for, and what it will do, I'll make bloody sure it's on time."

"Then I'll make sure the money is in your account on the eighteenth," replied Michel, shaking Bobby's hand.

Lewis and Michel left the house, and Bobby returned to the poky one-bed studio flat on the first floor of the house. He stood looking at his easel which was leaning up against the wall in the corner of his room near the window. It was covered in a muslin cloth, gathering dust. He hadn't painted anything for what seemed like an age. He walked over to the easel and removed the cloth. He sat on the little stool in front of the blank canvas. He blew on the easel and the room was suddenly filled with dust. He took a pouch of tobacco from his cardigan pocket and a packet of cigarette papers from the table beside him, rolled a cigarette and lit it. He again stared at the blank piece of canvas in front of him. He took a large photo from his pocket that Michel had given him, and, using a small bulldog clip that was sitting on the edge of the table, he pinned it to the top right-hand corner of the canvas.

"Right," he said to himself as the cigarette slowly burned between his lips. He leaned over and picked up his palette and brush. "Best get to work," he mumbled as he focused in on the photograph.

It was a photo of the Bontemps painting from Michel's restaurant, and it was now the subject of Bobby Thewlis' latest masterpiece.

CHAPTER FORTY-SIX

Outskirts of Paris, present day.

As the de la Rue brothers and their film crew approached their final food festival before arriving in Paris and the closing banquet, there was an air of excitement among the group. The festival, La Fête de la Gastronomie, was an annual event with lots of food on show, as well as live music, and a number of amusement arcade rides and stalls. Donald's plan was to film the brothers working their way through the festival getting shots of them on the Ferris wheel, tucking into food, and interacting with the locals amidst the many beer tents on the site. As the crew arrived in Rosny-sous-Bois, parking was at a premium. Olly, who was driving the crew van, used all of his local knowledge and some rather coarse French language, to wangle his way into a nearby service yard in the grounds of the Parc Jean Decesari. The crew unloaded their equipment, and Donald was prepping his shot list, when Michel sat in beside him in the crew van.

"Can I have a quick word?" Michel asked.

"Sure, what's up?"

"I need to take a couple of hours off later, there's something I need to attend to."

Donald looked up from his notes and frowned.

"Take some time off?" he said. "This isn't *Cool Hand Luke*, Michel, you don't have to ask my permission to leave for an hour or two, as long as you're back before the camera rolls it's fine."

"No," replied Michel. "I realize that, but I need you to come with me, I need your, em, *expertise*."

Donald looked puzzled. "My *expertise*?"

"Yes," replied Michel. "And your microphones."

"Why?"

Michel took a deep breath before he spoke.

"I need you to come with me, fit me with one of those radio mics, and secretly record a meeting I'm going to have with my ex-girlfriend, a journalist from *Le Monde*, and a high-ranking officer from Interpol."

Silence.

Donald's face froze. After a long moment he spoke.

"Did you just say Interpol?"

Michel nodded.

"Well, forgive me for asking. And believe me there are about sixty-two questions I *could* ask you right now, but why do you need me to come with you, why am I afforded the chance to become an accomplice to whatever the hell you're involved in?"

Michel took a pack of cigarettes from his pocket, lit one and offered one to Donald.

"Antoine isn't fully aware of what's really going on here," Michel replied, "and I'd rather it stayed that way, at least until we get to Paris, *then* I can fill him in."

"Right," replied Donald, taking a long drag on his cigarette. "Well *I'm* going to need to know what the fuck is going on before I even *think* about tagging along, let alone bring a fucking microphone with me."

"Of course. I'll fill you in on the way over there later."

"Over where?"

"To the meeting. Now let's get this sequence shot so we can get the hell out of here." He jumped out of the crew van and headed over to his brother and the crew. Michel stopped and leaned back in the van window.

"And please, let's keep this between us, okay?" he said as he walked away. Donald sat in his seat, watching Michel help Phil as they carried his equipment over to where the first setup was going to be.

"It's always the fucking quiet ones," he muttered to himself. He flicked his cigarette out of the window and jumped out of the crew van.

Despite Michel's bizarre request to Donald, the day's filming went perfectly. The brothers carried out every direction and instruction thrown at them by Donald, which meant that his shot list was complete, and they could call it a day earlier than planned. Donald watched the brothers mingle and schmooze with the locals and tourists, and paid close attention to Michel. He didn't seem to be a man who was preoccupied with anything in particular, didn't seem jumpy or jittery. Donald concluded that this was probably some sort of final-day shooting prank, a wind-up instigated by Michel, that the rest of the crew were more than likely in on. As the crew were wrapping up the equipment and loading their van,

Donald approached with his arms filled with portions of candy floss, a little treat for the crew.

"Here we go, chaps," Donald said as he started dishing out the sweet treats. "Courtesy of what's left in the petty cash envelope."

"Almost there then," said Stephen the sound operator. As the crew sat around munching on candy floss. "Only two days to go, huh?"

"You know what," said Phil. "Been a really good job this." He picked his teeth with the empty candy floss stick in his hand. "I didn't expect much when I met you fellas back in Calais." He nodded over at Antoine and Michel. "But you're alright in my book."

"Fucking hell," said Olly. "That's as close to a marriage proposal as you'll get from him." The crew all laughed.

"Been a pleasure for us too," said Antoine. "Right, little brother?"

Michel didn't answer. He now seemed lost in his own world. The enormity of what lay ahead of him over the next two days looked like it was sitting heavily on his shoulders all of a sudden. Antoine nudged his brother.

"Eh?" said Michel. "No, right, yes, it's been great."

Donald watched Michel. This meeting tonight was definitely a wind up he thought, and now was his chance to prove it, let the gang know that he was in on the "joke" too.

"Right then," Donald said, standing up and brushing himself down. "If we're all done, it's time to get Michel here miked up and over to his secret meeting with Interpol!" Not a flicker or response from the crew.

"His meeting with who?" Antoine asked.

"You know," replied Donald. "The big secret meeting with the journalist and Interpol and his ex-girlfriend, the one he wants me to secretly record?" The crew looked at each other, and then to Michel, who stood there looking like a sheep caught in the headlights.

"Christ," Michel said. "What happened to keeping it between us?" Antoine stood and walked toward his brother.

"What's going on, kiddo? Sounds like you've something you need to tell me." Michel looked at his brother and then back to Donald, who now realized that this wasn't a set-up, and that he'd just broken one of his own cardinal rules of filming: keep the talent happy.

"Sorry, Michel, I thought it was a wind up!" Donald said.

"You're right, Antoine," Michel said. "Bear with me, and I'll fill you in on the way." He looked at his watch. "We need to go." He moved to the driver's door and stopped looking back at the group of now more than fascinated men. "Get in, all of you," Michel said as he opened the door and started the van. The crew all stood and looked at each other for a moment, and then they piled into their van. Antoine, however, didn't move. He stood firm on the same spot. "Give me a minute," Michel shouted at the crew as he stepped toward his brother.

"Are you in some sort of trouble?" Antoine asked.

"No. At least I don't *think* I am."

"We don't keep secrets from each other, Michel, we never have," Antoine said sternly. "So, I'll ask you again, are you in trouble?"

"No. Now if you'll get in the van, I'll tell you everything, we have to go, now." Antoine looked at Michel, then slowly started walking toward the campervan and jumped in. As the two vans pulled away from their parking spot in the service yard, an air of silence filled the interior of both of them.

"Does this mean we're not going for pints tonight?" said Olly in the back of the crew van.

"Shush!" shouted Donald and pointed at his ears.

"What?" replied Stephen.

"My headphones, give me my headphones, now!" he shouted.

"Why?" said Stephen as he handed Donald the headphones.

"They've still got their radio mics on from filming; turn them both on so I can hear what the fuck is being said in that van!" he screamed. Stephen scrambled for his recording pack, and quickly flicked both mics on. Donald, Olly, and Stephen, *all* now wearing headphones, were tuned in to the conversation happening in the van in front of them.

"Where are we headed?" asked Antoine.

"Our old stomping ground," replied Michel. "Over to Rue Pavée, to the library."

"That's a forty-five-minute drive in this traffic," said Antoine, looking at his watch. "Should give you time to tell me what the hell is going on."

Michel looked in the rearview mirror at the film crew in the van behind. They were all staring back at him, as was Antoine, all waiting for him to start talking.

"Press record," said Donald as the two vans turned onto the motorway and drove toward Paris and the city center.

CHAPTER FORTY-SEVEN

OVER THE NEXT FORTY minutes Michel spoke, and everyone listened. Antoine sat in the passenger seat in taking every word in, glued to his brother, only breaking out of the trance occasionally to swear at a motorist or pedestrian who was impeding their progress. Michel started at the very beginning, explaining to Antoine that soon after he'd met Deschamps for the first time at a charity lunch, he began looking in to Deschamps and his businesses.

"Due diligence," Antoine said.

"Served us well thus far, hasn't it?"

Michel began to explain that he discovered Deschamps wasn't the saintly, generous philanthropist that his public image portrayed. He was in fact a criminal, with a past, something that was confirmed to Michel when he called in the services of their friend Lewis Ralph. He explained that he and Lewis had spoken at length about the court case that saw Lewis and Alain come face-to-face, which ultimately resulted in Bobby Thewlis being sentenced to six years. Michel noted Lewis and his colleagues disgust at the authorities effectively letting Deschamps walk free after negotiating a plea bargain. Deschamps was also willing to give the authorities more than just Bobby Thewlis on a plate, he gave up numerous criminals across the globe, former associates of Deschamps that had wronged him at some point. As a result, authorities across the continent sent numerous criminals to prison for a total of almost three hundred years.

As Alain gave up one after another, he felt he had banked some sort of goodwill currency with the authorities. After all, the authorities had their pound of flesh jailing these career criminals, which gave the public the opinion that they were hard at work catching and prosecuting major felons across the continent. At the same time, they had removed a large majority of Deschamps's competition. It was a masterstroke by Deschamps.

Antoine was gripped by what Michel was telling him about Deschamps, but also growing more and more frustrated with his brother.

"Why the hell did you agree to put us through this trip then? We're working for an archcriminal for Christ's sake!"

Michel put his hand in the air to shush his brother.

"Shut up and listen, I'm getting to that," he replied. Antoine fell quiet again and lit another cigarette.

Michel carried on talking, telling Antoine that after Alain walked away from all charges leveled against him, he presumed that the investigation into him and his businesses ceased that day. It didn't. Lewis Ralph and the rest of the legal team had never dropped the investigation into Alain. Further research and conversations with Mr. Ralph and his contacts, led Michel down another line of interest. He started to look into the paintings that went through Deschamps's gallery over the years, and they began to notice patterns, certain clients buying certain types of paintings, by certain artists. Almost always these sales went through one particular auction house in Paris, the Hôtel Drouot, the same auction house that Alain used while taking Bobby Thewlis down, and the same auction house where Alain Deschamps was planning to unveil all six of the *Obscurum Amicis* collection.

Digging further into the art, the paintings, and the artists, Michel ended up steeping himself in the world of Jewish art, specifically stolen art from World War Two, as this was where most of the works in Deschamps's gallery either started, ended up, or passed through. Working closely alongside Mr. Ralph, and some allies of his among the intelligence community, Michel was soon made aware of the legend of the *Obscurum Amicis*.

"I don't understand where this is all going?" said Antoine.

"There's more you need to know," replied Michel. "And I promise, I'll tell you *everything*, after I get this meeting out of the way."

"You haven't even told me *who* you're meeting?"

"Someone from Interpol," said Michel. "There's also a journalist tagging along." He paused before he lets Antoine know the name of the other attendee. "And Lucy."

"Lucy?" shouted Antoine.

"Who the fuck is Lucy?" Donald said to himself as he sat in the van behind the brothers, pressing the headphones over his ears.

"What has Lucy got to do with all of this?" asked Antoine, now losing his patience.

"She works for Alain," he said, watching Antoine put his heads in his hands, now totally overloaded with what he was hearing. "She's not *involved* though," Michel said, in an attempt to calm his brother down. "According to Lewis, she's got nothing to do with the underbelly of the Deschamps organization. Lewis had run Lucy's name through all of his contacts to see if she had any hand act or part in Alain's below-the-line dealings, and her name come back clean."

Antoine pulled alongside the curb and stopped just down the road from the library. Michel grabbed his rucksack and jumped out of their campervan. Antoine joined him at the back of the van.

"You have to trust me Antoine, just let me get through this next hour, and I'll finish explaining everything," Michel said.

Donald and the crew pulled up in their van right behind the brothers.

Antoine stood for a moment trying to digest all that he had been told.

"I'm going in there with you," Antoine said. "I'm not letting you walk into something like this, *alone*, even though I still don't know what the fuck is going on."

Michel stared at his brother and recognized that look Antoine was giving him. It reminded him of his father. Antoine was not just the brother who *looked* most like their father, but he was the one that *behaved* most like him. Antoine was stubborn, just like their father. Michel knew that this was an argument he wasn't going to win. He nodded at his brother, as Donald now joined them at the back of the campervan.

"Better make sure the batteries on these are charged," Antoine said to Donald as the rest of the crew emerged from the back of their van.

"Stephen, change the batteries in both mic packs," Donald ordered. Stephen moved behind the two brothers and started fiddling with their mic packs which they both still had clipped to their belts from filming earlier. Watching Stephen, Michel now realized that both he and Antoine had been wearing the mics all along.

"So, no need for me to explain anything to *you* then," he said, looking at Donald and the crew.

"Nope," Donald replied, tapping the headphones that were still on his head.

"Look, I've no idea how this is going to go," said Michel. "I have a plan that I want to run by these people. Let me do the talking and we'll see if they go for it."

Donald looked at Antoine.

"And if they don't go for it?" said Antoine. Michel paused, zipped up his jacket, and turned to look down toward the library where he'd spent so many happy hours.

"Well then you'd better ring TF1," Michel said to Donald. "See if they can recommend a good lawyer because we are about to accuse their newest shareholder of being one of the biggest criminal masterminds in Europe." He started to walk down the street toward the library.

Antoine jogged up behind his brother and put his arm around him in a sign of unity. Michel felt a change in himself. His brother, his protector, was at his side, where he belonged.

CHAPTER FORTY-EIGHT

INSIDE THE BUILDING THE librarian on duty, Ms. Martial, was behind her desk trying to catch up on some college work she'd failed to hand in earlier that week. The job of night clerk could hardly be classed as hard labour. Her duties included the odd bout of stamping books in and out, and a twice nightly replacing of books that had been read and spread across the vast room in the center of the building. One of the meeting rooms had been booked on behalf of a Mr. Pieters and as result there was more activity in the building than usual.

An hour ago, two police cars had arrived, delivering Mr. Pieters and a number of guests, among them Lucy and Fabian. As the group entered the room, four uniformed officers replaced Ms. Martial at her desk, despatching her to start her book collection rounds a little earlier than normal. Inside the meeting room, Pieters and a number of the Interpol operatives had set up two notice boards in the room, and pinned all sorts of photos, lists, maps, and other paraphernalia there. Pieters was going to lay everything out for Michel, under the presumption that he knew nothing of what Alain Deschamps was planning.

Lucy and Fabian sat a table in the center of the room, watching Pieters operative's scurry around getting in each other's way as they set up the temporary field office.

"Is all of this totally necessary?" asked Fabian pointing to the notice boards. Pieters stopped what he was doing and came to the table and sat down.

"Michel de la Rue is a target of Alain Deschamps," Pieters said. "And it's my job this evening to gain his confidence to make sure that he agrees to work with us."

Lucy shook her head. "How do you know this won't spook Michel, make him run a kilometer and a half in the opposite direction?"

"Well you know him better than anybody else in this room, will it?" Pieters replied.

Lucy stood from the table and went to help herself to a coffee from the small flasks that had been set up in the room for them.

"You're right," she said. "I do know Michel better than you. He's much *like* you, Mr. Pieters, a man of detail and precision, and Michel knows the value of information. I've no doubt that Michel will sit attentively and listen to what you're going to tell him, but don't think for a second that he'll just jump when you ask him to, he's a man who likes to make his own mind up. I know that to my cost."

Pieters smiled at Lucy.

"I appreciate that," he said. "And that's why it was important for us that *you* are here in the room. I want him to feel comfortable enough to make an informed decision, quickly, as I'm sure you've realized by now, time is against us. Michel needs to know that we're all on the same side here."

Lucy sat back down at the table, point taken.

"What's the latest from you, Fabian," Pieters said. "It's been a couple of days, have you heard from Deschamps?" Lucy spoke before Fabian got a chance to answer.

"He hasn't been seen at the office in days," Lucy said. "Hasn't been seen since he got back from Geneva," she added.

Fabian reached for his bag, pulled his laptop out, opened it, and clicked on the keyboard.

"Hold on, he did touch base with my editor; he got an email from Deschamps," he said. "Wanted an update on how his profile piece was coming along."

"And?" asked Pieters.

Fabian spun the laptop around so both Pieters and Lucy could read the screen. "My editor sent Alain a rough draft of the piece that I'd started working on, which he then added to, all nice and light, nothing that Deschamps would object to. My editor is more than happy to play his part in your plan."

"Good," replied Pieters.

"Plan?" asked Lucy. Fabian looked at Pieters and gave him a look to suggest that it was time to let Lucy in on a little more of what was going on. She needed to know why Fabian was there, and what part he was playing in this investigation.

"Fabian's editor is a good friend of mine, and a good friend of Interpol's," Pieters said. "His editor had commissioned a profile piece on Deschamps for *Le Monde*." Pieters stood and brought the laptop over to Lucy so she could see what Fabian and his editor had written about Alain. "This piece is not the piece that will be published. This was a piece written to keep Alain happy, the *real* article, which Fabian is currently writing, will document Deschamps's downfall, arrest, and finally his prosecution." Lucy quickly skimmed through the article on the screen.

Pieters continued, "During their first interview some weeks ago, Deschamps told Fabian that he was planning to donate some paintings to an auction house, paintings that *we've* been looking for years."

"Okay," replied Lucy. "And how is that a crime?"

Pieters took a file from one of his colleagues and put it in front of Lucy.

"The crime is that the paintings he's planning to donate are fakes, or at least that's what I believe, but I also believe that Deschamps has the genuine paintings hidden away, and is planning to sell *those* to an unnamed buyer. Having received glorious press coverage about the paintings through *Le Monde*, the article in the paper would be the signal that the unknown buyer was waiting for, to let him know Deschamps had gathered all the genuine paintings together, and was ready to sell. Michel, we believe, is in possession of the final remaining painting that Alain needs to complete this collection." Lucy started to flick through the file and looked up at Fabian who nodded, confirming to her that what Pieters was telling her was true.

"We believe that Deschamps is planning to steal that painting from Michel's restaurant in London," said Fabian. "That's why he's had Michel and Antoine running around France for the past number of weeks." Lucy looked up from the file at the wall of notice boards in front of her. The operatives had pinned large photos of the paintings up there, and as they put the final one up beside the other five, her eyes widened.

"That's Michel's mother's painting," she said. The operative stepped back revealing *Veiller Sur Toi* on the notice board.

"Correct," said Pieters.

One of the uniformed policemen keeping guard outside, knocked at the door and entered the room.

"He's here, sir," he said. "And he's not alone."

"Send them through," replied Pieters.

He clicked his fingers and told the operative to remove the photo of Michel's parents' painting from the notice board. He didn't want to alert Michel as soon as he came into the room. He wanted to build to that reveal; clearly there was an inner showman in Mr. Pieters.

The door to the room opened and the policeman was now accompanied by Michel and Antoine.

"Please, come in gentlemen, have a seat," said Pieters. He pointed to the table and beckoned to the officer to leave the room.

"Antoine!" said Lucy as she moved to greet him.

"Lucy, so good to see you," Antoine said as he hugged Lucy warmly.

"Michel," said Lucy as she turned to the younger brother. Michel threw the bag he was carrying to Antoine. He and Lucy hugged, awkwardly at first, and then a little longer than the hug that was afforded to Antoine, which surprised no one in the room, least of all Antoine.

"Sorry about this," Michel whispered in Lucy's ear. "I didn't want to get you mixed up in all of this."

Pieters remained standing as the brothers and Lucy sat.

"My brother, Antoine," said Michel. Pieters shook his hand, then Michel's.

"A pleasure to meet you both," Pieters replied. "We appreciate you coming to meet us, Michel."

"I'm gathering you didn't call me over here to recommend something from the fiction section," said Michel.

Pieters smiled.

"I'm afraid it's a little more serious than that."

Another knock at the door saw the policeman again stick his head into the room.

"There's another one outside, insisting he comes in," he said. "Said he's with Mr. de la Rue?" Pieters took a moment to think.

"You have room for one more at the table, don't you?" Michel said.

"You invited your lawyer along?" said Pieters.

"Not my lawyer, no," replied Michel. "Someone who I think you need to meet, again."

Pieters looked puzzled.

The door opened to reveal Lewis Ralph standing there.

"What the hell is this, a reunion?" Antoine said as he nudged his little brother.

"Come in, Lewis," said Michel as he pulled another chair over to the table.

"Lewis Ralph," said Pieters. "My word, how long has it been?" He got up from the table and shook Lewis' hand.

"Too long, good to see you again, Lorenzo," said Lewis as he joined the others at the table. "I think you're going to enjoy talking to my friend Michel here, he just might be able to help pull a thorn from your side."

Pieters was now more intrigued with Michel de la Rue. This was going be an interesting meeting, to say the least.

Antoine looked over at Michel. Michel said nothing, he just winked back at his big brother. Pieters walked around the room, talking for more than fifteen minutes. Michel, Antoine, Lucy, Fabian, and Lewis all passed the files and photos amongst each other, studied them, and listened attentively to what Pieters had to say. Lorenzo ended his presentation by showing the group another range of photos, mug shots of the London crew Alain had instructed Hassan to put together for this final robbery.

As Michel looked through the mug shots, he immediately recognized Mr. Hassan, but didn't know any of the other three.

"I know this is a lot to take in," said Pieters as he joined the group at the table. "But after months of investigation on our behalf, we now feel that we are close to finally understanding what Deschamps is undertaking, and I'm afraid to say it involves a piece of property belonging to you and your family."

Pieters pointed at the photographs of the five paintings on the notice board and began explain details of the *Obscurum Amicis* collection.

Antoine hung on every word that came out of Pieters mouth as he expanded on his theory. Michel, on the other hand looked decidedly smug. He already knew *most* of the things that were being explained to them, so he just sat there, waiting for Pieters to finish, so he could present the results of his *and* Lewis Ralph's research.

Pieters handed the group another photograph.

"This was taken a number of weeks ago," Pieters said. "When our journalist Mr. Ritzier here, visited Deschamps in his Paris office." The group were looking at the photo that Fabian had taken of Alain standing in front of the five paintings in the private viewing room located behind his office in Paris.

"So, he already has five paintings from this *Obscurum Amicis* collection?" said Antoine.

"Yes, and no," replied Pieters. "We believe that the five paintings in the photo are fakes, copies, but that he *has* the genuine paintings in his possession in a location we have yet to pinpoint, and when he *completes* the collection, he plans to sell them."

"So why not just go to his office and arrest him then?" asked Antoine.

"Proof, Antoine, proof," replied Pieters. "He hasn't committed a crime as yet, we haven't enough evidence gathered for an arrest. We need proof that those five *are* forgeries, that he has the genuine paintings, *and* that he's planning to steal the sixth painting." Pieters then pointed to the operative standing nearest the notice board. The operative took another photo and pinned it on the board beside the other five.

"That's our painting!" said Antoine.

"And that, is the final piece of the *Obscurum Amicis* that is missing from Alain's collection," replied Pieters.

"That thing, really?" said Antoine.

"That *thing*, as you so eloquently put it, is worth around half a million pounds," Pieters said. Antoine froze in his chair.

"And this bastard is planning to steal it from us?" Antoine shouted.

"That is what we *think*, Antoine. We think that is why he has lured you and your brother away from your home, giving him and his team the time and opportunity to steal it." Antoine was beginning to get very uncomfortable in his seat and looked like he could blow at any moment. Michel put his hand on his brothers' arm, to calm him down.

"Our concern is that we are not sure when Deschamps is going to make his move," Pieters said. Michel raised his hand.

"He already has," said Michel.

The room fell silent.

CHAPTER FORTY-NINE

"I BEG YOUR PARDON?" replied Pieters.

"He already has, and I have all the proof you need." Michel stood up from the table and took his bag out from under Antoine's chair.

He placed several files in the middle of the table. Mr. Ralph put his briefcase on the table and followed suit. Michel launched into a speech that by the time he was finished would leave Pieters reeling.

"When I first met Alain Deschamps, he approached me with an offer of work, for me and my brother. He knew of my financial situation, our financial problems, because he had picked the brains of my former girlfriend, Lucy. It wasn't Lucy's fault that she got dragged into this; she was clearly of use to Deschamps, having been so close to me and my brother. Deschamps used her as bait, to get a private meeting with me at a charity lunch in London."

Michel spoke for more than ten minutes, telling Pieters and those gathered about how he'd started digging into Deschamps's background, and how it raised sufficient alarm bells to call in help from ex-British embassy staffer Mr. Ralph.

Pieters was impressed not just by the amount of information Michel had gathered, but by how he was delivering that information to this more than expectant gathering.

"Ever thought of a career in the police?" asked Pieters as Michel took his seat again at the table.

"I couldn't live on the salary," Michel replied, which gave the entire room cause to laugh.

"What you and your friend have uncovered is very impressive," Pieters said. "I do wish you it mentioned when we first spoke on the phone; you would have saved me going through the motions when you first came in here."

"Well, like you, Mr. Pieters, I wanted to make sure we were all on the same side, that we all had the same objective."

"We are, Michel, I can assure you," replied Pieters.

"Hang on," Antoine chirped in. "Pieters, you said Deschamps was *planning* to steal the painting from our restaurant. And then, Michel, you said, he already *had*?" he said pointing at his brother.

"Good point, Antoine," replied Pieters. He turned to Michel. "What did you mean by that?"

Mr. Ralph tapped Michel on the shoulder.

"If I may, Michel?" he said as he reached into his briefcase and pulled out an envelope, opened it, and laid two photographs onto the table. Pieters picked the photos up which featured the familiar Mr. Hassan. One photo showed him dressed in a British gas uniform, accompanied by three other men, entering the brother's restaurant in Soho. The other showed the same group exiting the restaurant; this time Hassan was carrying a large portfolio in his hands.

"And these were taken when?" asked Pieters.

"Forty-eight hours ago," said Michel. "From the roof of an apartment across the road from our restaurant, taken by a good friend of mine, who runs a photography studio there, and is a highly accomplished photographer as you can see. I've had him watching our building since we left London six weeks ago."

Antoine looked at his brother, with a puzzled look on his face.

"So that's that then, the painting is gone, they've already taken it?" Antoine asked. Pieters thumped his fist on the table, disgusted that he'd let the criminals get steps ahead of him and his team. He wasn't a fan of giving criminals the edge over him.

"Not *exactly*," replied Lewis.

Pieters raised his eyebrows and looked up at Lewis.

Michel he reached down to his bag again and pulled out a long cardboard tube. The group stood and watched as Michel popped the lid at the bottom of the tube, pulled out the contents, and carefully laid it out on the table. As he unrolled the contents, Antoine gasped. He and the group could now see a painting in front of them. The painting from their restaurant. All of the people gathered around the table looked between each other, and then over at Michel and Mr. Ralph.

"Is that what I think it is?" Fabian asked.

"It is, *this* is the sixth painting," replied Michel as he took the photo of Mr. Hassan and pointed at the portfolio case in Hassan's hands. "What he's carrying in *there*, is a copy, a forgery. Lewis and I swapped the paintings out the night before we left for France."

Pieters shook his head in both disbelief and admiration. The rest of group shared looks between them as they digested this latest revelation. Stunned, Antoine locked eyes with his little brother. A modest smile broke across Michel's face.

CHAPTER FIFTY

Lorenzo paced the room, slowly rubbing his stubbled chin. The others didn't move a muscle.

"The work that these two men have done," Pieters said as he pointed at Michel and Lewis, "May have brought us closer to putting Deschamps in jail, but believe me, we need to tread lightly. We have new information now that we will act upon straight away." He clicked his fingers to call two of the operatives over to the table. "Put eyes on the ports and airports, and circulate Hassan's photo to all border crossings." The two operatives scurried away out of the room.

"We need to let this play out," Pieters continued. "We let Deschamps take delivery of the fake painting; we need to see what his next move is from there. We have a list of possible locations where Deschamps may have the genuine paintings stashed, but we'll need time to work through it. This will help, no doubt, but Deschamps has properties all over the world, could be anywhere."

Michel put his hand on Pieters shoulder.

"Well, we've been working on that, too, haven't we?" Michel said to Lewis.

"We have," replied Lewis. "We'll explain all, perhaps after some tea, it's been a long day."

"Certainly, Mr. Holmes," replied Lorenzo, impressed by this newest of crime fighting double acts.

"I'm Watson in this arrangement, he's Sherlock," he added, pointing to Michel. Pieters walked to the door, opened it and beckoned a uniformed policeman into the room.

"Can you arrange some fresh tea and coffees?" he said to the officer.

"Right away, sir."

"Let's hear it then, gentlemen." He said to Lewis and Michel.

"Lorenzo, could you get me a map of eastern Germany, please?" Lewis asked.

Lorenzo smiled as he turned back toward the door to add another item to the tea and coffee order.

CHAPTER FIFTY-ONE

THE PRIVATE DINING AREA in the plush surroundings of the renowned Fermette Marbeuf restaurant near the Champs-Élysées, provided Alain with the perfect central location in which to hold meetings that required a little more privacy and panache than his Paris headquarters could offer. Alain's operations and business dealings were now so far and wide, he needed more people to manage them, and that meant there were more people that he had good reason to suspect, and fewer he could trust.

Bribery was rife in his business, border guards, local politicians, police sergeants, judges, and low-level criminals, all needed paying off in order to facilitate the uninterrupted movement of Alain's goods around the world. It was a huge operation; the day-to-day minutiae was handled by a small efficient team of people based in Germany, whom Alain implicitly trusted, while special operations like the robberies of paintings, and the removal of rival dealers, were handled by his most trusted ally, Mr. Hassan. Having watched Hassan and his squad carry out his latest special operation in London last night, Alain now needed to expedite the next and most crucial part of the plan. This was to be handled by Alain himself.

He sat at the table, trimming tiny leaves from a cigar he'd just cut for himself.

"Your usual, Mr. Deschamps?" said the waiter approaching the table.

"Yes, thank you, Davide," replied Alain. "But hold the main course until my guests have arrived and ordered." The waiter scuttled away toward the kitchen. Alain checked his watch. It was 1:37; his guests were late. Alain hated tardiness, particularly when a meeting held more than the regular level of importance, and if Alain was at the meeting, it was very important. As he fidgeted at the table, his phone rang.

"Yes," said Alain into the phone.

"My boy," said the voice on the other end of the line. "Are we on schedule?" It was Alain's uncle Karsten, calling from Germany, inquiring about the details of the cargo that was en route to him.

"It should be with you in two days, providing there are no obstacles."

"Knowing you, I'd imagine you've already smoothed the path for a safe journey."

"Indeed. And by the way, have the guest wing in the house made up." There was a pause on the line.

"Are you gracing us with a visit?"

"I'll be there to greet the cargo, to make sure my investment has arrived safe and sound."

"I look forward to seeing you," Karsten said as he hung up.

This last painting, the last part of his lifelong mission was almost complete, and Alain wanted to see it out to the end, personally. He was giving this operation, above all others, his undivided attention.

As Alain hung up, his guests arrived. He stood and greeted both men fondly.

"How was your flight?" Alain asked as the men took their seats at the table.

"Late departure, terrible seats, and the food was appalling," replied one of the men.

"Well, you do insist on flying coach, why, I'll never know," replied the other.

"Discretion, my boy, discretion," the first man replied.

The two men that sat opposite Alain were part of his inner circle, those select few that Alain trusted most with his business dealings, both of whom had profited hugely from their association with him over the years.

Arnold Silvestre was an elderly gentleman, held the post of general manager at Hôtel Drouot auction house in Paris for over thirty years. His relationship with Alain began through Alain's father, whom he had first met and began dealing with soon after Delitzsch Sr.'s arrival in Paris. He and Delitzsch Sr. struck up an affiliation that helped the Delitzsch family establish themselves on the art scene in Paris and across Europe. Silvestre could have been a poster boy for corruption, willing to take any risk in order to feather his own nest. Alain had put more forgeries through Silvestre's auction house than his father had, and that was some feat. This highly respected but utterly corrupt man, had the utmost respect for Alain. Alain had after all, with the proceeds from those many deals, put most of Silvestre's grandchildren through college.

The other man at the table, was like Alain in many ways. A similar age and upbringing, he too learned from the best in his business. Alberto Di Bona, a native of Alcamo, a coastal village in Sicily, had sat at his father's feet watching and learning. His father Pietro was known locally as *l'uomo specchio*, or "the mirror man." His father's gift was being able to replicate any document put in front of him, from just one quick viewing, with incredible dexterity and precision. Over the years his father had forged passports, driving licenses, marriage and death certificates, anything that was requested of him, for a small fee. His son Alberto carried on this trade, and spread his wings moving into art forgery, becoming one of the most sought after, and *hunted* forgers in the world. The key to Alberto's success was his anonymity. He'd never been arrested. He'd managed to avoid the authorities so well over the years, they didn't even have a photograph of him on file.

Alberto Di Bona's levels of professionalism and working methods soon brought him to the attention of Alain Deschamps. With the help of Mr. Hassan, Alain had tracked him down and recruited him to the small stable of forgers he had put together. After Alain had relinquished himself of Bobby Thewlis' services as a master forger, he needed to replace him. Alain moved quickly to elevate Alberto through the ranks and secure his exclusive services, flying to Sicily to meet with Alberto in person. At the end of a raucous lunch in the marina in Alcamo, they had struck a deal. Alberto was now going to reproduce paintings *exclusively* for Alain, for a much larger commission than the paltry two percent Bobby Thewlis was paid, but in Alain's eyes, it was worth every penny.

"It's been a while," said Alain to his guests.

"We are all busy men," replied Silvestre.

"Please, all you do now is play golf and top up your safety deposit boxes in Berne once a month," Alain said, which brought a laugh from the other men at the table. The waiter appeared at the table.

"Gentlemen, are we ready to order?" he said politely.

"Let me guess," said Arnold. "He's having the chateaubriand, medium rare." He gestured to Alain. The waiter nodded. "Well, I'd better go for the escargots then, no point in me ordering a steak too, because you'll give him the better cut, am I right?" Alain nodded; he was spot on.

"And for you, sir?" the waiter asked Alberto.

"The taglionini," said Alberto quickly.

"You can take the man out of Sicily, but not the Sicily out of the man," Alain said.

"We could show you French boys how to cook properly, if you came down off your culinary high horses for long enough," Alberto replied. The men laughed again. Alain leaned forward, to the conversation in a new direction.

"To business," he said. The smiles slowly rolled off the other men's faces. "Everything set on your end, Arnold?" Alain asked.

"Everything is on schedule, the exhibition followed by the sale are scheduled for the same day as requested, and we've already garnered interest in the pieces from Asia, the US, and of course, Russia," he answered.

"Perfect, the last piece is due to arrive here from London later this afternoon. I'd like you to come with me to check it over," Alain said, gesturing to Di Bona.

"Of course, I'd like to compare, see how good a job I've done," Di Bona replied.

"Speaking of," said Alain. "How's the mirror image?"

"Came in this morning through Milan, should be at your office by now," Di Bona answered.

"Gentlemen, I love dealing with people who know what they're doing," Alain said as he raised his glass to toast the company. The three men clinked glasses as the amuse-bouche arrived. "Thank you, Davide," said Alain as the maître d' laid the plates on the table.

"Bon appetite," said Alain as he sliced into the food on his plate.

Later that afternoon, Alain and Alberto left his office in a chauffeur driven car, having collected Alberto's cargo. They were now heading toward a warehouse in the Bassin de l'Arsenal area of Paris, one of several industrial properties Alain owned around the French capital. It was where he had arranged to meet Mr. Hassan and his newest acquisition, which had arrived in from London. Hassan had taken the car ferry from the UK and driven down toward Paris. Alain and Hassan preferred this method of transport, as the border security was somewhat looser than at the major airports, that and the fact that Deschamps had most of the border guards on the French side of the crossing on his payroll, which made it a swift passage through for Hassan and whatever illicit cargo he was transporting. Alain's car pulled into the warehouse car park. Both men left the car and headed into the building. It was a vast space, some ten thousand square feet, with rows of empty storage racks seemed to stretch for kilometers filling the space. Alain and Alberto headed for the offices on the premises, where they were greeted by Hassan.

"All good?" asked Alain.

"Like clockwork," Hassan replied. He showed Alain into the office and gave him his first glimpse of the recently arrived painting.

Hassan had mounted it on an easel in the corner. Alain moved toward it, barely believing that he was about to lay his eyes on it.

"Incredible," Alain said as he stood gazing at the painting in all its glory. "Not the finest piece of art in the world, but boy am I glad to see it, to finally *have* it." Alberto joined Alain and asked if he could take it from the easel and put in on the table in the office to examine it further.

"Please do." Alain watched Alberto carefully lift the painting and place it on the table. Then, using a small torch he'd taken from his pocket, he skimmed over the painting, leaning in so close that his nose was almost touching the paint on the canvas.

"Well?" asked Alain.

"It's beautiful," replied Alberto. "Simple, but beautiful."

Alain nodded to Hassan, who took the painting from the table and put it back on the easel.

"I've shown you mine, now show me yours," said Alain. Alberto took the portfolio case that they'd collected from Alain's office and put it up on the table, unzipping it carefully. He pulled out his painting, and the three men stood looking down at Alberto's forgery of the Pierre Bontemps *Veiller Sur Toi*. It was immaculately done. Alain shook his head, marveling at the skill that was on display in front of him.

"Incredible," he said as he moved to shake Alberto's hand. "Your father would be proud."

"All in a day's work," Alberto replied. "Or in this case, two months." Alain turned to Hassan and signaled him.

"Two hundred thousand, as agreed," Alain said. Hassan typed on a laptop, and nodded that a bank transfer was in progress.

"Pleasure as always," Alberto replied. Alain took the forged painting from the table and handed it to Hassan.

"Get this over to the viewing room in my office, put it with the others," he said. "And make sure *this* one leaves here tonight," Alain added, pointing at the genuine painting now back on the easel.

"In all the years I've worked for you, I still never know where my pieces end up," said Alberto.

"Ignorance is bliss," replied Alain.

"This one is headed for where, some oligarch's mansion wall, or the private vault of an exiled dictator?" asked Alberto.

"I've never known you to get sentimental about your work, Alberto," said Alain, questioning Alberto's sudden curiosity.

"I'm just interested," replied Alberto. "I like knowing where things finish up, how things end."

"Very prophetic."

"Prophetic?"

"That you want to know how things end." Alain answered. "For you, badly." He nodded to Mr. Hassan. In a heartbeat, Hassan pulled a gun from his belt and fired two shots into Alberto's body, one in the chest, and one in the head, throwing him violently against the office wall.

"Clean this up and get moving with the paintings." Alain clicked on the laptop, cancelling the money transfer, and left the office. As they pulled out of the industrial park, his phone rang.

"Everything check out?" asked Arnold Silvestre.

"Perfectly," replied Alain.

"And Alberto?"

"I don't think the pasta agreed with him; he should have ordered the snails." Alain hung up the phone. Minutes later as Alain sped toward central Paris, Mr. Hassan left the warehouse, carrying the two portfolios. He quickly loaded them into the boot of his car and climbed into the driver's seat. He had a ten-hour drive ahead of him. He had to drop the forged painting at Alain's office, and then head west with what he thought was the genuine painting. He had a long night ahead of him. As he sped past the lay-by at the exit from the industrial park, two men in a car watched him. One of the men picked up his phone and dialed.

"He's just left; he's on the move," the man said into the phone.

"Off you go then, don't let him out of your sight," replied Lorenzo Pieters on the other end of the line.

CHAPTER FIFTY-TWO

SO FAR, THE INFORMATION that Michel and Mr. Ralph had provided Pieters and his team had all checked out. Mr. Ralph took center stage in the library as he started his explanation to Pieters and the gathered group about their theory on where the genuine *Obscurum Amicis* collection were currently located. One of the Interpol operatives entered the room with a laptop in hand, opened it and punched up a map on the screen. As Lewis Ralph scanned the map, he pointed toward the district of Bavaria, in the southeast of the country. Lewis quickly focused in, and tapped on the screen with his index finger.

"Here," he said.

He was pointing to an area marked Berchtesgaden, close to the border in Austria.

"While researching Deschamps's father and his extended family, I discovered that his mother had passed away a little over a year ago," said Lewis as he addressed the group. "I was soon able to find out where she had been buried, and it was here in a family plot alongside Alain's father, Karl Delitzsch, in the small cemetery in Berchtesgaden."

The cemetery was the final resting place not only of Deschamps's parents, but of other key figures in and around the Nazi party. It was the burial place of Dietrich Eckart, the anti-Semitic novelist and poet, who had a huge influence on Hitler; and Paul Giesler, a key figure in the German army, a former minister of Bavaria, and a man who alongside his wife took his own life, on the eighth of May 1945, the day the Nazi's capitulated to the Allied forces. Lewis Ralph had requested information about Mrs. Deschamps's death, funeral, and burial, from a connection in the Bavarian government. Having received details of her burial, he looked through the list of mourners who had signed a book of condolence in the local church on the day she was put to rest. It contained only two names. Two people turned up at her funeral. Her son Alain, and his uncle Karsten. Karsten Delitzsch then became the person who Mr. Ralph focused on.

Lewis discovered that Karsten had held various positions of power in the town. He decided to investigate further and contacted local police on the ground in Berchtesgaden. Having spoken to the sergeant in the local police station there, Mr. Ralph was able to secure low-level surveillance on Karsten, which threw up nothing out of the ordinary. Except that three times a week, like clockwork, he would head to the now defunct salt mines near the town center, and disappear for hours within the vast complex there.

"This," Mr. Ralph told the room. "Was odd to say the least because Karsten didn't work at the mines, didn't seem to have any connection to them, and yet had access to what seemed to be an area of the mines that was off-limits to the general public."

"That deserves further investigation in my books," said Pieters as he followed Mr. Ralph's story carefully. All the while Pieters whispered instructions to the nearest operative, who then scuttled off to complete whatever task they'd been given.

And that was what took place over the next twenty-four hours: further discreet investigations led by Pieters, and coordination with police on the ground in and around Berchtesgaden led to more light being shed on Karsten's thrice weekly trips to the salt mines.

When the meeting in the library finished, all parties dispersed, all having given instructions by Pieters.

When Fabian, Pieters, Lucy, Michel, Lewis, and Antoine met again, the day before the auction, there was a firm plan in place. The group met in the hotel where Fabian had taken Lucy a couple of days earlier. With the updated information on the walls and screens, they could see that Interpol now had eyes on both Mr. Hassan and Karsten Delitzsch. And it looked like Lewis Ralph and Michel were right on the money again as Pieters led the group through some footage he was playing on the monitor in the main part of the hotel suite.

"This is our friend, Mr. Hassan," said Pieters, "arriving in Berchtesgaden some hours ago." The group watched a combination of video footage taken by operatives in the German town and photos taken by the unit who had followed Hassan in his car all the way from Paris. He clicked his fingers and an operative brought a new set of images up on the screen. The group were now looking at photos of Hassan meeting Karsten, handshakes abound, with Hassan taking Karsten into his car, which was now headed toward the salt mines. When the pair arrived at the mine, Hassan was seen taking one of the portfolios out of his car, the other having been deposited in the Hôtel Drouot's auction rooms as per Alain's request. The group watched on as Hassan and Karsten headed down into the mines.

"This is where we now believe that Deschamps is housing the entire *Obscurum Amicis* collection," Pieters declared. "Although what he doesn't know, is that the painting he had Mr. Hassan drive all the way from Paris and deposit in the mine, is a forgery, courtesy of Bobby Thewlis."

"Correct," replied Lewis Ralph as Michel put his arm around his shoulder.

"Great work, my friend," said Michel.

"What happens now then?" asked Antoine. "What happens with the auction tomorrow, are you just going to go and arrest Deschamps now?"

"This is where we need to be patient," replied Pieters. "We need to let things play out, so Deschamps doesn't get alerted." Antoine looked puzzled.

"If I may," said Mr. Ralph. "Antoine, Deschamps hasn't yet committed a crime. And what Mr. Pieters needs above anything else is proof, preferably to catch him in the act of a crime." Antoine nodded; everything was slowly starting to make sense.

"Our plan will not bring us the required result unless we all play our part," said Pieters. The group nodded in agreement. "Firstly, we are going to let the auction happen as scheduled, let Deschamps present the paintings, have them taken in by the auction house, verified by the assembled experts, viewed by the public, and sold," Pieters said. "Then the first crime will have been committed. He will then have supplied an auction house with paintings of which we now know at least one is forged."

Michel put his hand in the air. Pieters nodded at Michel.

"We have proof that at least three of the submitted paintings are forgeries," he said.

"Care to share that proof with those of us in the cheap seats?" Lucy asked. Michel smiled at Lucy and took a letter from his pocket and held it up to the group.

"This is a signed statement from Bobby Thewlis, Alain's former master forger, until he sold him down the river some years ago. This letter confirms that he painted two of the paintings that Deschamps will have had submitted to the auction house."

Lucy and Antoine both looked at each other, impressed with Michel's level of detail; he appeared to have every base covered. Pieters continued to be surprised by Michel too.

"Thank you, Michel, so we will have Deschamps on at least *three* counts of knowingly supplying forged works, but we want more," Pieters said. He again addressed the group, now ready to hand out specific instructions to each of them.

"Lucy, you will go to work as normal tomorrow and escort Alain to the auction. Fabian will be there also, upon request from Alain to photo and document his handing over of the collection to the gallery." Both Fabian and Lucy nodded. "Michel, Antoine, you two need to complete your filming as per Alain's schedule, we have no doubt that he's tracking your movements closely, so stick to your schedule, which means you should be finishing up your filming at the British ambassador's residence at the time of the auction, so business as usual." Michel and Antoine both agreed. "Lewis will remain with me where he will, with the help of the police and our operatives on the ground in Germany, confirm the location of the genuine paintings."

Lewis gave Pieters a thumbs-up. Everyone now had their instructions, their own tasks and duties to bring this operation to a close. The group began to make their way out of hotel suite.

Fabian had jumped in a taxi and was headed back to his newspaper office to bring his editor up to speed. Lewis headed for the metro, which left Michel, Antoine, and Lucy on the steps of the hotel.

"I don't know how you've done all that," said Antoine. He was in awe of what Michel had achieved, not only over the past two days, but the past two months in fact. "You did all of that research, all of the detective work, with the noose of bankruptcy dangling over our necks."

"That's *why* I did it, Antoine. To cut that free and get us back on our feet."

"I just don't know how you have room in there for all of that," Antoine said tapping him on his head.

"It's what I love to do, brother: read, research, dig, make sure I know who and what I'm dealing with. Can you excuse us for one minute?" he asked Lucy, who stood and lit a cigarette.

"Sure, I'll flag a taxi," she replied.

"Just wait one minute," Michel said to her.

"Okay, I'll wait," she replied.

Michel took Antoine to one side.

"Look, I need to talk to Lucy, I need to explain a few things, get things straightened out, I never did that after we broke up."

"I hear you, little brother," Antoine replied. "Bring her to dinner, talk, you should."

"You get back to the film crew at the hotel; I'm sure Donald is pacing the corridor like an expectant father, waiting for us. You get back there and make sure everything is set for tomorrow's banquet."

"*Bien sur, mon petit choux*," Antoine replied as he moved back toward Lucy. "Right, for the first time in my life I'm going to have an early night." Antoine hugged Lucy. "See you tomorrow, should be fun and games, right?" He jumped in the taxi that Lucy had hailed for herself.

"What's going on now?" Lucy asked Michel.

"I think we should talk. You hungry?" Lucy stood and looked at Michel; she could see in his eyes that this was coming from the right place, and yes, she thought, they did need to talk.

"I've no appetite," she replied. "But I'll happily sit and watch you fumble your way through a bowl of moules mariniére and an apology." Michel raised his eyebrows.

"You think there's an apology coming?" he said with a smile on his face.

"Well, there's certainly one due." Lucy said as she stepped off the curbside onto the street and whistled for another taxi.

CHAPTER FIFTY-THREE

Across Paris, Alain sat behind his desk in his office. The room was dark, illuminated only by the light coming from the streetlights outside. He leaned back in his chair and lit a cigar and looked out at the view of the Paris nighttime landscape. He took his phone from his pocket and dialed.

"Hello?" said Mr. Hassan. "Did I forget something?"

"No, I did." Alain stood from the chair and walked through the door and down the corridor toward his private viewing room.

"I need you to call Knowles in London; there's a loose end I need to tie up." Alain stopped in front of the five paintings. "I want it done now, tonight."

"A loose end?" replied Hassan. "I'm not sure I know what you mean."

"Our original mirror man," said Alain.

"Ah, of course," replied Hassan. "I'd forgotten about him."

"I hadn't," said Alain as he leaned forward and put his cigar out on the glass case covering one of his paintings. "Get it done tonight, quickly and quietly."

"Of course," replied Hassan.

Alain hung up the phone and stood back from the paintings. He noticed his reflection in the glass case. He smiled at himself. He never forgot anything.

In London, Frank Knowles sat at the bar of the Pig and Whistle in Islington, quietly nursing a whisky. The noise of fruit machines and the hum of football commentary coming from the television hanging off the wall filled the room. As Frank drained his glass his phone lit up in front of him. He noticed the number and quickly stepped outside the bar onto the street before answering.

"Yes, sir?"

Hassan spoke quickly and briefly.

"No problem, send me the address," Frank said as Hassan hung up on the call.

Seconds later Frank quickly read the text that landed on his phone and jogged across the street to his car.

He pulled up outside 16 Waldegrave Road less than twenty minutes later. He rolled down his window and looked at the property. No lights were on, the house looked quiet. He looked in the rearview mirror and saw a young couple exiting the nearby Strawberry Hill Park. He waited for them to pass his car and disappear into the distance before he leaned forward to grab something under his seat. He checked his phone and opened the picture that Hassan had sent him along with the earlier text. He pulled his SIG Sauer pistol from under the seat and checked the clip. It was full, six bullets, primed and ready for use. He opened the glove box and pulled out a small silencer, which he attached to the gun. He stepped out from the car, putting the gun into his belt under his jacket. He looked up and down the street, no movement, so he entered through the small gate and onto the driveway of the house. When he got to the door, he looked at the panel of buzzers that was mounted on the wall. He noticed a small bowl on the porch which was half filled with the remnants of a tin of cat food. He reread the text on his phone and then pressed number four. Nothing. He pressed again. A voice crackled through the small speaker.

"Who is it?" said the voice.

Frank pulled a handkerchief from his pocket, put it over his mouth, and leaned into the buzzer.

"I think I've got your cat. He was in my garden next door."

There was a moments silence before the buzzer crackled into life again.

"Bloody thing, okay, I'm coming down," said the voice.

Frank stood back from the door and slowly pulled the gun out, holding it down by his side. He checked the street again, still no signs of life. A minute later he heard footsteps shuffling in the hallway of the house. The door moved as the locks were being opened. When the door opened fully Frank saw his target.

It was Bobby Thewlis. Without a moment's hesitation, Frank raised the gun and fired three shots into Bobby's chest, sending him flying back down the hall. His small frail body lay lifeless on the floor. Frank moved closer to him and took his phone out. He quickly took a photograph, then moved back down the hallway. He closed the front door behind him, wiping the handle and door buzzer with his handkerchief, and returned to his car. Before he pulled away, Frank took his phone out and sent the picture of the prone Bobby Thewlis to Hassan. Seconds later he received a text back.

"Good work, stand down, I'll be in touch," it read.

CHAPTER FIFTY-FOUR

LUCY AND MICHEL SAT outside La Rose de France, a small restaurant which backed onto the leafy Place Dauphine Square, not far from Lucy's apartment. This opportunity to have time together, this chance to talk, to reminisce, to explain, hadn't happened *nearly* enough in the weeks and months leading up to their split.

"You said you wanted to talk," Lucy said as they sat over their post-dinner coffees. Michel had wanted this opportunity to sit with Lucy for a long time, but now that it was here, in front of him, he was struggling. His hand was placed flat across his stomach, as if the food had caused him pain. It wasn't the food. This was Michel's "tell" as poker players would call it, that physical signature that showed everything was not what it seemed. He had tried to speak during the meal, he'd eaten practically nothing, just spent the entire time pushing food around the plate and looking up every once in a while, to try and catch Lucy's eyes.

"Honestly," he said. "I don't know where to start."

Lucy waited; she knew Michel too well to know that he wouldn't have asked her for this chance to talk, and have nothing to say. The last time she'd seen him like this was years ago, the night she'd left his apartment. In equal measures she desperately wanted to have this conversation but was terrified of what he was going to say. She sat forward, fixed Michel with a glare, and opened her eyes wide. Finally, Michel opened up.

"At home in London, there's a bunch of letters in the writing desk in my bedroom," he said. "Letters that I wrote to you not long after I'd left Paris. I never sent them, never posted them. I was too afraid you'd ignore them, or worse still, reply." Michel began to grow in his seat, as if a weight was being lifted from his shoulders, like a freedom had just arrived, his speech was flowing, he couldn't stop. "I didn't grieve my mother's death properly, come to think of it, I didn't grieve my father's passing either. On both occasions I just upped roots and ran as far as I could away from the situation." He spoke in a slow, soft tone;

sometimes the words cracked a little as he fought through the emotions that were coursing through his veins.

"Everybody told me, *time* will be your best friend, that it will go some way to healing the pain. And the truth is they were right, I think I've got to that point now, but I'm still grieving. I haven't stopped grieving since that night you left the apartment. Time hasn't helped me with that, it's made it worse, but what it did make me realize, is that I've never gotten over *you*. I don't think I ever will."

Lucy was now looking at the back of Michel's head as he leaned forward in the chair, almost turning himself away from her, not wanting her to see the hurt and the pain. But she could hear it in his voice.

"Do you know how many times I cried myself to sleep those first few months in Dubai?" she asked. "You weren't the only one who was in pain, Michel."

Michel slowly sat back in the chair, looking up at Lucy.

"At least when you went back to London you had family around you, you had Antoine beside you. I was alone in Dubai; I had nobody there for me. All these years apart, did you not think I wanted to share those big moments with you, your restaurant opening, did you not think I wanted to be sitting beside you holding your hand when you won your Michelin star, share *that* moment with you? I should have been, I wanted to, but you never gave me the opportunity, you took that away from me, from us, you killed our relationship stone dead when you decided not to move to Dubai with me."

Michel squirmed in the chair; what she was saying was true, and it hurt like hell. The waiter arrived at the table with the bill, and saw that the couple were clearly in the middle of something significant, and backed away attempting to make himself invisible.

"I know I hurt you, Lucy. That's what has given me the most amount of pain over the years, knowing that I hurt you; it wasn't your fault that we spilt up. I was pigheaded and selfish, and the fact that it has never been resolved kills me a little more each day."

Lucy crossed her arms as she tried to soak in this apology. She knew how hard this was for Michel; she'd never heard him apologize for anything in his personal life. He'd spent his professional life apologizing thirty times a day to disgruntled guests, but this was very different.

"When I saw you in London months ago at that lunch with Alain," Michel said. "I didn't know what to say, seeing you there, everything just came flooding back. All of those memories, I didn't know where to begin. I didn't know how to act around you.

"After Alain made the proposal to me and Antoine, I started digging into his business, not because I wanted to find out more about you. I thought that because you worked closely with him, that if I said yes to the offer of the TV project, that we would *probably* get the chance to meet again, to discuss the project, or the filming schedule, anything. And I saw that as an opportunity to make *sure* that we'd meet up again, and when we did, I was going to apologize properly to you, like I've just tried to do, all of this other stuff with the painting was information that I discovered after the fact. And me agreeing to do the TV show, and talking Antoine into doing it, which was no easy feat, was just a ruse for me to get closer to you, to have the chance to talk to you again. But once I'd discovered the information about Alain and the paintings, I had to keep digging, which drove me to bring in Lewis Ralph, and that's led us all here and now."

"Wow," replied Lucy after she'd taken a few minutes to take all of that information in. She called the waiter over, placed her credit card in the folder, and handed it to him.

"Look," she said. "All of this business with the painting, with Alain, Interpol, Fabian, I mean honestly, Michel, I don't know where my head is at the moment. I'm probably going to be out of a job however this all plays out." She was reeling from all that Michel had just told her.

"Lucy, all I want is for you to think about what I just said," Michel replied. "I meant every word of it; let's just get tomorrow out of the way, and maybe we can talk again."

"Let's just get tomorrow out of the way?" Lucy laughed. "You say that like you're planning to spend the day painting your dining room. When actually, tomorrow, you, me, your brother, as well as most of the staff of Interpol's Paris office, and a film crew, and a journalist from *Le Monde*, are hoping to bring a criminal mastermind and his entire organization to justice."

With that, the waiter arrived back with her receipt, and the pair made their way out of the restaurant and onto the banks of the Seine, heading back in the direction of Lucy's apartment. They walked in silence, both trying to get their heads around what just happened back at the restaurant, and what lay ahead of them tomorrow. When they got to Lucy's apartment, they stopped, and hugged. Lucy said good night, and started to walk to her front door. As she turned the key, Michel spoke.

"I was thinking duck egg blue for the restaurant dining room, by the way," Michel shouted up the steps to her. Lucy didn't turn around but smiled as she went through her front door. Duck egg blue was her favorite color.

Michel hailed a taxi to take him back to the hotel where he, Antoine, and the rest of the film crew were staying. He and his brother were sharing a room in the hotel, that was as far as the budget stretched on this less-than-epic TV shoot. Donald had booked the hotel as a treat for the brothers and the film crew having reached the end of the filming schedule. *Better than sleeping in that godforsaken campervan*, Michel thought, as he sat in the back of taxi that was weaving its way through the traffic. When Michel got back to the room, Antoine was still awake, lying on his bed, wearing a silk dressing gown, smoking, and reading.

"How did that go then?" Antoine asked as Michel got to his bed, kicked off his shoes, and threw himself back on the mattress.

"I don't know to be honest."

"Want one?" Antoine threw his cigarette packet over to Michel.

"You know you can't smoke in here?" said Michel pointing to the large no-smoking sign on the back of the room door. Antoine pointed upward, to the smoke alarm, which now had a shower cap strapped around it.

"I've got it covered, literally," Antoine replied winking at his brother. He reached over, grabbed his duffel bag from the side of the bed, and pulled out a bottle of red wine. He grabbed two plastic cups and poured each of them a glass. "Been some trip."

"And it's not over yet," replied Michel. "How were the crew when you got back here?"

"I spoke to Donald, told him that it was business as usual tomorrow with the final lunch. He's a little concerned about you, thinks you'll be distracted tomorrow, that your mind will be over at the auction house instead of the ambassador's lunch."

"He needn't worry about that," Michel replied. "There's nothing more we can do about what's going to happen at the auction, those wheels are in motion. Where's the bag?" He looked around the room for his bag containing the cardboard tube and their *genuine* painting.

"Stuck it under your bed," Antoine replied. "Can I ask you something?"

"Sure," replied Michel. Antoine put his cigarette out and sat on the edge of the bed as he watched Michel pull his bag from under his bed, take out the tube, and roll the painting out on his bed.

"Why didn't you tell me what was going on, what you were planning? You could have told me everything back in London; you could have brought me to meet Lewis, I could have helped."

Michel looked back at his brother with raised eyebrows. "You could have helped? Antoine you've barely been able to look after *yourself* the past two years. I wasn't going to throw you off the edge by getting you involved in something you didn't need to be."

Antoine lay back on his bed. It was a fair point; he wasn't good with fragile information, and at the rate he'd been drinking over the last six months, any secrets that had been bestowed on him would have made it out into the open via most of the drinking dens in Soho.

"You know that I'm doing this for us," Michel said. "For Mum and Dad. They had no clue what this painting meant, or who it really belonged to. But if everything goes to plan tomorrow, I can try and put things right and get this back where it belongs."

"It belongs on the wall of our restaurant," Antoine said.

"No, brother, it doesn't."

Antoine sat back in his bed. He closed his eyes and rubbed his temples, as if to calm himself down. "Well, where the hell *does* it belong then?"

"Not to us," Michel replied.

Antoine sat up in the bed. "Hang on a second, you're telling me that this painting, if it is what everyone thinks that it is, is worth about, what, a couple of hundred thousand?

Michel nodded yes.

"And you are planning to give it away?"

"I'm not going to give it away," Michel replied. "We're going to give it *back*." He rolled the painting up, put it back in the tube, and back under his bed. He climbed onto his bed and turned off the light above it. "Get some sleep, Antoine."

Antoine shook his head and mumbled to himself as he climbed into his bed and killed the lights. As the two brothers lay in the dark, he spoke. "I hope you're doing the right thing, Michel." His voice was soft. Michel didn't answer back, he just lay there, looking up at ceiling, watching the flashing red light on the smoke alarm as it illuminated Antoine's shower cap.

"We'll soon find out," Michel mumbled to himself as his eyes closed.

CHAPTER FIFTY-FIVE

THE FILM CREWS CALL-TIME was six a.m. Donald wanted all of them fed and watered before heading over to the location for the final day's filming. He was even more uptight than usual today; this was a big deal for him. They were to film at the exquisite Hôtel de Charost, the building that has been home to the British ambassador to Paris since the early nineteenth century. Filming on such a property brought a new and long set of rules. The crew were only allowed access to certain rooms; they had an allotted time in which to get their filming completed; and because the segment was to finish with a lunch with invited dignitaries, the crew had to be fully vetted by the French police.

They also needed to be dressed smartly, so when Stephen arrived at the breakfast room looking like an extra from *Bill & Ted's Excellent Adventure*, complete with a long sweater, shorts, and flip flops, Donald quickly marched him up to his room, where he decked him out in his spare suit. Stephen now looked like an extra from *Honey I Shrunk the Kids!*, but it was an improvement. The film crew stood in a line in the lobby, like a group of cadets at a passing-out parade, and were being inspected by Donald, who himself was dressed in an immaculate three-piece morning suit.

"Jesus, Phil, you look like your about to start smuggling molasses in from Canada." Donald pointed to Phil's shiny gangster-like suit, which he'd borrowed from his father.

Having given the crew his seal of approval, Donald dispatched them off in the crew van, bound for the embassy, while he waited in the lobby for Antoine and Michel. Antoine was the first down, resplendent in his chef whites. Donald was relieved to see Michel quickly follow his brother into the reception area. Michel looked sharp, in his best front-of-house two-piece suit.

"Tell you what, chaps," he said. "The two you look like you belong in a Michelin star establishment."

"Never a truer word spoken," replied Antoine as he patted his brother on the back. Michel smiled as the three men headed out to the campervan and set off for Rue du Faubourg Saint-Honoré, and their appointment with the British ambassador.

When they arrived, they were directed around the back of the building, to the staff car park, where Michel parked the campervan. The three men made their way into the kitchen area at the rear of this majestic building. Built in 1720, this palatial residence was just a few doors down from the Élysée Palace and was at one time home to the Duke of Wellington. The menu Antoine had put together for this banquet paid honor to the former owner of the building, with Beef Wellington pride of place as the main course.

"Nice touch," noted Michel as Antoine read the menu to the staff.

"You're not the only one who likes to do his research," Antoine replied, winking at his little brother.

At the back of the building were beautifully maintained gardens, which were flanked on both sides by ornate glass-built orangeries, one of which was to be the setting for the lunch. The first part of the sequence was to be filmed in the kitchen, where the crew had already set up. Donald's plan was to film Antoine busy at work, prepping the lunch menu, and setting out his plan for the food as it was to leave the kitchen. While he was doing this, Donald was aiming to send a second camera with Michel as he moved around the house discussing its architecture and history with the head butler, a Mr. Entibe. That way, by using two cameras at the same time, Donald hoped he complete his filming day on schedule. Before they began filming on the camera in the kitchen, Donald pulled Michel aside.

"I know there's a lot going on elsewhere today," he said. "But we really need this day to go without a hitch."

"Donald," Michel replied, "you just concentrate on what you're being paid to do. Which by the way you are doing brilliantly. We'll be fine, trust me."

"You sure you're okay to continue filming today?" Donald asked Michel, seeing the strain, stress, and worry that was written all over his face.

"Of course I am. Look, what's happening elsewhere, as you put it, is out of my hands; all we can do is our jobs, let the rest look after itself." Donald nodded. He was satisfied that Michel was going to deliver for him. Michel walked away from Donald and headed to the main reception area of the house where he met Mr. Entibe. As he got there, he stopped and took his phone out of his pocket. He typed in a message and hit send. He took a deep breath as Mr. Entibe approached.

"Monsieur Entibe, I presume, Michel de la Rue, a pleasure," he said as he greeted him with a firm handshake.

On the other side of Paris, Alain Deschamps paced the lobby of his office block. He was expecting a visitor. Late last night, Mr. Hassan had sent the final piece of the *Obscurum Amicis* the version painted by Alberto Di Bona, now deceased, over to the Paris auction rooms, before heading to Germany with the other version of the painting. After Alain left the warehouse last night, he returned to his office to finalize plans for the six paintings that hung on the wall of the salt mine in Berchtesgaden.

When Alain last met Fabian Ritzier, he had told him many lies, but one truth was buried in there. Alain had left one detail of his plan out, and that was his plan to leave the business, completely. Unlike his father, Alain didn't want to spend his final days looking over his shoulder, being driven demented by whispers and rumors. Alain wanted out and away from it all. The completion of this mission would signal the end. He planned to travel to Germany, collect the six genuine paintings, and arrange their sale to an already lined up buyer. This would be his biggest triumph, and his biggest payday. After that, he was selling up and getting out. Deschamps International Holdings had a number of buyers lined up; he wasn't particularly fussy as to who took the business over, just as long as he got the right price. He wanted away from all the nefarious connections he'd made over the years, away from his father's legacy, and to live an anonymous life. No one, with the exception of Mr. Hassan knew of Alain's true scheme. The money Alain would raise through the combined sales of the paintings and his company would more than fund his exit.

He was planning to head south, to Argentina, a route taken by many people with connections to the Nazi party. But he wasn't going to the bustling Buenos Aires, or another similar city; he wanted anonymity, and he would get it, a lot of it, on *La Sistina,* a 1,730-acre island, located just over three hundred kilometers southwest of the Argentinian capital, in Laguna del Monte. From there, he could live out his days in the splendor of true isolation. That was his plan. His connection to the *Obscurum Amicis* was nothing more than financial. He wasn't truly concerned about clearing his family's name. He simply saw this collection as a meal ticket. He knew that the authorities were closing in on his business, and he wanted to get away, quickly and cleanly. A new identity had already been lined up thanks to the German ambassador he'd greased in Dubai.

His escape plan was set, ready, and almost time to initiate. Just the small matter of a major art auction to get out of the way.

Finally, twenty minutes late, Alain's visitor arrived. Fabian skipped into the lobby offering apologies.

"Sorry, Mr. Deschamps," said Fabian. "I couldn't get away from the office, a terrorist attack in Yemen has the newsroom in meltdown."

"You're here now. Shall we?" Alain said as he led the way toward the lifts. They made their way up to Alain's office, and when they entered, Alain introduced Fabian to the person waiting for them. "You remember Lucy Carter," Alain said. "I believe she took good care of you, deputising for me, on your last visit to our offices?" Lucy and Fabian shook hands. Fabian noticed that Lucy's hands were sweaty; she was feeling the nerves as much as he was.

"Indeed, she was more than accommodating," Fabian said.

Alain stared at Lucy. She was motionless, not a flicker. She didn't take her eyes off Fabian. She seemed a little off guard, which Alain found odd. He wasn't quite able to put a finger on what was going on between Lucy and his guest, but something wasn't quite right. Eventually, he moved on.

"Right," announced Alain. "Let's get to it. I've read the piece you've written; your editor sent it through to me last week, not bad, paints a reasonable picture of me and my business, nothing too salacious in there."

"Glad you liked it," replied Fabian.

"Lucy here tells me that you're planning to head to the auction later today, to get some photographs over there, to fill the piece out."

"Yes, I am."

"Good, Ms. Carter will accompany you, I won't be able to make it, my attention is required elsewhere." He waited to gauge a reaction from both.

Fabian looked at Lucy.

"No problem," replied Fabian. Lucy politely smiled back at him.

"So to complete your profile piece, I told you some weeks ago that I was awaiting just one more painting to complete my collection," Alain said. Fabian nodded. "Follow me and let me show you, before these are moved over to the auction house for the viewing." Deschamps accessed the panel to the sliding door, and soon the three were heading down the corridor toward the private viewing room.

When they entered the room, Alain took up a position in front of the six paintings, and asked Fabian to replicate the photo he'd taken some weeks ago, when there were only five. Fabian obliged, only too happy to, knowing that this was even more proof of the crime Alain was about to commit. Alain didn't realize it, but he was handing Lorenzo Pieters pieces of concrete evidence which would make up the case for his prosecution. Deschamps posed, pointing to the sixth painting, as Fabian clicked away. They returned to Alain's office, and he thanked Fabian for coming over on such short notice.

"My pleasure, Alain," said Fabian as they shook hands.

"Enjoy the auction," Alain said. He watched Fabian as he checked his camera back to make sure he'd got the shot. Lucy stood close, looking at the screen on Fabian's camera. She seemed overly interested in what image he'd captured.

"I look forward to seeing your final piece in the newspaper, next Saturday, is it?" Alain asked Lucy. She jumped to attention, like a child in a classroom.

"Em, Sunday, Mr. Deschamps, the editor confirmed it with me this morning, two-page spread, plus the photos obviously," she answered.

"Perfect," said Alain. "My mother would be so proud, god rest her soul." He paused to bless himself. "Now if you don't mind," he added, showing Fabian the door.

"Good to see you again, Alain," Fabian said as he began to leave.

"I'll, em, show Mr. Ritzier out," Lucy offered. Alain nodded, and watched closely as Fabian and Lucy headed back downstairs to the lobby.

"I don't think I've ever been so nervous in my life," Lucy said as she walked across the reception area.

"Almost there," replied Fabian. "I'll meet you over at the auction house in an hour, I want to get these photos uploaded and over to Pieters ASAP." He looked up to notice Bruno standing watching him from across the lobby, he was talking into his phone. Fabian shook Lucy's hand and left. Bruno quickly headed for the lift, throwing a daggered look at Lucy as the lift doors closed in front of him. Lucy thought about going back upstairs to her office but changed her mind when saw Bruno. Instead, she approached the receptionist at the counter.

"If anyone is looking for me they can get me on my phone," she said.

"Of course, Ms. Carter," replied the receptionist.

Lucy left the office and headed toward her apartment nearby. She had an hour to kill before the auction, and she didn't want to spend it worrying each time the door to her office opened.

CHAPTER FIFTY-SIX

THROUGH A WARREN OF side streets not far from the impressive Boulevard Haussmann, was the renowned Paris institution Hôtel Drouot, which had temporarily housed some of the greatest works of art in the world. The main auction room, complete with its stunning red velvet walls, had taken delivery of the fabled *Obscurum Amicis* from the offices of Alain Deschamps. The six paintings sat side by side along the left-hand side of the room, under heavy guard. The strict two-hour public viewing period was almost over, and soon the room would be cleared of the mildly interested and nosey onlookers, and the real bidders would be shown into the room. In a couple of hours the potential buyers both in the room and on the internet would have the chance to make a bid and attempt to purchase one, or all of this fabled collection.

When the paintings arrived, they were met by a group of people led by Arnold Silvestre, the auction house manager and off-the-books employee of Alain Deschamps. He escorted the small but important group of people into the room where the paintings were displayed. Among the group were various experts on the numerous artists on show. After two hours of perusing, poking, sniffing, and scratching, the experts certified the collection as genuine, and fit for sale. Arnold Silvestre showed the group into his office for coffee as a way of thanking them. As the group were leaving Mr. Silvestre held back the self-appointed chairman of the group and whispered in his ear.

"Alain is very grateful for your work here today," Arnold said. The man shook his hand. Silvestre's work was done. Those experts had been paid off, and the sale could go ahead. Alain was another small step closer to La Sistina.

"MORE SALT," SAID ANTOINE to one of the house chefs. He was busy tasting the sauces the chefs had prepared for the starter course, Dover sole served with a buerre noisette, but he wasn't happy. Donald had been filming Antoine and the chefs for two hours. There had been laughs, rows, spillages, burns, and even a visit to the kitchen from one of the ambassador's dogs, all of which provided Donald with ample content to make this a impressive final episode.

Michel had turned up trumps too, moving at ease with Mr. Entibe through the main building, discussing the architecture on show, as well as making Mr. Entibe comfortable enough to share the odd tidbit of gossip about some of the previous ambassadors who had once served the crown here. A bell rang in the kitchen which signaled that the guests had taken their seats at their tables in the orangeries. The guest list for the lunch included the British Ambassador, the right honorable George Dunscombe; the head of the French tourist board Claire Henry; and the head of development at TF1 who had commissioned the TV series, Jules Tallon. All of the guests had been sent invites through TF1, except one. Lewis Ralph had added another guest to the list, and it was approved by those at TF1, who saw it merely as another high-profile name and organization that would be represented at the lunch. This guest was invited by Lewis Ralph, not only to enjoy the surroundings, the esteemed company, and the lavish banquet, but to meet Michel de la Rue.

Anna Herschel, was head of an organization that had many small offices dotted across the globe. The United Restitution Organization carried out work on behalf of those Jewish families whose treasures had been stolen by the Nazis during both world wars. Lewis had found her after an exhaustive search and was adamant that she and Michel meet, here, in Paris, on this most important day, the day of the auction.

The rest of the filming went smoothly, and at the end of the meal the de la Rue brothers were brought into the dining room to meet and take the plaudits from their guests. The British ambassador gave a rousing speech and thanked the brothers for the incredible banquet that he and his guests had just enjoyed. Mr. Ralph had joined the group just as the brothers were taking their bow and made straight for Michel.

"The auction begins in just over an hour, we need to get moving," he said as the crew started wrapping up their equipment.

"Have you spoken to Mrs. Herschel yet, explained everything to her?" Michel asked, having only had the chance to shake her hand a little earlier.

"I'm about to," replied Mr. Ralph. "You get yourself and Antoine and the crew over to the auction house as soon as you can, I'll bring Anna." Michel agreed and started to help the crew gather their equipment and load the two vans.

"Donald, a word," Michel said as he threw his bag into the campervan. "I need you and the crew to come with me, and keep filming."

"Come where?" Donald answered. "We've just completed filming, Michel, the job is done."

"Your job is, but mine isn't," Michel said. "I've a great idea for one final piece to camera, a great location, lots of color, just what you want, I promise." He pointed to his watch and signaled to Antoine. Antoine nodded, and jumped into the campervan and started the engine.

"Alright," replied Donald. "Lead the way." He and the rest of the crew got into their van and followed the brothers out of the car park and across Paris.

"This is it then, brother," Antoine said as they drove toward Notre Dame en route to the auction house. The two brothers were nervous, hoping that Pieters and Michel's plan had gone smoothly so far, and that this, the final act, would conclude in a similar manner.

"Almost there," replied Michel as he lit two cigarettes and passed one to his brother.

"There's the precious cargo," Antoine said, pointing behind him.

Michel looked behind at the bag that had the large cardboard tube sticking out of it. He smiled to himself.

By the time the two vans arrived at the auction house, the public and private viewings had just finished, and the auction was about to begin. Only accredited attendees, the official bidders, a number of handpicked journalists, and officials from the gallery, were allowed access into the room where the sale was going to take place. The famous red room was the venue for the sale. This room, steeped in history, had some of the greatest works of art pass through it over the years, and it had seen its share of scandal too. Forgeries had been through the room, and sold, but it normally wasn't until well after the physical sale that these fraudulences were discovered. Today was going be different, at least that's what Lorenzo Pieters hoped.

CHAPTER FIFTY-SEVEN

LUCY PULLED THE DOOR to her apartment building closed and stepped down onto the street. She had changed out of her usual office attire and made herself more comfortable in her favorite jeans and oversized sweater. She wasn't going back to the office that afternoon. In fact, she'd decided that she wasn't going back there ever again. Today was going to be a fresh start for her. Get to the auction, get through this day, and reassess. She couldn't work for a man like Alain Deschamps, not after discovering what she had. She was fed up being taken for a fool. It was time for her to take control of her life. All this was ahead of her, but right now she needed cigarettes.

At the end of her quiet street was a small kiosk selling newspapers and tobacco. She checked her phone again; she had time. She ran down the street and threw twenty euro on the small counter of the kiosk. She didn't even have to speak; the vendor popped a pack of Gauloises beside the money and smiled at one of his favorite regulars. Lucy thanked the man and moved behind the kiosk to open the pack. She took a cigarette out when a voice called out.

"Excuse me, Madam, have you a light?" they asked.

As Lucy turned to offer her cigarette lighter, she was punched square in the face, knocking her clean out. In a flash, her assailant grabbed her and dragged her toward a nearby car, dumping her in the back seat and slamming the door. The driver quickly jumped in the front and sped away from the scene.

"Lucy, your change?" said the vendor as he popped his head out of the kiosk looking around for his customer. She'd gone. In a heartbeat. He looked up and down the street, shrugged his shoulders, pocketed the change, and moved back into his kiosk.

Minutes later the car came to a stop at a deserted underpass near the Pont de Bir-Hakeim. As the pale green Metro passed overhead, the driver got out of his seat and opened the back door where Lucy lay prone on the back seat. He pulled her lifeless body up toward him and took a handkerchief from his pocket, which he stuffed into her mouth. He wrapped some tape around her mouth, dampening any sounds that would follow when she came to. Working quickly, he pulled two sets of cable ties from his pocket and tied them tightly around her hands and her feet. Lucy began to come too. Her eyes opened slowly. Her head throbbed with pain. She barely caught a glimpse of her captor's dark hair before he slipped a hood over her head plunging her vision into complete darkness. She tried to scream but nothing came out, just a muffled noise. The man lay her back down on the seat. She could hear a clicking noise, and then silence. She squirmed furiously, but couldn't sit up. Her heart thumped in her chest; she was struggling to breathe. Suddenly she felt a pinch in her thigh; she was being injected with something. She tried to scream but within seconds her struggling body stopped moving. She fell unconscious again.

Another train rattled on the tracks overhead as the car pulled out slowly and made its way toward the nearby slip road onto the main carriageway.

Thirty minutes later Lucy began to stir. Her hood had been removed and she opened her eyes to take in her surroundings. The first thing that hit her was the smell. Dampness. She could hear water dripping nearby. Still tied up, she lay on a small stone ledge in what seem to be some sort of cavern. The stone floor was covered in dirt and sand, and the walls looked thick and solid. She raised her head and looked straight in front of her and noticed two arches opposite her, with a small guardrail spanning the width of the room. Behind the railing sitting on a chair facing her was a heavily armed man wearing a balaclava. His eyes were locked on Lucy. She was startled when she saw him, and quickly moved herself up into a sitting position. Above her head she noticed a marking on the wall: "IR 1879". Her head was banging with pain. She could taste blood on her lips, and her mouth was bone dry. She coughed to clear her throat.

"Who are you, what do want?" she said feebly.

The man in the chair said nothing, he stood slowly and moved toward the railing. A black attaché case lay on the floor near the man. He picked it up and slowly began to open it.

"Whatever you're thinking of doing, please don't do it," Lucy pleaded. She trembled. The man lifted something from the bag and looked at Lucy. He put his fingers to his lips to quieten her down. He jumped the guardrail and placed the item on the rail facing Lucy. She squinted her eyes to focus on what he was doing. The man had placed a large iPad on the rail, pressed a button on the screen, and moved to stand beside Lucy. The screen lit up as the man pulled a gun from his belt and held it to the side of Lucy's head. Tears fell from her eyes as she watched the screen. Eventually a face came into focus. It was Alain.

"Put the gun down, give her some space," said Alain.

The man lowered the gun and returned to his seat facing Lucy.

"Lucy," Alain said in a low voice. "Just stay calm and everything will be okay."

"Fuck you," Lucy answered, barely able to get the words out.

"This will all be over soon, Lucy, I just need you to tell me more about your new circle of friends," said Alain is a slow calculated tone.

"What you're talking about?"

Alain shook his head.

"Show her," he said.

Her captor went to the attaché case and pulled out a file. He stood behind the rail and held up some photographs for Lucy to see. The first photograph showed her and Fabian leaving Alain's office. Lucy sat motionless on the ledge, her eyes flicking between the photos and Alain's face on the screen. The man showed her another photo, of her and Fabian arriving at a hotel in Paris, and then another of them leaving, followed by Lorenzo Pieters from Interpol.

"Lucy," said Alain, "you need to tell me what's going on, what you've told them."

Lucy stared at the screen. She didn't budge. Her eyes screamed "Fuck you!" but she kept it inside, biting her lips. Alain stared back at her. He leaned into the screen and whispered.

"You need to start talking or I'll let my colleague there do what he does best."

Lucy shook her head in defiance.

"Talk," said Alain in a grave tone.

Her captor, Knowles, put the photos away and moved slowly toward Lucy. She scampered along the stone bench until the wall stopped her moving away any farther.

"You have two hours," Alain said, and hung up. The screen on the iPad went black.

Knowles towered over Lucy and smiled as he reached for his gun.

CHAPTER FIFTY-EIGHT

THE AUCTION ROOM QUICKLY filled up with thirty bidders jostling for seats. At a table along the right-hand side of the room five gallery staff were poised, phones at their ears, each connected to a separate bidder across the world. This was an old-fashioned sale room, no electronic screens behind the auctioneer displaying sums of money in different currencies ticking upward like a fruit machine. Things were done at a slower pace here. That was the way auctions had been carried out here for centuries, and that was the way it was being carried out today.

The auctioneer, Jules Lemont, a seasoned professional, moved around the room shaking hands with familiar faces, happy to run through details in the catalogue if any of them had any questions about the items that were up for sale. At the back of the room, there was a small area reserved for press and invited spectators, and today among them were journalists from Europe, the UK, Asia, and the US. Lorenzo Pieters and a small number of his team were there under the guise of a bi-monthly spot check visit, which of course he was entitled to do, being head of Interpol's Stolen Works of Art Unit. In the row behind Pieters was Mr. Ralph, accompanied by Anna Herschel, having gained access through a former colleague at the British embassy.

Antoine, Michel, and the film crew were in the main reception area of the auction house, along with a number of local press teams, waiting to hear the outcome of the sale. The door into the sale room was closed and guarded by a number of hefty gallery security staff. The brothers had to sit this one out and hope that everything on the other side of that door went as they'd hoped.

Fabian entered the reception area and made his way over to the brothers.

"You're cutting it close," Michel said as he pointed at his watch. "I thought Lucy was coming with you?"

"She's not here?" Fabian asked. "I told her I'd meet her here."

"Maybe she got held up at the office," Michel said. "I'll give her a call." He took his phone out and dialed. "Voicemail," he said and hung up.

"I'll keep trying her," Fabian said, heading for the auction room. Michel nodded and moved back to Antoine who was busy trying to get a decent peek into the auction room. Donald was chatting to the press officer from the gallery and told him that he was here with a film crew, as part of a documentary they were shooting, the subjects of which were the two brothers whom he quickly pointed out. After a short chat and the offer of two tickets to the late show at the Moulin Rouge, Donald had been granted permission to film in the building, just the reception area, but on the premises at least.

"Everything okay?" asked Michel as Donald approached.

"No problem," he answered. "How did you know he'd go for those tickets?"

"Those tickets are better than currency," Michel answered.

He'd secured the tickets earlier on that week from an old friend who now worked in the ticket office at the Moulin Rouge who'd owed him a favor.

"Well, look," said Donald. "I've told him that we want to film a quick piece to camera here, and that we'd be out of his hair in thirty minutes."

"Perfect." Michel replied. "That should give us plenty of time." He glanced at his watch.

"Chaps?" interrupted Antoine. "It's hammer time."

"Get the film crew to set up and follow my lead when I give you the signal." Michel said.

"Give me a signal?" Donald said. "Sounds like we're going to war." Michel nodded his head. *Donald wasn't far off the mark,* he thought to himself. Again, Michel looked at his watch. He was clearly agitated.

"Relax, brother," Antoine said. "Don't get yourself into a knot." As well as being anxious about Lucy, Michel was waiting for someone else; this whole plan would fall through if that person didn't turn up.

Inside the auction room, Mr. Lemont took to the small stage, and stood in front of the podium. He adjusted the microphone for his height—he was only about one hundred and sixty-seven centimeters—banged his gavel on the podium to bring the room to his attention, cleared his throat, and began.

"Ladies and gentlemen," said Mr. Lemont. "Welcome to Hôtel Drouot; it is so good to see so many familiar faces, and some new ones here today, for what promises to be a most exhilarating sale. These six paintings, recently recovered and donated to us, feature some of the most sought after works this auction house has had the pleasure of handling. Missing, presumed lost, for more than seventy years, we are proud to present this collection to you today." There was a ripple of applause followed by an audible hush around the room as Mr. Lemont spoke.

Out in the reception area Michel paced in front of the door into the auction room, trying to hear what was going on inside. He dialed Lucy's phone again, still no answer. Just then, his final guest arrived in the reception area. Michel moved quickly to greet him.

"This place hasn't changed," said Bobby Thewlis as he shook Michel's hand warmly.

"Boy, am I glad to see you Bobby, you okay?" Michel wore a wide grin on his face. Bobby nodded.

"A few bruises, but nothing some painkillers and the odd dram of whiskey couldn't sort out," he answered. Michel hugged Bobby warmly.

Bobby Thewlis was the final piece of the puzzle for Michel, Lewis, and Lorenzo Pieters. Their plan was to let the paintings go under the hammer, therefore Alain would have committed the initial crime of presenting known forgeries to an auction house for sale. They would be made known as forgeries not long after the gavel dropped. Whereupon Pieters would make himself known to the room and present Bobby Thewlis. Pieters would then show the auction a signed sworn affidavit, in which Thewlis confessed to having painted three of the six paintings just sold. An arrest warrant would then be immediately issued for Alain Deschamps, and the forged paintings would be taken into custody by Interpol. Part two of the plan was poised and ready to go on Pieters' signal, some eight hundred kilometers away in Berchtesgaden.

Lewis Ralph had paid Bobby a second visit to his flat in London to check in on the progress of his version of *Veillier Sur Toi*, and to warn him that Deschamps could possibly make an attempt on his life. Bobby took the warning seriously.

"Look, I've still got it on," said Bobby as he opened his coat to reveal a bulletproof vest to Michel. "I need to thank Lewis for the heads-up."

"I'm glad you took his advice," said Michel. "He's inside the auction room, you can thank him when this is all over, and probably best to take that off, can't see you needing it in here."

"I feel like James Bond," said Bobby as he headed to the gents to take his precious piece of lifesaving attire off.

Michel breathed a huge sigh of relief. Their intricate plan was coming to fruition, Bobby had made it to Paris. He took his phone out again and dialed.

"Come on, Lucy, pick up," he whispered to himself.

Inside the auction room there was a hushed silence as the first lot came under the hammer.

CHAPTER FIFTY-NINE

Alain Deschamps sat in the back of his chauffeur driven car having left Paris early that morning after his meeting with Fabian. Something had struck him about the way Lucy and Fabian had behaved in his company, and his instinct was right. After speaking to his assistant, Alain learned that Lucy and Fabian had left together after they'd met in Alain's office some weeks ago. Alain thought it suspicious. Further surveillance of Lucy over the past week confirmed that she was communicating with Interpol through Lorenzo Pieters. Alan quickly made the decision to not let Lucy get near the auction room that day. He'd instructed Hassan to get Frank Knowles to Paris, and hours later Knowles was sitting outside Lucy's apartment, waiting. Now that Lucy was being held securely off-site, Alain could push on with his plan. He wasn't going to dispose of Lucy just yet though, she may prove useful to him at some point before his exit to the southern hemisphere.

Alain was due to arrive in Berchtesgaden in a couple of hours to meet Mr. Hassan and his uncle Karsten and head down into the salt mine to view the six paintings together. Alain had already lined up a buyer for the collection, having spent three months flaunting them on the black market. He had agreed on a price, just under thirty million euro, which would be transferred to one of his accounts as soon as the paintings changed hands between him and their new owner.

This was more than enough to cover his self-determined retirement plan, which included the purchase of the private island in South America, as well as the staff and security required to keep him safe over the proceeding years. The sale of his company, Deschamps International Holdings would yield him close half a billion, but the money he was about to make on the sale of the *Obscurum Amicis* collection would be the sweetest money he'd ever earned. It seemed a fair price Alain thought to himself, having put years of work into wrangling this collection together. These paintings had already commanded a higher price. Many lives had been lost surrounding their movements over the years, from the lives of the two German soldiers Müller and Weber, who first stole them from the Rothstein's apartment in Paris in 1942, to the countless others that Mr. Hassan and his teams had disposed of around the world while stealing them back. Thirty million euro seemed like chicken feed in comparison to that.

Mr. Hassan and Karsten Delitzsch stood at the entrance to the salt mine awaiting the arrival of their boss. Karsten had already put the final painting in position on the wall of the dark room where its five companions were hanging.

"What time is he due here?" asked Karsten.

"Another hour or so," replied Mr. Hassan,

"Let's head back in, it's fucking freezing out here." The two men headed back in toward the heat of the tunnel entrance. Click went the cameras in the car parked opposite the mine entrance.

Two Interpol operatives from Pieters' division sat photographing Hassan and Karsten heading back into the mines. They had been on Hassan's tail since he'd left Paris, and watched on as Hassan and Karsten took the portfolio from Hassan's car, containing what Hassan thought to be the genuine Pierre Bontemps painting, down into the mine.

Meanwhile as Deschamps's car approached the autobahn Berchtesgaden bound, two other operatives were close behind in another car, tailing him. It seemed like the net was closing in on the biggest scalp of Lorenzo Pieters career.

CHAPTER SIXTY

Paris

The power of restitution. What did it mean to those who were reunited with articles that had once belonged to their long since gone family members. That feeling of being handed back a necklace, a piece of ceramic, a painting, or a book, that you knew had once been in the hands of your parents or grandparents. Something that was more than an object, a piece of your family's history, something that was woven into the tapestry of your family tree, and that had been violently ripped from it. The reactions, the faces of those family members who now clung to those objects as tightly as if they were clinging to their ancestors themselves, was beyond touching.

This was the driving force behind Anna Herschel and the many people who worked as volunteers in the organization, the United Restitution Organization. Anna, the daughter of an Auschwitz survivor, made it her life goal to rescue as many of these pieces as possible and get them back into the hands of their original owners' families. She traveled the world in search of these items, in search of documents, in search of the full provenance that would confirm that these objects did once belong to the living ancestors of those Jewish families who so brutally had them taken away from them. It took a toll on her, but every time that she felt that she'd reached a dead end, a brick wall, the smallest piece of information, an anonymous phone call, a letter, a tip-off from a museum or gallery, something would lead to a breakthrough for her and the members of her team, which would suddenly reinvigorate her. Not long afterward, in most cases, she and her team completed their search, which ultimately led to her handing something back. It made it all of their efforts worthwhile. Persistence. Anna had it in spades. She never gave up the hunt, the chase. Over the years she had sat with children, grandchildren, cousins, and distant relatives of those original owners, and every time she revealed not just the piece, but the story as to how she'd located and secured them, it was met with unbridled emotions. More often than not a stunned, silent joy as the family member looked into the heart of the object in their hands, and saw the faces of those cherished relatives.

When Anna received a phone call from Lewis Ralph inviting her to a luncheon at the British ambassador's residence in Paris, and subsequent invite to accompany Lewis to an auction on the same day, little did she know that she was now close to one the biggest acts of restitution in her organization's history. She, like most of the attendees in the auction room, was more than familiar with the art that was going up for sale. Anna had heard of the rumors of the collection known as the *Obscurum Amicis*, but until this moment, she didn't believe it to be true, there were so many stories of mythical collections, it was hard to tell truth from fiction. As she stood beside Lewis Ralph in the auction room, now linking his arm, she watched with bated breath.

Michel was consumed with righting the wrongs of his grandfather, Ronin Kohl, whom he'd never met, but now knew, through the legend of the *Obscurum Amicis*. He had near-as-concrete proof that his grandfather had stolen this painting, this painting that his mother discovered and loved, a painting that she'd been bequeathed by way of Mrs. Rothstein. Michel was determined to get it back into the right hands, the hands of the family that originally owned it, the family his godmother Mrs. Rothstein, had married in to.

Michel stood in the reception area of the auction house, dressed in his finest morning suit which he'd been wearing for the filming earlier that day, with a bag draped over his shoulder. In the bag, was the now battered cardboard tube, which contained the key to all of the mayhem and madness of the past two months. He clung to the bag, gripping it like his life depended on it, waiting for the signal from inside the sale room to reveal its contents.

"Sold, for one point two million euros," declared Mr. Lemont as the hammer went down on the second to last painting in the collection, *River Landscape* by Salomon Van Ruysdael.

"Last one," Lewis said to Anna. She stood and watched as the final painting was moved onto the easel closest to the auctioneer.

"A beautiful, simple piece this," said Mr. Lemont from the podium. "A portrait, featuring a woman and two young men, a mother and two sons we believe, from the hand of Pierre Bontemps, grandson of the famous Italian sculptor, circa 1894." He raised his gavel. "Where shall we start? Two hundred thousand?" Silence, and then a bid from the phones, and then another from the floor. The bidding picked up pace, and after some back and forward, the painting was nearing a sale.

"For the third and final time then, the bid is with you in the room, at six hundred and twenty thousand euros." He drove the gavel down onto his podium. "Sold!" he said. "Ladies and gentlemen that concludes today's sale, thank you for your attendance." Applause again broke across the room.

Pieters quickly made his move, maneuvering toward the podium, and taking Mr. Lemont by the arm. Pieters whispered in the auctioneer's ear for a long moment, at which point Pieters called out.

"Clear the room!" he said, and the security men quickly pounced into action, clearing the crowd from the space. Utter confusion spread throughout the building. Pieters stood at the podium with Mr. Lemont and beckoned toward Lewis and Anna.

Mr. Lemont shouted over to the security men, and within seconds Anna and Lewis were brought forward to the auctioneer. "There are some more in the reception area," said Pieters to Lemont, and signaled to his Interpol colleagues to go and fetch them. The doors of the sale room swept open as the crowd filed out through the reception area, watched by Michel, Antoine, Bobby, and the film crew. The Interpol operatives called over to Michel, and escorted his group into the sale room, where the doors were shut behind them.

"Can you please tell me what the hell is going on, Mr. Pieters?" asked Mr. Lemont. "We are in the process of concluding a sale here, this is beyond inappropriate." Pieters took the Bontemps painting off the easel and put it back on the stand along with the other five paintings.

"None of these paintings are leaving the hands of Interpol, Mr. Lemont," he said.

"Oh really?" replied Lemont as the door to the sale room burst open, and Arnold Silvestre was led in, handcuffed, by two uniformed officers.

"Ah, Mr. Silvestre," said Pieters. "Thank you for joining us."

"Put that down man, you can't do that in here!" he shouted. Mr. Lemont screamed at Phil the cameraman, who was now filming every move in the room.

"Yes, he can," replied Pieters. "He has permission, given to him by Police Commissioner Barthez himself. These paintings that you have just sold, are, I'm afraid, forgeries." Lemont put his hand over his mouth, stunned by the very thought of it.

"Here is a sworn affidavit, by convicted forger Bobby Thewlis, confessing to having painted at least three of the six paintings in front of you," Pieters said producing the document from his pocket.

"Impossible," said Silvestre. "Thewlis has been off the grid for years, who knows if the man is even still alive?" Pieters looked at the group standing in front of him and nodded.

"I'm very much alive, Mr. Silvestre, thanks to these men," said Bobby as he stood out from the group. Lewis Ralph smiled at Bobby; the relief was palpable on his face. Bobby nodded back at him. Lemont and Silvestre both looked like they had just seen a ghost. Pieters continued.

"Within these documents are details of meetings with you, Mr. Silvestre, in which you concluded deals for all three paintings with their broker, Mr. Alain Deschamps."

The blood drained from Silvestre's face as he slumped to the floor. Mr. Lemont moved quickly to help the officers pick Silvestre up off the floor and onto a nearby chair.

"But these paintings were all authenticated by a committee of experts," said Lemont. "How can they be forgeries?"

"A committee assembled by Mr. Silvestre here, whom we can now prove are also on the payroll of Deschamps, and have been for years," Pieters said. "Rest assured they are being taken into custody by members of Interpol as we speak."

Lemont quickly let go of Silvestre's arm, leaving him to the officers.

"How could you, Arnold?" said Lemont. "After all of your years of service here?" Silvestre couldn't think, let alone speak. Lemont moved back to join Pieters at the podium.

"Naturally we will need the names and contact details of all of the buyers of these paintings," Pieters said. "My colleagues here will save you the embarrassment of having to call them yourself with the bad news." Mr. Lemont, an innocent party in all of this, shook with fear, this was the type of scandal that could close any auction house completely, even one as respected as this.

"There is one more thing that we'd like to show you, Mr. Lemont," said Pieters. "Just so you can say that you handled at least one *genuine* painting today." Michel walked to the podium, took the bag from his back, opened the cardboard tube, and revealed the genuine *Veiller Sur Toi*, laying it carefully on the floor in front of the podium. Donald stood open-mouthed as he pushed Phil in closer to the action to get a better shot of the painting.

The room fell silent as Anna Herschel walked toward the painting on the floor.

"She's beautiful," she said as she stared at the lady in the painting.

"Isn't she," replied Michel in a quiet voice. "And it's yours."

Anna looked at him. "Well, my organization will certainly do our best to find out who it belongs to and get it back to them," she said taking Michel's hand.

"No need, I've done all the legwork for you," said Michel. "It's yours."

Anna looked at Michel and frowned.

"Your father," Michel said. "He was a survivor?"

Anna stood frozen and looked around at Lewis Ralph.

"Let him explain," Lewis said. Michel moved Anna to the front row of chairs and sat down with her.

"Your father, Isaac Herschel, was a survivor?" Michel said. Anna nodded, not able to speak a word. "And his family, do you know anything about what happened to them?"

"He, em, he was from a family of six children, all of whom were taken and killed." Her voice cracked. "His, em, my family were just wiped away."

"Not all of them it seems," said Michel. Fabian frantically took notes of the conversation. Antoine stood transfixed beside Pieters and Bobby.

"Did you know that your father had a cousin, Edsel Rothstein?" asked Michel.

"Rothstein? That was mother's maiden name."

"Your mother was Edsel Rothstein's cousin. But like your fathers' family, Edsel's family too were taken away from her in the dead of night, and so she knew nothing of her extended family. She was transported to London to start a new life, knew nothing of the fate of her mother and father, so she presumed she was on her own."

Anna could hardly breath. Given her job and her heritage, she had taken a deep dive into her own family and their history, but had come up with nothing more than the little information she'd just relayed to Michel. Like most survivors the thoughts of talking about the events of those days were too painful. Any family that hadn't been seen for a period of time were presumed to have met the same fate as so many others.

"You are the *only* living direct descendant of Edsel Rothstein," Michel said as he knelt on the floor and slowly rolled up the painting. "So, this is yours." In tears, he handed Anna the painting. "It was stolen by my grandfather, Ronin Kohl, in Paris in 1942. But thanks to the French Resistance, it ended up in a house in London that was to become Edsel Rothstein's home, and through another series of events, the house became *our* family home, and Edsel was to become our godmother. My mother discovered this painting in the cellar, and fell in love with it, but she had no idea that her own father had stolen it. It was never truly hers to love."

Anna began to break down. Lewis quickly moved in to comfort her.

Antoine came and stood with Michel, who was now physically and mentally spent. The atmosphere in the room was one of reverence, of respect, and remembrance. And Donald and the film crew, had captured every moment of it on camera.

"Take him away," said Pieters gravely as he pointed at Silvestre. Pieters moved and sat with the brothers. "I know this may be difficult to hear, but the job is only half-done," he said to them. "We should get word from Germany any moment now."

Michel and Antoine nodded.

As the police officers proceeded with the arrest of Silvestre, Anna sat in silence. Lewis and Fabian sat either side of her, Lewis offering his handkerchief, which she took and wiped away tears from her face. There was a somber mood in the room, far from a celebratory one, this was history. Old wounds were being opened, and scandals were revealed, and you could see it on the face of everyone in the room.

Pieters suddenly ran and grabbed Michel, his phone in his hand.

"We've got a problem, it's Lucy," he said as they started moving toward the door.

As the two men moved quickly through the crowd, Michel's stomach turned. This was far from over.

CHAPTER SIXTY-ONE

LESS THAN AN HOUR later, Pieters and the assembled group sat in what was known as the "bull-pen" area of Interpol's Paris office, at the National Crime Bureau. Every agent in the building had gathered to watch the final moments of this mammoth, multi-agency operation unfolding on the large bank of screens which dominated the space. Pieters and his team had now linked up with their operatives on the ground in Germany, and via bodycams, live pictures were being fed onto the screens, giving the watching crowd instant feedback on what was happening in Berchtesgaden.

In the time that had elapsed since the end of the auction, Arnold Silvestre had been taken into custody, warrants had been issued and were being executed for the remaining members of the committee who had verified the forged paintings, and the forged paintings had now been secured and moved to a secure holding room within the Interpol building. Michel paced at the back of the room near Antoine as they looked up at the giant screens. They watched as dozens of Interpol officers moved in and around the entrance to the salt mines, awaiting the arrival of Alain Deschamps.

Fabian, who had now been joined by his editor, frantically tapped away on his laptop, documenting every extraordinary moment of the past twelve hours. Lewis and Anna were also there, and along with Bobby Thewlis, these three stood to the side of the main body of onlookers, with Anna now clutching the cardboard tube that contained her painting, her birthright.

Michel couldn't hold himself any longer and moved to join Pieters who was deep in conversation with members of his team and local detectives.

"Anything?" he asked. Pieters dismissed his team.

"Nothing as yet," he answered. "Last sighting of her was by a local kiosk owner on the street where she lives, we're checking CCTV in the surrounding area as we speak."

Michel felt physically ill. He stumbled into the nearest chair.

"I'll never forgive myself..." he said, unable to finish the sentence.

"Don't think like that," replied Pieters. "Let my people do their work. We'll find her."

Michel nodded. Pieters didn't mention the CCTV footage he'd seen of Lucy being bundled into a car. He wanted his team to confirm that it was indeed Frank Knowles, one of Deschamps's trusted crew that he'd seen taking Lucy, before letting Michel know.

"Let's get Deschamps into custody, and I guarantee you, if he had anything to do with Lucy's disappearance, I'll get it out of him," Pieters added.

Michel moved to the back of the room where Antoine stood. His brother put his arm around his shoulder, and both looked around at the organized chaos in the room.

Donald and the film crew took up a position at the back of the room, and quickly set up the cameras to capture the events that were about to unfold. Another set of international arrest warrants had been issued, for Alain Deschamps, Ahmed Hassan, Karsten Delitzsch, and Frank Knowles. Interpol had the backing and support of the local police force in Germany, who had joined them in and around the entrance of the mine, and all were out of sight as they awaited the arrival of Deschamps's car. Pieters spoke out loudly, addressing the gathered crowd.

"Please, let's keep this civil, respectful, our people here and on the ground in Germany have work to do," he said. "This operation will not conclude until we find the original paintings, which to this point we only *believe* to be in this location." Proof. Pieters wanted proof before he celebrated. "We need to be aware that we are also dealing with a missing person here, who *could* be on-site, and if she is, her rescue becomes priority one."

Michel looked over at Lewis Ralph, who gave him a reassuring look. One of the operatives clicked away at a computer terminal in front of the screens, and voices could now be heard by all in the room.

"Communication link is up, sir," he said to Pieters. Lorenzo spoke into a headset that the operative had handed him, giving him a direct line to the lead Interpol officer on the ground in Germany.

"This is Pieters, can you read me?" he said.

"Loud and clear, sir," replied the operative. "Should have a visual in two minutes."

The room went silent as they watched the screens and saw four different camera angles all trained on the entrance to the salt mines. Two figures suddenly appeared in one of the screens. Mr. Hassan and Karsten Delitzsch had returned back out to the entrance, and could be seen standing together, talking, with Hassan constantly checking his watch. A minute later the operative on the ground in Germany spoke again.

"Vehicle approaching from the west side," he said as a black car could now be seen approaching the entrance to the mine. "Visual confirmed. It's Deschamps's car." The atmosphere in the room in Paris suddenly went cold. The celebratory mood that had enveloped the room after the success at the auction house, was now replaced by tension.

The screens filled with the image of Deschamps's car pulling up to where Mr. Hassan and Karsten were standing waiting. The camera moved in closer to the car, filming the driver getting out and opening the back door, revealing Deschamps. He greeted Hassan with a handshake, and then turned to hug his Uncle Karsten.

"Any other people in the car?" asked Pieters. A moment's silence in the room.

"Negative, sir, just the driver and Deschamps," replied the operative on the ground.

"Fuck," whispered Pieters to himself.

Michel put his head in his hands, Antoine rubbed his back, comforting his brother. Lewis Ralph and Anna looked nervously at each other. Concern was growing amongst everyone in the room for Lucy.

On the screen they watched as Deschamps and his uncle smiled, as if they were congratulating each other. The three men headed into the entrance and down into the mine.

"Follow in," said Pieters.

"Copy that," replied the operative.

"Maintain distance," Pieters added as the operatives and local police started to change their positions and move closer to the entrance of the mine.

Three of the Interpol operatives now took the lead, and they could be seen reaching the entrance of the mine and heading down after Deschamps. As the operatives moved through the warren of corridors, the screens showed the mines in all of their dark, damp glory. Ahead of them, Karsten reached the door to the heavily secured room. As he unlocked the door, little did Hassan, Karsten, and more importantly Deschamps know, that the painting that Hassan had recently brought from Paris, was a copy, a fake, a mirror image of the one that Anna Herschel now held tightly in her hands back in the Interpol office. Karsten turned the key, and the three men entered the room. They stood and looked at the collection of paintings on the wall. The Interpol officers hung back, less than ninety meters from the room.

"Unbelievable," said Alain.

Hassan put his hand on the shoulder of his boss.

"Your father would be very proud," said Karsten.

Alain looked at him, his face showing no emotion.

"My father was nothing more than a sheep," Alain said. "He just carried out orders, blindly. He had no creativity, no vision, no class. He was a thug in a uniform." Karsten looked at his nephew, upset by this change of tone, and angered by the way his brother was being spoken about.

"He lifted these out of a crate in an attic, he was a cat burglar in a uniform, nothing more," Alain continued. "With the protection of an entire army behind him. I didn't have an army. But I did have the competence, intelligence, and the wherewithal to spend my life and my money, tracking these down. You, Karsten, and my father, have no idea of the levels of work and commitment that have gone in to getting these back together. It puts what my father did to shame. My peers never respected me, not many in my family did either, including you." He took a step closer to his father's brother. "All I had was the loyalty and vision of one good friend." He looked at Hassan. "This is the end. All of this, these paintings, my father, his name, his so-called legacy, I'm done with it." He nodded to Hassan.

Hassan immediately pulled his gun from his belt and fired all six bullets into Karsten. The gun was silenced, but the shots could be heard more than eight hundred kilometers away.

Everyone in the Paris office froze.

"Shots fired, shots fired!" whispered the operative aggressively down the corridor.

"Move in!" said Pieters as the operatives and the armed police force behind them moved quickly down through the maze of corridors toward the room. The crowd in the room in Paris held their collective breaths.

"The fuck is that?" Hassan said to Alain as they heard the noise of footsteps approaching, quickly trying to look around and size up their options. As the operatives approached the room where Alain and Hassan were standing over Karsten's body, the volume increased.

"Police, don't move, drop the weapon, hands above your heads!" shouted the Interpol operatives. Alain looked at Hassan, they were trapped, nowhere to go, no escape route. They were out of options. Hassan didn't even have a bullet left in his gun to fight back with.

Two of the operatives in the tunnel approached the open door of the room.

"Don't move, put the weapon down," they said, their automatic rifles trained on both Hassan and Alain.

Those two men stood frozen to the spot. Hassan slowly put his weapon on the ground. The two operatives moved in through the doorway. On the big screens in the Interpol office, the crowd could now see both Hassan and Alain, standing either side of Karsten's dead body. Caught, trapped.

Michel looked over at Pieters, who was glued to the screens.

"Check the paintings," Pieters said into his headset.

The two operatives in the doorway called in the armed police behind them who quickly placed Alain and Hassan in handcuffs. As one of operatives moved past Alain and Hassan, his bodycam revealed on the screens what he was looking at. The other five genuine *Obscurum Amicis* paintings.

"My god," whispered Anna Herschel as she looked up at these stunning pictures. Lewis Ralph put his arm around her. Anna could now see, for the first time, her parent's entire collection of art. Michel stood and joined Pieters in front of the screens.

"Incredible," Pieters said. "You've no idea what you have accomplished here Michel." Pieters and Michel watched Alain Deschamps and Mr. Hassan being led away out of the mine and into the awaiting police cars. But Michel wasn't celebrating, neither was Pieters.

The rest of people in the room went into raptures. For Pieters' team this was the culmination of years of work. He and his group of investigators had invested so much, and finally they had their man, and their paintings.

"People, please calm down!" Pieters said as he watched Michel start to cry. "I want Deschamps in a holding cell and on a video call with me within fifteen minutes," he said into his headset. "The mission in not complete."

The room slowly fell silent again.

"Copy that," said the team leader on the ground in Germany. "We'll notify you as soon as the video link us up, sir."

Pieters approached Michel and put his arm around him,

"Come with me," he said moving quickly through the room. "You too." He pointed at Lewis Ralph. "I want you two in the room with me when I speak to Deschamps."

Antoine watched as his brother moved through the room, he hadn't seen him cry since they were children. He quickly followed them toward a secure interrogation room on the same floor. There were still plenty of questions to ask, and Pieters hoped Deschamps could provide the answers. Antoine sat outside the interrogation room while Lewis joined Pieters and Michel inside.

"Don't worry, Antoine, I've got him," Lewis said as he shut the door.

CHAPTER SIXTY-TWO

True to their word, Interpol officers had Deschamps in a secure cell in the nearest police station in Berchtesgaden within fifteen minutes of his arrest. Inside the cell, Alain sat at one end of a table, his hands cuffed and linked to a chain that was attached to a bar in the middle of the table. Two Interpol officers sat at the opposite end of the table. They had set up a laptop facing Deschamps, and were set to make the call.

In Paris, an operative spun a laptop around for Pieters. "All set on our end," he said as left the interrogation room.

"Leave the talking to me," Pieters said to Lewis and Michel. "*Listen*, but don't talk." Pieters had Lewis and Michel sit at the far end of the table, behind the laptop screen. He didn't want Deschamps seeing them. No distractions, this was between him and Alain. Both Lewis and Michel nodded as the sound of a call ringing filled the tiny room. The operative in Germany clicked on the laptop and the call was connected. Deschamps could now see Pieters, and Pieters faced the man he'd been chasing for years.

"Inspector," offered Alain after a moments silence. "I'd like to say it's nice to see you, but I won't.

"I can assure you the feeling is mutual," replied Pieters.

Michel and Lewis looked at each other. Michel's toes tapped on the floor. He was exhausted, filled with tension and rage. Lewis put his hand on Michel's knee, and Michel stopped tapping his feet.

"You've got me, well done," said Alain. "Why the phone call, a victory lap is it?"

"I have got you," replied Pieters. "And my colleagues on the ground in Germany have possession of the paintings. Just like your father, you've lost them." Alain scowled at Pieters' riposte. "But you've got something else that doesn't belong to you, and I want to know where she is."

"I have no idea what you're talking about," said Alain, with a smug grin on his face.

Pieters' expression darkened. He leaned into the screen.

"Deschamps, I've known for years what you are, and what you are capable of, but now thanks to this operation and the help of certain individuals, including your old friend Bobby Thewlis, you'll be spending the rest of your days in a maximum-security facility. The closest you'll get to art will be the looking at the drawings your cellmates have drawn on the shower walls."

Alain took this in for a moment. He smiled.

"Thewlis?" replied Alain, laughing smugly. "I'm not quite sure what evidence a corpse can provide in court?"

Pieters smiled back at Alain.

"I can assure you he can provide plenty. Bobby Thewlis is very much alive and well, thanks to a bulletproof jacket, and your man Knowles' eagerness to leave the scene without checking to see if his intended target was dead or alive. This same man was seen abducting a young lady earlier today here in Paris." Michel sat bolt upright in his chair. Pieters looked at with stern expression. Lewis again calmed Michel, putting his arm around him.

Deschamps shifted in his seat.

"As I was saying," said Pieters. "You have something else that doesn't belong to you."

Deschamps was quickly running out of options. Nonetheless, he was never one to give in without a fight.

"I presume your referring to my *former* head of special operations," he said calmly.

Michel's blood ran cold.

"Where is she, Alain?" Pieters asked. "Tell me where she is, *and* if she's okay."

Alain leaned into the screen.

"Fuck you, *and* Bobby Thewlis," he said coldly.

Michel stood, not able to contain his emotions any longer. Lewis grabbed him and pulled him back down into his seat.

"Try a different answer," said Pieters.

"What's she worth to you? Or more importantly what is she worth to me?" Alain asked.

Pieters smiled into the camera. He looked down the table at Michel and Lewis.

"You think this a negotiation Alain? It's not. You don't want to play games with me, trust me," said Pieters.

"You know me, Lorenzo, I'm a gambler," replied Alain. "You didn't think I'd do all this without having some form of an insurance policy, did you? Ms. Carter is my insurance policy. She is my pile of chips, and I'm willing to cash them in, in return for a level of leniency when it comes to my impending trial and sentencing."

Michel took a pen from his jacket pocket and grabbed a notepad from the table and wrote something on the page. He held the notebook up to face Lorenzo. Pieters read the message and looked at Michel. Michel tapped on the notepad.

"Always willing to sell someone down the river to save yourself, Alain, just like you did with Bobby Thewlis all those years ago," Pieters said. Alain didn't respond, just looked back at Pieters calmly.

"Your insurance policy, as you so eloquently put it, could save you from receiving the death sentence, is that what you're hoping?" Lorenzo said. Deschamps laughed.

"In 1981, Inspector, France abolished the death penalty," Alain replied.

Lorenzo stared at Alain on the screen.

"Correct, but they still have it in the US, Alain," he replied. "And given the fact your *former* head of special operations was born in the US, thus making her a US citizen, I think the might make the DA in Washington interested in your extradition."

Michel slid the notebook toward Lewis. He tapped on the page. Lewis read the note. "Extradition—Lucy was born in Washington." Lewis smiled broadly at Michel and patted his shoulder.

Alain's face dropped slightly. He tried not to show Pieters that he'd missed this vital piece of information, but the fact was, he had. His "insurance policy" was worthless, And now it could cost him his life.

"So, you better start talking, or the next call I make is to the FBI in Washington," Lorenzo said.

Alain sat back in his chair. He needed a moment to consider his next move. Lucy was expendable in his eyes, most people were to him. And there was no way he was going to give Pieters an easy win. He sat forward in his chair.

"You want to know where she is?" he said. "I'm only going to tell you two things. If you can work it out from that, good for you. If you don't, well I'll take my chances with the legal system in the US. I'm now *agreeing* to help you, and according to my very expensive legal team, that will be considered a form of cooperation, which always counts for something when determining sentencing, especially in the United States."

Pieters looked down the table at Lewis and Michel. This was as good as it was going to get.

"Talk," he said to the screen.

"I'd rather write it down," Alain said.

"Give him something to write on," Pieters said. The two operatives in the room with Alain quickly produced a sheet of paper and a pen and placed them in front of him. Alain looked at the screen, smiled, and started writing. This was still a game for him. And he wasn't going down easily. Michel, Lewis, and Pieters sat impatiently as Alain scribbled on the sheet. When he finished, Alain held the sheet up in front of the screen. Pieters read aloud.

"Lucy is not alone; she's surrounded by the six million. If you want to find her, think about taking a pedicure."

Lewis frantically wrote down what he'd just heard.

"Now you'd better hurry. Mind you, there's no guarantee that *if* you find her, she'll still be alive, after all, I'm not responsible for the actions of my colleagues. That's all I'm saying. Next time you hear me utter another word, it will be in the presence of my extensive team of lawyers."

Pieters looked at Alain on the screen.

"You'd better hope she's still alive Deschamps because if she's not, I can't guarantee your safe arrival on US soil, after all, I cannot be responsible for the actions of my colleagues either," Pieters said. "Now take him away." He hung up the call. The operatives in the room with Alain unchained him from the desk and headed for the cells.

The three men in the interrogation room sat and looked at the piece of paper. None of them spoke. Michel was close to tears; the thought of Lucy suffering, or worse, was too much to bear.

"Any thoughts?" asked Pieters. "She's only been missing for a few hours, she could be still be here in Paris somewhere," said Pieters.

"Give me a few minutes," replied Lewis.

"We don't fucking have a few minutes, Lewis!" Michel screamed.

Lewis and Pieters looked at Michel. Pieters moved toward him with his hands out.

"Calm, Michel, calm," he said. "That's what we need here, give us some time to figure this out, we're on it, I promise you. Maybe go and grab us all some coffees, eh?"

"Fine," replied Michel. He started to leave the room.

"Michel, I'll work this out, trust me," Lewis said.

Michel nodded and left the room. Pieters pulled his chair close to Lewis as both men studied the notes again.

"Any ideas?" he asked.

"Open that laptop, pull up a map of Paris for me," replied Lewis.

CHAPTER SIXTY-THREE

The interrogation room was filled with smoke as Pieters, Lewis, and Michel were now surrounded by empty coffee cups and a brimming ashtray. Lewis was anxiously scrolling through various websites and crossing off names on a list he'd written on his notepad.

"It's been forty minutes since the call," Michel pointed out as he paced around the table.

"We're aware of that," said Pieters lighting another cigarette.

"Can't you just got call Deschamps again, or beat it out of him?" Michel said.

Pieters poured milk into his already cold cup of coffee and looked up at Michel.

"We're not dealing with a low-level criminal here. This man has walked away from huge charges before. He's clearly thought this move with Lucy would enable him to do that again. If I go in heavy-handed, his lawyers will use it against us, and the bastard *will* walk away."

"I understand that," said Michel. "But is it not worth trying?"

"Please, Michel, let me know do my job here," replied Pieters.

Lewis slapped the desk and stood.

"Here!" he shouted. "Les Catacombes, on Place Denfert-Rochereau."

"Where?" asked Michel.

"Here, it has to be here," said Lewis. He pulled up a website as Michel and Pieters moved in beside him. He scrolled through pictures as he spoke.

"Alain said she's surrounded by the six million. I presumed he was referring to World War Two, but he's not," said Lewis as he pointed at the screen. "Les Catacombes in Paris were built in the late eighteenth century after there were problems with the city's cemeteries. They decided to transfer their contents to an underground site. Popular opinion reckons that there are over six million skulls down there, the walls down there are literally built from skulls. I've been down there several times, an incredible place." Lewis became more animated with each word.

"And the pedicure reference?" Michel asked.

Lewis stopped scrolling and pointed to an image on the screen. They were looking at a sunken spiral staircase, cut into the stone walls, and at the bottom lay a well, a footbath. The photo was titled *Bain de pied des carriers*, or "the quarry foot bath."

Pieters sprang into action, ran out into the corridor shouting in both directions. Within minutes two GIGN teams were scrambled, and Pieters, Lewis Ralph, and Michel, were in a convoy of six police cars tearing through Paris toward Place Denfert-Rochereau.

As they reached the entrance to the catacombs, police had already cleared the area of locals, staff, and tourists, and had the area cordoned off. Pieters jumped from the car and was immediately surrounded by armed uniformed officers as they approached the entrance. Michel and Lewis followed close behind.

"No, wait here," Pieters said to them both. "Let me and my men handle this, stay in the car, the radio is there, you can track us on that."

"No fucking way," said Michel as he barged his way toward Pieters and the entrance.

"Michel," said Pieters heading him off." I'm not asking you; I'm telling you. We've no idea what's down there, what other insurance policies Deschamps may have in place." He shoved Michel back toward the police car. Lewis grabbed Michel and they both sat into the back of the car.

"Let them do their jobs, it's out of our hands now," Lewis said. Michel reluctantly agreed. They sat and looked out the window of the car as Pieters and his team entered the catacombs. When they had disappeared out of sight, Michel leaned forward and turned the police radio in the car up. They could hear voices but couldn't make out what they were saying.

"What the fuck is wrong with this thing?" Michel shouted as he thumped the radio. Lewis reached over and pulled Michel back into the seat.

"Hey, these guys are going hundreds of feet underground," he said. "It's not the radio that's the problem, it's the thousands of tons of earth between it and them." They sat back and listened. Crackled voices. Silence. More crackled sounds. Then nothing. For what seemed an age. Michel glanced over at the entrance. Not a movement. Dozens of armed police took up positions, their guns all trained on the entrance. Silence on the radio in the car.

Bang! Bang! Bang!

The loud gunshots filled the car and caused both men to jump out of their skin. More radio silence. Then screams.

Bang! Bang!

Michel leapt from the car with Lewis in pursuit. Michel was headed toward the cordon around the entrance. A member of the GIGN team stopped him.

"Quiet!" the officer screamed and pointed to the radio on his vest.

The two men stopped in their tracks.

"We're coming up," said Pieters over the radio. "Have the medics standing by."

The GIGN team straightened up and fixed their guns on the entrance. Michel and Lewis took cover behind a nearby police car. Moments later the door swung open, and two GIGN team members came through, carrying a body.

"Stand down, stand down!" shouted Pieters as he emerged into the Paris daylight.

Michel sprinted toward the men carrying the body. Lewis hung back, too scared to move. As Michel approached the men he slowed down, now fearful of what he might see. The GIGN team laid the body on the ground and moved away revealing the face.

It was Frank Knowles. Hie eyes were open, his body lifeless. He was covered in blood, bullet wounds dotted across his torso. Killed by the GIGN team.

As Michel turned around toward the entrance, more of the GIGN team came out carrying Lucy. Michel ran to her side, Pieters joined him.

"She's going to be okay, Michel," he said as he put his arm around him. "Couple of cuts and bruises, nothing serious."

The GIGN team carried Lucy toward a nearby ambulance. As they laid her on the stretcher, the paramedics started to work on her and moved her into the back of the vehicle. Michel jumped in, and the ambulance pulled away, sirens blaring. Through the small windows in the back of the ambulance Michel looked back and observed the chaos of the scene. He watched as Pieters approached Lewis Ralph, and the two men shook hands. Michel took Lucy's hand in his as the tears flowed down his face. It was over, and all of the emotions of the past twenty-four hours, the past four *years*, poured out.

CHAPTER SIXTY-FOUR

TWO DAYS LATER, AT the hotel where the brothers and the film crew had been staying, there was a party in full swing. A wrap party, arranged to mark the crew reaching the end of the filming of the TV documentary series. Donald had organized some food and drinks to be served in the function room, and as the main guests of honor arrived into the room, a huge cheer went up. Michel and Antoine entered arm in arm, exhausted, relieved, and elated. Not only had they managed to play their part in the downfall of one of the biggest organized crime syndicates in Europe, they had also completed their first ever TV series. Not bad for a burned-out chef and an overworked maître d'. The film crew took their opportunity to surround and congratulate the brothers. Donald approached the brothers and handed them both a glass of champagne.

"Hope you don't mind, but I invited a few others," he said as all three took a sip from their glasses. With that, the door behind the bar opened, and in filed some of the people they'd met along their filming journey—Françoise the truffle farmer; two of their fellow naked chefs from the festival at Oye-Plage, thankfully both fully clothed; as well as the owner of the ancient flour mill they'd filmed at. Also, the goat farmer who led the boys through a goat yoga class, as well as some of the senior executives from TF1, followed by Anna, Fabian, Bobby, and Lewis Ralph. The entire cast of their adventure had assembled in the room to celebrate.

Thewlis faced no criminal charges, he was offered a similar deal to the one Deschamps had taken years previously, recommended and sanctioned by Lorenzo Pieters himself. The deal also included a request from Pieters that Bobby would now take on a role within his division, as a consultant, helping Pieters' team identify the genuine from the fake. Bobby Thewlis proudly accepted the post, and had finally come in from the cold. His future work and contributions to Interpol would now be recognized, for all the *right* reasons.

As the party was in full flow, Anna Herschel sat beside Michel in a corner booth. She talked about the work her organization had done and was continuing to do. Michel talked about wanting to be a part of this work with her.

"I wondered if I could help, in terms of similar collections to the *Obscurum Amicis,* to help bring *them* home?" he asked.

"We'd be honored to have someone like you on our team," Anna replied, smiling proudly.

"Consider it done." Michel and Anna hugged and clinked their champagne glasses. Donald called Antoine and Michel over to a corner of the room; he also had a proposal he wanted to put forward to Michel, and his brother.

"Listen, I just wanted to say thank you," he said to the brothers. "I know it's been tough, you're a couple of TV rookies, but you did it, the series is in the can, and it's a series that you can both be very proud of. It's got a very different ending to the one we originally planned, but it'll be one hell of a series. I've no idea how you got through it all, Michel, with all of this other stuff going on in your world."

"That makes two of us," Antoine replied. "I thought I was the one that provided the surprises in our family, boy did I get that wrong." He put his arm around his little brother. Michel was embarrassed. He didn't like the limelight. He did what he did for his own reasons, not for any kind of gratitude or in pursuit of plaudits. Donald beckoned over to one of the TV executives from TF1.

"You didn't get a chance to talk to Jules Tallon at the banquet earlier this week," said Donald as he introduced him to the brothers. "But I've been talking to him for most of the evening, you see Jules is the commissioning editor at TF1."

"A pleasure, and thank you for the opportunity," replied Michel as he shook his hand.

"It was our pleasure. You both have done a great job, all three of you in fact. You've delivered a bizarre, gripping, bonkers, but ultimately superb TV product for us," Jules replied. "Has Donald spoken to you about Discovery?"

Michel and Antoine looked blankly at Donald.

"I was just about to," replied Donald.

"Discovery?" asked Michel.

"The spaceship?" asked Antoine.

"No, the TV channel," replied Donald as he and Jules laughed. "You're not the only one with connections, Michel. Jules not only commissions TV shows for TF1, but also for the Discovery channel in the US, and he has a proposal for you."

"We're listening," replied Antoine, even though no one was talking to him.

"Donald got in touch with me a couple of days ago, explained what was going on, what you were all a part of, and after what has transpired, we wondered if you would like to tell this story to a wider audience," Jules said.

"What story?" asked Michel.

"The story of restitution, we want to take the footage of you and your brother, with your permission of course, and finish *that* story. We would like to follow you, and the people who work with Anna at her organization, and see other objects being returned to their rightful owners."

Michel looked at his brother and then back at Jules and Donald.

"You mean you'd pay me to travel around the world, hunting down the owners of other stolen works, trying to reunite them?" he said.

"Trying to get them *home*," replied Jules. "Yes, we think it would make an incredible series, and Anna's organization would receive a healthy fee, and the well needed publicity."

"He'll need to think about it," said Antoine.

"Of course, take all the time you need," replied Jules. "Donald has my contact details, get in touch whenever you're ready to talk." He shook their hands and went back to the party.

"There you go," said Donald. "Only thing I ask is that you might think of hiring me and the crew for the shoot?" Michel and Antoine laughed out loud.

"Consider it done my friend," said Michel, shaking Donald's hand. Donald left the brothers' company and headed back to his film crew, who were opening another bottle of champagne. The brothers watched the crew as they got stuck into the bottle, laughing and hugging each other.

"What a trip," Michel said putting his arm around his brother.

"Life changing," replied Antoine. He walked his brother over to a couple of empty seats at the bar. The two sat and Antoine ordered a couple of whiskeys. As the drinks landed in front of them Antoine raised his glass. "I want to make a toast," he declared. Michel nodded and raised his glass.

"To my protector, my biggest supporter, my bailiff, my psychiatrist, my accountant, my family, my little brother, and my best friend," Antoine said, his eyes locked on Michel. Michel sat frozen, tears filled his eyes. "You're all those things to me, Michel, always have been. You've always had my back, been there for me, and I'm eternally grateful to have you in my life." Antoine continued. "You never cease to amaze me, and if your even hesitating about taking that new TV job, I'll kick your arse from here to the Sorbonne. Take it, you deserve it, I mean that. Let me get things going back in London, I won't let you down this time, I promise."

Michel was speechless. He knew his brother loved him, that was a given, but he could see a change in Antoine over the last few weeks, and now right in front of him, and this filled his heart. Michel, still with his glass raised, looked at his brother.

"To the new Rien Mais les Meilleur, and it's phenomenal head chef, my big brother, *my* family," he said. The boys clinked their glasses, put their arms around each other, and downed their whiskeys in one clean shot.

"By the way," said Antoine. "That horse? The one I put my last forty pounds on before we left London? Larry the limp texted me last night. Came in at thirty-three to one. Fancy hitting the nearest casino?" The two brothers laughed riotously as Michel pulled Antoine into a headlock.

Later as the party began to wind down, Michel sat on the front steps of the hotel, smoking, his head spinning with all that had gone on. What a journey they had all been on. As he sat and looked around at the streets of Paris, his mind wandered, and soon he was picturing his mother and father walking those same streets, happy together, and then he thought about his grandfather, Ronin Kohl, whom he'd never met but now knew so much about, sneaking through those same streets with his army unit alongside him, pilfering and pillaging hundreds of pieces of art from the bounty that sat in the Jewish apartments nearby.

His thoughts then turned to his godmother, Edsel Rothstein. He had spent a lot of time as a boy in her small apartment in London, at his mother's side, as she and Edsel prepared lunch for him and his brother. He thought about Edsel being loaded into the back of a truck and whisked away at such a young age, and then he thought of *Veiller Sur Toi*, the piece of art that also suffered that same fate, loaded into a truck in the dark of night, and dispatched across Europe. His heart ached when he thought that Edsel and this painting ended up in the same building in London, without either being aware of each other's presence or existence. Finally, he thought about Edsel's parents, Rebecca and Laurence Rothstein, and pictured them walking the streets, with their newly purchased paintings under their arms, bringing them home.

His thoughts were broken by the lights of a taxi that pulled up in front of the hotel. He watched as the back door of the cab opened. Lucy stepped out, gingerly. Michel leapt to her aid.

"What the hell are you doing here?" he asked. "You weren't supposed to get out of the hospital until tomorrow morning!"

"Takes more than a few bruised ribs for me to miss a party, Michel," Lucy replied. Michel smiled as they reached the steps in front of the building. Lucy stopped.

"Before we go in, can I have a cigarette?" she asked. "They're kind of funny about you smoking in the hospital."

Michel laughed and helped Lucy sit on step beside him. He lit two cigarettes and passed her one. They sat and smoked, in silence.

"Penny for them?" said Lucy. Michel smiled at her.

"Just thinking about fate," Michel said.

"Is that right?" replied Lucy as she took a drag from the cigarette.

"It's a strange thing, isn't it? I mean, this little painting has seen and done so much in its life. It's seen people torn apart and seen people brought back together." He stared at Lucy. She took the moment and that statement in and looked back at Michel. These two were meant to be together, they both knew it, but just didn't know how to tell each other.

"What are you going to do now?" she asked.

Michel looked back at the Paris skyline. He began to fill Lucy in on the conversation he'd just had with the TV executive. Lucy listened and nodded along, loving the way he spoke. His face was filled with excitement, hope, and passion, as he talked about Anna's organization and the incredible work they did. This was the Michel she used to know, the Michel she loved, and, oh, it was good to see him again.

"I think I'll take that offer," Michel said. "Antoine is more than happy to get the business back up and running in London. I mean I'll help him set it up, get it going, I mean I'd have to, otherwise he'd have the place decked out like a TGI Fridays." They both laughed. "But he'll be fine." Michel continued. "He just needs time and a place to shine, and that's in our parents restaurant in London." Lucy and Michel stared out at the river Seine and sat in silence for a long moment.

"Then I dunno, maybe I'll set off in search of other paintings, and see where it takes me," Michel said. Lucy finished her cigarette, slowly stood up, and offered Michel her hand.

"Sounds like you could use a hand on that trip, an advisor maybe," she said looking into his eyes. Michel smiled back at her and nodded his head. "You know, you and me are very much like those paintings," she said.

"Oh, how so?" Michel replied.

"Well, even though we've been apart from each other for so long," Lucy replied. "We've ended up being put back together again, *Obscurum Amicis* of a sort." Michel stood, and took her face in his hands.

"*Obscurum Amicis,*" he whispered as they kissed, and walked back into the hotel together, hand in hand.

THE END

ACKNOWLEDGMENTS

In the world I spend most of my working days, the world of acting, there is a saying, "It takes a village to make a movie." Very true.

When I embarked on writing this novel, my first, I presumed it would be a solitary journey. How wrong I was. I needed more than a village to get this novel to where it is now, and I want to take this opportunity to thank those who helped, guided, and pushed me along the way.

Firstly, a huge thanks to those friends of mine who read my early scribblings, and encouraged me to keep going, namely Simon O'Gorman and Aidan Power. Their enthusiasm for those early chapters kept me writing, which was key to getting toward the finish line.

When I finished the original manuscript, I knew it needed help, I needed to find an editor. I was beyond lucky to find the brilliant author Anthony J Quinn, who over the course of six months, helped me whip the book into shape. His notes, his advice, and again his encouragement were invaluable to me. To have such an accomplished author pour over your work was daunting and exciting, and ultimately so rewarding.

A huge thank you to my literary agent, Tracy Brennan, who took my manuscript and tried to find it a home, a publisher, and she did. The lovely people at Rare Bird Books took the leap, and here we are. Thank you to Tyson Cornell and all the team at Rare Bird, especially Hailie Johnson, who took this greenhorn's hand and guided me through the lengthy but thoroughly enjoyable editing process.

Of course I had encouragement at home, and without Lisa and my boys pushing me along, this book would never have been finished. I am truly a lucky man, to have family and friends that support, encourage, and push me toward my end goals. Without them, there would be no book, there would be no me.

Thanks also to my acting agents Lorraine, Bex, and Meg, in particular Lorraine, who has been on this journey with me for over twenty years, she is more than my agent, she is one of my best friends, who's advice and counsel I will always treasure.

And last but not least, thank you. Thank you for taking the time to read my work. I am so excited to share these characters with you, and can't wait to share more with you in the future.